Evil Lurks Below

In intermittent flashes of light and darkness, George picked out the details of the hell he'd walked into.

Anne and Helen knelt beside a great copper vat. Some *thing* in the vat moved restlessly, throwing up ropes of doughy matter, sending slime creeping up the women's arms. Their faces, in the beam of the trembling flashlight, showed unapproachable joy and total horror.

God! George thought. *It's feeding on them!*

Yulian gripped his shoulder from behind. Fingers with the strength of steel propelling him effortlessly, irresistibly, toward the vat.

"George," the vampire remarked, "I want you to meet something. . . ."

TOR BOOKS BY BRIAN LUMLEY

THE NECROSCOPE SERIES
Necroscope
Necroscope: Vamphyri!
Necroscope: The Source
Necroscope: Deadspeak
Necroscope: Deadspawn
Blood Brothers
The Last Aerie
Bloodwars
Necroscope: The Lost Years
Necroscope: Resurgence
Necroscope: Invaders
Necroscope: Defilers
Necroscope: Avengers

THE TITUS CROW SERIES
Titus Crow Volume One: The Burrowers Beneath &
The Transition of Titus Crow
Titus Crow Volume Two: The Clock of Dreams &
Spawn of the Winds
Titus Crow Volume Three: In the Moons of Borea & Elysia

THE PSYCHOMECH TRILOGY
Psychomech
Psychosphere
Psychamok

OTHER NOVELS
Demogorgon
The House of Doors
Maze of Worlds
Khai of Khern

SHORT STORY COLLECTIONS
Fruiting Bodies and Other Fungi
The Whisperer and Other Voices
Beneath the Moors and Darker Places
Harry Keogh: Necroscope and Other Weird Heroes!

Brian Lumley
NECROSCOPE II:
VAMPHYRI!

TOR®

A TOM DOHERTY ASSOCIATES BOOK
NEW YORK

This is a work of fiction. All the characters and events portrayed in this book are either fictitious or used fictitiously.

VAMPHYRI!

Copyright © 1988 by Brian Lumley

Cover art by Bob Eggleton

A Tor Book
Published by Tom Doherty Associates, LLC
175 Fifth Avenue
New York, NY 10010

www.tor.com

Tor® is a registered trademark of Tom Doherty Associates, LLC.

ISBN 0-812-52126-9
EAN 978-0-812-52126-9

First edition: April 1989

Printed in the United States of America

20   19   18   17   16   15   14

For Dave and Pete and all the blokes
I met at the House on the Borderland
in July 1986. Cheers!

Many and multiform are the dim horrors of Earth, infesting her ways from the prime. They sleep beneath the unturned stone; they rise with the tree from its root; they move beneath the sea and in subterranean places; they dwell in the inmost adyta; they emerge betimes from the shutten sepulchre of haughty bronze and the low grave that is sealed with clay. There be some that are long known to man, and others as yet unknown that abide the terrible latter days of their revealing. Those which are the most dreadful and the loathliest of all are haply still to be declared. But among those that have revealed themselves aforetime and have made manifest their veritable presence, there is one which may not openly be named for its exceeding foulness. It is that spawn which the hidden dweller in the vaults has begotten upon mortality . . .

CLARK ASHTON SMITH
(As by Abdul Alhazred)

*They say foul beings of Old Times still lurk
In dark forgotten corners of the world,
And Gates still gape to loose, on certain nights,
Shapes pent in Hell . . .*

ROBERT E. HOWARD
(As by Justin Geoffrey)

Chapter One

Afternoon of the fourth Monday in January 1977; the
Château Bronnitsy off the Serpukhov road not far out of
Moscow; 2:40 P.M. middle-European time, and a telephone
in the temporary Investigation Control Room ringing . . .
ringing . . . ringing.

The Château Bronnitsy stood central on open, peaty
ground in the middle of a densely wooded tract now white
under drifted snow. A house or mansion of debased heri-
tage and mixed architectural antecedents, several recent
wings were of modern brick on old stone foundations,
while others were cheap breeze blocks camouflaged in
grey and green paint. A once-courtyard in the "U" of
polyglot wings was now roofed over, its roof painted to
match the surrounding terrain. Bedded at their bases in
massive, steeply gabled end walls, twin minarets raised
broken bulbous domes high over the landscape, their boarded
windows glooming like hooded eyes. In keeping with the
generally run-down aspect of the rest of the place, the
upper sections of these towers were derelict, decayed as

1

rotten fangs. From the air, the Château would seem a gaunt old ruin. But it was hardly that, even though the towers were not the only things in a state of decay.

Outside the roofed courtyard stood a canopied ten-ton Army truck, the canvas flaps at its rear thrown back and its exhaust puffing acrid blue smoke into the frosty air. A KGB man, conspicuous in his "uniform" of felt hat and dark grey overcoat, stared in across the truck's lowered tailgate at its contents and shuddered. Hands thrust deep in his pockets, he turned to a second man dressed in the white smock of a technician and grimaced. "Comrade Krakovitch," he grunted, "what the hell are they? And what are they doing here?"

Felix Krakovitch glanced at him, shook his head, said, "You wouldn't understand if I told you. And if you understood, you wouldn't believe." Like his ex-boss, Gregor Borowitz, Krakovitch considered all KGB low life-forms. He would keep information and assistance to the barest minimum—within certain limits of prudence and personal safety, of course. The KGB weren't much for forgiving and forgetting.

The blocky Special Policeman shrugged, lit a stubby brown cigarette and drew deeply on its cardboard tube. "Try me anyway," he said. 'It's cold here but I am warm enough. See, when I go to report to Comrade Andropov— and I am sure I need not remind you of his Politburo status—he will want some answers, which is why I want answers from you. So we will stand out here until—"

"Zombies!" said Krakovitch abruptly. "Mummies! Men dead for four hundred years. You can tell that from their weapons, and—" For the first time he heard the insistent ringing of the telephone, turned towards the door in the corrugated iron façade of the covered courtyard.

"Where are you going?" The KGB man came alive, took his hands out of his pockets. "Do you expect me to tell Yuri Andropov that the—the *mayhem*—here was done by dead men?'' He almost choked on the last two words, coughed long and loud, finally spat on the snow.

"Stand there long enough," Krakovitch said over his shoulder, "in those exhaust fumes, smoking that shredded rope, and you might as well climb in the truck with them!" He stepped through the door, let it slam shut behind him.

"Zombies?" The agent wrinkled his nose, looked again at the truckload of cadavers.

He couldn't know it but they were Crimean Tartars, butchered *en masse* in 1579 by Russian reinforcements hastening to a ravaged Moscow. They had died and gone down in blood and mire and bog, to lie part-preserved in the peat of a low-lying field—and to come up again two nights ago to wage war on the Château! They had won that war, the Tartars and their young English leader, Harry Keogh, for after the fighting only five of the Château's defenders still lived. Krakovitch was one of them. Five out of thirty-three, and the only enemy casualty Harry Keogh himself. Amazing odds, unless one counted the Tartars. But one could hardly count them, for they had been dead before it started . . .

These were Krakovitch's thoughts as he entered what long ago had been a cobbled courtyard—now a large area of plastic-tiled floor, partitioned into airy conservatories, small apartments and laboratories—where E-Branch operatives had studied and practised their esoteric talents in comparative comfort, or whatever condition or environment best suited their work. Forty-eight hours ago the place had been immaculate; now it was a shambles, where bullet-holes patterned the partition walls and the effects of blast and fire could be seen on every hand. It was a wonder the place hadn't been burned to the ground, completely gutted.

In a mainly cleared area—the so-called Investigation Control Room—a table had been erected and supported the ringing telephone. Krakovitch made his way towards it, pausing to drag aside a large piece of utility wall which partly blocked his path. Underneath, lying half-buried in crumbled plaster, broken glass and the crushed remains of a wooden chair, a human arm and hand lay like a huge grey salted slug. Its flesh was shrivelled, the colour of leather, and the bone where it projected in a knob at the shoulder was shiny white. It was almost a fossil. There'd be many more fragments such as this yet to be discovered, scattered throughout the Château, but apart from their repulsive looks they'd be harmless—now. Not so on the night of the horror. Krakovitch had seen portions like this one, without heads or brains to guide them, crawling, fighting, killing!

He shuddered, moved the arm aside with his foot, went to the telephone. "Hello, Krakovitch?"

"Who?" the unknown caller snapped back. "Krakovitch? Are you in charge there?" It was a female voice, very efficient.

"I suppose I am, yes," Krakovitch answered. "What can I do for you?"

"For me, nothing. For the Party Leader, only he can say. He's been trying to contact you for the last five minutes!"

Krakovitch was tired. He hadn't slept since the nightmare, doubted if he'd ever sleep again. He and the other four survivors, one of them a raving madman, had only come out of the security vault on Sunday morning, when the air was finished. Since then the others had made their statements, been sent home. The Château Bronnitsy was a High Security Establishment, so their stories wouldn't be for general consumption. In fact Krakovitch—being the only genuinely coherent member of the survivors—had demanded that the case *in toto* be sent direct to Leonid Brezhnev. That was Standing Orders anyway: Brezhnev was the top man, personally and directly responsible for E-Branch, despite the fact that he'd left all of it to Gregor Borowitz. But the branch had been important to the Party

Leader, and he'd seen everything that came out of it (or at least anything of any importance). Also, Borowitz must have told him quite a bit about the branch's paranormal work—literally ESPionage—so that Brezhnev should be at least part-qualified to pass judgement on what had happened here. Or so Krakovitch hoped. In any case, it had to be better than trying to explain it to Yuri Andropov!

"Krakovitch?" the phone barked at him. (Was this really the Party Leader?)

"Er, yes, sir, Felix Krakovitch. I was on Comrade Borowitz's staff."

"Felix? Why tell me your first name? You expect me to call you by your first name?" The voice had a hard edge, but it also sounded like its owner was eating something mushy. Krakovitch had heard several of Brezhnev's infrequent speeches; this could only be him.

"I . . . no, of course not, Comrade Party Leader." (How the hell did one *address* him?) "But I—"

"Listen, are you in charge there?"

"Yes, er, Comrade Party—"

"Forget all that stuff," Brezhnev rasped. "I don't need reminding who I am, just answers. Is there no one left who is senior to you?"

"No."

"Anyone who's your equal?"

"Four of them, but one's a madman."

"Eh?"

"He went mad when . . . when it happened."

There was a pause; then, the voice went on, a little less harshly: "Do you know Borowitz is dead?"

"Yes. A neighbour found him in his dacha at Zhukovka. The neighbour was ex-KGB and got in touch with Comrade Andropov, who sent a man here. He's here now."

"I know another name," Brezhnev's thick, gurgling voice continued. "Boris Dragosani. What of him?"

"Dead," and before Krakovitch could check his tongue, "thank God!"

"Eh? You're glad one of your comrades is dead?"

"I . . . yes, I'm glad." Krakovitch was too tired to answer in any way but truthfully, straight from the heart. "I think he was probably part of it; at least, I believe he brought it down on us. His body is still here. Also the bodies of our other dead—and that of Harry Keogh, a British agent, we think. And also—"

"The Tartars?" Brezhnev was quiet now.

Krakovitch sighed. The man wasn't a slave to convention after all. "Yes, but no longer . . . animate," he answered.

Another pause. "Krakovitch—er, Felix, did you say? —I've read the statements of the other three. Are they true? No chance of an error, mass hypnotism or delusion or something? Was it really as bad as that?"

"They are true—no chance of an error—it *was* as bad as that."

"Felix, listen. Take over there. I mean *you*, take over. I don't want E-Branch shut down. It has been more than beneficial to our security. And Borowitz was more valuable to me personally than many of my generals would ever believe. So I want the branch rebuilt. And it looks like you've got the job."

Krakovitch felt like a swatted fly: knocked off his feet, lost for words. "I . . . Comrade . . . I mean—"

"Can you do it?"

Krakovitch wasn't crazy. It was the chance of a lifetime. "It will take years—but yes, I'll try to do it."

"Good! But if you take it on, you'll have to do more than just try, Felix. Let me know what you need and I'll see you get it. The first thing *I* want is answers. But I'm the only one who gets those answers, you understand? This one has to be screwed down. It mustn't leak. And that reminds me—did you say there was someone from the KGB with you right now?"

"He's outside, in the grounds."

"Get him," Brezhnev's voice was harsh again. "Bring him to the phone. Let me speak to him at once!"

Krakovitch started back across the floor, but at that moment the door opened to admit the man in question. He squared his shoulders, looked at Krakovitch in a surly, narrow-eyed manner, said, "We haven't finished, Comrade."

"I'm afraid we have," Krakovitch felt shored up, buoyant as a cork. It must be his fatigue beginning to work on him. "There ... someone on the phone for you."

"Eh? For me?" The other pushed by him. "Who is it, someone ... m the office?"

"Not sure," Krakovitch lied. "Head office, I think."

The KGB man frowned at him, scowled, snatched up the phone from the table. "Yanov here. What is it? I'm busy down here, and—"

His face immediately underwent rapid changes of expression and colour. He jerked visibly and almost staggered. Only the phone seemed to be holding him up. "Yessir! Oh, yes, sir. Yes, sir! Yes, yessir! No, sir. I will, sir. Yes, sir. But I—no, sir. *Yessir!*" He looked sick, held out the phone for Krakovitch, glad to be rid of it.

As Krakovitch took the instrument from him, the agent hissed viciously: "Fool! That's the Party Leader!"

Krakovitch let his eyes go big and round, made an "O" with his mouth. Then he said casually into the mouthpiece, "Krakovitch here," and at once held the phone towards the KGB man, let him hear Brezhnev's voice:

"Felix? Has that prick gone yet?"

It was the Special Policeman's turn to make an "O."

"He's going now," Krakovitch answered. He nodded sharply towards the door. "Out! And do try to remember what the Party Leader told you. For your own good."

The KGB operative shook his head dazedly, licked his lips, headed for the door. He was still white-faced. At the door he turned, thrust his chin out. "I—" he began.

"Goodbye, comrade," Krakovitch dismissed him. "Now

he's gone,'' he finally confirmed, after the door had slammed shut.

"Good! I don't want them interfering. They didn't fool about with Gregor, and I don't want them fooling with you. Any problems from them and you get straight back to me!''

"Yes, sir.''

"Now, here's what I want . . . But first, tell me—have the branch records survived?''

"Almost everything's intact, except for our agents. There's damage, a lot. But records, installations, the Château itself—in decent order, I think. Manpower's a different story. I'll tell you what we have left. There's myself and three other survivors, six more on holiday in various parts, three fairly good telepaths on permanent duty in connection with the British, American and French embassies, and another four or five field agents out in the world. With twenty-eight dead, we've lost almost two-thirds of our staff. Most of the best men are gone.''

"Yes, yes,'' Brezhnev was impatient. "Manpower is important, that's why I asked about records. Recruitment! That's your first task. It will take a long time, I know, but get on it. Old Gregor once told me that you have special sorts who can spot others with the talent, right?''

"I've still got one good spotter, yes,'' Krakovitch answered, giving an unconscious nod. "I'll start using him at once. And I'll commence studying Comrade Borowitz's records, of course.''

"Good! Now then, see how quickly you can get that place cleaned up. Those Tartar corpses: burn 'em! And don't let anyone see them. I don't care how that's done, but do it. Then put in a comprehensive works chit for repairs on the Château. I'll have it actioned at once. In fact, I'll have a man here, on this number or another number he'll give you, who you can contact at any time for anything. That's from right now. You'll keep him informed and he'll keep me informed. He'll be your only boss, except he'll deny you nothing. See how highly I prize you, Felix? Right, that should get things started. As for the rest: Felix Krakovitch, I want to know *how* this happened! Are they that far ahead, the British, the Americans, the Chinese? I mean, how *could* one man, this Harry Keogh, do so much damage?''

"Comrade," Krakovitch answered, "you mentioned Boris Dragosani. I once watched him work. He was a necromancer. He sniffed out the secrets of dead men. I've seem him do things to corpses that gave me nightmares for months! You ask how Harry Keogh could do so much damage? From what little I've so far been able to discover, it seems he was capable of almost anything. Telepathy, teleportation, even Dragosani's own necromancy. He was their best. But I think Keogh was many steps ahead of Dragosani. It's one thing to torture dead men and drain their secrets from their blood and brains and guts, but it's quite another to call them up out of their graves and make them fight for you!''

"Teleportation?" For a moment the Party Leader was thoughtful, then came on impatient: "You know, the more I hear the less I'm inclined to believe. I *wouldn't* believe, except I saw Borowitz's results. And how else am I to explain a couple of hundred Tartar corpses, eh? But right now . . . I've spent enough time with you on this. I have other things to do. In five more minutes I'll have your go-between on this line. Think about it and tell him what you want done, anything you need. If he can come up with something he will. He's had this kind of assignment before. Well, not exactly *this* kind! One last thing . . .''

"Yes?" Krakovitch's head was whirling.

"Let me make it quite clear: I want the answers. As soon as possible. But there has to be a limit, and that limit's a year. By then the branch will be working at 100 percent efficiency, and you and I will know everything. And we'll understand everything. You see, when we have all the answers, Felix, then we'll be as smart as the people who did this. Right?''

"That seems logical, Party Leader."

"It is, so get to it. Good luck . . ." The phone emitted a continuous buzzing tone.

Krakovitch replaced it carefully in its cradle, stared at it for a moment, then started for the door. In his head he made lists—in loose order of precedence—of things to be done. In the western world such a massive tragedy could never be covered up, but here in the USSR it wouldn't be nearly so difficult. Krakovitch wasn't sure whether that was a good thing or not.

1. The dead men had families. They would now have to be told some sort of story—maybe there had been a "castastrophic accident." That must be his go-between's responsibility.

2. All E-Branch personnel must be recalled at once, including the three who knew what had happened here. They were in their homes right now, but they knew enough to say nothing.

3. The bodies of twenty-eight E-Branch colleagues would have to be gathered up, coffined, prepared as best as possible for burial. And that would have to be done here, by the survivors and those returning from leave of absence.

4. Recruitment must be started at once.

5. A Second in Command must be appointed, so that Krakovitch could begin a proper, *complete* investigation from scratch. That was something he must do himself, just as Brezhnev had ordered it.

And, 6 . . . he would think of 6 when the first 5 were working! But before any of that—

Outside he found the driver of the Army truck, a young Sergeant in uniform. "What's your name?" he asked, listlessly. He must get some sleep soon.

"Sergeant Gulharov, *sir!*" he slammed to attention.

"First name?"

"Sergei, *sir!*"

"Sergei, call me Felix. Tell me, did you ever hear of Felix the Cat?"

The other shook his head.

"I have a friend who collects old films, cartoons," Krakovitch told him, shrugging. "He has connections. Anyway, there's a funny American cartoon character called Felix the Cat. He's a very wary fellow, this Felix. Cats usually are, you know? In the British Army, they call bomb disposal officers Felix, too—they have to tread so very warily. Ah! Maybe my mother should have called me Sergei, eh?"

The Sergeant scratched his head. "Sir?"

"Never mind," said Krakovitch. "Tell me: do you carry spare fuel?"

"Only what's in the tank, sir. About fifty litres."

Krakovitch nodded. "Right, let's get in the cab and I'll tell you where to drive." He directed him around the Château to a bunker near the helicopter landing area, where they kept the Avgas. It was very close, but better to take the truck to the Avgas than bring the Avgas to the truck. On their way, bumping over the rough ground, the Sergeant asked, "Sir, what happened here?"

For the first time Krakovitch noticed that his eyes had a glazed look. He had helped load his truck's awful cargo. "Never ask that sort of question," Krakovitch told him. "In fact as long as you're here—which will probably be a long, long time—don't ask *any* questions. Just do as you're told."

They loaded the cans of Avgas just inside the truck's tailgate and drove to a wooded corner of the Château's grounds where the earth was very boggy. Sergei Gulharov protested, but Krakovitch made him drive on until the truck was quite bogged down in churned up snow and mud. When they could go no farther, Krakovitch said, "This will do."

They got out and unloaded the Avgas and, still protesting, the Sergeant helped Krakovitch pour the aviation fuel all around and into the truck. When they were through, Krakovitch asked, "Anything in the cab that you want?"

"No, sir." Gulharov was agitated. "Sir, er, Felix—you can't do this. We must *not* do this! I'll be court-martialled, shot even! When I get back to barracks, they'll—"

"Are you married or single?" Krakovitch poured a thin trail of Avgas from the truck well back into the trees. It cut a dark groove in the snow.

"Single."

"Me too. Good! Well, you're not going back to barracks, Sergei. From now on you work with me, always."

"But—"

"No buts. The Party Leader has ordered it. You should feel honoured!"

"But my Sergeant-Major, and the Colonel, they—"

"Believe me," Krakovitch again interrupted, "they'll be proud of you. Do you smoke, Sergei?" He patted the pockets of his now less than white smock, found cigarettes.

"Yes, sir, sometimes."

Krakovitch offered him a cigarette and put one in his own mouth. "I seem to have forgotten my matches."

"Sir, I—"

"Matches," Krakovitch repeated, holding out his hand.

Gulharov surrendered, began to reach into a deep pocket. If Krakovitch was crazy, it would work out all right in the end. They'd lock him away and Sergeant Sergei Gulharov would be exonerated. Of course, he could always assume that he was mad and jump on him right here and now. That way, if he *was* mad, he'd be a hero. He readied himself.

Krakovitch saw it coming, only seconds away. That was his talent: precognition, to see in advance. In situations like this it was as good as telepathy; he could almost feel the young Sergeant's muscles bunching. "If you do that," he said very quickly and earnestly, staring straight into the other's eyes, "then they really will court-martial you!"

Gulharov bit his lip, clenched and unclenched a fist, shook his head and backed off a pace.

"Well?" Krakovitch was patient. "Do you really think I'd take the Party Leader's name in vain?"

The Sergeant took out a box of matches and handed them over. They moved away from the Avgas trail. Then Krakovitch lit their cigarettes, cupped his hand over the flame until the entire match was burning, and finally tossed it towards the lethally scarred snow.

Blue, near-invisible flames leaped back towards the truck thirty yards away. The snow along the groove collapsed in upon itself under the sudden intense heat. And the truck ignited in a blinding flash of fire and brilliant blue light.

The two men backed off, watched the flames roar higher. They could hear the crackling, hissing and popping of its ancient corpse cargo, which seemed to be burning nicely. *Back where you came from, lads,* thought Krakovitch, *and no way anyone can ever disturb you again!* "Come on," he said out loud. "Let's get away before the truck's fuel tank goes up."

They ran clumsily through the snow, back towards the Château. Oddly, it wasn't until they were in the shade of the Château itself that the tank did go, and by then the truck was a blazing shell anyway. Hearing the thunderous roar and feeling something of its concussion, they looked back. Cab and chassis and superstructure had all flown apart; bits of blazing debris were falling in the snow; a mushroom of smoke shot with flame was uncurling itself high over the trees. It was done . . .

Krakovitch spoke for some time on the telephone to his go-between, an anonymous voice which seemed hardly interested in what he was saying, yet precise and cutting as a razor when its owner required more information. He finished off by saying: "Oh, and I've a new assistant here, a Sergeant Sergei Gulharov, from the supply and transport barracks in Serpukhov. I'm keeping him on. Can you get him permanently posted to the Château, as of now? He's young and strong and I'll have plenty of work for him.''

"Yes, I'll do that," came the cool, clear answer. "He'll be your odd-job man, you say?"

"And my bodyguard," said Krakovitch, "eventually. I'm not much physically."

"Very well. I'll check out the chances of getting him on a military close protection course. Weapons, too, if he's not up to scratch. Of course, we could take a shortcut and get you a professional . . ."

"No," Krakovitch was firm. "No professionals. This one will do. He's fairly innocent and I like that. It's refreshing."

"Krakovitch," said the voice on the other end, "I need to know this. Are you a homosexual?"

"Of course not! Oh! I see. No, I need him genuinely— and he looks about as gay as a shipyard welder! I'll tell you why I want him right now—because I'm alone here. And if you were here you'd know what I mean."

"Yes, I'm told you've had to weather quite a lot. Very well, leave it with me."

"Thank you," said Krakovitch. He broke the connection.

Gulharov was impressed. "Just like that," he said. "You have a lot of power, sir."

"It seems that way, doesn't it?" Krakovitch smiled tiredly. "Listen, I'm dead on my feet. But there's one more thing to do before I can sleep. And let me tell you, if you think what you've seen so far is unpleasant, what you're about to see is far worse! Come with me."

He led the way through the chaos of shattered rooms and piled rubble, from the covered-in courtyard area into the main, original building, then up two flights of time-hollowed stone stairs into one of the twin towers. This was where Gregor Borowitz had had his office, which Dragosani had turned into his control room on the night of the horror.

The stairwell was scarred and blackened, with tiny fragments of shrapnel, flattened lead bullets and copper cases lying everywhere. The stink of cordite was still heavy in the air. That would be from blast grenades, tossed down here from above when the tower came under attack. But none of this had stopped Harry Keogh and his Tartars. On the second floor landing the door to a tiny anteroom stood open. The room had served as an office for Borowitz's secretary, Yul Galenski. Krakovitch had known him personally: a generally timid man, a clerk with no extrasensory talent. Just staff.

Between the open door and the stairwell's safety rail, face down on the landing, lay a corpse in the Château's duty uniform: grey coveralls with a single diagonal yellow stripe across the heart. Not Galenski (he had been a "civvies only" man) but the Duty Officer. The corpse's face lay quite flat on the floor in a pool of blood. Flatter than it should. That was because there was very little of actual face left, just a raw flat mess.

Krakovitch and Gulharov stepped carefully over the body, entered the little office. Behind a desk, crumpled in one corner, Galenski sat clutching a rusty curved sword where it stuck out of his chest. It had been driven home with such force that he was pinned to the wall. His eyes were still open, but no longer terrified. From some people, death steals all emotion.

"Mother in heaven!" Gulharov whispered. He'd never seen anything like this. He wasn't even a combat soldier, not yet.

They went through a second door into what had been Borowitz's office.

It was spacious, with great bullet-proof bay windows looking out and down from the tower's curving stone wall toward distant woodland. The carpet was burned and stained here and there. A massive block of a desk in solid oak stood in one corner, receiving light from the windows and protection from the stone wall at its back. As for the rest of the room: it was a shambles—and a nightmare!

A shattered radio spilled its guts onto the floor; walls

were pockmarked and the door splintered from the impact of sprayed bullets; the body of a young man in Western styled clothes lay where it had fallen, ripped by machine gun fire, almost in two pieces behind the door. It was glued to the floor with its own blood. This was Harry Keogh's body: nothing much to look at, but there was no fear or pain on his white, unmarked face.

As for the nightmare: that lay propped against the wall on the other side of the room.

"Boris Dragosani," said Krakovitch, pointing. "The thing pinned to his chest is what controlled him, I think." He stepped carefully across the room to stand gazing down on what was left of Dragosani and his parasite creature; Gulharov was right behind him, not wanting to get too close.

Both of Dragosani's legs were broken and lay at weird angles. His arms hung slack down the wall to the skirting, elbows just off the floor, forearms at ninety degrees and hands projecting well beyond the cuffs of his jacket. They were hands like claws, big, powerful and grasping, frozen in Dragosani's final spasm. His face was a rictus of agony, made worse by the fact that it was hardly a human face at all, and worse still by the gash that split his skull ear to ear.

But his *face!*

Dragosani's jaws were long as some great hound's, gaping open to display curving needle teeth. His skull was misshapen, and his ears were pointed where they curved forward and lay flat against his temples. His eyes were ruptured red pits above a nose long and wrinkled and flattened to show gaping nostrils, like the convoluted snout of some great bat. That was how he looked: part man, part wolf, part bat. And the thing pinned to his chest was worse.

"What . . . what *is* that?" Gulharov gasped out the question.

"God help me," Krakovitch shook his head, "I don't

know! But it lived in him. I mean, inside him. It only came out at the end.''

The trunk of the thing had the form of a great leech some eighteen inches long, but tapering to a tail. There were no limbs; it seemed to cling to Dragosani's chest by suction, and was held there by a sharp stake formed of the splintered hardwood stock of a heavy-duty machine gun; its skin was grey-green, corrugated. Gulharov saw that its head, flat and cobra-like—but eyeless, blind—lay on the carpet a little apart.

"Like . . . like some gigantic tapeworm?'' Gulharov's horror was plain on his face.

"Something like that,'' Krakovitch nodded grimly. "But intelligent, evil, and deadly.''

"Why have we come up here?'' Gulharov's Adam's apple bobbed. "There are fifty million better places to be.''

Krakovitch's face was white, pinched. He could fully appreciate Gulharov's feelings. "We've come up here because we have to burn this, that's why.'' His talent again, warning him that both Dragosani and his symbiont *must* be destroyed, utterly. He looked around, saw a tall steel filing cabinet standing against the wall to one side of the door. He and Gulharov tore out the shelving, turning the cabinet into a metal coffin. They lowered it onto its back and dragged it across the floor to Dragosani.

"You take his shoulders, I'll take his thighs,'' said Krakovitch. "Once we've got him in here we can close the door and slide the cabinet down the steps. Frankly, I don't fancy touching him. I'll touch him as little as possible. This way has to be best.''

They gingerly lifted the corpse, strained to get it over the rim of the cabinet, lowered it inside. Gulharov went to close the door and the projecting stake got in the way. He grasped the splintered stock in both hands—and the mental warning hit Krakovitch like a fist in his heart!

"Don't touch that!'' he yelled, but too late.

As Gulharov wrenched the stake free, so the leech-thing—headless as it was—came alive. Its hideous slug-like body began to lash in a frenzy, so that it almost ejected itself from the cabinet. At the same time its leathery skin broke open in a dozen places, putting out protoplasmic tentacles that writhed and vibrated in a sort of mindless agony. These pseudopods whipped out, struck the sides of the cabinet and recoiled, settled on Dragosani's body. They passed through clothing and dead flesh and burrowed into him. More of them sprouted from the main body; they formed barbs, hooked themselves into Dragosani's flesh. One of the tentacles found his chest cavity; it thickened rapidly to the diameter of a man's wrist; the rest dissolved their barbs, released their holds, withdrew and followed the main branch *into* him. With a final sucking *plop* the entire organism drew itself down into Dragosani's body. His trunk began to heave and throb where it lay in the cabinet.

While all of this occurred, Gulharov had danced away and clambered up onto the desk. He was mouthing half-inarticulate obscenities, shrieking like a woman. And he was pointing at something. Krakovitch, almost numb with shock and horror, saw the leech-creature's flat cobra head vibrating on the floor, flipping and flopping like a stranded flatfish. He gave a cry of loathing, began to panic, then gripped himself tight and drove the panic out. Finally he slammed the cabinet door shut and shot the bolt.

He grabbed a metal drawer from the cabinet's scattered guts, yelled: "Well, *help* me!"

Gulharov got down off the desk. He still had the stake, was hanging on to it like grim death. Prodding the flopping head, and cursing all the time under his breath, finally he juggled the thing into Krakovitch's drawer. Krakovitch slammed a section of shelving down on top of it, and Gulharov brought a pair of heavy ledgers to put on top of that. Both cabinet and drawer shuddered and shook for a few seconds more, then were still.

Like a pair of ghosts Krakovitch and Gulharov faced each other, both of them panting, white as sheets and round-eyed. Then Krakovitch snarled, reached out and slapped the other's face. "Bodyguard?" he shouted. "Bloody bodyguard?" He slapped him again, hard. *"Bloody hell!"*

"I . . . I'm sorry. I didn't know what to . . ." Gulharov was trembling like a leaf, looked like he was going to faint.

Krakovitch calmed down. He could hardly blame him. "It's all right," he said. "It's all right. Now listen: we'll burn the head up here. We'll do that first, right now. Go quickly, fetch Avgas."

Staggering a little, Gulharov went.

He was back in record time, carrying a jerrycan. They slid the shelving over the drawer open a crack, poured Avgas. There was no movement from inside the drawer. "Enough!" said Krakovitch. "Any more and there'll be one hell of an explosion. Now then, help me drag the cabinet through into the other room." In a moment they were back, and Krakovitch tipped out the drawers of Borowitz's desk. He found what he was looking for: a small ball of string. He snapped off a ten foot length, soaked it in Avgas, carefully dangled one end through the crack into the drawer. Then he laid the string out on the floor in a straight line towards the door and took out Gulharov's matches. They shielded their eyes as he lit the fuse.

Blue fire raced across the floor, leaped into the drawer. There was a dull *thump* and shelving, ledgers and all hit the ceiling, then fell back to the floor. The metal drawer was an inferno, in which the flat snake-head danced and skittered—but not for long. As the drawer began to buckle under the heat and the carpet about it blackened and burst into flames, so the thing in the drawer puffed up, split open and quickly became liquescent. And then it, too, burned. But Krakovitch and Gulharov waited a full minute more before they put out the fire.

Krakovitch gave a curt nod. "Well, at least we know the thing burns!" he said. "It was probably dead anyway, but by my books when a thing's dead it lies still!"

They bumped the cabinet downstairs, two flights to the ground floor, then out through the battle-torn building into the grounds. Krakovitch stood guard on it while Gulharov went back for the Avgas. When he returned, Krakovitch said, "This will be the tricky bit. First we pour some of this stuff around the cabinet. That way, when we open it, if what's inside is—active—we just jump back out of range and toss a match. Until it's quiet. And so on . . ."

Gulharov seemed uncertain, but he was far more alert now.

They poured Avgas on to and around the cabinet, and then Gulharov got well back out of it. Krakovitch slid back the bolt, threw the door clangingly open. Inside, Dragosani stared into the sky. His chest stirred a little, but that was all. As Krakovitch began to pour Avgas carefully into the cabinet near Dragosani's feet, Gulharov came forward. "Don't use too much," it was the Sergeant's turn to caution. "Or it will go off like a bomb!"

When the fuel swirled almost an inch deep around Dragosani's prone form, evaporating furiously, the dead man's chest gave another sudden lurch. Krakovitch stopped pouring, stared, backed off a little. Outside the circle of danger, Gulharov stood with a match ready to strike. A slickly shining, grey-green tendril sprouted upwards from Dragosani's chest. Its tip formed a knob as big as a fist, which in turn formed an eye. Just seeing that orb, Krakovitch knew there was no thought behind it, no sentience. It was vacant, staring, made no connections and carried no emotions. Krakovitch doubted if it even saw. Certainly there was no longer any brain for it to relay its message to. The eye melted back into protoflesh, was replaced by small jaws which clashed mindlessly. Then it sank down again out of sight.

"Felix, get out of there!" Gulharov was nervous.

Krakovitch backed out of the circle; Gulharov struck a match, tossed it; in a moment the cabinet was an inferno. Like the oblong mouth of a jet engine on test, the cabinet hurled a pale blue sheet of fire roaring into the cold air, a shimmering column of intense heat. And then Dragosani sat up!

Gulharov clutched Krakovitch, clung to him. "Oh God! Oh, mother—he's alive!" he croaked.

"No," Krakovitch denied, tearing himself free. "The thing *in* him is alive, but mindless. It's all instinct with no brain to govern it. It would flee but doesn't know how to, or even what it's fleeing from. If you spear a sea-cucumber it reacts, spills out its guts. No mind, just reaction. Look, look! It's melting!"

And indeed it seemed that Dragosani was melting. Smoke curled upward from his blackened shell; layers of skin peeled away, bursting into flame; the fats of his body ran like candle wax, and were consumed by the fire. The thing inside him felt the heat, reacted. Dragosani's trunk shuddered, vibrated, convulsed. His arms shot out straight, then fell to dangle over the sides of the blazing cabinet, where all the while they jerked and twitched. His clothing was completely burned away by now, and as Krakovitch and Gulharov watched and shuddered, so his crisped flesh burst open here and there, putting out frantic, whipping tendrils that melted and slopped down into the furnace.

In a very little while he fell back and was still, and the two men stood in the snow and watched the fire until it burned itself out. It took all of twenty minutes, but they stood there anyway . . .

3:00 P.M., 27 August 1977.

The big London hotel, within easy walking distance of Whitehall, contained rather more than its exterior might suggest. In fact the entire top floor was given over to a company of "international financial entrepreneurs," which was the sum total of the hotel manager's knowledge about it. The company had its own elevator at the rear of the building, private stairs, even its own fire escape. Indeed the company owned the top floor, which was therefore entirely outside the hotel's sphere of control and operation.

In short, the top floor was the headquarters of the most secret of all British secret services: namely INTESP, the British equivalent of that Russian organization housed just outside Moscow at the Château Bronnitsy. But the hotel was only the headquarters; there were also two "factories," one in Dorset and the other in Norfolk, direct-linked to each other and to the HQ by telephone, radio-telephone and computer. Such links, though top-security screened, were open to sophisticated abuse, of course; a clever hacker might get in one day. Hopefully before that happened the branch would have developed its telepaths to such an extent that all of this technological junk would be unnecessary. Radio waves travel at a mere 186,000 miles per second, but human thought is instantaneous and carries a far more vivid and finished picture.

Such were Alec Kyle's own thoughts as he sat at his desk and formulated Security Standing Orders for the six Special Branch officers whose sole task in life was the personal security of an infant boy just one month old, a child called Harry Keogh. Harry Jr.—the future head of INTESP.

"Harry," said Kyle out loud, to no one in particular, "you can have the job right now, if you still want it."

No, came the answer at once, startlingly clear in Kyle's mind. *Not now, maybe not ever!*

Kyle's mouth fell open and he started upright in his swivel chair. He knew what this was, had known something very much similar at a time some eight months ago. It was telepathy, yes, but it was more than telepathy. It was the "infant" he'd just been thinking about, the child whose mind housed all that was left of the greatest ESP talent in the world: Harry Keogh.

"Christ!" Kyle whispered. And now he knew what it had been about, "it" being the dream or nightmare he'd had last night—when he'd been covered with leeches as big as kittens, whose mouths had fastened on him to drain his blood, while he had leaped and gibbered in a glade of stirless trees, until he'd been too weak to fight any longer. Then he'd fallen on the earth amidst the pine needles, and the leeches had clung to him, and he'd known that he was *becoming* a leech!

And that, mercifully, had scared him wide awake. As for the dream's meaning: Kyle had long since given up trying to read meanings into such precognitive glimpses. That was the trouble with them: they were usually cryptic, rarely self-elucidating. But certainly he'd known that the dream was one of *those* dreams, and now he guessed that this had something to do with it, too.

"Harry?" he breathed the query into the suddenly frigid atmosphere of the room. His breath actually plumed in the air; in the space of mere seconds the temperature had taken a plunge. Just like last time.

Something was forming in the middle of the room, in front of Kyle's desk. The smoke of his cigarette trembled there and the air seemed to waver. He got up, crossed quickly to the window and adjusted the blinds. The room grew dim, and the figure in front of his desk took on more form.

Kyle's intercom buzzed urgently and he jumped six inches. He leaped to his desk, hit the receive button, and a breathless voice said, "Alec, there's something here!" It was Carl Quint, a top-rank psychic sensitive, a "spotter."

Kyle pressed the send button, held it down. "I know. It's with me now. But it's OK, I've been half-expecting it." Now he pressed the command button, spoke to the entire HQ. "Kyle here. I don't want to talk to anybody for—for as long as it takes. No messages, no incoming calls, and no questions. Listen in if you like, but don't try to interfere. I'll get back to you.'' He pressed the secure button on his desk computer keyboard, and door and window locks audibly snapped shut. And now he and Harry Keogh were completely alone.

Kyle forced himself to relax, stared at the—ghost?—of Keogh where it confronted him across his desk. And he thought an old thought, one which had never been far away, not since the first day he'd come here to work for INTESP:

Funny bloody outfit. Robots and romantics. Super science and the supernatural. Telemetry and telepathy. Computerized probability patterns and precognition. Gadgets . . . and ghosts!

No ghost, Alec, Keogh answered with a wan, immaterial smile. *I thought we went into all of that last time?*

Kyle thought about pinching himself but didn't bother. He'd gone through all of *that* last time, too. "Last time?" he spoke out loud, because that was easier for him. "But that was eight months ago, Harry. I had started to think we'd never hear from you again."

Maybe you wouldn't have, said the other, his lips moving not at all, *for believe me I've plenty to keep me occupied. But . . . something's come up.*

Kyle's awe was ebbing, his pulse gradually slowing to its norm. He leaned forward in his chair, looked the other up and down. Oh, it was Keogh, all right. But not exactly the same as the last time. Last time Kyle's first thought had been that the—apparition—was supernatural. Not merely paranormal or ESP-engendered but actually supernatural, extra-mundane, not of this world. Just like now, the office scanners had failed to detect it; it had come and told Kyle a fantastic true story, and gone without leaving a trace. No, not quite, for he'd written down all that had been said. Even thinking about *that*, his wrist ached. But you couldn't photograph the thing, couldn't record its voice, couldn't harm or interfere with it in any way. The entire HQ was now listening in on Kyle's conversation with this, this . . . with Harry Keogh—and yet they'd hear only Kyle's voice. But Keogh *was* here: at least the central heating's thermostat knew it. The heating had just come on, turning itself up several notches to compensate for the sudden drop in temperature. Yes, and Carl Quint knew it, too.

The figure seemed etched in pale blue light: insubstantial as a moonbeam, less than a puff of smoke. Incorporeal, yet there was a power in it. An unbelievable power.

Taking into account the fact that his neon-limned feet weren't quite touching the floor, Keogh must be about five-ten in height. If his flesh were real instead of luminous filament, he would weigh maybe nine and a half to ten stone. Everything about him was now vaguely fluorescent, as if shining with some faint inner light, so Kyle couldn't be sure about colouring. His hair, an untidy mop, might be sandy, his face slightly freckled. He would be twenty-one, twenty-two years old.

His eyes were interesting. They looked *at* Kyle and yet seemed to look right through him, as if he were the apparition and not the other way about. They were blue, those eyes—a startling, almost colourless blue neon—but more than this, there was that in those eyes which said they knew more than any twenty-two year old had any right to know. The wisdom of ages seemed locked in them, the knowledge of centuries lying just beneath the shimmer of blue haze which covered them.

Apart from that: his features would be fine, like blue porcelain and seemingly equally fragile; his hands slim, tapering; his shoulders drooped a little; his skin in general, apart from the freckles, pale and unblemished. But for those eyes, you probably wouldn't look twice at him on the street. He was just . . . a young man. Or had been.

And now? Now he was something more. Harry Keogh's body had no real, physical existence now, but his mind went on. And his mind was housed in a new—quite literally new—body. Kyle found himself starting to examine *that* part of the apparition, quickly checked himself. What was there to examine? In any case it could wait, wasn't important. All that mattered was that Keogh was here, and that he had something important to say.

"Something's come up?" Kyle repeated the Keogh projection's statement, made it a question. "What sort of something, Harry?"

Something monstrous! Right now I can give you only the barest outline—I simply don't know enough about it, not yet. But do you remember what I told you about the Russian E-Branch? And about Dragosani? I know there was no way you could check it all out, but have you looked into it at all? Do you believe *what I told you about Dragosani?*

While Keogh spoke to him, so Kyle had stared fascinated at that facet of him which was different, that addition to him since the last time he'd seen or sensed him. For now, superimposed over the apparition's abdomen—suspended in midair and slowly spinning on its own axis, turning *in* the space that Keogh's body occupied—there floated a naked male baby, or the ghost of one, just as insubstantial as Keogh himself. The child was curled like a foetus floating in some invisible, churning fluid, like some strange biological exhibit, like a hologram. But it was a real baby, and alive; and Kyle knew that it, too, was Harry Keogh.

"About Dragosani?" Kyle came back to earth. "Yes, I believe you. I have to believe you. I checked out as much as I could and it was all exactly as you said. And as for Borowitz's branch—whatever you did there, it was devastating! They contacted us a week later, the Russians, and asked us if we wanted you . . . I mean—"

"My body?"

"—if we wanted it back, yes. They contacted *us*, you understand. Direct. It didn't come through diplomatic channels. They weren't ready to admit that they existed, and didn't expect us to admit that we existed. Therefore *you* didn't exist, but they asked us if we wanted you back anyway. With Borowitz gone they have a new boss, Felix Krakovitch. He said we could have you, if we'd tell them how. How you did what you did to them. *What*, exactly, you'd done to them. I'm sorry, Harry, but we had to deny you, tell them we didn't know you. Actually, *we* didn't know you! Only I knew you, and Sir Keenan before me. But if we'd admitted you were one of ours, what you'd done might be construed as warfare.''

Actually, it was mayhem! said Keogh. *Listen, Alec, this can't be like the last time we talked. I may not have the time. On the metaphysical plane I have comparative freedom. In the Möbius continuum I'm a free agent. But here in the physical now I'm a virtual prisoner in little Harry. Right now he's asleep and I can use his subconscious mind as my own. But when he's awake his mind's his own, and like a magnet I'm drawn back to it. The stronger he gets—the more his mind learns—the less freedom for me. Eventually I'll be forced to leave him entirely for an existence along the Möbius way. If I get the chance I'll explain all of that later, but for now we don't know how long he'll sleep and so we have to use our time wisely. And what I have to say can't wait.*

''And it somehow concerns Dragosani?'' Kyle frowned. ''But Dragosani's dead. You told me that yourself.''

Keogh's face—the face of his apparition—was grave now. *Do you remember what he was, this Dragosani?*

''He was a necromancer,'' said Kyle at once, no shadow of doubt in his mind. ''Much like you.'' He saw his mistake immediately and could have bitten his tongue.

Unlike me! Keogh corrected him. *I was, I am, a necroscope, not a necromancer. Dragosani stole the secrets of the dead like . . . like an insane dentist yanking healthy teeth—without an anaesthetic. Me: I talk to the dead and respect them. And they respect me. But very well, I know that was a slip of the tongue. I know you didn't mean that. So yes, he was a necromancer. But because of what the old Thing in the ground did to him, he was more than that. He was worse than that.*

Of course. Now Kyle remembered. ''You mean he was also a vampire.''

Keogh's shimmering image nodded. *That's exactly what I mean. And that's why I'm here now. You see, you're the only one in the world who can do anything about it. You and your branch, and maybe your Russian counterparts. And when you know what I'm talking about, then you'll have to do something about it.*

Such was Keogh's intensity, such the warning in his mental voice, that gooseflesh crept on Kyle's spine. ''Do something about what, Harry?''

About the rest of them, the apparition answered. *You see, Alec, Dragosani and Thibor Ferenczy weren't the only ones. And God only knows how many more there are!*

''Vampires?'' Kyle thrilled with horror. He remembered only too well that story Keogh had told him some eight months ago. ''You're sure?''

Oh yes. In the Möbius continuum—looking out through the doors of time past and time to come—I've seen their scarlet threads. I wouldn't have known them, might never have come across them, but they cross young Harry's blue life thread. Yes, and they cross yours, too!

Hearing that, it was as if the cold blade of a psychic knife lanced into Kyle's heart. ''Harry,'' he said stumblingly, ''you'd . . . you'd better tell me all you know, and then what I must do.''

I'll tell you as much as I can, and then we'll try to decide what's to be done. As to how I know what I'm about to tell you . . . The apparition shrugged. *I'm a necroscope, remember? I've talked to Thibor Ferenczy himself, as I once promised him I would, and I've talked to one other. A recent victim. More of him later. But mainly the story is Thibor's . . .*

Chapter Two

THE OLD THING IN THE GROUND TREMBLED HOWEVER MINUTELY, shuddered slightly, strove to return to his immemorial dreaming. Something was intruding, threatening to rouse him up from his dark slumbers, but sleep had become a habit which satisfied his every need . . . almost.

He clung to his loathsome dreams—of madness and mayhem, the hell of living and the horror of dying, and the pleasures of blood, blood, blood—and felt the cold embrace of the clotted earth closing him in, weighing him down, holding him here in his darkling grave. And yet the earth was familiar and no longer held any terrors for him; the darkness was like that of a shuttered room or deep vault, an impenetrable gloom entirely in keeping; the forbidding nature and location of his mausoleum not only set him apart but kept him protected. He was safe here. Damned forever, certainly—doomed for all time, yes, barring some major miracle of intervention—but safe, too, and there was much to be said for safety.

Safe from the men—mere men, most of them—who had

put him here. For in his dreaming the wizened Thing had forgotten that those men were long dead. And their sons, dead. And theirs, and theirs . . .

The old Thing in the ground had lived for five hundred years, and as long again had lain undead in his unhallowed grave. Above him, in the gloom of a glade beneath stirless, snow-laden trees, the tumbled stones and slabs of his tomb told something of his story, but only the Thing himself knew all of it. His name had been . . . but no, the Wamphyri have no names as such. His host's name, then, had been Thibor Ferenczy, and in the beginning Thibor had been a man. But that had been almost a thousand years ago.

The Thibor part of the Thing in the ground existed still, but changed, mutated, mingled and metamorphosed along with its vampire "guest." The two were one now, inseparably fused; but in dreams that spanned a millennium, still Thibor could return to his roots, go back to the immensely cruel past . . .

In the very beginning he had not been a Ferenczy but an Ungar, though that was of no account now. His forefathers were farmers who came from a Hungarian princedom across the Carpathians to settle on the banks of the Dniester where it flowed down to the Black Sea. But "settling" was hardly the word for it. They had had to fight Vikings (the dreadful Varyagi) on the river, where they came exploring from the Black Sea, the Khazars and vassal Magyars from the steppes, finally the fierce Pechenegi tribes in their constant expansion west and northwards. Thibor had been a young man then, when at last the Pechenegi wiped out the rude settlement he called home and he alone survived. After that he'd fled north to Kiev.

Never much of a farmer, indeed, far more suited for war with his massive size—which in those days, when most men were small, made Thibor the Wallach something of a giant—in Kiev he sold himself into the service of Vladimir I. The Vlad made him a small *Voevod* or warrior chief and gave him a hundred men. "Go join my Boyars in the south," he commanded. "Fend off and kill the Pechenegi, keep 'em from crossing the Ros, and by our new Christian God I'll give you title and banner both, Thibor of Wallachia!" Thibor had gone to him when he was desperate, that much was clear.

In his dream, the Thing in the ground remembered how he'd answered: "Title and banner, keep them, my Lord— but only give me one hundred men more and I shall kill you a thousand Pechenegi before returning to Kiev. Aye, and I'll bring you their thumbs to prove it!"

He got his hundred men; also, like it or not, his banner: a golden dragon, one forepaw raised in warning. "The dragon of the true Christ, brought to us by the Greeks," Vlad told him. "Now the dragon watches over Christian Kiev—Russia itself—and it roars from your banner with the voice of the Lord! What mark of your own will you put on it?" On that same morning he had asked this question of half-a-dozen other fledgling defenders, five Boyars with their own followers and one band of mercenaries. All of them had taken a symbol to fly with the dragon. But not Thibor.

"I'm no Boyar, sire," the Wallach had told him with a shrug. "That's not to say my father's house was not honourable, for it was, and built by a decent man—but in no way royal. No lord's or prince's blood flows in my veins. When I've earned myself a mark, then I'll set it over your dragon."

"I'm not sure I like you especially, Wallach." The Vlad had frowned then, uneasy with this great, grim man before him. "Your voice sounds out perhaps a trifle loud from a heart as yet untried. But—" and he, too, had given a shrug, "—very well, choose a device for yourself when you return in triumph. And Thibor—bring me those thumbs or I'll likely string you up by yours!" And that day at noon seven polyglot companies of men had set out from Kiev, reinforcements for the ensieged defensive positions on the Ros.

One year and one month later Thibor returned with nearly all of his men, plus another eighty recruited from peasants hiding in the foothills and valleys of the southern Khorvaty. He made no plea for audience but strode into the Vlad's own church where he was at worship. He left his weary men outside and took in with him only one small sack that rattled, and approached Prince Vladimir Svyatoslavich at his prayers and waited for him to finish. Behind him Kiev's civilian nobles were deathly silent, waiting for their prince to see him.

Finally the Vlad and his Greek monks turned to Thibor. The sight they saw was fearsome. Thibor had soil on him from the fields and forests; dirt was ingrained in him; he bore a freshly healed scar high on his right cheek to the middle of his jaw, which made a pale stripe of scar tissue that cut almost to the bone. Also, he had gone away as a peasant and returned something else entirely. Haughty as a hawk, with his nose slightly hooked under bushy eyebrows that very nearly came together in the middle, he gazed out of yellow, unblinking eyes. He wore moustaches and a scraggy, twisting black beard; also the armour of some Pechenegi chief, chased in gold and silver, and an earring set with a gemstone in the lobe of his left ear. He had shaved his head with the exception of black forelocks that hung one to each side, in the manner of certain nobles; and in all his mien, there was no sign that he knew he stood in a holy place or even considered his whereabouts.

"I know you now," the Vlad hissed, "Thibor the Wallach. Don't you fear the true God? Don't you tremble before the cross of Christ? I was praying for our deliverance, and you—"

"And I have brought it to you." Thibor's voice was deep, doleful. He tipped out his sack onto the flags. The prince's retinue and the nobles of Kiev where they stood back from him who ruled over them gasped and gaped. Bones clattered white in a heap at the Vlad's feet.

"What?" he choked. "What?"

"Thumbs," said Thibor. "I had the flesh boiled off them, lest their stink offend. The Pechenegi are driven back, trapped between the Dniester, the Bug and the sea. Your Boyar army hems them in. Hopefully they can deal with them without me and mine. For I have heard that the Polovtsy are rising like the wind in the east. Also, in Turkey-land, armies wax for war!"

"You have heard? *You* have heard? And are you some mighty Voevod, then? Do you set yourself up as the ears of Vladimir? And what do you mean, 'you and yours?' The two hundred men you marched with are mine!"

At that Thibor took a deep breath. He paced forward—then paused. Then he bowed low, if inelegantly, and said, "Of course they are yours, Prince. Also the four-score refugees I've gathered together and turned into warriors. All are yours. As for being your ears: if I have heard falsely, then strike me deaf. But my work is finished in the south and I thought you had more need of me here. Soldiers are few in Kiev this day, and her borders are wide . . ."

The Vlad's eyes remained veiled. "The Pechenegi are at bay, you say—and do you give yourself credit for this?"

"In all modesty. This and more."

"And you've brought my men back with you, without casualty?"

"A handful are fallen." Thibor shrugged. "But I found eighty to replace them."

"Show me."

They went to the great doors, out onto the wide steps of the church. There in the square, Thibor's men waited in silence, some upon horses but most afoot, all armed to the teeth and looking very fierce. They were the same sorry bunch the Wallach had taken away with him, but no longer sorry. His standard flew from three tall flagstaffs: the golden dragon, and upon its back a black bat with eyes of carnelian.

The Vlad nodded. "Your mark," he commented, perhaps sourly. "A bat."

"The black bat of the Wallachs, aye," said Thibor.

One of the monks spoke up, "But atop the dragon?"

Thibor grinned at him wolfishly. "Would you have the dragon pissing on my bat?"

The monks took the prince aside while Thibor stood waiting. He could not hear what was said, but he'd imagined it often enough in times since:

"These men are utterly loyal to him! See how proud they stand beneath his banner?" the senior monk would have whispered in that sly Greek way. *"It could be a nuisance."*

And Vlad: *"Does it trouble you? I have five times their number right here in the city."*

The Greek: *"But these men have been tried in battle; they are warriors all!"*

Vlad: *"What are you saying? I should fear him? I've Varyagi blood in me and fear no man!"*

Greek: *"Of course you don't. But . . . he sets himself above his station, this one. Can we not find him a task— him and a handful of his men—and keep the rest of them back here to bolster the city's defences? This way, in his absence, their loyalty will surely swing more rightly to you."*

And Vladimir Svyatoslavich's eyes narrowing more yet. Then—his nod of approval: *"I have the very thing. Yes, and I believe you're right—best to be rid of him. These Wallachs are a tricky lot. Far too insular . . ."* And out loud to the Voevod: "Thibor, I'm honouring you tonight at the palace. You and five of your best. Then you can tell me all about your victories. But there'll be ladies there, so see you're washed and leave your armour in your lodgings and tents."

With a stiff little bow Thibor backed off, went down the steps to his mount, led his men away. At his command, as they left the square, they rattled their weapons and gave a single, sharp, ringing shout: "Prince Vladimir!" Then they were gone into the autumn morning, gone into Kiev, called the City at the Edge of the Woods . . .

Despite the disturbance, the unknown intrusion, the Thing in the ground continued to dream. Night would soon fall, and Thibor was sensitive to night as a rooster is to the dawn, but for now he dreamed.

That night at the palace—a huge place with stone chimneys in every room, and wood fires blazing, sprinkled with aromatic resins—Thibor had worn clean but common clothes under a rich red robe taken from some high-ranking Pechenegi. His flesh was washed and perfumed, tanned like leather, and his forelocks freshly greased. He was an imposing sight. His officers, too, were spruce. Though they obviously stood in awe of him, still he spoke to them with some familiarity; but he was courteous to the ladies, attentive to the Vlad.

It was possible (so Thibor had later reckoned) that the prince found himself in two minds: the Wallach would seem to have proved himself a warrior, a Voevod indeed. By rights he should be made a Boyar, given lands of his own. A man will fight even harder if he fights to protect that which is his. But there was that sombre something about Thibor which the Vlad found disquieting. So perhaps his Greek advisors were right.

"Now tell me how you dealt with the Pechenegi, Thibor of Wallachia," Vladimir finally commanded, when all were feasting. Their dishes were several: Greek sausages wrapped in vine leaves; joints roasted in the Viking fashion; goulashes steaming in huge pots. Meads and wines came by the gallon. All at table stabbed and speared with their knives at smoking meats; short bursts of conversation would erupt now and then amidst the general clatter of eating. Thibor's voice, though he hardly raised it at all, had carried over all of that. And gradually the great table had grown quieter.

"The Pechenegi come in parties or tribes. They are not

like a mighty army; there is little of unity; they have their
own chiefs who vie with each other. The earthworks and
fortifications on the Ros at the edge of the wooded steppe
have stopped them *because* they are not united. If they
came as an army they could cross river and battlements
both in a day, carrying all away before them. But they
merely probe around our defences, contenting themselves
with whatever they can pillage in short, sharp forays to
east and west. This is how they sacked Kolomyya on the
west flank. They crossed the Prut by day, crept forward in
the forests, rested overnight and attacked at first light. It is
their way. And so they gradually encroach.

"This is how I saw the situation: because the defences
are there, our soldiers use them: we hide behind them. The
earthworks act as a border. We have been content to say,
'South of these works lies the territory of the Pechenegi,
and we must keep him out.' Wherefore the Pechenegi,
barbarian that he is, in fact holds *us* in siege! I have sat on
the walls of our forts and seen our enemies make camp,
unafraid. Smoke from his fires goes up, all untroubled,
because we don't molest him on 'his' ground.

"When I left Kiev, Prince Vladimir, you said: 'Fend off
the Pechenegi, keep him from crossing the Ros.' But *I*
said, 'Pursue the fiend and kill him!' One day I saw a
camp of some two hundred; they had their women, even
their children with them! They were camped across the
river, to the west, quite apart from the other encampments.
I split my two hundred in half. Half went with me across
the river in the dusk. We stole up on the Pechenegi fires.
They had guards out but most of them were sleeping—and
we cut their throats in the night without them ever knowing who killed them! Then we set about the camp—but all
in silence. I had daubed my men in mud. Any man not
daubed was Pechenegi. In the darkness we slew them,
flitting from tent to tent. We were like great bats in the
night, and it was very bloody.

"When the camp was awakened half were already dead.

The rest gave chase. We led them back to the Ros; and them hounding us, eager to catch us at the river, all of them shouting and screaming their warcries! But we shouted and screamed not at all. At the river, on the Pechenegi side, my second hundred lay in waiting. They were daubed in mud. They struck not at their silent, muddy brothers but trapped the howling pursuers. Then we rose up, turned in upon the Pechenegi, slew them to a man. And we cut off their thumbs . . ." He paused.

"Bravo!" said Vladimir the prince, faintly.

"Another time," Thibor continued, "we went to Kamenets which was under siege. Again I had half my men with me. The Pechenegi about the town saw us, gave chase. We led them into a steep-sided gulley where, after we had scrambled through, my other half rained down an avalanche upon them. I lost many thumbs that time, buried under the boulders—else I would have brought you back another sackful!"

Now there was almost total silence about the table. It was not so much the reporting of these deeds that impressed but the stony delivery, which lacked all emotion. When the Pechenegi had raided, raped and razed this man's Ungar settlement, they had turned him into an utterly pitiless killer.

"I've had reports, of course," Svyatoslavich broke the silence, "if somewhat vague until now and few and far between. But this is something to chew on. And so my Boyars have driven the Pechenegi back, you say? A recent turn of events? Perhaps they learned something from you, eh?"

"They learned that standing guard behind high walls achieves nothing!" said Thibor. "I spoke to them and said: 'Summer is at an end. The Pechenegi far to the south are grown fat and idle from the little work they've had to do; they do not think we'll come against them. They are building permanent settlements, winter homes for themselves. Like the Khazars before them, they are putting aside the sword in favour of the plough. If we strike now they'll fall like grass beneath the scythe!' Then, all the Boyars banded together, crossed the river, struck deep into the southern steppes. We killed the Pechenegi wherever we found them.

"But by then I had heard rumours of a greater peril in the making: to the east the Polovtsy are rising up! They spill over from the great steppes and deserts, expand westward— soon they'll be at our doors. When the Khazars fell they left the way open for the Pechenegi. And after the Pechenegi? Which is why I thought—why I dared to think—that perhaps the Vlad would give me an army and send me east, to put down our enemies before they wax too strong . . ."

For long moments Prince Vladimir simply sat and stared at him from eyes half-lidded. Then he quietly said, "You've come a long way in a year and a month, Wallach . . ." And out loud, to his guests: "Eat, drink, talk! Honour this man. We owe him that much." But as the feasting contin- ued he got up, indicating that Thibor should walk with him. They went out into the grounds, into the cool autumn evening. The wood smoke was fragrant under the trees.

A little way from the palace, the prince paused. "Thibor, we'll have to see about this idea of yours—this eastward invasion, for that's what it would be—for I'm not sure we're ready for that. It's been tried before, you know." He nodded bitterly. "The Grand Prince himself tried it. First he tackled the Khazars—Svyatoslav ground them down and the Byzantines swept up their pieces—and then he had a go at Bulgaria and Macedonia. And while he was at it the nomads laid siege to Kiev itself! And did he pay for his zeal? Aye, however many sagas are written about him. Nomads sank him in the river rapids and made his skull into a drinking cup! He was hasty, you see? Oh, he got rid of the Khazars, all right, but only to let in the damned Pechenegi! And shall I be hasty too?"

The Wallach stood silent for a moment in the dusk. "You'll send me back to the southern steppe, then?"

"I might, and I might not. I *might* stand you down from the fighting entirely, make you a Boyar, give you land and men to look after it for you. There's a lot of good land here, Thibor."

Thibor shook his head. "Then I'd prefer to return to Wallachia. I'm no farmer, Prince. I tried that and the Pechenegi came and made a warrior of me. Since then— all my dreams have been red ones. Dreams of blood. The blood of my enemies, the enemies of this land."

"And what of *my* enemies?"

"They are the same. Only show them to me."

"Very well," said the Vlad, "I'll show you one of them. Do you know the mountains to the west, which divide us from the Hungarians?"

"My fathers were Ungars," said Thibor. "As for the mountains: I was born under them. Not in the west but in the south, in the land of the Wallachs, beyond the bend in the mountains."

The prince nodded. "So you have some experience of mountains and their treachery. Good. But on my side of those peaks, beyond Galich, in that area called the Khorvaty after a certain people, there lives a Boyar who is . . . not my friend. I claim him as one who owes allegiance to me, but when I called in all my little princelings and Boyars he came not. When I invite him to Kiev he answers not. When I express a desire to meet with him he ignores me. If he is not my friend then he can only be my enemy. He is a dog that comes not to heel. A wild dog, and his home is a mountain fastness. Until now I've had neither the time, the inclination, nor the power to winkle him out, but—"

"What?" Thibor was astonished, his gasp cutting the Vlad short. "I'm sorry, my Prince, but you—no power?"

Vladimir Svyatoslavich shook his head. "You don't understand," he said. "Of course I have power. Kiev has power. But all so extended as to be almost expended! Should I recall an army to deal with one unruly princeling? And in so doing let the Pechenegi come up again? Should I form up an army from farmers and officials and peasants, all unskilled in battle? And if I did, what then? An army could *not* bring this Ferenczy out of his castle if he did not wish to leave it. Even an army could *not* destroy him, his defences are so strong! What? They are the mountain passes themselves, the gorges, the avalanches! With a handful of fierce, faithful retainers, he could hold back any army I muster almost indefinitely. Oh, if I had two thousand men to spare, then I might possibly starve him with a siege, but at what expense? On the other hand, what an army cannot achieve might just be possible—for one brave and clever and loyal man . . .''

"Are you saying you want this Ferenczy taken from his castle and brought to you in Kiev?"

"Too late for that, Thibor. He has shown how he 'respects' me. How then should I respect him? No, I want him dead! His lands then fall to me, his castle on the heights, his household and serfs. And his death will be an example to others who might think to stand apart."

"Then you don't want his thumbs but his head!" Thibor's chuckle was throaty, without humour.

"I want his head, his heart, and his standard. And I want to burn all three on a bonfire right here in Kiev!"

"His standard? He has a symbol, then, this Ferenczy? Might I enquire the nature of this blazon?"

"By all means," said the prince, his grey eyes suddenly thoughtful. He lowered his voice, cast about in the dusk for a moment, as if to be doubly sure that no one heard. "His mark is the horned head of a devil, with a forked tongue that drips gouts of blood . . ."

Blood!

Gouts of blood soaking into the black earth.

The sun had touched the horizon and was burning red there like . . . like a great gout of blood. Soon the earth would swallow it up. The old Thing in the ground trembled again; its husk of leather and bone slowly cracked open like a desiccated sponge to receive the earth's tribute, the blood that soaked through leaf-mould and roots and black, centuried soil down to where the thousand-year-old Thibor-creature lay in his shallow grave.

Subconsciously Thibor sensed the seeping blood and knew, in the way all dreamers "know," that it was only part of the dream. It would be a different matter when the sun had set and the seepage actually touched him, but for now he ignored it, returned to that time at the turn of the tenth century when he'd been merely human and had gone up into the Khorvaty on a mission of murder . . .

They had travelled as trappers, Thibor and his seven, as Wallachians who followed the Carpathian curve on a trek designed to get them deep into the northern forests by the onset of winter. In fact they had simply come from Kiev through Kolomyya and so to the mountains, but they'd taken all the paraphernalia of the trapper with them, to substantiate their story. It had taken them three weeks of steady riding to reach the place in the very lee of the sheer mountains, (a "village," consisting of a handful of stone houses built into the hillside, half-a-dozen semi-permanent cabins, and a smattering of gypsy tents of cured skins with the fur inside) which the current incumbents called Moupho Alde Ferenc Yaborov, a mouthful they invariably short-ened to Ferenc, which they made to sound like "Ferengi." It meant "Place of the Old One," or "of the Old Ferengi," and the gypsies spoke of it in lowered tones and with a deal of respect.

There were maybe a hundred men there, some thirty women and as many children. Half of the men were trappers passing through, or prospective settlers uprooted by Pechenegi raids, on their way to find homes further north. Many of the latter group had their families with them. The remainder were either peasant inhabitants of Ferengi Yaborov, or gypsies come here to winter it out. They'd been coming since time immemorial, apparently, for "the old devil" who was Boyar here was good to them and turned none away. Indeed, in times of hardship he'd even been known to supply his wandering occasional tenants with food from his own larder and wine from his cellars.

Thibor, asking about food and drink for himself and the others, was shown a house of timbers set in a stand of pines. It was an inn of sorts, with tiny rooms up in the rafters which could only be reached by rope ladders; the ladders were drawn up when the boarder wished to sleep. Down below there were wooden tables and stools, and at one end of the large room a bar stocked with small kegs of plum brandy and buckets of sweet ale. One wall was built half of stone, where burned a fire in the base of a huge chimney. On the fire was an iron pot of goulash giving out a heavy paprika reek. Onions dangled in bunches from nails in the wall close to the fire; likewise huge coarse-skinned sausages; black bread stood in loaves on the tables, baked in a stone oven to one side of the fire.

A man, his wife and one scruffy son ran the place; gypsies, Thibor guessed, who'd chosen to settle here. They could have done better, he thought, feeling cold in the shadows of the looming rocks, the mountains whose presence could be felt even indoors. It was a gloomy place this, frowning and foreboding.

The Wallach had told his men to speak to no one, but as they put away their gear, ate and drank, spoke in muffled tones to each other, he himself shared a jug of brandy with his host. "Who are you?"' that gnarled old man asked him.

"Do you ask what I have been and where I have been?" Thibor answered. "That's easier to tell than who I am."

"Tell it then, if you feel like talking."

Thibor smiled and sipped brandy. "I was a young boy under the Carpatii. My father was an Ungar who wandered into the borders of the southern steppe to farm—him and his brothers and kin and their families. I'll be brief: came the Pechenegi, all was uprooted, our settlement destroyed.

Since then I've wandered, fought the barbarian for payment and what little I could find on his body, done what I
could where and whenever. Now I'll be a trapper. I've
seen the mountains, the steppe, the forests. Farming's a
hard life and blood-letting makes a man bitter. But in the
towns and cities there's money to be had from furs. You've
roamed a bit yourself, I'll vow?''

"Here and there," the other shrugged, nodded. He was
swarthy as smoke-grimed leather, wrinkled as a walnut
from extremes of weather, lean as a wolf. Not young by
any standards, still his hair was shiny black, his eyes too,
and he seemed to have all of his teeth. But he moved his
limbs carefully and his hands were very crooked. "I'd be
doing it still if my bones hadn't started to seize up. We
had a cart of two wheels wrapped in leather, which we'd
break down and carry when the way was rough. Upon the
cart we took our house and goods along with us: a big tent
with rooms, and cooking pots, and tools. We were—we
are—Szgany, gypsies, and became Szgany Ferengi when I
built this place here." He craned his neck and looked up,
wide-eyed, at one interior wall of the house. It was a look
half respectful, half fearful. There was no window but the
Wallach knew that the old man stared up at the mountain
peaks.

"Szgany Ferengi?" Thibor repeated. "You ally yourself to the Boyar Ferenczy in his castle, then?"

The old gypsy lowered his eyes from the unseen heights,
drew back a little, took on a suspicious look. Thibor
quickly poured him more of his own brandy. The other
remained silent and the Wallach shrugged. "No matter,
it's just that I've heard good things of him," he lied. "My
father knew him, once . . .''

"Indeed!" the old man's eyes widened.

Thibor nodded. "One cold winter, the Ferenczy gave
him shelter in his castle. My father told me, if ever I
passed this way, I should go up and remind the Boyar of
that time, and thank him on behalf of my father.''

The old man stared at Thibor for long moments. "So, you've heard good things of our master, have you? From your father, eh? And you were born under the mountains . . ."

"Is something strange?" Thibor raised a dark eyebrow.

The other looked him up and down. "You're a big man," he said, grudgingly, "and strong, I can tell. Also, you look fierce. A Wallach, eh, whose fathers were Ungars? Well, perhaps you are, perhaps you are."

"Perhaps I am what?"

"It's said," the gypsy whispered, drawing closer, "that the old Ferengi's true sons always come home to roost. In the end they come here, seek him out—seek out their father! Would you climb up to see him?"

Thibor put on a look of indecision. He shrugged. "I might, if I knew the way. But these cliffs and passes are treacherous."

"I know the way."

"You've been there?" Thibor tried not to seem too eager.

The old man nodded. "Oh, yes, and I could take you. But would you go alone? The Ferengi's not one for too many visitors."

Thibor appeared to give it some little thought. "I'd want to take two of my friends, at least. In case the way gets rough."

"Huh! If these old bones can make it, surely yours can! Just two of them?"

"For assistance in the steep places."

Thibor's host pursed his lips. "It would cost you a little something. My time and . . ."

"That's understood," the Wallach stopped him.

The gypsy scratched his ear. "What do you know of the old Ferengi? What have you heard of him?"

Thibor saw a chance for knowledge. Getting information out of people such as these was like drawing the teeth of a bear! "I've heard he has a great company of men garrisoned with him, and that his castle is a fastness impenetrable. Because of this he swears no fealty, pays no taxes on his lands, for none may collect it.''

"Hah!" The old gypsy laughed out loud, thumped the bar, poured more brandy. "A company of men? Retainers? Serfs? He has none! A woman or two, perhaps, but no men. Only the wolves guard those passes. As for his castle: it hugs the cliff. One way in—for mere men—and the same way out. Unless some unwary fool leans too far from a window . . ."

As he paused his eyes because suspicious again. "And did your father tell you that the Ferengi had men?"

Thibor's father had told him nothing, of course. Nor had the Vlad, for that matter. What little he knew was superstitious twaddle he'd had from a fellow at court, a foolish man who didn't much care for the prince and who in turn was little cared for. Thibor had no time for ghosts: he knew how many men he'd killed, and not a man of them had come back to haunt him.

He decided to take a chance. He'd already learned much of what he wanted to know. "My father said only that the way was steep, and that when he was there, many men were camped in and about the castle."

The old man stared at him, slowly nodded. "It could be, it could be. The Szgany have often wintered with him." He came to a decision. "Very well, I will take you up—if he will see you." He laughed at Thibor's raised eyebrows, led him out of the house into the quiet of the afternoon. On their way the gypsy took a huge bronze frying pan from its peg.

A weak sun was poised, preparing itself for setting over the grey peaks. The mountains brought an early twilight here, where already the birds were singing their evening songs. "We are in time," the old man nodded. "And now we must hope that we are seen."

He pointed steeply upwards at the looming mountains, to where a high, jagged black crest etched itself against the grey of the ultimate peaks. "You see there, where the darkness is deepest?"

Thibor nodded.

"That's the castle. Now watch." He polished the bottom of the pan on his sleeve, then turned it towards the sun. Catching the weak rays, he threw them back into the mountains and traced a line of gold up the crags. Fainter and fainter the disc of light flickered with distance, jumping from scree to flat rock face, from fangs to fir clump, from trees back to crumbling shale as it climbed ever higher. And finally it seemed to Thibor that the ray was answered; for when at last the gypsy held the pan stiffly in his gnarled hands, suddenly that dark, angular outcrop he'd pointed out seemed to burst into golden fire! The lance of light was so sudden, so blinding, that the Wallach threw up his hands before his eyes and peered through the bars of his fingers.

"Is that him?" he gasped. "Is it the Boyar himself who answers?"

"The old Ferengi?" The gypsy laughed uproariously. Carefully he propped up the pan on a flat rock, and still the beam of light glanced down from on high. "No, not him. The sun's no friend of his. Nor any mirror, for that matter!" He laughed again, and then explained. "It's a mirror, burnished bright, one of several which sit above the rear wall of the keep where it meets the cliff. Now, if our signal is seen, someone will cover the mirror—which merely shoots back our beam—and the light will be snuffed out. Not gradually, as by the sun's slow descent, but all at once—*like that!*"

Like a candle snuffed, the beam blinked out, leaving Thibor almost staggering in what seemed a preternatural gloom. He steadied himself. "So, it would seem you've established contact," he said. "Plainly the Boyar has seen that you have something to convey, but how will he know what it is?"

"He *will* know," said the gypsy. He grasped Thibor's

arm, stared up into the high passes. A glaze came suddenly over the old man's eyes and he swayed. Thibor held him up. And:

"There, *now* he knows," the old man whispered. The film went from his wide eyes.

"What?" Thibor was puzzled; he felt troubled. The Szgany were queer folk with little-understood powers. "What do you mean when you say—"

"And now he will answer 'yes'—or 'no,' " the gypsy cut him off. Even as he finished speaking there came a single, searing beam of light from the high castle, which in the next moment died away.

"Ah!" the old gypsy sighed. "And his answer is 'yes,' he will see you."

"When?" Thibor accepted the strangeness of it, fought down the eagerness in his voice.

"Now. We set off at once. The mountains are dangerous at night, but he'll have it no other way. Are you still game?"

"I'll not disappoint him, now that he's invited me," said Thibor.

"Very well. But wrap yourself well, Wallach. It gets cold up there." The old man fixed him with a brief, bright, penetrating stare. "Aye, cold as death . . ."

Thibor chose a pair of burly Wallachs to accompany him. Most of his men were out of his old homeland, but he'd personally stood alongside these two in his war with the Pechenegi, and he knew they were fierce fighters. He wanted real men at his back when he went up against this Ferenczy. And it could well be that he'd need them. Arvos, the old gypsy, had said the Boyar had no retainers; who, then, had answered the mirror signal? No, Thibor couldn't see a rich man living up there all alone with a mere woman or two, fetching and carrying for himself. Old Arvos lied.

In the event that there was only a handful of men up in

the mountains with their master . . . But it was no good speculating, Thibor would have to wait and see what were the odds. If there were many men, however, then he would say that he came as an envoy of Vladimir, to invite the Boyar to the palace in Kiev. It would be in connection with the war against the Pechenegi. Either way, his course was now set: he had a mountain to climb, and at the top a man to kill, depending on conditions.

In those days Thibor had been in a way naïve; it had not once crossed his mind that the Vlad had sent him on a suicide mission, from which he was not expected to return to Kiev.

As for the climb: at first the going had been easy, and this despite the fact that the way was unmarked. The track (there was no real track, merely a route which the old gypsy knew by heart) climbed a saddle between foothills to the base of an unscalable cliff, then followed a rising apron of sliding scree to a wide crevice or chimney in the cliff, which elevated steeply through a fissure on to a false plateau beneath a second line of even steeper hills. These hills were wild and wooded, their trees massive and ancient, but by now Thibor had seen that indeed there was a path of sorts. It was as if some giant had taken a scythe and cut a straight line through the trees; their wood had doubtless provided much of the village's timber, and perhaps some of it had been hauled up into the mountains for use in the construction of the castle. That might possibly have been hundreds of years ago, and yet no new trees had grown up to bar the way. Or if they had, then someone had uprooted them to keep the path free.

Whichever, the climb along the track through the rising woods was fairly easy going, and as twilight grew towards night a full moon rose to lend the way its silvery light. Saving their breath for the climbing, the three men and their guide spoke not at all and Thibor was able to turn his mind to what little he'd heard of the Boyar Ferenczy from his foppish court contact.

"The Greeks fear him more than Vladimir does," that loose-tongue had informed. "In Greek-land they've long sought all such out and put them down. They call such as the Ferenczy 'vrykolax,' which is the same as the Bulgarian 'obour' or 'mouphour'—or 'wampir'!"

"I've heard of the wampir," Thibor had answered. "They have the same myth, and the same name for it, in my old country. A peasant superstition. And I'll tell you something: the men I've killed rot in their graves, if indeed they have graves. They certainly don't bloat there! Or if they do it's from rotten gasses, not the blood of the living!"

"Nevertheless this Ferenczy is said to be just such a creature," Thibor's informant had insisted. "I've heard the Greek priests talking: saying how there's no room in any Christian land for such as that. In Greek-land they put stakes through their hearts and cut off their heads. Or better still, they break them up entirely and burn all the pieces. They believe that even a small part of a wampir can grow whole again in the body of an unwary man. The thing is like a leech, but on the inside! Hence the saying that a wampir has two hearts and two souls—and that the creature may not die until both facets are destroyed."

Thibor had smiled, humourlessly, scornfully. He'd thanked the man, saying, "Well, wizard or witch or whatever, he's lived long enough. Vladimir the Prince wants this Ferenczy dead, and I've been given the job."

"Lived long enough!" the other had repeated, throwing up his hands. "Aye, and you don't know how true that is. Why, there's been a Ferenczy up in those mountains as long as men remember. And the legends have it that it's the *same* Ferenczy! Now you tell me, Wallach, what sort of man is it who watches years pass like hours, eh?"

Thibor had laughed at that, too; but now, thinking back on it—several things connected, it seemed.

The "Moupho" in the name of the village, for instance—which sounded a lot like "mouphour," or wampir. "Vil-

lage of the Old Ferenczy Vampire?'' And what was it
Arvos the Szgany had said? ''The sun's no friend of his.
Nor any mirror, for that matter!'' Weren't vampires things
of the night; afraid of mirrors because they showed no
reflection, or perhaps a reflection more nearly the reality?
Then the Wallach gave a snort of derision at his own
imaginings. It was this old place, that was all, working
on his imagination. These centuried woods and ageless
mountains . . .

At which point his party came out of the trees and on to
the crest of domed hills where the soil was thin as a
whisper and only the lichens grew; beyond which, in a
shallow depression, a jumbled plain of stony rubble and
brittle scree reached perhaps half a mile to the inky shadows of dark cliffs. To the north it reached up high, that
black boundary, forming horns; and to these horns in the
light of the moon, old Arvos now pointed a crooked
finger.

''There!'' He chuckled as at some joke. ''There broods
the house of the old Ferengi.''

Thibor looked—and sure enough he saw distant windows lit like eyes in the darkness under the horns. And it
was for all the world as if some monstrous bat squatted
there in the heights, or maybe the lord of all great wolves.

''Like eyes in a face of stone,'' growled one of Thibor's
Wallachs, a man all chest and arms, with short stumpy
legs.

''And not the only eyes watching us!'' whispered the
other, a thin, hunched man who always went with his head
aggressively forward.

''What's that you say?'' Thibor was at once alert, casting about in the darkness. Then he saw the feral, triangular
eyes, like blobs of gold, seeming to hang suspended in the
darkness at the edge of the woods. Five pairs of eyes:
wolves' eyes, surely?

''Ho!'' Thibor shouted. He unsheathed his sword, stepped

forward. "Away, dogs of the woods! We've nothing for you."

The eyes blinked sporadically in pairs, drew back, scattered. Four lean, grey shapes loped off, flowing under the moon like liquid, lost in the jumble of boulders on the plain of scree. But the fifth pair of eyes remained, seemed to gain height, floated forward out of the darkness without hesitation.

A man stepped from the shadows, as tall as, if not taller than, Thibor himself.

Arvos the gypsy staggered, seemed about to faint. The moon showed his face a ghastly, silvery-grey. The stranger reached out a hand and gripped his shoulder, stared deep into his eyes. And slowly the old man straightened up and the trembling went out of him.

In the manner of the warrior born, Thibor had placed himself in striking distance. His sword was still in his hand, but the stranger was only one man. Thibor's men—astounded at first, perhaps even a little afraid—were on the point of drawing their own weapons but he stopped them with a word, sheathed his sword. If anything, this was a simple show of defiance, a gesture which in one move showed his strength and possibly his contempt. Certainly it showed his fearlessness. "Who are you?" he said. "You come like a wolf in the night."

The newcomer was slender, almost fragile-seeming. He was dressed all in black, with a heavy black cape draped about his shoulders and falling to below his knees. There could be weapons concealed under the cape, but he kept his hands in view, resting them on his thighs. He now ignored old Arvos, looked at the three Wallachs. His dark eyes merely fell upon Thibor's henchmen and moved on, but they rested on Thibor himself for long moments before he answered: "I am from the house of the Ferenczy. My master sent me out to see what manner of men would visit him this night." He smiled a thin smile. His voice had a soothing effect on the Voevod; strangely, his unblinking eyes also, which now reflected moonlight. Thibor found himself wishing there was more natural light. There was that about the features of this one which repulsed him. He felt that he gazed upon a misshapen skull, and wondered that this didn't disturb him more. But he was held as by some mysterious attraction, like a moth to the devouring flame. Yes, attracted and repulsed at one and the same time.

As that idea dawned—that he was falling under some strange malaise or enticement—he drew himself more upright, forced himself to speak. "You may tell your master I'm a Wallach. Also that I come to speak of important things, of summonses and responsibilities."

The man in the cape drew closer and the moon shone fully in his face. It was a man's face after all and not a skull, but there was that which was wolfish about it, an almost freakish longness of jaws and ears. "My master supposed it might be so," he said, a certain hard edge creeping into his voice. "But no matter—what will be will be, and you are but a messenger. Before you pass this point, however, which is a boundary, my master must be sure that you come of your own free will."

Thibor had regained his self-control. "No one dragged me up here," he snorted.

"But you were sent . . .?"

"A strong man may only be 'sent' where he wishes to go," the Wallach answered.

"And your men?"

"We're with Thibor," said the hunched one. "Where he ventures, we venture—willingly!"

"Even to see one who sends out wolves to do his bidding," Thibor's second companion, the apish one, added.

"Wolves?" The stranger frowned and cocked his head on one side quizzically. He glanced sharply all about, then smiled his amusement. "My master's dogs, you mean?"

"Dogs?" Thibor was certain he'd seen wolves. Now, however, the idea seemed ridiculous.

"Aye, dogs. They came out to walk with me, for it's a fine night. But they're not used to strangers. See, they've run off home."

Thibor nodded, and eventually he said: "So, you've come to meet us half-way, then. To walk with us and show us the way."

"Not I," the other shook his head. "Arvos can do that well enough. I came only to greet you and to count your numbers—also to ensure that your presence here was not forced. Which is to say, that you came of your own free mind and will."

"I say again," Thibor growled, "who could force me?"

"There are pressures and there are pressures," the other shrugged. "But I see you are your own man."

"You mentioned our numbers."

The man in the cape raised his eyebrows. They peaked like gables. "For your accommodation," he answered. "What else?" And before Thibor could reply: "Now I must go on ahead—to make preparation."

"I'd hate to crowd your master's house," said Thibor quickly. "Bad enough to be an unexpected guest, but worse far if others are obliged to vacate their rightful positions to make room for me."

"Oh, there's room enough," the other answered. "And you were not entirely unexpected. As for putting others out: my master's house is a castle, but it shelters fewer human souls than you have here." It was as if he'd read Thibor's mind and answered the question he'd found there.

Now he inclined his head towards the old Szgany. "Be warned, however, that the path along the cliff is loose and the way a little perilous. Be on your guard for rock falls!" And once more to Thibor he said, "Until later, then."

They watched him turn and make off after his master's "dogs" across the narrow, jumbled, boulder-strewn plain.

When he'd gone into the shadows, Thibor grabbed Arvos by the neck. "No retainers?" he hissed into the old gypsy's face. "No servants? What, and are you a simple liar or a very great liar? The Ferenczy could harbour an army up there!"

Arvos tried to snatch himself back and found the Wallach's grip like iron on his throat. "A . . . a manservant or two," he choked. "How was . . . was I to know? It's been many a year . . ." Thibor released him, thrust him away.

"Old man," he warned, "if you'd see another day, just be sure you guide us carefully along this perilous cliff path."

And so they had crossed the stony depression to the cliff, and started up the narrow way carved in its sheer face . . .

Chapter Three

THE PATH CLUNG TO THE BLACK ROCK OF THE CLIFFS LIKE A silver snake under the moon. Its surface was wide enough to take a small cart, no more; but in places the rim had fallen away, and then the track narrowed to little more than the width of a man. And it was in just such narrow spots that the night breeze off the forests picked up to a bluster, seeming to tug at and threaten the men who toiled up like insects towards that unknown aerie which was their destination.

"How long is this damned path, anyway?" Thibor snarled at the Gypsy, after maybe half a mile of slow, careful climbing.

"The same distance again," Arvos at once replied, "but steeper from now on. Once they brought carts up here, I'm told, but that was a hundred years or more ago and the way has not been well kept."

"*Huh!*" Thibor's apish aide snorted. "Carts? I wouldn't bring goats up here!"

At that the other Wallach, the hunched one, gave a start

and pressed more closely to the cliff. "I wouldn't know about goats," he whispered hoarsely, "but if I'm not mistaken we have company of sorts: the Ferenczy's 'dogs'!"

Thibor looked ahead to where the path vanished round the curve of the cliff. Silhouetted against the starry void of space, hump-shouldered wolf-shapes stood with muzzles lifted, ears pointed and eyes ferally agleam. But there were only two of them. Gasping his shock, then a harsh curse, Thibor looked back into the deepest shadows—and saw the other two; or rather, he saw their triangular moon-silvered eyes. "Arvos!" he growled, gathering his wits, reaching for the old gypsy. *"Arvos!"*

The sudden rumbling might well have been thunder, except the air was crisp and dry and what few clouds there were scudded rather than boiled; and thunder seldom makes the ground shudder beneath a man's feet.

Thibor's thin, hunched friend was hindmost, bringing up the rear at a point where the path was the merest ledge. It required but a step to bring him to safety. "Rock fall!" he cried hoarsely, making to leap forward. But as he sprang, so the boulders rained down and swept him away. It was as quick as that: he was there—arms straining forward, face gaping white in the light of the moon—and he was gone. He did not cry out: clubbed by boulders, doubtless he'd been unconscious or dead even as he fell.

When the last pebble and plume of dust had fallen and the rumbling was an echo, Thibor stepped to the rim and looked down. There was nothing to see, just darkness and the glint of the moon on distant rocks. Up and down the trail, of wolves there was no sign.

Thibor turned to where the old gypsy shivered and clung to the face of the cliff.

"A rock fall!" The old man saw the look on his face. "You can't blame me for a rock fall. If he'd jumped instead of shouting his warning . . ."

Thibor nodded. "No," he agreed, brows black as the night itself, "I can't blame you for a rock fall. But from now on blame doesn't come into it. From now on if there's any problem at all—from whatever cause or quarter—I'll just toss you off the cliff. That way, if I'm to die, I'll know that you died first. For let's have something clearly understood, old man. I don't trust the Ferenczy, I don't trust his 'dogs,' and I trust you least of all. There'll be no further warnings.'' He jerked his thumb up the path. "Lead on, Arvos of the Szgany—and nimble about it!''

Thibor did not think that his warning would carry much weight; even if it weighed on the gypsy, it certainly wouldn't weigh on his master in the mountain. But neither was the Wallach a man to issue idle threats. Arvos the Szgany belonged to the Ferenczy, no doubt of that. And so, if more trouble was on the way from that quarter (Thibor was sure that the avalanche had been arranged) then he would see that it came to Arvos first. And trouble *was* coming: it waited in the defile where the cliff was split by a deep chasm, at the back of which sat the castle of the Ferenczy.

This was the sight they saw, Thibor and his simian Wallach friend, and the now sinister gypsy Arvos, when they reached the cleft. Back in the dim mists of time the mountains had convulsed, split apart. Passes had been formed through the ranges, of which this might have been one. Except that in this case the opening had not gone all the way through. The cliff whose face they'd traversed had led finally to a high crest which reared now a half mile away. The crest was split into twin peaks—like the ears of a bat or a wolf. And there, straddling the defile where it narrowed to a fissure—clinging to both opposing faces and meeting centrally in a massive arch of masonry—there sat the manse of the Ferenczy. As before, two windows were lighted, like eyes under the sharp black ears, and the fissure below seemed to form a gaping mouth.

"No wonder he runs wolves, this one!" Thibor's squat companion grunted. His words acted like an invocation. They came down the cliff-hugging track from the castle, and not just four of them. A flood of them, a wall of grey fur studded with yellow jewel eyes. And they came at the lope, full of purpose.

"A pack!" cried Thibor's friend.

"Too many to fight off," the Voevod shouted back. Out of the corner of his eye he saw Arvos start forward, *towards* the oncoming wolves. He reached out a leg, tripped the old gypsy.

"Grab him!" Thibor commanded, drawing his sword.

The squat Wallach lifted Arvos as easily as he would lift the dead, dry branch of a tree, swung him out over the abyss and held him there. Arvos howled his terror. The wolves, scant paces away, came to an uneasy halt. Their leaders threw up pointed muzzles, howled mournfully. It was for all the world as if they waited upon some command. But from whom?

Arvos stopped his yelling, turned his head and gazed wide-eyed at the distant castle. His gullet bobbed spastically with his gulping.

The man who held him glanced from the wolves to Thibor. "What now? Do I drop him?"

The huge Wallach shook his head. "Only if they attack," he answered.

"You think the Ferenczy controls them, then? But . . . is it possible?"

"It seems our quarry has powers," said Thibor. "Look at the gypsy's face."

Arvos' gaze had become fixed. Thibor had seen that look before, when the old man used the frying-pan mirror down in the village: as if a film of milk had been painted on each eyeball.

Then the Gypsy spoke: "Master?" Arvos' mouth scarce moved. His words were the merest breath, vying with the mountain breeze at first but rapidly growing louder. "Master? But Master, I have always been your faithful—" He paused suddenly, as if cut short, and his filmed eyes bulged. "No, master, *no!*" His voice was now a shriek; he clawed at the hands and brawny arms that alone sustained him against gravity, shifted his once more clear gaze to the ledge and the wolves where they gathered themselves.

Thibor had almost felt the surge of power emanating from the distant castle, had almost tasted the rejection which had surely doomed the Szgany to his death. The Ferenczy was finished with him, so why delay it?

The leading pair of wolves, massive beasts, crept forward in unison, muscles bunching.

"Drop him!" Thibor rasped. Utterly pitiless, he urged, "Let him die—and then fight for your own life! The ledge is narrow—side by side we've a chance."

His companion tried to shake the old man loose but couldn't. The gypsy clung like thorns to his arms, fought desperately to swing his legs back onto the ledge. But already it was too late for both men. Heedless of their own lives, the pair of great grey wolves sprang as one creature, as if triggered. Not at Thibor—not even looking at him— but directly at his squat comrade where he tried to break Arvos' grip. They struck together, dead weight against a lurching double-silhouette, and bore the apish Wallach, Arvos, and themselves out over the rim and down into darkness.

It was beyond Thibor. He gave it only a moment's thought. The pack leaders had sacrificed themselves in answer to a call he had not heard—or had he? But in any case, they'd died willingly for a cause he could not possibly comprehend. He still lived, however, and he wouldn't sell his life cheaply.

" All of you, then!" he howled at the pack, almost in its own tongue. "Come on, who'll be first to taste my steel?" And for long moments not a beast of them moved.

Then—

Then they *did* move, but not forward. Instead they turned, slunk away, paused and looked back over lean shoulders.

"Cowards!" Thibor raged. He took a pace towards

them; they slunk further away, looked back. And the Wallach's jaw dropped. He knew—suddenly *knew*—that they weren't here to harm him, only to ensure that he came on alone!

For the first time he began to understand something of the true power of the mysterious Boyar, knew why the Vlad wanted him dead. And now, too, he wished he hadn't scoffed so much at the warnings of his court informant. Of course, he could always go back to the village and bring up the rest of his men—couldn't he? Behind him, pale tongues lolling, a crush of furry bodies crowded the track cut from the face of the cliff.

Thibor took a pace their way; they didn't move an inch, but their dog grins at once turned to snarls. A pace in the other direction, and they crept after. He had an escort.

"My own free will, eh?" he muttered, and looked at the sword in his hand. The sword of some warrior Varyagi—a good Viking sword—but useless if the pack should decide to attack in a body. Or if that were decided for them. Thibor knew it, and he suspected that they knew it, too.

He sheathed the weapon, found nerve to command: "Lead on, then, my lads—but not too close or I'll have your paws for lucky charms!" And so they took him to the castle in the riven rock . . .

In his shallow grave, the old Thing in the ground shivered again, this time from fear. However monstrous a man may become in this world, when he dreams of his youth the things which frightened him then frighten him anew. So it was with the Thibor-creature, and now his dream was carrying him to the edge of terror itself.

The sun was down, its rim forming the merest red blister on the hills; but still its rays lanced across the earth and gleamed fitfully on land where shadows visibly lengthened, quickly blotting out the sun's golden stains. But even when the sun was fully down, burning on other lands, still Thibor might not "waken" in the sense that men waken; for he was one who might dream for many a year between bouts of that black hatred called waking. It is not pleasant to be a Thing in the ground awake, alone, immobile, undead.

But the rich blood which soaked the earth would waken him, certainly, in that instant when it touched him. Even now the nearness of that warm, precious liquid roused passions in him. His nostrils gaped for its scent; his desiccated heart urged his own ancient blood faster in his veins; his vampire core moaned soundlessly in the sleep it shared with him.

Thibor's dream, however, was stronger. It was a magnet of the mind, luring him to a conclusion he knew and dreaded of old but which he must always experience again. And down in the cold earth in the glade of stirless trees, where the stones of his mausoleum lay broken and matted with lichens, the nightmare Thing dreamed on . . .

The way widened, grew into an avenue of tall dark pines atop a broad levelled rim of ages-impacted scree. On Thibor's left hand, beyond the straight boles of the pines, smooth black rocks rose vertical through hundreds of feet to an indigo sky strewn with stars; on his right the trees massed, marched down the no longer sheer "V" of the gorge and steeply up the other side. At the bottom water gushed and gurgled, invisible beneath a night-black canopy. The Vlad had been right: given a handful of men—or wolves—the Ferenczy could easily defend his castle against an army. Inside the castle itself, however, things might be different. Especially if the Boyar were indeed a man alone or nearly so.

Finally the ancient pile itself loomed. Its stonework was massive, but pitted, rotten. On both sides of the defile huge towers rose up eighty feet and more; square and very nearly featureless at their broad bases, higher up there were arched, fortified windows, ledges and balconies with deep embrasures, and gaping stone spouts projecting from the mouths of carved gargoyle or kraken heads. At the top of each tower, more embrasures fronted tiled pyramid spires; but with gaping holes showing through, where repairs were badly needed; and over everything a heavy miasma of decay, a dank and clinging patina, as if the very stone issued a cold and clammy sweat.

Half-way up, the inward-facing walls sprouted flying buttresses almost as massive as the towers themselves, which met across the gorge in a single span—like a stone bridge some eighty or ninety feet from tower to tower. Supported by the buttresses, a long single-storey hall with small square windows was constructed of timbers. It had a peaked roof of heavy slates; hall and roof both were in the same generally poor condition as the towers. But for the fact that two of the windows were lit with a flickering illumination, the entire pile might seem deserted, derelict. It was not how Thibor imagined the residence of a great Boyar should look; on the other hand, if he were a super-stitious man, certainly he might believe that demons lived there.

The ranks of wolves began to thin out as they drew closer to the castle's walls. Moving forward, it was not until the Wallach stood in the very shadow of those walls that he saw the castle's simple defences: a trench fifteen feet wide and fifteen deep, excavated right down to solid rock, the bottom furnished with long pointed stakes set so close to each other that any man falling in must surely be speared. Then, too, he saw the door: a heavy, oak-boarded, iron-banded affair extended at its top to form a draw-bridge. And even as he looked, so the door was creakingly lowered, heavy chains rattling as the trench was bridged.

In the opening thus revealed stood a cloaked figure holding before him a flaring torch. Behind the glare of that brand, little could be seen of features but a blur; all that Thibor could make of them was their paleness, and a vague awareness of grotesque proportions. He had his suspicions, however, and more than suspicions—which were fully borne out on the instant that the figure spoke: "And so you have come—of your own free will."

Thibor had often been accused of being a cold man with a cold, emotionless voice. It was something he had never denied. But if his voice was cold, *this* voice might have issued from the grave itself. And where Thibor had found the voice soothing in the first instance, now it grated on his nerves like the ache of a rotten tooth, or cold steel on a living bone. It was old—hoary as the mountains, and possibly entrusted with as many secrets—but it was certainly not infirm. It held the authority of all dark knowledge.

"My own free will?" Thibor dared to look away from the figure, saw that he was quite alone. The wolves had melted into the night, into the mountains. Perhaps a single pair of yellow eyes gleamed for a moment under the trees, but that was all. He turned back to face his host. "Yes, of my own free will . . ."

"Then you are welcome." The Boyar fixed his torch in a bracket just inside the doorway, bowed a little from the waist, stood to one side. And Thibor crossed the drawbridge, made to enter the house of the Ferenczy. But in the moment before he entered, he glanced up, saw the legend burned into the age-blackened oak of the arched lintel. He couldn't read or write, but the cloaked man saw his glance and translated for him:

"It says that this is the house of Waldemar Ferrenzig. There is also a sign which dates it, showing that the castle is nearly two hundred years old. Waldemar was . . . he was my father. I am Faethor Ferrenzig, whom my people call 'the Ferenczy'."

There was a fierce pride now in that dark voice, and for the first time Thibor felt himself unsure. He knew nothing of the castle; there might easily be many men lying in wait; the open door gaped like the maw of some unknown beast.

"I have made preparations," said Thibor's host. "Food and drink, and a fire to warm your bones." He deliberately turned his back, took a second torch from a dark niche in the wall and lit it from the first. As flames caught hold, so the shadows fled. The Ferenczy glanced once at his guest, unsmiling, then led the way inside. And the Wallach followed.

They passed quickly through dark corridors of stone, anterooms, narrow doorways, into the heart of the tower; then up a spiralling stone stairway to a heavy trapdoor in a floor of stone flags supported by great black timbers. The trapdoor stood open and the Ferenczy gathered up his cloak before climbing through into a well lighted room. Thibor followed close behind, allowing the other no time to be on his own. As he emerged into the room he shivered. It would have been so very easy for someone to spear him or lop off his head as he came up through the trapdoor. But apart from the pile's master, the room was empty of men.

Thibor glanced at his host, looked all around. The room was long, broad, high. Overhead, a ceiling of timbers was badly gapped; flickering firelight showed a slate roof above the ceiling; missing tiles permitted a glimpse of stars swimming in smoke from the fire. The place was somewhat open to the weather. In winter it would be bitterly cold. Even now it would not be warm if not for the fire.

The fire was of pine logs, roaring in a huge open fireplace with a chimney built at an angle to pass through an exterior wall. The logs burned on a cradle of warped iron bars, twisted with the heat of many such fires. At the fire's front, six spitted woodcocks were roasting over red ashes. Sprinkled with herbs, the smell of their flesh was mouth-watering.

Close to the fireplace stood a heavy table and two chairs of oak. On the table were wooden platters, eating knives, a stone pitcher of wine or water. In the centre of the table the roasted joint of some beast still smoked. There was a bowl of dried fruits, too, and another containing slices of coarse dark bread. It was not intended that Thibor should starve!

He glanced again at the wall with the fireplace; its base was of stone, but higher up it was of timber. There was also a square window, open to the night. He crossed to the window, looked out and down on a dizzy scene: the ravine, dark with close-packed firs, and away in the east the vast black forests. And now the Voevod knew that he was in a room of the castle's central span where it crossed the narrow gorge between the towers.

"Are you nervous, Wallach?" Faethor Ferenczy's soft voice (soft now, aye) startled him.

"Nervous?" Thibor slowly shook his head. "Bemused, that's all. Surprised. You *are* alone here!"

"Oh? And did you expect something else? Didn't Arvos the gypsy tell you I was alone?"

Thibor narrowed his eyes. "He told me several things— and now he's dead."

The other showed not the slightest flicker of surprise, nor of remorse. "Death comes to all men," he said.

"My two friends, they're also dead." Thibor hardened his tone of voice.

The Ferenczy merely shrugged. "The way up is hard. It's cost many lives over the years. But friends, did you say? Then you are fortunate. I have no friends."

Thibor's hand strayed close to the hilt of his sword. "I had fancied an entire pack of your 'friends' showed me the way here . . ."

His host at once stepped close to him, less a step than a flowing motion. The man moved like liquid. A long hand, slender but strong, rested on the hilt of Thibor's sword *under* his own hand. Touching it was like touching living snakeskin. Thibor's flesh crawled and he jerked his hand away. In the same moment the Boyar unsheathed his sword, again with that flowing, liquid motion. The Wallach stood disarmed, astonished.

"You can't eat with this great thing clanging about your

legs," the Ferenczy told him. He weighed the sword like a toy in his hands, smiled a thin smile. "Ah! A warrior's weapon. And are you a warrior, Thibor of Wallachia? A Voevod, eh? I've heard how Vladimir Svyatoslavich recruits many warlords—even from peasants."

Again Thibor was caught off guard; he hadn't told the Ferenczy his name, hadn't mentioned the Kievan Vlad. But before he could find words for an answer:

"Come," said his host, "you'll let your food grow cold. Sit, eat, and we'll talk." He tossed Thibor's sword down on a bench covered with soft pelts.

Across his broad back, Thibor carried a crossbow. He shrugged its strap from his shoulder, handed it to the Ferenczy. In any case, the weapon would take too long to load. Useless at close quarters, against a man who moved like this one. "Do you want my knife, too?"

Faethor Ferenczy's long jaws gaped and he laughed. "I desire only to seat you comfortably at my table. Keep your knife. See, there are more knives within reach—to stab the meat." He tossed the crossbow down with the sword.

Thibor stared at him, finally nodded. He shrugged out of his heavy jacket, let it fall in a heap to the floor. He took a seat at one end of the table, watched the Ferenczy arrange all the food within easy reach. Then his host poured two deep iron goblets of wine from the pitcher before seating himself opposite.

"You won't eat with me?" Thibor was suddenly hungry, but he would not take the first bite. In the palace in Kiev, they always waited for the Vlad to lead the way.

Faethor Ferenczy reached along the top of the table, showing an enormous length of arm, and deftly sliced off a corner of meat. "I'll take a woodcock when they're cooked," he said. "But don't wait for me—you eat whatever you want." He toyed with his food while Thibor fell to with some zeal. The Ferenczy watched him for a little while, then said, "It seems only right that a big man should have a big appetite. I, too, have . . . appetites, which this place restricts. That is why you interest me, Thibor. We could be brothers, do you see? I might even be your father. Aye, big men both of us—and you a warrior, and quite fearless. I suspect there are not many such as you in the world . . .'' And after a short pause, and in complete contrast: ''What did the Vlad tell you about me, before he sent you to bring me to his court?''

Thibor had determined not to be taken by surprise a third time. He swallowed what was in his mouth, and returned gaze for gaze across the table. Now, in the light from the fire and flickering flambeaux in jutting brackets, he allowed himself a more detailed inspection of the castle's master.

It would be pointless, Thibor decided, to make any sort of guess at the age of this man. He seemed to *exude* age like some ancient monolith, and yet moved with the incredible speed of a striking serpent and the lithe suppleness of a young girl. His voice could sound harsh as the elements, or soft as a mother's kiss, and yet it too seemed hoary beyond measure. As for the Ferenczy's eyes: they were deep-seated in triangular sockets, heavy-lidded, and their true colour was likewise impossible to fathom. From a certain angle they were black, shiny as wet pebbles, while from another they were yellow, with gold in their pupils. They were educated eyes and full of wisdom, yet feral too and brimming with sin.

Then there was the nose. Faethor Ferenczy's nose, along with his pointed, fleshy ears, formed the least acceptable part of his face. It was more a muzzle than a nose proper, yet its length stayed close to the face, flattening down towards the upper lip, and pushed back from it with large nostrils slanting upwards. Directly underneath it—too close, in fact—the man's ridgy mouth was wide and red against his otherwise pale, coarse flesh. When he spoke, his lips parted just a little. But his teeth, what the Wallach had seen of them when the Ferenczy laughed, were big and square and yellow. Also glimpsed: incisors oddly curved and sharp as tiny scythes, but Thibor couldn't be sure. If it was so, then the man would seem even more wolf-like.

And so he was an ugly man, this Faethor Ferenczy. But . . . Thibor had known ugly men aplenty. And he had killed plenty of them, too.

"The Vlad?" Thibor carved more meat, took a swig of red wine. It was vinegary stuff, but no worse than he was used to. Then he looked again at the Ferenczy and shrugged. "He told me that you live under his protection but swear him no allegiance. That you occupy land but concede no taxes. That you could muster many men but choose to sit here brooding while other Boyars fight off the Pechenegi to keep your hide whole."

For a moment the Ferenczy's eyes went wide, seemed flecked in their corners with blood, and his nostrils gaped in an audible grunt. His top lip wrinkled and curled back a little, and his jagged peaked eyebrows crushed together on his pale, high forehead. Then . . . he sat back, seemed to relax, grinned and nodded.

Thibor had stopped eating, but as the Ferenczy brought himself under control, so he carried on. Between mouthfuls he said, "Did you think I'd flatter you, Faethor Ferenczy? Perhaps you also thought your trickery would scare me off?"

The castle's master frowned, wrinkled his nose into ridges. "My . . . trickery?"

Thibor nodded. "The Prince's advisors—Christian monks out of Greek-land—think you're some sort of demon, a 'vampire.' I believe he thinks so too. But me, I'm just a common man—a peasant, aye—and I say you're only a clever trickster. You speak to your Szgany serfs with mirror signals, and you've a trained wolf or two to do your bidding, like dogs. Hah! Mangy wolves! Why, in Kiev there's a man leads great bears around on a leash—and he dances with them! And what else do you have, eh? Nothing! Oh, you make shrewd guesses—and then pretend that your eyes have powers, that they see over woods and mountains. You cloak yourself in mystery and superstition up here in these dark hills, but that only works with the superstitious. And who are *most* superstitious? Educated men, monks and princes, that's who! They know so much— their brains are so bursting with knowledge—that they'll believe anything! But a common man, a warrior, he only believes in blood and iron. The first to give him strength to wield the second, the second to spill the first in a scarlet flood.''

A little surprised at himself, Thibor paused, wiped his mouth. The wine had loosened his tongue.

The Ferenczy had sat there as if turned to stone; now he rocked back in his chair, slapped the table with a long, flat hand, roared his mirth. And Thibor saw that indeed his eye-teeth were like those of a great dog. ''What? Wisdom from a warrior?'' the Boyar shouted. He pointed a slender finger. ''But you are so *right*, Thibor! Right to be outspoken, and I like you for it. And I'm glad you came, whatever your mission. Wasn't I right to say you could be my son? Indeed, I *was* right. A man after my own heart—in perhaps more ways than one, eh?''

His eyes were red again (only an effect of the fire's glow, surely?) but Thibor made sure that a knife lay close at hand. Perhaps the Ferenczy was mad. Certainly he looked mad, when he laughed like that.

The fire flared up as a log turned on its side. A smell of burning wafted to Thibor's nostrils. The woodcocks! Both he and his host had forgotten them. He decided to be charitable, to let the hermit eat before killing him. ''Your birds,'' he said, or tried to say, as he made to get to his feet. But the words tangled themselves up on his tongue, came out slurred and alien sounding. Worse, he couldn't force himself upright; his hands seemed glued to the table top, and his feet were heavy as lumps of lead!

Thibor looked down at his straining, twitching hands, his nearly paralyzed body, and even his horrified glance was slow, filled with an unnatural languor. It was as if he were drunk, but drunker than he'd ever been. It would require only the slightest shove, he was sure, to send him sprawling.

Then his eyes fell upon his goblet, the red wine from the pitcher. Vinegary, yes. That and worse. He was poisoned!

The Ferenczy was watching him closely. Suddenly he sighed and stood up. He seemed even taller now, younger, stronger. He stepped lithe to the fire, toppled the spit and steaming birds into the flames. They hissed, smoked, caught fire in a moment. Then he turned to where Thibor sat watching him. Not a muscle of Thibor's body would answer his mind's desperate commands. It was as if he were turned to stone. Droplets of cold sweat started out upon his brow. The Ferenczy came closer, stood over him. Thibor looked at him, at his long jaws, his misshapen skull and ears, his crushed snout of a nose. An ugly man, yes, and perhaps more than a man.

"P-p-*poisoned!*" The Wallach finally spat it out.

"Eh?" the Ferenczy cocked his head, looked down on him. "Poisoned? No, no," he denied, "merely drugged. Isn't it obvious that if I wanted you dead, then you'd *be* dead—along with Arvos and your friends? But such bravery! I showed you what I could do, and yet you came on. Or are you simply stubborn? Stupid, maybe? I'll give you the benefit of the doubt and say that you're brave, for I've no time to waste on fools."

With a great effort of will, Thibor forced his right hand spastically towards a knife where it lay on the table. His host smiled, took up the knife, offered it to him. Thibor sat and trembled with the strain of his effort, but he could no more take that knife than stand up. The entire room was beginning to swim, to melt, to flow together in a dark, irresistible whirlpool.

The last thing he saw was the Ferenczy's face, more terrible than ever, as he leaned over him. That bestial, animal face—jaws open in a gaping laugh—*and the crim-*

*son forked tongue that vibrated like a crippled snake in the
cavern of his throat!*

The old Thing in the ground sprang awake . . . !

His nightmare had awakened him, and something else.

For a moment the Thibor-creature thrilled with the horror of his dream, before remembering where, who and
what he was. And then he thrilled again, the second time
with ecstasy.

Blood!

The black soil of his grave was drenched, gorged with
blood! Blood touched him, seeped like oil through leaf-
mould, rootlets and earth and touched him. Drawn by the
instant capillary action of his myriad thirsting fibres, it
soaked *into* him, filled his desiccated pores and veins, his
spongy organs and yawning, aching alveolate bones.

Blood—life!— filled the vampire, set centuries-numbed
nerves leaping, brought incredible, inhuman senses instantly alert.

His eyes cracked open—closed at once. Soil. Darkness.
He was buried still. He lay in his grave, as always. He
opened the sinuses of his gaping nostrils, and immediately
closed them—but not entirely. He smelled the soil, yes,
but he also smelled blood. And now, fully awake, he
carefully, far more minutely, began to examine his
surroundings.

He weighed the earth above him, probed it with instinct.
Shallow, very shallow. Eighteen inches, no more. And
above that, another twelve inches of compact leaf-mould.
Oh, he'd been buried deep enough that time, but in the
centuries between he'd wormed his way closer to the
surface. That had been when he had the strength to do so.

He exerted himself, extended pseudopods up into the
soil like crimson worms—and snatched them back. Oh,
yes, the earth was heavily saturated with blood, and human blood at that, but . . . how could that be? Could this
be—could it possibly be—the work of Dragosani?

The Thing reached out its mind, called softly: *Drago-saaaniiii? Is it you, my son? Have you done this thing, brought me this fine tribute, Dragosaaaniiii?*

His thoughts touched upon minds—but clean minds, innocent minds. Human minds which had never known his taint. But people? Here in the cruciform hills? What was their purpose here? Why had they come to his grave and baited the earth with—

Baited the earth!

The Thibor-creature whipped back his thoughts, his protoplasmic extrusions, his psychic extensions and cringed down into himself. Terror and hatred filled his every nerve. Was that the answer? Had they remembered him after all these years and come to put paid to him at last? Had they let him lie here undead for half a millennium simply to come and destroy him now? Had Dragosani perhaps spoken of him to someone, and that someone recognized the peril in what was buried here?

Senses thrilling, the Thing lay there, his scarcely human body trembling with tension, listening, feeling, smelling, tasting, using all of his heightened vampire senses except that of sight. Aye, and he could use that, too, if he dared.

But for all his fear, the one thing he did not sense was danger. And he would know the smell of danger as surely as he knew the smell of blood.

What hour would it be?

His trembling stilled as he gave the problem of the hour a moment's thought. Hour? *Hah!* What month would it be, what season, year, decade? How long since the boy Dragosani—that child of Thibor's every hope and evil aspiration—how long since he'd visited him here? But more importantly, was it day now . . . or was it night?

It was night. The vampire could feel it. Darkness seeped down through the soil like the rich, dark blood it accompanied. It was night, *his* time, and the blood had given him a strength, an elasticity, a motivation and a mobility almost forgotten through all the centuries he'd lain here.

He put out his thoughts again to touch upon the minds of the people in the glade of stirless trees directly above him where he lay. He did not think *at* them, made no effort to communicate, merely touched their thoughts with his own. A man and a woman. Only the two of them. Were they lovers? Is that what they were doing here? But in winter? Yes, it was winter, and the ground cold and hard. And what of the blood? Perhaps it was . . . murder?

The woman's mind was . . . full of nightmares! She slept, or lay unconscious, but panic was fresh in her mind and her heart beat fitfully, in a fever of fear. What had frightened her?

As for the man: he was dying. It was his blood the old Thing had absorbed, which fuelled his vampire system even now. But what had happened to these two? Had he lured her here, attacked her, and had she in turn cut him open before he could use her?

Thibor tried to explore the dying man's mind a little deeper. There was pain—too much pain. It had closed the man's mind down, so that now all was growing numb, succumbing to an aching void. It was the ultimate void, called Death, which would swallow its victim utterly.

But pain, yes—indeed agony. The Thing in the ground put out extrusions like flexible, fleshy antennae to trace the man's seeping life fluid; red worms of inhuman flesh extended from his ages-wrinkled face, hollow chest, shrivelled limbs, burrowing upward like tube-worms or the siphons of some loathsome mollusc; they followed the scarlet trace, converging upon its source.

The man's right leg was broken above the knee. Sharply fractured bone had sliced open arteries like a knife, arteries which even now pumped thin splashes of steaming scarlet on to the cold, dead earth. But *that* was a thought which was too much; it stirred the true beast in the Thibor-creature; he was ravening in a moment. His great dog's jaws cracked open in the hard earth, crusted lips quivered and salivated, flaring nostrils gaped like black funnels.

From its neck the Thing sent up a thick snake of surging protoplasm, which pushed aside rootlets and pebbles and dirt until it emerged, nodding like some vile, animated mushroom, in the glade of Thibor's mausoleum. He formed a rudimentary eye in its tip, expanded its pupil the better to see in the darkness.

He saw the dying man: a large, handsome man, which might explain the good strong blood, its quality and quantity. An intelligent man, high browed. And yet crumpled here on the hard earth, with his life leaking out of him down to the last few droplets.

Thibor couldn't save him, wouldn't if he could. But neither would he let him go to waste. A cursory glance of his obscene eye, to ensure that the woman was not coming out of her faint, and then he sent up a score of tiny red snouts from his gaping face: hollow tubes like little pouting mouths, to slide into the raw wound and draw on the last of the hot juices which flooded there. Then—

All of Thibor's hellish being surrendered itself to the sheer ecstasy—the black joy, the unholy rapture—of feeding, of drawing red sustenance direct from a victim's veins. It was . . . it was indescribable!

It was a man's first woman. Not his first fumbling, hurried, uncontrolled eruption on to some girl's belly or into her pubic hair, but the first pumping of salving semen into the hot core of a groaning, sated woman. It was a man's first kill in battle, when his enemy's head leaps free or his sword strikes home in heart or throat. It was the sharp, stinging agony of a douse in some mountain pool; the sight of a battlefield, where the piled bodies of an army reek and steam; the adoration of warriors hoisting high a man's colours in recognition of his victory. It was as sweet as all of these things—but alas, it was over all too quickly.

The man's heart no longer pumped. His blood, what little remained, was still. The great blotches of crimson were hardening and turning leaf-mould to clotted crusts.

Almost before it had begun, the marvellous feast was . . . over?

Perhaps not . . .

The Thibor-thing's sight extension turned its eye upon the woman. She was pale, attractive, fine-boned. She looked like the fine toy lady of some rich Boyar, full of thin aristocratic blood. Feverish highlights of colour gave her cheeks a fresh appearance, but the rest of her skin was pale as death. Cold and growing colder, exposure would kill her if the old Thing in the ground did not.

The eye-stalk extended, elongated out of the earth. Its colour was grey-green, mottled, but blood-red veins pulsed in it now, just beneath the surface of its protoplasmic skin. It swayed closer to the woman where she lay, poised itself before her face. Her breath, shallow, almost gasping, filmed the eye over and caused it to draw back. In her neck, a pulse fluttered like an exhausted bird. Her breast rose and fell, rose and fell.

The phallic eye swayed close to her throat, lidlessly observed the soft pulse of the jugular. Slowly the eye dissolved away and the red veins in the leprous nodding mushroom shuddered beneath its skin and turned a deeper scarlet. A reptilian mouth and jaws formed, taking the place of the eye, so that the tentacle might well seem a blind, smooth, mottled snake. The jaws yawned open and a forked tongue flickered between many rows of needle-sharp fangs. Saliva trickled from the distended jaws, slopped on the scummy earth. The "head" of the awful member drew back, formed a deadly "S" like a cobra about to strike, and—

—And the Thibor-creature gave himself a great mental shake and froze all his physical parts to instant rigidity. In the last possible moment he had realized what he was about to do, had recognized the extreme danger of his own naked lust.

These were not the old times but the new. The Twentieth Century! Except in ancient, crumbling records, his tomb here under the trees was forgotten. But if he took this woman's life, what then? Ah! He *knew* what then!

Search parties would come out looking for them both. They would be found sooner or later, here in the stirless glade, by the crumbling mausoleum. Someone would remember. Some old fool would whisper: "But—that place is forbidden!" and another would say, "Aye, for they buried something there long, long ago. My grandfather's grandfather used to tell tales about the thing buried on those cruciform hills, to put fear in his children when they were bad!"

Then they'd read the old records and remember the old ways, and in broad, streaming daylight they'd come, cut down the trees, uproot the ancient slabs, dig in the rotting soil until they found him. They'd stake him down again, but this time . . . this time . . . *this time they'd take his head and burn it!*

They'd burn all of him . . .

Thibor fought a fearsome battle with himself. The vampire in him, which had formed the major part of him for nine hundred years, was almost beyond reason. But Thibor *himself* could still think like a man, and his reasoning was sound. The vampire-Thibor was greedy for the moment, but the man-Thibor could see far beyond that. And he had already laid his plans. Plans which hinged on the boy Dragosani.

Dragosani was at school in Bucharest now, a mere lad in his teens, but the old Thing in the ground had already corrupted him. He'd taught him the art of necromancy, shown him how to divine the secrets only dead things know. And Dragosani would always return, would always come back here in his search for new knowledge, because the ancient Thing in the putrid earth was the very font of all dark mystery.

Meanwhile, a vampire seed or egg—the Thibor-creature's filthy, leech-like clone—was growing in him where he lay, a single drop of alien fluid which carried the complex code of the new vampire. But that was a slow, slow process. One day Dragosani, grown to a man, would come up here into these hills and the egg would be ready. A man would come up here full of monstrous talent, seeking the ultimate secrets of the Wamphyri . . . but when he went away, he would carry a fledgling vampire with him, *inside* him.

After that he would come again—would have to come again—by which time Thibor would be ready for the final phase of his plan. Dragosani would come, Dragosani *and* Thibor would leave—together. At last the cycle would be complete, the wheel turned full circle, when again the immemorial vampire would walk the earth—this time to conquer it!

That was how the old Thing in the ground had planned it, and that was how it would be. He *would* rise up from here and go out again into the world. The world would be his! But not if he killed this woman here and now. No, for that would be total madness, the very end of him and all his dreams . . .

The vampire in him succumbed to common sense, reluctantly allowed the twisted but human mind of Thibor to take ascendancy. Blood-lust receded, was replaced by curiosity, which in turn gave way to dormant, ages-repressed urges. New feelings, entirely human feelings, awakened in the old Thing in the ground. He was neither male nor female, now, Thibor—he was of the Wamphyri—but he had once been a man. A lustful man.

He had known women, many women, in the five hundred years that his scourge had terrified Wallachia, Bulgaria, Moldavia, Russia and the Ottoman. Some had been his willingly, but most had not. There was no way a woman could be had which was unknown to him, no pleasure or pain a woman could offer that he had not been offered, or taken by force, times without number.

In the mid-fifteenth century, as a mercenary Voevod of Vlad Tepes the so-called "impaler," he had crossed the Danube with his forces and taken an emissary of the Sultan

Murad. The sultan's representative, his escort of two hun
dred soldiers, and his harem of twelve beauties were taken
in the night in the town of Isperikh. Thibor had shown
leniency of a sort towards the Bulgarian townspeople: they
were allowed to flee while his troops sacked the town and
burned it, looting and raping when the inhabitants were
slow off the mark.

But as for the sultan's emissary: Thibor had had him
impaled, him and his entire two hundred, on tall, thin
stakes. "In their own fashion," he'd gleefully commanded
his executioners. "The Turkish way. They like buggering
little lads, this lot, so let 'em die happy, the way they've
lived!" But the women of the harem: he'd had all twelve
the same night, going from one to the next unstintingly,
and carrying on all through the following day. Ah! He'd
been a satyr in those days.

And now . . . now he was just an old Thing in the
ground. For the moment. For a few more years. But he
could still dream, couldn't he? He could still remember
how it had been. Indeed, perhaps he could do more than
just remember . . .

The mucus matter of his probe underwent another metamorphosis. The snake jaws, fangs and tongue melted back
into the body of the tentacle, whose tip flattened and
spread out, becoming bluntly spatulate. The flat paddle
split into five stubby grey-green worms—a rudimentary
thumb and four fingers—and the central digit grew a small
eye of its own which fixed itself in moist fascination upon
the rise and fall of the unconscious woman's breast. Thibor
flexed his "hand," made it sensitive, thickened and elongated the stalk which was its "arm."

With the tiny glistening eye to guide it, the trembling
gelatinous hand found its way inside the woman's jacket,
under layers of clothing to her flesh. She was still warm
but the sensitive hand could feel the heat gradually leaking
out of her. Her breasts were soft, large-nippled, more than
amply proportioned. When Thibor had been alive as op-

posed to undead, they had been the sort of breasts he enjoyed. His hand fondled then, growing rough in its teasing. She moaned a little and stirred the merest fraction of an inch.

Beneath the old Thing's hand, her heart was beating more strongly now, perhaps stimulated by his touch. A strong beat, yes, but desperate, panicked. She knew she should *not* be lying here, doing nothing, and strove to rise up from her faint. But her body was not answering her needs, her limbs were cooling; when her blood also began to cool, then shock would kill her.

Now the Thibor-creature also panicked a little. She must not be allowed to die here! In his mind he saw again the searchers finding the bodies of the man and woman, saw them peering narrow-eyed at his crumbling tomb, their knowing glances. Then he saw them digging, saw their pointed hardwood stakes, their chains of silver, their bright axes. He saw the very hillside blazing up in a bonfire of felled trees, and for a single agonizing instant felt his alien flesh melting, liquefying into fat and foul ichor where it boiled in the putrid earth.

No, she must not be allowed to die here. He must bring her back to consciousness. But first . . .

His hand left her breasts, began to crawl lustfully down across her belly—and froze!

Lying here through all the centuries, the Thibor-creature's senses, his awareness, had not been dulled but had amplified many times over. Deprived of all else, he had developed a super-sensitivity. In the many springtimes he had felt the green shoots rising, listened to birds mating in distant trees. He had smelled the warmth of all the summers, had crouched down deep, snarling his hatred of stray beams of sunlight where they penetrated the glade to fall glancingly upon his tomb. Autumns, and the brown, sere leaves falling against the earth had sometimes sounded like thunder; and when the rain came, streamlets roared like mighty rivers. And now—

Now the tiny, insistent, almost mechanical beat he "heard" through his hand where it rested on the woman's belly told a story, tapped out a code, one that other creatures could not possibly detect. It told of new life, of a being unborn, as yet the merest foetus.

The woman was pregnant!

Ahhhh! said Thibor, if only to himself. He stiffened his pseudohand and pressed it harder against the woman's flesh. A child-to-be—pure innocence—a single instant of intense pleasure solidified into a seed, growing here in its dark, warm womb.

Evil instinct took over—part vampire, part human, but all evil. Night-dark logic replaced lust. The tentacle elongated more yet and its hand lost substance; it grew smaller and slimmer as it proceeded with renewed purpose, indeed with an entirely *new* purpose. Its destination had been the woman's most secret place, the core of her female identity. Not to harm but simply to know, and to remember. But now there was a new destination.

Down in the ground, under powdery leaf-mould and hard, cold earth, the vampire's jaws cracked open in a blind, monstrous smile. He must lie here forever, or until a time when Dragosani should come to free him; but here at last might be an opportunity, a chance to send at least *something* of himself out into the world.

He entered the woman—carefully, delicately, so that even awake she might not have suspected he was there—and wrapped curling, frond-like fingers about the new life in her womb. His very touch was a taint as for an instant of time he weighed the tiny thing, that minute blob of almost featureless flesh, and felt the thud of its foetal heart. And:

Rememberrrr! said the old Thing in the ground. *Know what you are, what I am. More than that, know where I am. And when you are ready, then seek me out. Remember meeee!*

The woman moved, and moaned again, louder this time.

Thibor withdrew from her, made his hand heavier, more solid. He struck her, a ringing slap across her pale face. She cried out, shook herself, opened her eyes. But too late to see the leprous appendage of the vampire as it was sucked down swiftly into the earth.

She cried out again, cast about with frightened eyes in the gloom, saw the still, crumpled shape of her husband. Galvanized, she drew breath, cried, "Oh God!" as she flew to him. It took only a moment more to accept the unacceptable truth.

"No!" she cried. "Oh, God, *no!*" Horror gave her strength. She would not faint again; indeed she loathed herself that she'd fainted the first time. Now she must act, must do . . . something! There was nothing she could do, not for him, though for the moment that fact hadn't registered.

She got her arms hooked under his, dragged him a few stumbling paces under the trees, down the slope. Then she tripped on a root, flew backwards, and her husband's corpse came tumbling after her. She was brought up short when she collided with the bole of a tree, but not him. He went sliding, lolling and flopping past her, a loose bundle of arms and legs. He hit a patch of snow crusted over with ice, and went tobogganing away out of sight, down the hill, shooting into steep shadows.

The crashing of undergrowth came back to her where she got to her feet and gaspingly drew breath. And it was all useless, her efforts all totally worthless.

As that fact dawned she filled her lungs—filled them to bursting—and stumbling blindly after him down the hill, under the trees, let it all out in a long, piercing scream of mental agony and self-reproach.

The cruciform hills echoed her scream, bouncing it to and fro until it fell to earth and was absorbed. And down below the old Thing heard it and sighed, and waited for whatever the future would bring . . .

* * *

In an office in London, on the top floor of a hotel which was rather more than a hotel, Alec Kyle glanced at his watch. It was 4:05, and the Keogh apparition wasn't finished yet. The story it told was fascinating, however morbid, and Kyle guessed it would also be accurate—but how much more of it would there be? Time must surely be running out. Now, while the spectral thing which was Keogh paused, and while yet the image of his child host turned on its axis in and through his mid-section, Kyle said, "But of course we know what happened to Thibor: Dragosani put an end to him, finally beheaded and destroyed him there under the motionless trees on the cruciform hills."

Keogh had noticed him looking at his watch. *You're right,* he said, with a spectral nod. *Thibor Ferenczy is dead. That's how I was able to speak to him, there on those selfsame hills. I went there along the Möbius route. But you're also right that time is running down. So while we have time we must use it. And I've more to tell you.*

Kyle sat back, said nothing, waited.

I said there were other vampires, Keogh continued. *And there may be. But there are certainly creatures which I call half-vampires. That is something I'll try to explain later. I also mentioned a victim: a man who has been taken, used, destroyed by one of these half-vampires. He was dead when I spoke to him. Dead and utterly terrified. But not of being dead. And now he is undead.*

Kyle shook his head, tried hard to understand. "You'd better get on. Tell it your way. Let it unfold. That way I'll understand it better. Just tell me one thing: when did you . . . speak . . . to this dead man?"

Just a few days ago, as you measure time, Keogh answered without hesitation. *I was on my way back from the past, travelling in the Möbius continuum, when I saw a blue life-line crossed, and terminated, by a line more red than blue. I knew a life had been taken, and so I stopped and spoke to the victim. Incidentally, my discovery wasn't*

an accident: I had been looking for just such an occur-
rence. In a way I even needed this killing, horrible as that
may seem. But it's how I gain knowledge. You see, it's
much easier for me to talk to the dead than to the living.
And in any case, I couldn't have saved him. But through
him I might be able to save others.

"And you say he'd been taken by a vampire, this
man?" Still groping in the dark, Kyle was horrified. "Recently? But where? How?"

That's the worst of it, Alec, said Keogh. *He was taken*
here—here in England! As for how he was taken—let me
tell you . . .

Chapter Four

YULIAN HAD BEEN A LATE BABY, LATE BY ALMOST A MONTH, though in the circumstances his mother considered herself fortunate that he hadn't been born early. Or *very* early and dead! Now, on the spacious back seat of her cousin Anne's Mercedes, on their way to Yulian's christening at a church in Harrow, Georgina Bodescu steadied the infant in his portable cot and thought back on those circumstances: on that time almost a year before when she and her husband had holidayed in Slatina, only eighty kilometres from the wild and ominously rearing bastions of the Carpatii Meridionali, the Transylvanian Alps.

A year is a long time and she could do it now—look back—without any longer feeling that she too must die, without submitting to slow, hot tears and an agony of self-reproach bordering on guilt. That's how she had felt for long, long months: guilty. Guilty that she lived when Ilya was dead, and that but for her weakness he, too, might still be alive. Guilty that she had fainted at the sight of his blood, when she should have run like the wind to fetch help. And poor Ilya lying there, made unconscious by his pain, his life's blood leaking out of him into the dark earth, while she lay crumpled in a swoon like . . . like some typically English shrinking violet.

Oh, yes, she could look back now—indeed she had to—for they had been Ilya's last days, which she had been part of. She had loved him very, very much and did not want to lose grasp of her memory of him. If only in looking back she could conjure all the good things without invoking the nightmare, then she would be happy.

But of course she couldn't . . .

Ilya Bodescu, a Romanian, had been teaching Slavonic languages in London when Georgina first met him. A linguist, he moved between Bucharest, where he taught French and English, and the European Institute in Regent Street where she had studied Bulgarian (her grandfather on her mother's side, a dealer in wines, had come from Sofia). Ilya had only occasionally been her tutor—when standing in for a huge-breasted, moustachioed matron from Pleven—at which times his dry wit and dark, sparkling eyes had transformed what were otherwise laborious hours of learning into all too short periods of pure pleasure. Love at first sight? Not in the light of twelve years' hindsight—but a rapid enough process by any estimation. They had married inside a year, Ilya's usual term with the Institute. When the year was up, she'd gone back to Bucharest with him. That had been in November of '47.

Things had not been entirely easy. Georgina Drew's parents were fairly well-to-do; her father in the diplomatic service had had several prestigious postings abroad, and her mother too was from a monied background. An ex-deb turned auxiliary nurse during the First World War, she had met John Drew in a field hospital in France where she nursed his bad leg wound. This kept him out of the rest of the fighting until she could return home with him. They married in the summer of 1917.

When Georgina had introduced Ilya to her parents, his reception had been more than a little stiff. For years her father, severely British, had been "living down" the fact that his wife was of Bulgarian stock, and now here was his daughter bringing home a damned gypsy! It hadn't been *that* open, but Georgina had known what her father had thought of it all right. Her mother hadn't been quite so bad, but was too fond of remembering how "Papa never much trusted the 'Wallachs' across the border," a distrust which she put forward as one of the reasons he'd emigrated to England in the first place. In short, Ilya had not been made to feel at home.

Sadly, within the space of eight more years—split evenly for Georgina and Ilya between Bucharest and London—time had caught up with both of her parents. All squabbles were long forgotten by then and Georgina had been left fairly well off—which was as well. In those early years Ilya certainly wasn't earning enough from his teaching to keep her in her accustomed style.

But it was then that Ilya had been offered a lucrative position as an interpreter-translator with the Foreign Office in London; for while in life Georgina's father had once been something of a pain, in death his legacy included an excellent introduction to diplomatic circles. There was one condition: to secure the position Ilya must first become a British citizen. This was no hardship—he'd intended it anyway, eventually, when the right opportunity presented itself—but he did have a final term's contract at the Institute, and one more year to complete in Bucharest, before he could take up the position.

That last year in Romania had been a sad one—because of the knowledge that it *was* the last—but towards the end of his term Ilya had been glad. The war was eleven years in the past and the air of the reviving cities had not been good for him. London had been smog and Bucharest fog, both were laden with exhaust fumes and, for Ilya, the taint of mouldering books in libraries and classrooms too. His health had suffered a little.

They could have come back to England as soon as he'd fulfilled his duties, but a doctor in Bucharest advised against it. "Stay through the winter," he'd counselled, "but not in the city. Get out into the countryside. Long walks in the clean, fresh air—that's what you need. Evenings by a roaring log fire, just taking it easy. Knowing that the snow lies deep without, and that you're all warm within! There's a deal of satisfaction in that. It makes you glad you're alive."

It had seemed sound advice.

Ilya wasn't due to start working at the Foreign Office until the end of May; they spent Christmas in Bucharest with friends; then, early in the new year, they took the train for Slatina under the Alps. In fact the town was on the slopes gentling up to the foothills, but the locals always spoke of it as being "under the Alps." There they hired an old barn of a place set back from the highway to Pitesti, settling in just before the coming of the first real snows of the year.

By the end of January the snowploughs were out, clearing the roads, their blue exhaust smoke acrid in the sharp, smarting air; the townspeople went about their business with a great stamping of feet; they were muffled to their ears, more like great bundles of clothing than people. Ilya and Georgina roasted chestnuts on their blazing, open hearth fire and made plans for the future. Until now they'd held back from a family, for their lives had seemed too unsettled. But now . . . now it felt right to start.

In fact they'd started almost two months earlier, but Georgina couldn't be sure yet. She had her suspicions, though.

Days would find them in town—when the snow would allow—and nights they were here in their rambling hiring, reading or making languid love before the fire. Usually the latter. Within a month of leaving Bucharest Ilya's irritating

cough had disappeared and much of his former strength
had returned. With typical Romanian zeal, he revelled in
expending much of it on Georgina. It had been like a
second honeymoon.

Mid-February and the impossible happened: three con-
secutive days of clear skies and bright sunshine, and all of
the snow steaming away, so that on the morning of the
fourth day it looked almost like an early spring. "Another
two or three days of fair weather," the locals nodded
knowingly, "and then you'll see snow like you've *never*
seen it! So enjoy what we've got while you can." Ilya and
Georgina had determined to do just that.

Over the years and under Ilya's tuition, Georgina had
become quite handy on a pair of skis. It might be a very
long time before they got the chance again. Down here on
the so-called steppe, all that remained of the snow were
dark grey piles heaped at the roadsides; a few kilometres
up country towards the Alps, however, there was still
plenty to be found.

Ilya hired a car for a couple of days—a beat-up old
Volkswagen beetle—and skis, and by 1:30 P.M. on that
fateful fourth day they had motored up into the foothills.
For lunch they stopped at a tiny inn on the northern
extreme of Ionesti, ordering goulash which they washed
down with thick coffee, followed by a single shot each of
sharp slivovitz to clean their mouths.

Then on higher into the hills, to a region where the
snow still lay thick on the fields and hedgerows. And there
it was that Ilya spied the hump of low grey hills a mile or
so to the west, and turned off the road on to a track to try
to get a little closer.

Finally the track had become rutted under the drifted
snow, and the snow itself deeper, until at last Ilya had
grunted his annoyance. Not wanting to get bogged down,
revving the little car's engine, he'd bumpily turned it about
in its own tracks, the better to make an easy getaway when
they were through with their sport.

"Landlaufen!" he'd declared, getting down their skis from the roofrack.

Georgina had groaned. "Cross-country? All the way to those hills?"

"They're white!" he declared. "Glittery with dust over the hard, firm crust. Perfect! Maybe half a mile there, a slow climb to the top and a controlled, enjoyable slalom through the trees, then back here just as the twilight's coming down on us."

"But it's after three now!" she'd protested.

"Then we'd better get a move on. Come on, it'll be good for us . . ."

"Good for us!" Georgina sadly repeated now, his picture still clear in her mind a year later, tall and darkly handsome as he lifted the skis from the beetle's roof and tossed them down in the snow.

"What's that?" Anne Drew, her younger cousin, glanced back at her over her shoulder. "Did you say something?"

"No," Georgina smiled wanly, shaking her head. She was glad for the intrusion of another into her memories, but at the same time sorry. Ilya's face, fading, hung in the air, superimposed over her cousin's. "Daydreaming, that's all."

Anne frowned, turned back to her driving. *Daydreaming*, she thought. Yes, and Georgina had done a lot of that over the last twelve months. There'd seemed to be something in her, something other than little Yulian, that is, which hadn't come out of her when he had. Grief, yes, of course, but more than that. It was as if she'd teetered for twelve months on the very edge of a nervous breakdown, and that only Ilya's continuation in Yulian had kept her from toppling. As for daydreams: sometimes she'd seemed so very far away, so detached from the real world, that it had been difficult to call her back. But now, with the baby . . . now she had something to cling to, an anchor, something to live for.

Good for us, Georgina said again, but this time to herself, bitterly.

It hadn't been "good" for them, that last fatal frolic in the snow on the cruciform hills. Anything but. It had been terrible, tragic. A nightmare she'd lived through a thousand times in the year gone by, with ten thousand more to come, she was sure. Lulled by the car's warmth and the purr of its motor, she slipped back into her memories . . .

They'd found an old firebreak in the side of the hill and set out to climb it to the top, pausing now and then with their breath pluming, shielding their eyes against the white blaze. But by the time they'd pantingly reached the crest the sun had been low and the light starting to fade.

"From now on it's all downhill," Ilya had pointed out. "A brisk slalom through the saplings grown up in the firebreak, then a slow glide back to the car. Ready? Then here we go!"

And the rest of it had been . . . disaster!

The saplings he'd mentioned were in fact half-grown trees. The snow, drifted into the firebreak, was far deeper than he might have guessed, so that only the tops of the pines—looking like saplings—stood proud of the powdery white surface. Half-way down he'd skied too close to one such; a branch, just under the surface, showing as the merest tuft of green, had tangled his right-hand ski. He'd upended, bounced and skittered and jarred another twenty-five yards in a whirling bundle of white anorak, sticks and skis, flailing arms and legs before grabbing another "sapling" and bringing his careening descent to a halt.

Georgina, well to his rear and skiing a little more timidly, saw it all. Her heart seemed to fly into her mouth and she cried out, then formed a snowplough of her skis and drew up alongside her husband where he sprawled. She'd stepped out of her clamps at once, dug her skis in so that she couldn't lose them, gone down on her knees beside him. Ilya held his sides as he laughed and laughed, the tears of laughter rolling down his cheeks and freezing there.

"Clown!" She'd thumped his chest then. "Oh, you *clown!* You very nearly frightened the life out of me!"

He had laughed all the louder, grabbing her wrists, holding her still. Then he'd looked at his skis and stopped laughing. The right ski was broken, hanging by a splinter where it had cracked across its width some six inches in front of the clamp. "Ah!" he had exclaimed then, frowning. And he'd sat up in the snow and looked all about. Georgina had known, then, that it was serious. She could see it in his eyes, the way they narrowed.

"You go back to the car," he'd told her. "But carefully, mind you—don't be like me and go banging your skis up! Start the car and get the heater going. It's not much more than a mile, so by the time I get back you'll have that old beetle good and warm for me. No point both of us freezing."

"No!" She'd refused point-blank. "We go back together. I—"

"Georgina." He'd spoken quietly, which meant that he was getting angry. "Look, if we go back together, it means we'll *both* get back wet, tired, and very, very cold. Now that's OK for me, and I deserve it, but you don't. My way you'll soon be warm, and I'll be warm a lot sooner! Also, night is coming on. You get back to the car now, in the twilight, and you'll be able to put on the lights as a marker. You can beep the horn now and then to let me know you're safe and warm, and to give me an incentive. You see?"

She had seen, but his arguments hadn't swayed her. "If we stick together, at least we'll *be* together! What if I did fall down and get stuck, eh? You'd get back to the car and I wouldn't be there. What then? Ilya, I'd be frightened on my own. For myself and for you!"

For a second his eyes had narrowed more yet. But then he'd nodded. "You're right, of course." And again he'd looked all about. Then, taking off his skis: "Very well, this is what we'll do. Look down there."

The firebreak had continued for maybe another half kilometre, running steeply downhill. To both sides full-grown trees, some of them hoary with age, stood thick and dark, with the snow drifted in banks under them where they bordered the firebreak. They stood so close that over-head their branches often interlooked. They hadn't been cut for five hundred years, those trees. Beneath them the snow was mostly patchy, kept from the earth by the thick fir canopy, which it covered like a mantle.

"The car's over there," said Ilya, pointing east, "around the curve of the hill and behind the trees. We'll cut through the trees downhill to the track, then follow our own ski-tracks back to the car. Cutting off the corner will save us maybe half a kilometre, and it will be a lot easier than walking in deep snow. Easier for me, anyway. Once we're back on the track you can go on skis, a gentle glide; and when the car's in sight, then you can go on ahead and get her going. But we'll have to get a move on. It will be gloomy now under those trees, and in another half-hour the sun will be down. We won't want to be in the wood too long after that."

Then he'd hoisted Georgina's skis to his shoulder and they'd left the firebreak for the shelter and the silence of the trees.

At first they'd made good headway, so good in fact that she had almost stopped worrying. But there was that about the hillside which oppressed—a quiet too intense, a sense of ages passing or passed like a few ticks of some vast clock, and of something waiting, watching—so that she only desired to get down off the hill and back out into the open. She supposed that Ilya felt it, too, this strange *genius loci*, for he had said very little and even his breathing was quiet as they made their way diagonally down through the trees, moving from bole to black bole, avoiding the more precipitous places as much as possible.

Then they had reached a place where leaning stumps of stone, the bedrock itself, stuck up through the soil and leaf-mould; following which they had to negotiate an almost sheer face of crumbling rock down to a levelled area. And as he helped her down, so they had noticed the handiwork of man there under the dark trees.

They stood upon lichen-clad stone flags in front of . . . a mausoleum? That's what the tumbled ruins had looked like, anyway. But here? Georgina had nervously clutched Ilya's arm. This could hardly be considered a holy place or hallowed ground, not by any stretch of the imagination. It seemed that unseen presences moved here, lending their motion to the musty air without disturbing the festoons of cobwebs and dangling fingers of dead twigs that hung down from higher areas of gloom. It was a cold place—but lacking the normal, invigorating cold of winter—where the sun had only rarely broken through in . . . how many centuries?

Hewn from the raw stone of the hillside itself, the tomb had long since caved in; most of its roof of massive slabs lay in a tangle of broken masonry, where the flags of the floor were cracked and arched upwards from the achingly slow groping of great roots. A broken stone joist, leaning now against the thickly matted ruin of a side wall, had once formed the lintel above the tomb's wide entrance; it bore a vague motif or coat of arms, hard to make out in the gloom.

Ilya, who had always had a fascination for antiquities of all sorts, had gone to kneel beside the great sloping slab and gouge dirt from its carved legend. "Well, now!" his voice had sounded hushed. "And what are we to make of this, eh?"

Georgina had shuddered. "I don't want to make any-thing of it! This is an entirely horrid place. Come away, let's go on."

"But look—there are heraldic markings here. At least I suppose that's what they are. This one, at the bottom is . . . a dragon? Yes, with one forepaw raised, see? And above it—I can't quite make it out.''

"Because the sun is setting!" she'd cried. "It's getting gloomier by the moment." But she had gone to peer over his shoulder anyway. The dragon had been quite clearly worked, a proud-looking creature chipped from the stone.

"And that's a bat!" Georgina had said at once. "A bat in flight, over the dragon's back.''

Ilya had hurriedly cleaned away more dirt and lichen from the old chiselled grooves, and a third carved symbol had come to light. But the great lintel, which had seemed firmly enough bedded, had suddenly shifted, starting to topple as the rotting wall gave way.

Pushing Georgina back, Ilya had thrown himself off balance. Trying to scramble backwards himself, he'd somehow got his leg sticking straight out in front of him, directly under the toppling lintel. Still sprawling there as the slab fell, his cry of agony and the nerve-grating *crunch* as his leg broke and jagged bone sheared through his flesh came simultaneous with Georgina's scream.

Then, perhaps mercifully, he had lost consciousness. She had leaped to free him from the lintel, only to discover that while it had broken his leg, it had not trapped him. The lower part of his leg flopped uselessly and fell at an odd angle when she touched it, but miraculously it was not pinned. Then Georgina had seen and felt the break, the splintered bone projecting through red flesh and cloth, and the repetitive spurt of blood against her hands and jacket.

And that, until the moment of her awakening, had been the last that Georgia saw, felt or heard. Or rather, she had seen one other thing, and then forgotten it once she slumped to the ground. The thing she saw had remained forgotten, or more properly suppressed: it was the third symbol, carved above the dragon and the bat, which had seemed to leer at her even as the blackness closed in . . .

* * *

"Georgy? We're there!" Anne's voice broke the spell.

Georgina, reclining in the back of the car, eyes almost closed in her suddenly pale face, gave a start and sat upright. She had been on the verge of remembering something about the place where Ilya died, something she hadn't wanted to remember. Now she gulped air gratefully, forced a smile. "There already?" She managed to get the words out. "I . . . I must have been miles away!"

Anne pulled the big car into the car park behind the church, braking to a gentle halt. Then she turned to look at her passenger. "Are you *sure* you're all right?"

Georgina nodded. "Yes, I'm fine. Maybe a little tired, that's all. Come on, help me with the carry-cot."

The church was of old stone, all stained glass and Gothic arches, with a cemetery to one side where the headstones were leaning and crusted with grey-green lichens. Georgina couldn't bear lichens, especially when they covered old legends gouged in leaning slabs. She looked the other way as she hurried by the graveyard and turned left around the buttressed corner of the church towards its entrance. Anne, almost dragged along on the other handle of the carry-cot, had to break into a trot to keep up.

"Goodness!" she protested. "You'd think we were late or something!" And in fact they were, almost.

Waiting on the steps in front of the church, there stood Anne's fiancé, George Lake. They had lived together for three years and only just set a date; and they were to be Yulian's godparents. There had been several christenings this morning; the most recent party of beaming parents, godparents and relatives was just leaving, the mother radiant as she held her child in its christening-gown. George skipped by them, came hurrying down the steps, took the carry-cot and said, "I sat through the entire service, four christenings, all that mumbling and muttering and splashing—*and* screaming! But I thought it was only right that one of us be here from start to finish. But the old vicar—Lord, he's a boring old fart! God forgive me!''

George and Anne might well have been brother and sister, even twins. *Toss opposites attracting out the window*, thought Georgina. They were both five-ninish, a bit plump if not actually fat; both blondes, grey-eyed, soft-spoken. A few weeks separated their birth-dates: George was a Sagittarius and Anne a Capricorn. Typically, he would sometimes put his foot in it; she had sufficient of her sign's stability to pull him out of it. That was Anne's interpretation of their relationship, she being a lifelong advocate of astrology.

Leaving Georgina's hands free to tidy herself up a little, they now took the carry-cot between them and made to enter the church. The twin doors were of oak under a Gothic arch, one standing half open outwards on to the landing at the head of the steps. A wind came up from nowhere, blew yesterday's confetti up in mad swirls and slammed the door resoundingly in their faces. Earlier there had been the odd ray of sunshine filtering through wispy grey clouds, but now the clouds seemed to mass, the sun was switched off like a light and it grew noticeably darker.

''Not cold enough for snow,'' said George, turning his eyes apprehensively up to the sky. ''My guess is it's going to chuck it down!''

''Chuck it or bucket?'' Anne was still reeling from the door's slamming, her expression puzzled.

''Fuck it!'' said George, irreverently. ''Let's get in!''

A moment more and the door was shoved open from inside by the vicar. He was lean, getting on a bit in years, close to bald. His one advantage was of great height, so that he could look down on them all. He had little eyes made huge by thick-lensed spectacles, and a veined beak of a nose that seemed to turn his head as if it were a weathercock. His thinness gave the impression of a mantis, but at the same time he managed to look owlish.

A bird of pray! thought George, and grinned to himself.

But at the same time he noted that the old vicar's handshake was warm and full of comfort, however trembly, and that his smile was a beam of pure goodness. Nor was he lacking in his own brand of dry wit.

"So glad you could make it," he smiled, and nodded over Yulian in his carry-cot. The baby was awake, his round eyes moving to and fro. The vicar chucked him under his chubby chin, said, "Young man, it's always a good idea to be early for one's christening, punctual for one's wedding, and as late as one can get for one's funeral!" Then he peered frowningly at the door.

The freak gust of wind had disappeared, taking its confetti with it. "What happened here?" the old man lifted his eyebrows. "That's odd! I had thought the bolt was home. But in any case, it takes a wind of some power to slam shut a door heavy as this one. Perhaps we're in for a storm." At the foot of the door a bolt dragged squealingly along the groove it had worn in old stone flags, and thudded down into its bolthole as the vicar gave the door a final push. "There!" He wiped his hands, nodded his satisfaction.

Not such a boring old fart after all, all three thought the identical thought as he led them inside and up to the font.

In his time, the old clergyman had baptized Georgina; he'd married her, too, and was aware that she was now a widow. This was the church her parents had attended for most of their declining years, the church her father had attended as a boy and young man. There was no need for long preliminaries, and so he began at once. As George and Anne put the cot down, and as Georgina took up Yulian in her arms, he began to intone: "Hath this child been already baptized, or no?"

"No," Georgina shook her head.

"Dearly beloved," the vicar began in earnest, "foreasmuch as all men are conceived and born in sin—"

Sin, thought Georgina, the old man's words flowing over her. *Yulian wasn't conceived in sin.* This had ever been a part of the service that got her back up. *Sin, indeed! Conceived in joy and love and sweetest sweet pleasure, yes—unless pleasure were to be construed as sin . . .*

She looked down at Yulian in her arms; he was alert, staring at the vicar as he mumbled over his book. It was a funny expression on the baby's face: not quite vacant, not exactly a drool. Somehow intense. They had all kinds of looks, babies.

". . . that thou wilt mercifully look upon this child; wash him, sanctify him with the Holy Ghost; that he, being—"

The Holy Ghost. Ghosts had stirred under those stirless trees on the cruciform hills, but in no way holy ones. Unholy ones!

Thunder rumbled distantly and the high stained glass windows brightened momentarily from a far flash of lightning before falling into deeper gloom. A light burned over the font, however, sufficient for the vicar's eyes behind their thick lenses. He shivered visibly as he read his lines, for suddenly the temperature had seemed to fall dramatically.

The old man paused for a moment, looked up and blinked. His eyes went from the faces of the three adults to the baby, paused there for a moment, blinked rapidly. He looked at the light over the font, then at the high windows. For all his shivering, sweat gleamed on his brow and upper lip. "I . . . I . . ." he said.

"Are you all right?" George was concerned. He took the vicar's arm.

"A cold," the old man tried to smile, only succeeding in looking sick. His lips seemed to stick to his teeth, which were false and rather loose, and he was immediately apologetic. "I'm sorry, but this is not really surprising. A draughty place, you know? But don't worry, I won't let you down. We'll get this finished. It just came on so quickly, that's all." The sick smile twitched from his face.

"After this," said Anne, "you should spend what's left of the weekend in bed!"

"I believe I will, my dear." Fumblingly, the vicar went back to his text.

Georgina said nothing. She felt the strangeness. Something was unreal, out of focus. Did churches frown? This one was frowning. It had been hostile from the moment they'd arrived. That's what was wrong with the vicar: he could feel it too, but he didn't know what it was.

But how do I know what it is? Georgian wondered. *Have I felt it before?*

". . . They brought young children to Christ, that he should touch them; and his disciples rebuked those that brought them . . ."

Georgian felt the church groaning around her, trying to expel her. No, trying to expel . . . Yulian? She looked at the baby and he looked back: his face broke into that unsmile which small babies smile. But his eyes were fixed, steady, unblinking. Even as she stared at him, she saw those darling eyes swivel in their sockets to gaze full upon the old vicar. Nothing wrong with that—it was just that it had looked so deliberate.

Yulian is ordinary! Georgina denied what she was thinking. She'd had this feeling before and denied it, and now she must do it again. *He is ordinary!* It was her, not the baby. She was blaming him for Ilya. It was the only explanation.

She glanced at George and Anne, and they smiled back reassuringly. Didn't they feel the cold, the strangeness? They obviously thought she was concerned about the vicar, the service. Other than that, they felt nothing. Oh, maybe they felt how draughty the place was, but that was all.

Georgina felt more than the cold. And so did the vicar. He was skipping lines now, hurrying through the service almost mechanically, about as human as some gaunt robot penguin. He avoided looking at them, especially Yulian. Maybe he could feel the infant's eyes on him, unwaveringly.

"Dearly beloved," the old man was chanting at Anne

and George now, the godparents, "ye have brought this child here to be baptized . . ."

I have to stop it. Georgina's thought were growing wilder. She started to panic. *Have to, before it—but before what?—happens!*

". . . to release him of his sins, to sanctify him with . . ."

Outside, much closer now, thunder rumbled, accompanied by lightning that lit up the west-facing windows and sent kaleidoscopic beams of bright colours lancing through the interior. The group about the font was first gold, then green, finally crimson. Yulian was blood in Georgina's arms; his eyes were blood where they stared at the vicar.

At the back of the church, under the pulpit, almost unnoticed all of this time, a funereal man had been sweeping up, his broom scraping on the stone flags. Now, for no apparent reason, he threw the broom down, tore off his apron and rolled it up, almost ran from the church. He could be heard grumbling to himself, angry about something. Another flash of lightning turned him blue, green, finally white as an undeveloped photograph as he reached the door and plunged out of sight.

"Eccentric!" The vicar, seeming a little more in control of himself, frowned after him, blinked at his abrupt disappearance. "He cleans the church because he has a 'feel' for it! So he tells me."

"Er, can we get on?" George had apparently had enough of interruptions.

"Of course, of course," the old man peered again at his book, skipped several more lines. "Er . . . promise that you are his sureties, that he will renounce the devil and all his works, and constantly believe . . ."

Yulian had also had enough. He began to kick, gathered air for the howling session. His face puffed up and started to turn a little blue, which would normally mean that frustration and anger were coming to the boil just beneath the surface. Georgina couldn't keep back a great sigh of relief at that. What was Yulian but a helpless baby after all?

". . . the carnal desires of the flesh . . . was crucified, dead, and buried; that he went down into hell, and also did rise again the third day; that he . . ."

Just a baby, thought Georgina, *with Ilya's blood, and mine, and . . . and?*

". . . the quick and the dead?"

The church was thunder dark, the storm almost directly overhead.

". . . resurrection of the flesh; and everlasting life after death?"

Georgina gave a start as Anne and George answered in unison: "All this we steadfastly believe."

"Wilt he then be baptized in this faith?"

George and Anne again: "That is his desire."

But Yulian denied it! He gave a howl to raise the rafters, jerked and kicked with an astonishing strength where his mother cradled him. The old clergyman sensed trouble brewing—not the *real* trouble but trouble anyway— and decided not to prolong things. He took the baby from Georgina's arms. Yulian's white christening-gown was a haze of almost neon light, himself a pink pulsation in its folds.

Above the baby's howling, the old vicar said to George and Anne: "Name this child."

"Yulian," they answered simply.

"Yulian," he nodded, "I baptize thee in the name of—" He paused, stared at the baby. His right hand— practised, accustomed, of its own accord—had dipped into the font, lifted water, poised dripping.

Yulian continued to howl. Anne and George and Georgina heard his crying, only that. No longer touching her child, Georgina felt suddenly free, unburdened, separate from what was coming. It was not her doing; she was merely an observer; this priest must bear the brunt of his own ritual. She, too, heard only Yulian's crying—but she felt the approach of something enormous.

To the vicar the infant's howling had taken on a new note. It was no longer the cry of a child but a beast. His jaw dropped and he looked up, blinking rapidly as he peered from face to face: George and Anne smiling, if a little uncomfortably, and Georgina, looking small and wan. And then he looked again at Yulian. The baby was issuing grunts, animal grunts of rage! Its crying was only a cover, like perfume masking the stink of ordure. Underneath was the bass croaking of utter Horror!

Automatically, his hand trembling like a leaf in a gale, the old man splashed a little water on the infant's fevered brow, traced a cross there with his finger. The water might well have been acid!

NO! the thunderous croaking formed a denial. PUT NO CROSS ON ME, YOU TREACHEROUS CHRISTIAN DOG!

"What—!" the vicar suspected he'd gone insane. His eyes bulged behind the thick lenses of his spectacles.

The others heard nothing except the baby's crying—which now ceased on the instant. Old man and infant stared at each other in a deafening silence. "What?" the vicar asked again, his voice a whisper.

Before his eyes the skin of the baby's brow puffed up in twin mounds, like huge boils accelerated to instantaneous eruption. The fine skin split and blunt goat horns came through, curving as they emerged. Yulian's jaws elongated into a dog's muzzle, which cracked open to reveal a red cave of white knives and a viper's flickering tongue. The breath of the thing was a stench, an open tomb; its eyes, pits of sulphur, burned on the vicar's face like fire.

"Jesus!" said the old man. "Oh, my God—what *are* you?" And he dropped the child. Or would have—but George had seen the glazing of his eyes, the slackening of his body, the blood's rapid draining from his face. As the

old man crumpled, George stepped forward, took Yulian
from him.

Anne, also quick off the mark, had caught the old man
and managed to lower him a little less than gently to the
floor. But Georgina was also reeling. Like the other two,
she had seen, smelled, heard nothing—but she was Yulian's
mother. She had *felt* something coming, and she knew that
it had been here. As she, too, fainted, so there came a
thunderbolt that struck the steeple, and a cannonade of
thunder that rolled on and on.

Then there was only silence. And light gradually returning, and dust shaken down in rivulets from rafters high
overhead.

And George and Anne, white as ghosts, gaping at each
other in the church's lightening gloom.

And Yulian, angelic in his godfather's arms . . .

Georgina was a year making her recovery. Yulian spent
the time with his godparents, at the end of which they had
their own child to fuss over and care for. His mother spent
it in a somewhat select sanatorium. No one was much
surprised; her breakdown, so long delayed, had finally
arrived with a vengeance. George and Anne, and others of
Georgina's friends, visited her regularly, but no one mentioned the abortive christening or the death of the vicar.

That had been a stroke or some such. The old man's
health had been waning. He's lasted only a few hours after
his collapse in the church. George had gone with him in an
ambulance to the hospital, had been with him when he
died. The old man had come to in the final moments
before he passed forever from this world.

His eyes had focussed on George's face, widened, filled
with memory, disbelief. "It's all right," George had com-
forted him, patting the hand which grasped his forearm
with a feverish strength. "Take it easy. You're in good
hands."

"Good hands? Good hands! My God!" The old man

had been quite lucid. "I dreamed . . . I dreamed . . . there was a christening. You were there." It was almost an accusation.

George smiled. "There was *supposed* to be a christening," he'd answered. "But don't worry, you can finish it when you're up and about again."

"It was real?" the old man tried to sit up. "It *was* real!"

George and a nurse supported him in his bed, lowered him as he collapsed again on to his pillows. Then he caved in. His face contorted and he seemed to crumple into himself. The nurse rushed from the room shouting for a doctor. Still convulsing, the vicar beckoned George closer with a twitching finger. His face was fluttering, had turned the color of lead.

George put his ear to the old man's whispering lips, heard: "Christen it? No, no—you mustn't! First—*first have it exorcized!*"

And those were the last words he ever spoke. George mentioned it to no one. Obviously the old boy's mind had been going, too.

A week after the christening Yulian developed a rash of tiny white blisters on his forehead. They eventually dried up and flaked away, leaving barely visible marks exactly like freckles . . .

Chapter Five

"HE WAS A FUNNY LITTLE THING!" ANNE LAKE LAUGHED, shook her head and set her blonde hair flying in the breeze from the car's half-open window. "Do you remember when we had him that year?"

It was late in the summer of '77 and they were driving down to stay with Georgina and Yulian for a week. The last time they'd seen them was two years ago. George had thought the boy was strange then, and he'd said so on several occasions—not to Georgina and certainly not to Yulian himself, of course not, but to Anne, in private. Now he said so again:

"Funny little thing?" He cocked an eyebrow. "That's one way of putting it, I suppose. Weird would be a better way! And from what I remember of him last time we came down he hasn't changed—what was a weird baby is now a weird young man!"

"Oh, George, that's ridiculous. All babies are different from each other. Yulian was, well, more different, that's all."

"Listen," said George. "That child wasn't two months old when he came to us—and he had teeth! Teeth like little needles—sharp as hell! And I remember Georgina saying he was born with them. That's why she couldn't breast-feed him."

"George," said Anne warningly, a little sharply, reminding him that Helen sat in the back of the car. She was their daughter: a beautiful, occasionally precocious girl of sixteen.

Helen sighed, very deliberately and audibly, and said, "Oh, mother! I know what breasts are for—apart from being natural attractions for the opposite sex, that is. Why must you put them on your taboo list?"

"Ta-boob list!" George grinned.

"*George!*" said Anne again, more forcefully.

"Nineteen seventy-seven," Helen scoffed, "but you'd never know it. Not in this family. I mean, feeding your baby's natural, isn't it? More natural than letting your breasts be groped in the back row of some grubby flea-pit cinema!"

"Helen!" Anne half-turned in her seat, her lips compressing to a thin line.

"It's been a long time," George glanced at his wife, semi-ruefully.

"What has?" she snapped.

"Since I was groped in a flea-pit cinema," he said.

Anne snorted her exasperation. "She gets it from you!" she accused. "You've always treated her like an adult."

"Because she is an adult, very nearly," he answered. "You can only guide them so far, Anne my love, and after that they're on their own. Helen's healthy, intelligent, happy, good-looking, and she doesn't smoke pot. She's worn a bra for nearly four years, and every month she—"

"*George!*"

"Taboo!" said Helen, giggling.

"Anyway," George's irritation was showing now, "we weren't talking about Helen but Yulian. Helen, I submit, is normal. Her cousin—or cousin once removed, or whatever—is not."

"Give me a for-instance," Anne argued. "An example. Not normal, you say. Well then, is he *ab*normal? *Sub*normal? Where's his defect?"

"Whenever Yulian crops up," Helen joined in from the back, "you two always end up arguing. Is he really worth it?"

"Your mother's a very loyal person," George told her over one shoulder. "Georgina is her cousin and Yulian is Georgina's son. Which means they're untouchable. Your mother won't face simple facts, that's all. She's the same with all her friends: she won't hear a word against them. Very laudable. But I call a spade a spade. I find—and have always found—Yulian a bit much. As I said before, weird."

"You mean," Helen pressed, "a bit nine-bob notish?"

"*Helen!*" her mother protested yet again.

"I get *that* one from you!" Helen stopped her dead in her tracks. "You always talk about gays as nine-bobbers."

"I *never* talk about . . . about homosexuals!" Anne was furious. "And certainly not to you about them!"

"I've heard Daddy—in conversation with you, about one or two of his man-friends—say that so-and-so is gay as a defrocked vicar," said Helen matter-of-factly. "And you've replied: "What, so-and-so, nine-bobbish? Really?' "

Anne rounded on her and might well have lashed out physically if she could have reached her. Red-faced, she cried, "Then in the future we'll have to lock you in your bloody room before we dare have an adult conversation! You horrid girl!"

"Perhaps you better had." Helen was equally quick to rise. "Before I also start to swear!"

"All right, all *right!*" George quietened them. "Points taken all round. But we're on holiday, remember? I mean, it's probably my fault, but Yulian's a sore point with me, that's all. And I can't explain why. But he usually keeps out of the way most of the time we're there, and I can't help it but hope it's the same this time. For my peace of mind, anyway. He's simply not my type of lad. As for him being how's-your-father—'' (Helen somehow contrived not to snigger) ''—I can't say. But he did get kicked out of that boarding school, and—''

"He did *not!*" Anne had to have her say. "Kicked out, indeed! He got his qualifications a year early, left a year before the rest. I mean to say, do qualifications—does being intelligent above the average—certify someone as a raving . . . homosexual? Heaven forbid! Clever Miss Know-it-all here has a couple of second class 'A' Levels, which apparently make her near-omniscient; in which case Yulian has to be close to godlike! George, what qualifications do you have?"

"I fail to see what that has to do with it," he answered. "The way I hear it, more gays come out of the universities than ever came out of all the secondary moderns put together. And— ''

"George?"

"I was an apprentice," he sighed, "as you well know. Trade qualifications, I've got them all. And then I was a journeyman—an architect earning money for my boss, until I got into business for myself. And anyway—''

"What *academic* qualifications?" she was determined.

George drove the car, said nothing, wound down his window a little and breathed warm air. After a while: "The same as you, darling."

"None whatsoever!" Anne was triumphant. "Why, Yulian's cleverer than all of us put together. On paper, anyway. I say give him time and he'll show us all a thing or two. Oh, I admit he's quiet, comes and goes like a ghost, seems less active and enthusiastic about life than a boy his age should be. But give him a break, for God's sake! Look at his disadvantages. He never knew his father; was brought up by Georgina entirely on her own, and she's never been altogether with it since Ilya died, has lived in that gloomy old mansion of a place for twelve years of his young life. Little wonder he's a bit, well, reticent.''

She seemed to have won the day. They said nothing to dispute her logic, had apparently lost all interest in the argument. Anne searched her mind for a new topic, found nothing, relaxed in her seat.

Reticent. Helen turned her own thoughts over in her head. *Yulian, reticent?* Did her mother mean backward? Of course not, her argument had been all against that. Shy? Retiring? Yes, that's what she must have meant. Well, and he must seem shy—if one didn't know better. Helen knew better, from that time two years ago. And as for queer—hardly. She would greatly doubt it, anyway. She smiled secretly. Better to let them go on thinking it, though. At least while they thought he was a woofter they wouldn't worry about her being in his company. But no, Yulian wasn't entirely gay. AC, DC, maybe.

Two years ago, yes . . .

It had taken Helen ages to get him to talk to her. She remembered the circumstances clearly.

It had been a beautiful Saturday, their second day of a ten-day spell; her parents and Aunt Georgina gone off to Salcombe for a day's sea- and sun-bathing; Yulian and Helen were left in charge of the house, he with his Alsatian pup to play with and she to explore the gardens, the great barn, the crumbling old stables and the dark, dense copse. Yulian wasn't into bathing, indeed he hated the sun and sea, and Helen would have preferred anything rather than spend time with her parents.

"Walk with me?" she'd pressed Yulian, finding him alone with the gangling pup in the dim, cool library. He had shook his head.

Pale in the shade of this one room which the sun never seemed to reach, he'd lounged awkwardly on a settee, fondling the pup's floppy ears with one hand and holding a book in the other.

"Why not? You could show me the grounds."

He had glanced at the pup. "He gets tired if he walks too far. He's not quite steady on his legs. And I burn easily in the sun. I really don't much care for the sun. And anyway, I'm reading."

"You're not much fun to be with," she had told him, deliberately pouting. And she'd asked, "Is there still straw in the hayloft over the barn?"

"Hayloft?" Yulian had looked surprised. His long, not unhandsome face had formed a soft oval against the dark velvet of the back of the settee. "I haven't been up there in years."

"What are you reading, anyway?" She sat down beside him, reached for the book held loosely in his long-fingered, soft-looking hand. He drew back, kept the book from her.

"Not for little girls," he said, his expression unchanging.

Frustrated, she tossed her hair, glanced all about the large room. And it *was* large, that room; partitioned in the middle, just like a public library, with floor to ceiling shelves and book-lined alcoves all round the walls. It smelled of old books, dusty and musty. No, it *reeked* of them, so that you almost feared to breathe in case your lungs got filled with words and inks and desiccated glue and paper fibres.

There was a shallow cupboard in one corner of the room and its door stood open. Tracks in the threadbare carpet showed where Yulian had dragged a stepladder to a certain section of the shelving. The books on the top shelf were almost hidden in gloom, where old cobwebs were gathering dust. But unlike the neat rows of books in the lower shelves, they were piled haphazardly, lying in a jumble as if recently disturbed.

"Oh?" she stood up. "I'm a little girl, am I? And what does that make you? We're only a year apart, you know . . ." She went to the stepladder, started to climb.

Yulian's Adam's apple bobbed. He tossed his book aside, came easily to his feet. "You leave that top shelf alone," he said unemotionally, coming to the foot of the ladder.

She ignored him, looked at the titles, read out loud: "Coates, *Human Magnetism*, or *How to Hypnotize*. Huh! Mumbo-jumbo! *Lycan* . . . er, *Lycanthropy*. Eh? And . . . *The Erotic Beardsley!*" She clapped her hands delightedly. "What, dirty pictures, Yulian?" She took the book from the shelf, opened it. "Oh!" she said, rather more quietly. The black and white drawing on the page where the book had opened was rather more bestial than erotic.

"Put it down!" Yulian hissed from below.

Helen put down the Beardsley, read off more titles. "*Vampirism*—ugh! *Sexual Powers of Satyrs and Nymphomaniacs. Sadism and Sexual Aberration.* And . . . *Parasitic Creatures?* How diverse! And not dusty at all, these old books. Do you read them a lot, Yulian?"

He gave the ladder a shake and insisted, "Come down from there!" His voice was very low, almost menacing. It was guttural, deeper than she'd heard it before. Almost a man's voice and not a youth's at all. Then she looked down at him.

Yulian stood below her, his face turned up at a sharp angle just below the level of her knees. His eyes were like holes punched in a paper face, with pupils shiny as black marbles. She stared hard at him but their eyes didn't meet, because he wasn't looking at her face.

"Why, I do believe," she told him then, teasingly, "that you're quite naughty, really, Yulian! What with these books and everything . . ." She had worn her short dress because of the heat, and now she was glad.

He looked away, touched his brow, turned aside. "You . . . you wanted to see the barn?" His voice was soft again.

"Can we?" She was down the ladder in a flash. "I *love* old barns! But your mother said it wasn't safe."

"I think it's safe enough," he answered. "Georgina

worries about everything.'' He had called his mother Georgina since he was a little boy. She didn't seem to mind.

They went through the rambling house to the front, Yulian excusing himself for a moment to go to his room. He came back wearing dark spectacles and a floppy, wide-brimmed hat. "Now you look like some pallid Mexican brigand,'' Helen told him, leading the way. And with the black Alsatian pup tumbling at their heels, they made their way to the barn.

In fact it was a very simple outbuilding of stone, with a platform of planks across the high beams to form a hayloft. Next door were the stables, completely rundown, just a derelict old huddle of buildings. Until five or six years ago the Bodescus had let a local farmer winter his ponies on the grounds, and he'd stored hay for them in the barn.

"Why on earth do you need such a big place to live?'' Helen asked as they entered the barn through a squealing door into shade and dusty sunbeams and the scurry of mice.

"I'm sorry?'' he said after a moment, his thoughts elsewhere.

"This place. The whole place. And that high stone wall all the way round it. How much land does it enclose, that wall? Three acres?''

"Just over three and a half,'' he answered.

"A great rambling house, old stables, barns, an overgrown paddock—even a shady copse to walk through in the autumn, when the colours are growing old! I mean, why do two ordinary people need so much space just to live in?''

"Ordinary?'' he looked at her curiously, his eyes moistly gleaming behind dark lenses. "And do you consider yourself ordinary?''

"Of course.''

"Well I don't. I think you're quite extraordinary. So am I, and so is Georgina—all of us for different reasons.'' He sounded very sincere, almost aggressive, as if defying her to contradict him. But then he shrugged. "Anyway, it's not a question of why we need it. It's ours, that's all."

"But how did you get it? I mean, you couldn't have bought it! There must be so many other, well, *easier* places to live."

Yulian crossed the paved floor between piles of old slates and rusty, broken-down implements to the foot of the open wooden stairs. "Hayloft," he said, turning his dark eyes on her. She couldn't see those eyes, but she could feel them.

Sometimes his movements were so fluid it almost seemed as if he were sleep-walking. They were like that now as he climbed the stairs, slowly, step by deliberate step. "There *is* still straw," he said, voice languid as a deep pool.

She watched him until he passed out of sight. There was a leanness about him, a hunger. Her father thought he was soft, girlish, but Helen guessed otherwise. She saw him as an intelligent animal, as a wolf. Sort of furtive, but unobtrusive, and always there on the edge of things, just waiting for his chance . . .

She suddenly felt stifled and took three deep, deliberate gulps of air before following him. Going carefully up the wooden steps, she said, "Now I remember it! It was your great-grandfather's, wasn't it? The house, I mean."

She emerged into the hayloft. Three great bales of hay, blanched with age, stood dusty and withered in a pyramid. One end of the loft stood open, where projecting gables spared it from the elements. Thin, hot beams of sunlight came slanting in from chinks in the tiles, trapping dustmotes like flies in amber, forming yellow spotlights on the floorboards.

Yulian took out a pocket knife, sliced deftly at the binding of the uppermost bale. It fell to pieces like an ancient book, and he dragged great deep armfuls down onto the boards.

A bed for a gypsy, thought Helen. *Or a wanton.*

She threw herself down, was conscious that her dress

rode up above her knickers where she lay down. She did nothing to adjust it. Instead she spread her legs a little, wriggled her backside and contrived to make the movement seem perfectly unconscious—which it was not.

Yulian stood still for long moments and she could feel his eyes on her, but she simply cupped her chin in her hands and stared out of the open end of the loft. From here you could see the perimeter wall, the curving drive, the copse. Yulian's shadow eclipsed several discs of sunlight and she held her breath. The straw stirred and she knew he was right behind her, like a wolf in the forest.

His floppy hat fell in the straw on her left, his sunglasses plopped down into the hat; he got down beside her on her right, his arm falling casually across her waist. Casually, yes, and light as a feather, but she could feel it like a bar of iron. He lay not quite so far forward, propping his jaw in his right hand, looking at her. His arm, lying across her like that, must feel very awkward. He was taking most of its weight and she could feel it beginning to tremble, but he didn't seem to mind. But of course he wouldn't, would he?

"Great-grandfather's, yes," he finally answered her question. "He lived and died here. The place came down to Georgina's mother. Her husband, my grandfather, didn't like it and so they rented it out and lived in London. When they died it fell to Georgina, but by then it was on a life-lease to the old colonel who lived here. Eventually it was his turn to go, and then Georgina came down to sell it. She brought me with her. I wasn't quite five, I think, but I liked the place and said so. I said we should live here, and Georgina thought it a good idea."

"You really are remarkable!" she said. "I can't remember anything about when I was five." His arm had slid diagonally across her now, so that his fingers barely touched her thigh just below the curve of her bottom. Helen could feel an almost electric tingle in those fingers. They held no such charge, she knew, but that's how it felt.

"I remember everything almost from the moment I was born," he told her, his voice so even it was very nearly hypnotic. Maybe it *was* hypnotic. "Sometimes I even think I remember things from before my birth."

"Well, that might explain why you're so 'extraordinary' " she told him, "but what is it makes me different?"

"Your innocence," he at once replied, his voice a purr. "And your desire not to be." His hand caressed her rump now, the merest touch of electric fingers tracing the curve of her buttocks, to and fro, to and fro.

Helen sighed, put a piece of straw between her teeth, slowly turned over on to her back. Her dress rode up even more. She didn't look at Yulian but gazed wide-eyed at the sloping rows of tiles overhead. As she turned so he lifted his hand a fraction, but didn't take it away.

"My desire not to be? Not to be innocent? What makes you think that?" And she thought: *because it's so obvious?*

When he answered, Yulian's voice was a man's again. She hadn't noticed the slow transition, but now she did. Thick and dark, that voice, as he said, "I've read it. All girls of your age desire not to be innocent."

His hand fell on her belly, lingered over her navel, slipped down and crept under the band of her knickers. She stopped him there, trapping his hand with her own. "No, Yulian. You can't."

"Can't?" the word came in a gulp, choking. "Why?"

"Because you're right. I am innocent. But also because it's the wrong time."

"Time?" he was trembling again.

She pushed him away, sighed abruptly and said, "Oh, Yulian—I'm bleeding!"

"Bleed—?" He rolled away from her, snatched himself to his feet. Startled, she stared at him standing there. He shivered as if in a fever.

"Bleeding, yes," she said. "It's perfectly natural, you know."

There was no pallor in his face now: it was red with

blood, burning like a drunkard's face, with his eyes narrow slits dark as knife slashes. *"Bleeding!"* this time he managed to choke the word out whole. He reached out his arms towards her, hands hooked like claws, and for a moment she thought he would attack her. She could see his nostrils flaring, a nervous tic tugging the corner of his mouth.

For the first time she felt afraid, felt something of his strangeness: "Yes," she whispered. "It happens every month . . ."

His eyes opened up a little. Their pupils seemed flecked with scarlet. A trick of the light. "Ah! Ah—*bleeding!*" he said, as though only just understanding her meaning. "Oh, yes . . ." Then he reeled, turned away, went a little unsteadily down the steps and was gone.

Then Helen had heard the puppy's wild yelp of joy (it had been stopped by the steps, which it couldn't climb) and its whining and barking fading as it followed Yulian back to the house. And finally she started to breathe again.

"Yulian!" she'd called after him then. "Your sunglasses, your hat!" But if he heard, he didn't bother to answer.

She wasn't able to find him for the rest of the day, but then she hadn't really looked for him. And because she had her pride—and also because he had failed to seek her out—she hadn't much bothered with him for the rest of their holiday. Perhaps it had been for the best; for she *had* been innocent, after all. She wouldn't have known what to do, not two years ago.

But when she thought of him, she still remembered his hand burning on her flesh. And now, going back to Devon with the countryside speeding by outside the car, she found herself wondering if there was still straw in the hayloft . . .

George, too, had his secret thoughts about Yulian. Anne could say what she liked but she couldn't change that. He *was* weird, that lad, and weird in several directions. It wasn't only the creeping-Jesus aspect that irritated George, though certainly the youth's furtive ways were annoying enough. But he was sick, too. Not mental, maybe not even sick in his body, just generally *sick*. To look at him sometimes, to catch him unawares with a side-glance, was to look at a cockroach surprised by a switched-on light, or a jellyfish steaming away, stranded on the beach when the tide goes out. You could almost sense something seething in him. But if it wasn't mental or physical, and yet encompassed both, then what the hell was it?

Hard to explain. Maybe it was both mind *and* body—and soul too? Except George wasn't must of a one for believing in souls. He didn't disbelieve, but he would like evidence. He'd probably be praying when he died, just in case, but until then . . .

As for what Anne had said about Yulian at school: well, it was true, as far as it went. He had taken all of his exams early, and passed every one of them, but that wasn't why he'd left early. George had a draughtsman, Ian Jones, working for him in his London office, and Jones had a young son in the same school. Anne would hear none of it, of course not, but the stories had been wild. Yulian had "seduced" a male teacher, a half-way-gone gay he'd somehow switched on. Once over the top, the fellow had apparently turned into a raver, trying to roger every male thing that moved. He'd blamed Yulian. That was one thing. And then:

In his art classes, Yulian had painted pictures which caused a very gentle lady teacher to attack him physically; she'd also stormed his bed-space and burned his art folios. Out nature rambling (George hadn't known they still did that) Yulian had been found wandering on his own, his face and hands smeared with filth and entrails. Dangling from one hand he'd carried the remains of a stray kitten. Its carcass was still warm. He'd said a man had done it, but this was out on the moors, miles from anywhere.

That wasn't all. It seemed he walked in his sleep and had apparently scared the living shit out of the younger boys, until the school had had to put a night-guard on their dorms. But by then the head had spoken at length with Georgina and she'd agreed he could leave. It was that or expulsion—for the sake of the good name of the school.

And there'd been other things, lesser things, but that had been the gist of it.

These were some of the reasons why George didn't like Yulian. But of course there was one other thing. It was something very nearly as old as Yulian himself, but it had fixed itself in George's mind indelibly.

The sight of an old man clutching his sheets to his chest as he died, and his last whispered words: "Christen it? No, no—you mustn't! *First have it exorcized!*"

Anne could be strident if she had to be, but she was good through and through. She would never say a thing to hurt anyone, even though she might think certain things. To herself—if only to herself—she had to admit that she'd thought things about Yulian.

Now, lying back a little in her seat and stretching, feeling the cooling draught from the half-open window, she thought them again. Funny things: something about a big green frog, and something about the pain she'd get now and then in her left nipple.

The frog thing was hard to focus on; rather, she didn't *like* to focus on it. Personally she couldn't hurt a fly. Of course a child, a mere five-year old, wouldn't realize what he was doing. Would he? The trouble was that as long as she'd known Yulian he'd always seemed to know exactly what he was doing. Even as a baby.

She had called him a "funny little thing," but in fact George was right. Yulian had been more than just funny. For one thing, he never cried. No, not quite true, he had cried when hungry, at least when he was very small. And he had cried in direct sunlight. Photophobia, apparently, right from infancy. Oh, yes, and he'd cried at least one other time, at his christening. Though that had seemed more rage—or outrage—than crying proper. As far as Anne knew, he never had been properly christened.

She let her thoughts take hold, carrying her back. Yulian had just started to walk—to toddle, anyway—when Helen came along. That was a month or so before poor Georgina had been well enough to go home and take him back. Anne remembered that time well. She'd been heavy with milk, fat as butter and happier than at any other time in her life. And rosy? What a picture of health she'd been!

One day when Helen was just six weeks old, while she was feeding her, Yulian had come toddling like a little robot, looking for that extra ounce of affection of which Helen had robbed him. Jealousy even then, yes, for he was no longer all important. On impulse—feeling a pang of pity for the poor mite—she'd picked him up, bared her other breast to him, her left breast, and fed him.

Even remembering it, the twinge of pain in her nipple came back like a wasp sting to bother her. "Oh!" she said, stirring where she had fallen half-asleep.

"You all right?" George was quick to inquire. "Wind your window down a little more. Get some fresh air."

The steady purr of the car's engine brought her back to the present. "Cramp," she lied. "Pins and needles. Can we stop somewhere—the next café?"

"Of course," he answered. "There should be one any time now."

Anne slumped, returned half-reluctantly to her memories. Feeding Yulian, yes . . . She'd sat down with both babies, nodded off while they fed, Helen on the right, Yulian on the left. It had been strange; a sort of languor had come over her, a lethargy she hadn't the will to resist. But then, when the pain came, she'd come quickly awake. Helen had been crying, and Yulian had been—bloody!

She'd stared at the toddler in something close to shock. Those peculiar black eyes of his fixed unwaveringly on her face. And his red mouth, fixed like a lamprey on her breast! Her milk and blood had run down the curve of her breast, and his face had been smeared and glistened red with it; so that he'd looked like a dark-eyed gorging leech.

When she'd cleaned herself up, and cleaned up Yulian too, she'd seen how he'd bitten through the skin around her nipple; his teeth had left tiny punctures. The bites had taken a long time to heal, but their sting had never quite gone away . . .

Then there had been the frog episode. Anne didn't really want to dwell on that, but it formed a persistent picture in her mind, one she couldn't wipe clear. It had happened after Georgina had sold up in London, on the last day before she and Yulian had left the city and gone down to Devon to live in the old manor house.

George had built a pond in the garden of their Greenford home when Helen was one; since when, with a minimum of help, the pond had stocked itself. Now there were lilies, a clump of rushes, an ornamental shrub bending over the water like a Japanese picture, and a large species of green frog. There were water snails, too, and at the edges a little green scum. Anne called it scum, anyway. Mid-summer and there would normally be dragonflies, but that year they'd only seen one or two, and they'd been small ones of their sort.

She had been in the garden with the children, watching Yulian where he played with a soft rubber ball. Or perhaps "played" is the wrong word, for Yulian had difficulty playing like other children. He seemed to have a philosophy: a ball is a ball, a rubber sphere. Drop it and it bounces, toss it against a wall and it returns. Other than that it has no practical use, it cannot be considered a source of lasting interest. Others might argue the point, but that summed up Yulian's feelings on the subject. Anne really didn't know why she'd bought the ball for him; he never really played with anything. He *had* bounced it, however, twice. And he'd tossed it against the garden wall, once. But on the rebound it had rolled to the edge of the pond.

Yulian had followed it with eyes half scornful, until suddenly his interest had quickened. At the edge of the pond something leaped: a large frog, shiny green, poising itself where it landed, with two legs in the water and two on dry land. And the five-year old child froze, becoming still as a cat in the first seconds that it senses prey. It was Helen who ran to retrieve the ball, then skipped away with it up the garden, but Yulian had eyes only for the frog.

At that point George had called out from inside the house: something about the kebabs burning. They were to be the main course in a farewell meal for Georgina. George was supposed to be doing chef.

Anne had rushed to save the day, along the crazy-paving, under the arch of roses on their trellis to the paved patio area at the rear of the house. It had taken a minute, two at the outside, to lift the steaming meat from the grill onto a plate on the outside table. Then Georgina had come drifting downstairs in that slow get-there-eventually fashion of hers, and George had appeared from the kitchen with his herbs.

"Sorry, darling," he'd apologized. "Timing is everything, and I'm out of practice. But I've got it all together now and all's well . . ."

Except that all had not been well.

Hearing Helen's cry of alarm from the lower garden, Anne had breathlessly retraced her steps.

At first, as she reached the pond, Anne hadn't quite known what she was seeing. She thought Yulian must have fallen face down in the green scum. Then her eyes focussed and the picture firmed. And however much she'd tried to forget it, it had remained firm to this day:

The tiny white mosaic tiles at the edge of the pond, slimed with blood and guts; and Yulian slimed, too, his face and hands sticky with goo. Cross-legged by the pond like a buddha, Yulian, the frog like a torn green plastic bag in his inexpert hands, slopping its contents. And that child of—of innocence?—studying its innards, smelling it, *listening* to it, apparently astonished by its complexity.

Then his mother had come wafting up from behind, saying; "Oh dear, oh dear! Was it a live thing? Oh, I see it was. He does that sometimes. Opens things up. Curiosity. To see how they work."

And Anne, aghast, snatching up the whining Helen and turning her face away, gasping, "But Georgina, that's not some old alarm-clock—it's a frog!"

"Is it? Is it? Oh dear! Poor thing!" She fluttered her hands. "But it's a phase he's going through, that's all. He'll grow out of it . . ."

And Anne remembered thinking, *God, I certainly hope so!*

"Devon!" said George triumphantly, jogging her elbow, startling her. "Did you see the sign, the county boundary? And look, there's your café! Cream teas, fudge, clotted cream! We'll top the car up, have a bite to eat, and then we're on the last leg. Peace and quite for a whole week. Lord, how I can use it . . ."

Arriving at the house and turning off the Paignton road into its grounds, the party in the car found Georgina and Yulian waiting for them on the gravel drive. At first they very nearly failed to notice Georgina, for she was overshadowed by her son. As George stopped the car, Helen's jaw fell open a little. Anne simple stared. George himself thought, *Yulian? Yes, of course it is. But what's he been doing right?*

Getting out of the car, finally Anne spoke, echoing George's thought. "Yulian! My, but what a couple of years have done for you!" He held her briefly, taller by inches, then turned to Helen where she got out of the back seat and stretched.

"I'm not the only one who has grown," he said. His voice was that dark one Helen had heard on a previous occasion, apparently his natural voice now. He held her at arm's length, stared at her with those unfathomable eyes.

He's handsome as the devil, she thought. Or perhaps handsome was the wrong word for it. Attractive, yes— almost unnaturally so. His long, straight chin, not quite lantern-jaw, high brow, straight, flattish nose—and especially his eyes—all combined to form a face which might seem quite odd on anyone else's shoulders. But coupled with that voice, and with Yulian's mind behind it, the effect was quite devastating. He looked somehow foreign, almost alien. His dark hair, flowing naturally back and forming something of a mane at the back of his neck, made him seem even more wolfish than she'd remembered. That was it—wolfish! And he was getting tall as a tree.

"You're still slim, anyway," she finally found something to say, however uninspired. "But what's Aunt Georgina been feeding you?"

He smiled and turned to George, nodded and held out his hand. "George. Did you have a good journey? We've worried a little—the roads get so crowded down here in the summer."

George! George groaned inwardly. *First names, just like with Mummy, hey?* Still, it was better than being shied away from.

"The drive was fine," George forced a smile, checking Yulian out but unobtrusively. The youth topped him by a good three inches. Add his hair to that and he looked taller still. Seventeen and already he was a big man. Big-boned, anyway. But give him another stone in weight and he'd be like a barn door! Also, his handshake was iron. Hardly limp-wristed, no matter the length of his fingers.

George was suddenly very much aware of his own thinning hair, his small paunch and slightly stodgy appearance. *But at least I can go out in the sun!* he thought. Yulian's pallor was one thing that never changed; even here he stood in the shade of the old house, like part of its shadow.

But if the last two years had improved Yulian, they'd not been so kind to his mother.

"Georgina!" Anne had meanwhile turned to her cousin, hugging her. Beneath the hug she had felt how frail she was, how trembly. The loss of her husband almost eighteen years before was still taking its toll. "And . . . and looking so well!"

Liar! George couldn't help thinking. *Well? She looks like something clockwork that's about wound itself down!*

It was true—Georgina seemed like an automaton. She spoke and moved as if programmed. "Anne, George, Helen—so *good* to see you again. So glad you accepted Yulian's invitation. But come in, come in. You can guess what we've got for you, of course. A cream tea, naturally!"

She led the way, floating light as air, and went inside. Yulian paused at the door, turned and said, "Yes, do come in. Feel free. Enter freely and make yourselves at home." They way he said it, somehow ritualistically, made his welcome sound quite odd. As George, at the rear, made to pass him, Yulian added, "Can I bring in your luggage for you?"

"Why, thanks," said George. "Here, I'll give you a hand."

"Not necessary," Yulian smiled. "Just give me the keys." He opened the boot and took out their cases as if they were empty and weighed nothing. It wasn't just show, George could see that. Yulian was very strong . . .

Following him inside the house, and feeling just a shade useless, George paused on hearing a low growl of warning which came from an open cloakroom in an alcove to one side of the entrance hall. In there, in the deepest shadows behind a dark oak coatstand, something black as sin moved and yellow eyes glared. George looked harder, said, "What in—?" and the growling came louder.

Yulian, half-way down the corridor towards the stairs,

turned and looked back. "Oh, don't let him intimidate you, George. His bark is worse than his bite, I assure you." And in a harsher tone of command: "Come, boy, out into the light where we can see you."

A black Alsatian, almost full grown, (was this monster really Yulian's pup?) came slinking into view, baring its teeth at George as it slid by him. The dog went straight to Yulian, stood waiting. George noticed that it didn't wag its tail.

"It's all right, old friend," the youth murmured. "You make yourself scarce." At which the vicious-looking creature moved on into the house.

"Good Lord!" said George. "Thank goodness he's well trained! What's his name?"

"Vlad," Yulian answered at once, turning away, cases and all. "It's Romanian, I believe. Means "Prince" or something. Or it did in the old times . . ."

Yulian wasn't much visible for the next two or three days. The fact did not especially bother George; if anything he was relieved. Anne merely thought it odd that he wasn't around; Helen felt he was avoiding her and was annoyed about it, but she didn't let it show. "What does he do with himself all day?" Anne asked Georgina, for the sake of something to say, when they were alone together one morning.

Georgina's eyes seemed constantly dull, but only mention Yulian and they'd take on a startled, almost shocked brightness. Anne mentioned him now—and sure enough, there was that look.

"Oh, he has his interests . . ." She at once tried to change the subject, words tumbling out of her: "We're thinking about having the old stables down. There are extensive vaults under the grounds—old cellars, wine cellars my grandfather used—and Yulian thinks the stables will crash right through to them one day. If we have them down we'll sell the stone. It's good stone and should fetch a decent price."

"Vaults? I didn't know that. You say Yulian goes down there?"

"To check their condition," (more words babbling out of her). "He worries about maintenance . . . could collapse, make the house unsafe . . . just old corridors, almost like tunnels, and vaults opening off them. Full of nitre, spiders, rotten old wine racks . . . nothing of interest."

Seeing the sudden build-up of her—frenzy?—Anne got up, crossed to Georgina, laid a hand on her frail shoulder. The older woman reacted as if she'd been slapped, jerked away from Anne. Her eyes suddenly focussed. "Anne," she said, her voice a shivering whisper, "don't ask about that place below. And *never* go down there! It's not . . . not safe down there . . ."

The Lakes had come down from London on the third Thursday in August. The weather was very hot and showed no sign of letting up. On the Monday Anne and Helen drove off to buy straw sunhats for themselves in Paignton a few miles away. Georgina was having her noontime snooze and Yulian was nowhere to be found.

George remembered Anne mentioning the vaults under the house: wine cellars, according to Georgina. With nothing better to do he went out, walked around the house to the back, came face to face with a sort of shed built of old stone. He'd noticed it before, had long since concluded that it must be an old, disused outdoor loo and until now had had nothing more to do with it. It had a tiled, sloping roof and a door facing away from the house. Shrubbery grew rank, untended all about. The door was sagging on rotten hinges but George managed to drag it ajar. And squeezing inside, he knew at once that this must be an entrance to the alleged cellars. Narrow stone steps went down steeply on both sides of a ramp perfectly suited for the rolling of barrels. You could find covered delivery points like this in the yard of any old pub. He went carefully down the steps to a door at the bottom, began to push it squealingly open.

Vlad was in there!

His muzzle came through the first three inches of gap even as George pushed on the door. The snarl of rage preceded it by the merest fraction of a second, and snarl and snout both were the only warning George got. Shocked, he snatched back his hands, and only just in time. The Alsatian's teeth snapped on the door jamb where his fingers had been, tearing off long splinters of wood. Heart hammering, George leaned on the door, closed it. He'd seen the dog's eyes and they had looked quite hateful.

But why would Vlad be down there in the first place? George could only suppose that Yulian had put him there to keep him out of the way while guests were around. A wise move, for obviously Vlad's bark was *not* as bad as his bite! Maybe Yulian was down there with him. Well, they were a duo George could well do without . . .

Feeling shaken, he left the grounds and walked half a mile down the road to a pub at the crossroads. On the way, surrounded by fields and lanes, birdsong and the normal, entirely pleasant hum of insects in the hedgerows, his nerves slowly recovered. The sun was hot and by the time he reached his destination he was ready for a drink.

The pub was ancient, thatched, all oak beams and horse-brasses, with a gently ticking grandfather clock and a massive white cat overhanging its own chair. After Vlad, George could stand cats well enough. He ordered a lager, perched himself on a barstool.

There were others in the bar: a fashionable young couple seated well away from George at a corner table close to small-paned windows, who doubtless owned the little sports job he'd seen parked in the yard; local youths in another corner, playing dominoes; and two old-timers deep in conversation over their pints at a table close by. It was the muttered, lowered tones of this latter pair which attracted him. Sipping his ice-cold lager and after the bartender had moved on to other tasks, George thought he heard the word "Harkley" and his ears pricked up. Harkley House was Georgina's place.

"Oh, ar? That 'un up there, hey? A funny 'un, I'm told."

"Course there ain't a jot o' proof, but she'd bin seen wi' 'em, right enough. An' clean off Sharkham Point she went, down Brixham way. Terrible!"

A local tragedy, obviously, thought George. The Point was a headland of cliffs projecting into the sea. He glanced at the two old-timers, nodded and had his nod returned, turned back to his drink. But their conversation stayed with him. One of them was thin, ferret-faced, the other red and portly, the latter doing the story-telling.

Now he continued, "Carryin', o' course."

"Pregnant, were she?" the thin one gasped. "It were 'is, you reckon?"

"I reckons nuthin'," the first denied. "No proof, like I said. An' anyway, she were a rum 'un. But so young. 'Tis a pity."

"A pity's right," the thin one agreed. "But ter jump like that . . . what made 'er do it, d'you think? I mean, unwed an' carryin' these days ain't nuthin'!"

Out of the corner of his eye, George saw them lean closer. Their voices fell lower still and he strained to hear what was said:

"I reckon," said the portly one, "that Nature told 'er it weren't right. You know 'ow a ewe'll cast a puggled lamb? Suthin' like that, poor lass."

"It weren't right, you say? They opened 'er up, then?"

"Oh, ar, they did that! Tide were out an' she knew it. She weren't goin' in the water that one. She were goin' down on the rocks! Makin' sure, she were. Now 'ere, strictly 'tween you an' me, my girl Mary's at the hospital, as you know. She says that when they brung 'er in she were dead as mutton. But they sounded 'er belly, and it were still kickin' . . .!''

After a moment's pause: "The child?"

"Well what else, you old fool! So they opened 'er up. 'Orrible it were—but there's none but a handful knows of it, so this stops right 'ere. Well, doctor took one look at it an' put a needle in it. He just finished it there and then. An' into a plastic bag it went an' down to the hospital furnace. An' that was that."

"Deformed," the thin one nodded. "I've heard o' such."

"Well, this one weren't so much deformed as . . . as not much formed at all!" the florid one informed. "It were—'ow'd my Mary put it?—like some kind of massive tumour in 'er. A terrible sort of fleshy lump, and fibrous. But it were s'posed to 'ave been a child, for there was afterbirth and all. But for sure it were better off dead! My Mary said as 'ow there were eyes where there shouldn't be, an' things like teeth, an' 'ow it mewled suthin' terrible when the light fell on it!"

George had finished his lager, the last of it with a gulp. The door of the pub was flung open and a party of young people came in. Another moment and one of them had found a juke-box in some hidden alcove; rock music washed over everything. The barman came back, pulled pints for all he was worth.

George left, headed back down the road. Half-way back, his car pulled up and Anne shouted, "Get in the back."

She wore a straw hat with a wide black band, contrasting perfectly with her summer dress. Helen, sitting beside her, wore one with a red band. "How's that?" Anne laughed as George plumped down in the back seat and slammed the door. Mother and daughter tilted their heads coquettishly, showing off their hats. "Just like a couple of village girls out for a drive, eh?"

"Around here," George answered darkly, "village girls need to watch what they're doing." But he didn't explain his meaning, and in any case he wouldn't have mentioned

Harkley in the same breath as the story he'd overheard in the pub. He took it that he'd simply misinterpreted the first few words. However that may be, the unpleasantness of the thing stayed with him for the rest of the day.

The next morning, Tuesday, George was up late. Anne had offered him breakfast in bed but he'd declined, gone back to sleep. He got up at ten to a quiet house, made himself a small breakfast that turned out quite tasteless. Then, in the living-room, he found Anne's note:

Darling—
Yulian and Helen are out walking Vlad. I think I'll drive Georgina into town and buy her something. We'll be back for lunch—

Anne

George sighed his frustration, chewed his bottom lip angrily. This morning he'd meant to have a quick look at the cellars, just out of curiosity. Yulian could have perhaps shown him around down there. As for the rest of the day: he'd planned on driving the girls to the beach at Salcombe; a day by the sea might fetch Georgina out of herself. The salty air would be good for Helen, too, who'd been looking a bit peaky. Just like Anne to be cab-happy with the car the minute they were out of London!

Ah, well—maybe there'd still be time for the beach this afternoon. But what to do with himself this morning? A walk into Old Paignton, to the harbour, perhaps? It would be a fair bit of a walk, but he could always drop in somewhere for a pint along the way. And later, if he was tired or pushed for time, he'd simply come back by taxi.

George did exactly that. He took his binoculars with him and spent a little time gazing at near-distant Brixham across the bay, returned to Harkley by taxi at about 12:30 and paid the driver off at the gate. He'd enjoyed both the long walk and his glass of cold beer enormously, and it seemed he'd timed the entire expedition just perfectly for lunch.

Then, wandering up the drive where the curving gravel path came closest to the copse—a densely grown stand of beech, birch and alder, with one mighty cedar towering slightly apart—there he came across his car, its front doors standing open and the keys still in the ignition. George stared at the car in mild surprise, turned in a slow circle and glanced all about.

The copse had an overgrown crazy-paving path winding through its heart, and a once-elegant white three-bar fence running round it—like a wood in a book of fairy tales. The fence was leaning now and very much off-white, with rank growth sprung up on both sides. George looked in that direction but could see no one. Tall grasses and brambles, the tops of fenceposts, trees. And . . . maybe something big and black moving furtively in the undergrowth? Vlad?

It could well be that Anne, Helen, Georgina and Yulian were all walking together in the copse; certainly it would be leafy and cool under the canopy of the trees. But if it was only Yulian and the dog in there, or the bloody dog on his own . . .

Suddenly it came to George that he feared one as much as the other. Yes, feared them. Yulian wasn't like any other person he knew, and Vlad wasn't like any other dog. There was something wrong with both of them. And in the middle of a quiet, hot summer day George shivered.

Then he got a grip of himself. Frightened? Of a queer, freakish youth and a three-quarters grown dog? Ridiculous!

He gave a loud 'Hallooo!''—and got no answer.

Irritated now, his previously pleasant mood rapidly waning, he hurried to the house. Inside . . . no one! He went through the old place slamming doors, finally climbed the stairs to his and Anne's bedroom. Where the hell *was* everyone? And why had Anne left his car there like that? Was he to spend the entire day on his bloody own?

From his bedroom window he could see most of the grounds at the front of the house right to the gate. The barn and huddled stables interfered with the view of the copse, but—

George's attention was suddenly riveted by a splash of color showing in the tall grass this side of the fence where it circled the copse. It caught his attention and held it. He moved a fraction, tried to see beyond the projecting gables of the old barn. It wouldn't come into focus. Then he remembered his binoculars, still hanging round his neck. He quickly put them to his eyes, adjusted them.

Still the gables intervened, and he'd got the range wrong. The splash of color was still there—a dress?—but a flesh-pink tone was moving against it. Moving insistently. With viciously impatient hands, George finally got the range right, brought the picture close. The splash of summer colors was a dress, yes. And the flesh-colored tone was—flesh! Naked flesh.

George scanned the scene disbelievingly. They were in the grass. He couldn't see Helen—not her face, anyway—for she was face down, backside in the air. And Yulian mounting her, frantic in his rage, his passion, his hands gripping her waist. George began to tremble and he couldn't stop it. Helen was a willing party to this, had to be. Well, and he'd said she was an adult—but *God!*—there must be limits.

And there she was, face down in the grass, naked as a baby—George's baby girl—with her straw hat and her dress tossed aside and her pink flesh open to this . . . *this slime!* George no longer feared Yulian, if he ever had, but hated him. The weird-looking bastard would look a sight weirder when he was finished with him.

He snatched his binoculars from his neck, tossed them down on the bed, turned towards the door—and his muscles locked rigid. George's jaw fell open. Something he had seen, some monstrous thing burned on his mind's eye. With his hands numb to the bone he took up the binoculars, fixed them again on the couple in the long grass. Yulian had finished, lay sprawled alongside his partner. But George let the glasses slide right over them to the hat and disarrayed dress.

The straw hat had a wide black band. It was Anne's hat. And now that fact had dawned he saw that it was also Anne's dress.

The binoculars slipped from George's fingers. He staggered, almost fell, flopped down heavily on his bed. On their bed, his and Anne's. *Willing party . . . had to be.* The words kept repeating in his whirling head. He couldn't believe what he'd seen, but he had to believe. And she was a willing party. Had to be.

How long he sat there in a daze he couldn't tell: five minutes, ten? But finally he came out of it. He came out of it, shook himself, knew what he must do. All those stories from Yulian's school: they must be true. The bastard was a pervert! But Anne, what of Anne?

Could she be drunk? Or drugged? That was it! Yulian must have given her something.

George stood up. He was cold now, cold as ice. His blood boiled but his mind was a white snowfield, with the track he must take clearly delineated. He looked at his hands and felt the strength of both God and the devil flowing in them. He would tear out the black, soulless eyes of that swine; he would eat his rotten heart!

He staggered downstairs, through the empty house, reeled drunkenly, murderously towards the copse. And he found Anne's hat and dress exactly where he'd seen them. But no Anne, no Yulian. Blood pounded in George's temples; hate like acid corroded his mind, peeling away every layer of rationality. Still reeling, he scrambled his way through low brambles to the gravel drive, glared his loathing at the house. Then something told him to look behind. Back there, at the gates, Vlad stood watching, then started forward uncertainly.

Something of sanity returned. George hated Yulian now,

intended to kill him if he could, but he still feared the dog. There'd always been something about dogs, and especially this one. He ran back towards the house, and coming round a screen of bushes saw Yulian striding through the shrubbery towards the rear of the building. Towards the entrance to the cellars.

"Yulian!" George tried to yell, but the word came out as a gasping croak. He didn't try again. *Why warn the perverted little sod?* Behind him, Vlad put on a little speed, began to lope.

At the corner of the house George paused for a moment, gulped air desperately. He was out of condition. Then he saw a rusty old mattock leaning against the wall and snatched it up. A glance over his shoulder told him that Vlad was coming, his strides stretching now, ears flat to his head. George wasted no more time but plunged through the low shrubbery to the entrance to the vaults. And there stood Yulian at the open door. He heard George coming, turned his head and cast a startled glance his way.

"Ah, George!" He smiled a sickly smile. "I was just wondering if perhaps you'd like to see the cellars?" Then he saw George's expression, the mattock in his white-knuckled hands.

"The cellars?" George choked, almost entirely deranged with hatred. "Yes I fucking would!" He swung his pick-like weapon. Yulian put up an arm to shield his face, turned away. The sharper, rustier blade of the heavy tool took him in the back of his right shoulder, crunched through the lower part of the scapula and buried itself to the haft in his body.

Thrown forward, Yulian went toppling down the central ramp, the mattock still sticking in him. As he fell he said, "Ah! Ah!"— in no way a scream, more an expression of surprise, shock. George followed, arms reaching, lips drawn back from his teeth. He pursued Yulian, and Vlad pursued him.

Yulian lay face down at the bottom of the steps beside

the open door to the vaults. He moaned, moved awkwardly. George slammed a foot down in the middle of his back, levered the mattock out of him. "Ah! Ah!" again Yulian gave his peculiar, sighing cry. George lifted the mattock—and heard Vlad's rumbling growl close behind.

He turned, swung the mattock in a deadly arc. The dog was stopped in mid-flight as the mattock smacked flatly against the side of its head. It crumpled to the concrete floor, groaned like a man. George panted hoarsely, lifted his weapon again—but there was no sign of consciousness in the animal. Its sides heaved but it lay still, tongue protruding. Out like a light.

And now there was only Yulian.

George turned, saw Yulian staggering into the vault's unknown darkness. Unbelievable! With his injury, still the bastard kept going. George followed, kept Yulian's stumbling figure visible in the gloom. The cellars were extensive, rooms and alcoves and midnight corridors, but George didn't let his quarry out of sight for a single moment. Then—a light!

George peered through an arched entrance into a dimly illumined room. A single dusty bulb, shaded, hung from a vaulted ceiling of stone blocks. George had momentarily lost sight of Yulian in the darkness surrounding the cone of light; but then the youth staggered between him and the light source, and George picked him up again and advanced. Yulian saw him, swung an arm wildly at the light in an attempt to put it out of commission. Injured, he missed his aim, setting the lamp and shade dancing and swinging on their flex.

Then, by that wildly gyrating light, George saw the rest of the room. In intermittent flashes of light and darkness, he picked out the details of the hell he'd walked into.

Light . . . and in one corner a glimpse of piled wooden racks and cobwebbed shelving. Darkness . . . and Yulian an even darker shape that crouched uncertainly in the center of the room. Light—and along one wall Georgina, seated in an old cane chair, her eyes bulging but vacant and her mouth and flaring nostrils wide as yawning caverns. Darkness—and a movement close by, so that George put up the mattock to defend himself. Insane light—and to his right a huge copper vat, six feet across and seated on copper legs; with Helen slumped in a dining chair on one side, her back to the nitre-streaked wall, and Anne, naked, likewise positioned on the other side. Their inner arms dangling inside the rim of the bowl, and something in the bowl itself seeming to move restlessly, throwing up ropes of doughy matter. Flickering darkness—out of which came Yulian's laughter: the clotted, sick laughter of someone warped irreparably. The light again—which found George's eyes fixed on the great vat, or more properly on the women. And the picture searing itself indelibly into his brain.

Helen's clothing ripped down the front and pulled back, and the girl lolling there like a slut with her legs sprawled open, everything displayed. Anne likewise; but both of them grimacing, their faces working hideously, showing alternating joy and total horror; their arms in the vat, and the nameless slime *crawling* on their arms to their shoulders, pulsating from its unknown source!

Merciful darkness—and the thought in George's tottering mind: *God! It's feeding on them, and it's feeding itself to them!* And Yulian so close now that he could hear his rasping breathing. Light again, as the lamp settled to a jerky jitterbug—and the mattock wrenched from George's nerveless fingers and hurled away. And George finally face to visage with the man he'd intended to kill, who now he discovered to be hardly a man at all but something out of his very worst nightmares.

Fingers of rubber with the strength of steel gripped his shoulder and propelled him effortlessly, irresistibly towards the vat. "George," the nightmare gurgled almost conversationally, "I want you to meet something . . ."

Chapter Six

ALEC KYLE'S KNUCKLES WERE WHITE WHERE HIS HANDS gripped the rim of his desk. "God in heaven, Harry!" he cried, staring aghast at the Keogh apparition where bands of soft light flowed through it from the window's blinds. "Are you trying to scare the shit out of me before we even get started?"

I'm telling it as I know it. That's what you asked me to do, isn't it? Keogh was unrepentant. *Remember, Alec, you're getting it secondhand. I got it straight from them, from the dead—the horse's mouth, as it were—and believe me I've watered it down for you!*

Kyle gulped, shook his head, got a grip of himself. Then something Keogh had said got through to him. "You got it from 'them'? Suddenly I have this feeling you don't just mean Thibor Ferenczy and George Lake."

No, I've spoken to the Reverend Pollock, too. From Yulian's christening?

"Oh, yes," Kyle wiped his brow. "I see that now. Of course."

139

Alec! Keogh's soft voice was sharper now. *We have to hurry. Harry's beginning to stir.*

And not only the real child, three hundred and fifty miles away in Hartlepool, but also its ethereal image where it languidly turned, superimposed over and within Keogh's midriff. It too was stirring, slowly stretching from its foetal position, its baby mouth opening in a yawn. The Keogh manifestations began to waver like smoke, like the heat haze over a summer road.

"Before you go!" Kyle was desperate. "Where do I start?"

He was answered by the faint but very definite wail of a waking infant. Keogh's eyes opened wide. He tried to take a pace forward, towards Kyle. But the blue shimmer was breaking down, like a television image going wrong. In another moment it snapped into a single vertical line, like a tube of electric blue light, shortened to a point of blinding blue fire at eye-level—and blinked out.

But coming to Kyle as from a million miles away: *Get in touch with Krakovitch. Tell him what you know. Some of it, anyway. You're going to need his help.*

"The Russians? But Harry—"

Goodbye, Alec. I'll get . . . back . . . to . . . you.

And the room was completely still, felt somehow empty. The central heating made a loud *click* as it switched itself off.

Kyle sat there a long time, sweating a little, breathing deeply. Then he noticed the lights blinking on his desk communications, heard the gentle, almost timid rapping on his office door. "Alec?" a voice queried from outside. It was Carl Quint's voice. "It . . . it's gone now. But I suppose you know that. Are you all right in there?"

Kyle took a deep breath, pressed the command button. "It's finished for now," he told the breathless, waiting HQ. "You'd all better come in and see me. There's time for an 'O'-group before we knock it on the head for the day. There'll be things you're wanting to know, and things we have to talk about.'' He released the button, said to himself: "And I do mean 'things.' ''

The Russian response was immediate, faster than Kyle might ever have believed. He didn't know that Leonid Brezhnev would soon be wanting all the answers, and that Felix Krakovitch had only four months left of his year's borrowed time.

They were to meet on the first Friday in September, these two heads of ESPionage, on neutral ground. The venue was Genoa, Italy, a seedy bar called Frankie's Franchise lost in a labyrinth of alleys down in the guts of the city, less than two hundred yards from the waterfront.

Kyle and Quint got into Genoa's surprisingly ramshackle Christopher Columbus airport on Thursday evening; their minder from British Intelligence (whom they hadn't met and probably wouldn't) was there twelve hours earlier. They'd made no reservations but had no problems getting adjoining rooms at the Hotel Genovese, where they freshened up and had a meal before retiring to the bar. The bar was quiet, almost subdued, where half-a-dozen Italians, two German businessmen, and an American tourist and his wife sat at small tables or at the bar with their drinks. One of the Italians who sat apart, on his own, wasn't Italian at all; he was Russian, KGB, but Kyle and Quint had no way of knowing that. He had no ESP talent or Quint would have spotted him at once. They didn't spot him taking photographs of them with a tiny camera, either. But the Russian had not gone entirely undetected. Earlier he'd been seen entering the hotel and booking a room.

Kyle and Quint were in a corner of the bar, on their third Vecchia Romagnas, and talking in lowered tones about their business with Krakovitch tomorrow, when the bar telephone tinkled. "For me!" Kyle said at once, starting upright on his barstool. His talent always had that effect on him: it startled him like a mild electric shock.

The bartender answered the phone, looked up. "Signor—" he began.

"Kyle?" said Kyle, holding out his hand.

The bartender smiled, nodded, handed him the phone. "Kyle?" he said again into the mouthpiece.

"Brown here," said a soft voice. "Mr. Kyle, try not to act surprised or anything, and don't look up or go all furtive. One of the people in the bar with you is a Russian. I won't describe him because then you'd act differently and he'd notice it. But I've been on to London and put him through our computer. He's dressed Eyetie but he's definitely KGB, name of Theo Dolgikh. He's a top field agent for Andropov. Just thought you'd like to know. There wasn't supposed to be any of this stuff, was there?"

"No," said Kyle, "there wasn't."

"Tut-tut!" said Brown. "I should be a bit sharp with your man when you meet him tomorrow, if I were you. It really isn't good enough. And just for your peace of mind, if anything were to happen to you—which I consider unlikely—be sure Dolgikh's a goner too, OK?"

"That's very reassuring," said Kyle grimly. He gave the phone back to the barman.

"Problems?" Quint raised an eyebrow.

"Finish your drink and we'll talk about it in our rooms," said Kyle. "Just act naturally. I think we're on *Candid Camera*." He forced a smile, swallowed his brandy at a gulp, stood up. Quint followed suit; they left the bar unhurriedly and went up to their rooms; in Kyle's room they checked for electronic bugs. This was as much a job for their psychic sensitivity as for their five mundane senses, but the room was clean.

Kyle told Quint about the call in the bar. Quint was an extremely wiry man of about thirty-five, prematurely balding, soft-spoken but often aggressive, and very quick-thinking. "Not a very auspicious start," he growled. "Still, I suppose we should have expected it. This is what your common-or-garden secret agent comes up against all the time, I'm told.''

"Well, it's not on!" Kyle was angry. "This was supposed to be a meeting of minds, not muscle."

"Do you know which one of them it was?" Quint was practical about it. "I think I can remember all of their faces. I'd know any one of them again if we should bump into him."

"Forget it," said Kyle. "Brown doesn't want a confrontation. He's geared to get nasty, though, if things go wrong for us."

"Charmed, I'm sure!" said Quint.

"My reaction exactly," Kyle agreed.

Then they checked Quint's room for bugs and, finding nothing, called it a day.

Kyle took a shower, got into bed. It was uncomfortably warm so he pushed his blankets on to the floor. The air was humid, oppressive. It felt like rain, and if a storm blew up it would probably be a dandy. Kyle knew Genoa in the autumn, also knew that it has some of the worst storms imaginable.

He left his bedside light burning, settled down to sleep. A door, unlocked, stood between the two rooms. Quint was right next door, probably asleep by now. The city's traffic was giving it hell out beyond the louvred window shutters. London was a tomb by comparison. Tombs hardly seemed a fitting subject to go to sleep on, but . . . Kyle closed his eyes; he felt sleep pulling him down, soft as a woman's arms; and he felt—

—something else pulling him awake!

His lamp was still on, its shade forming a pool of yellow light on the mahogany bedside table. But there was now a second source of illumination, and it was blue! Kyle snatched himself back from sleep, sat bolt upright in his bed. It was Harry Keogh, of course.

Carl Quint came bounding through the joining door, dressed only in his pyjama bottoms. He pulled up short, backed off a pace. "Oh my God!" he said, his mouth hanging open. The Keogh apparition—man, sleeping child and all—turned through ninety degrees to face him.

Don't be alarmed, said Keogh.

"Can you see him?" Kyle wasn't quite awake yet.

"Lord, yes," Quint breathed, nodding. "And hear him, too. But even if I couldn't, I'd still know he was here."

A psychic sensitive, said Keogh. *Well, that helps.*

Kyle swung his legs out of bed, switched off the lamp. Keogh stood out so much better in the darkness, like a hologram of infinitely fine neon wires. "Carl Quint," Kyle said, his skin prickling with the sheer weirdness of this thing he'd never get used to, "meet Harry Keogh."

Quint stumblingly found a chair close to Kyle's bed and flopped into it. Kyle was wide awake now, fully in control. He realized how insubstantial it must sound, how hollow and commonplace when he asked: "Harry, what are you doing here?"

And Quint almost laughed, however hysterically, when the apparition answered: *I've been talking to Thibor Ferenczy, using my time to my best advantage—for there's precious little of it to waste. Every waking hour makes Harry Jr. stronger and me less able to resist him. It's his body and I'm being subsumed, even absorbed. His little brain is filling up with its own stuff, squeezing me out or maybe compacting me. Pretty soon I'll have to leave him, and then I don't know if I'll ever be corporeal again. So on the way back from Thibor, I thought I'd drop in on you.*

Kyle could almost feel Quint's near-hysteria; he glanced warningly at him in the light of the soft blue glow. "You've been talking to the old Thing in the ground?" he repeated. "But why, Harry? What is it you want from him?"

He's one of them, a vampire, or he was. The dead aren't much bothered with him. He's a pariah among the dead. In me he has, well, if not a friend, at least someone to talk to. So we trade: I converse with him, and he tells me things I want to know. But nothing's easy with Thibor

Ferenczy. Even dead he has a devious mind. He knows that the longer he strings it out, the sooner I'll be back. He used the same tactics with Dragosani, remember?

"Oh, yes," Kyle nodded. "And I also remember what happened to Dragosani. You should be careful, Harry."

Thibor's dead, Alec, Keogh reminded him. *He can do no more harm. But what he left behind might . . .*

"What he left behind? You mean Yulian Bodescu? I've got men watching the place in Devon until I'm ready for him. When we're sure of his patterns, when we've assessed everything you've told us, then we'll move in."

I didn't exactly mean Yulian, though certainly he's part of it. But are you telling me you've put espers on the job? Keogh seemed alarmed. *Do they know what they might have to deal with if they're marked? Are they fully in the picture?*

"Yes they are. Fully. And they're equipped. But if we can we'll learn a little more about them before we act. For all that you've told us, still we know so very little."

And do you know about George Lake?

Kyle felt his scalp tingle. Quint, too. And this time it was Quint who answered. "We know he's no longer in his grave in the cemetery in Blagdon, if that's what you mean. The doctors diagnosed a heart attack, and his wife and the Bodescus were there at his burial. So much we've checked out. But we've also been there and had a look for ourselves, and George Lake wasn't where he should be. We figure he's back at the house with the others."

The Keogh manifestation nodded. *That's what I meant. So now he's undead. And that will have told Yulian Bodescu exactly what he is! Or maybe not exactly. But by now he must be pretty sure he's a vampire. In fact, he's only a half-vampire. George, on the other hand—he's the real thing! He has been dead, so what's in him will have taken complete control.*

"What?" Kyle was bemused. "I don't—"

Let me tell you the rest of Thibor's story, Keogh cut in. *See what you make of that.*

Kyle could only nod his agreement. "I suppose you know what you're doing, Harry." The room was already colder. Kyle gave a blanket to Quint, wrapped another about himself. "OK, Harry," he said. "The stage is all yours . . ."

The last thing Thibor remembered seeing was the Ferenczy's bestial animal face, his jaws open in a gaping laugh, displaying a crimson forked tongue shuddering like a speared snake in its alien passion. He remembered that, and the fact that he'd been drugged. Then he'd gone down in an irresistible whirlpool, down, down to black lightless depths from which his resurgence had been slow and fraught with nightmares.

He had dreamed of yellow-eyed wolves; of a blasphemous banner device in the form of a devil's head, with its forked tongue much like Ferenczy's own, except that on the banner it had dripped gouts of blood; of a black castle built over a mountain gorge, and of its master, who was something other than human. And now, because he knew that he had dreamed, he also knew he must be waking up. And the thought came to him: how much was dream and how much reality?

Thibor felt a subterranean cold, cramps in all his limbs, a throbbing in his temples like a reverberating gong in some great sounding cavern. He felt the manacles on his wrists and ankles, the cold slimy stone at his back where he slumped, the drip of seeping moisture from somewhere overhead, where it hissed past his ear and splashed in the hollow of his collar-bone.

Chained naked in some black vault in the castle of the Ferenczy. And no need now to ask how how much of it had been dream. All of it was real.

Thibor came snarling to life, strained with a giant's strength against the chains that held him powerless, ignored the thunder in his head and the lancing pains in his limbs and body to roar in the darkness like a wounded bull. "Ferenczy! You *dog*, Ferenczy! Treacherous, misshapen, misbegotten—"

The Wallach warlord stopped shouting, listened to the echoes of his curses dying away. And to something else. From somewhere up above he had heard his bellowing answered by the slam of a door, heard unhurried footsteps descending towards him. And with his cold skin prickling and his nostrils flaring—from rage and terror both—he hung in his chains and waited.

The darkness was very nearly utter, streaks of nitre alone glowed with a chemical phosphorescence on the walls; but as Thibor held his breath and the hollow footsteps came closer, so too came a flickering illumination. It issued in an unevenly penetrating yellow glow from an arched stone doorway in what must otherwise be a solid wall of rock; and while Thibor watched with bated breath, so the shadows of his cell were thrown back more yet as the light grew stronger and the footsteps louder.

Then a sputtering lantern was thrust in through the archway, and behind it was the Ferenczy himself, crouching a little to avoid the wedge of the keystone. Behind the lantern his eyes were red fires in the shadows of his face. He held the lantern high, nodded grimly at what he saw.

Thibor had thought he was alone but now he saw that he was not. In the flare of yellow lamplight he discovered that there were others here with him. But dead or alive . . .? One of them seemed alive, at least.

Thibor narrowed his eyes as the glare from the Ferenczy's lantern brightened, lighting up the entire dungeon. Three other prisoners were with him here, yes, and dead or alive it wasn't hard to guess who they'd be. As to how or why the castle's master had brought them here—that was anybody's guess. There were of course Thibor's Wallach companions, and also old Arvos of the Szgany. Of the three, it seemed to be the stumpy Wallach who'd survived:

the one who was all chest and arms. He lay crumpled on the floor where stone flags had been laid aside to reveal black soil underneath. His body seemed badly broken, but still his barrel chest rose and fell with some regularity and one of his arms twitched a little.

"The lucky one," said the Ferenczy, his voice deep as a pit. "Or perhaps unlucky, depending on one's point of view. He was alive when my children took me to him."

Thibor rattled his chains. "Was? Man, he's alive now! Can't you see him moving? See, he breathes!"

"Oh, yes!" the Ferenczy moved closer, in that soundless, sinuous way of his. "And the blood surges in his veins, and the brain in his broken head functions and thinks frightened thoughts—but I tell you he is not alive. Nor is he truly dead. He is undead!" He chuckled as at some obscene joke.

"Alive, undead? Is there a difference?" Thibor yanked viciously on his chains. How he would love to wrap them round the other's neck and squeeze till his eyes popped out.

"The difference is immortality." His tormentor thrust his face closer yet. "Alive he was mortal, undead he 'lives' forever. Or until he destroys himself, or some accident does the job for him. Ah, but to live forever, eh, Thibor the Wallach? How sweet is life, eh? But would you believe it can be boring, too? No, of course not, for you have not known the ennui of the centuries. Women? I have had *such* women! And food?" His voice took on a slyness. "Ah! Gobbets you've not yet dreamed of. And yet for these last hundred—nay, two hundred—years, all of these thing have bored me."

"Bored with life, are you?" Thibor ground his teeth, put every last effort into wrenching his chains' staples from the sweating stone. It was useless. "Only set me free and I'll put an end to your—*uh!*—boredom."

The Ferenczy laughed like a baying hound. "You will? But you already have, my son. By coming here. For, you see, I have waited for one just such as you. Bored? Aye, that I have been. And indeed you are the cure, but it's a cure we'll apply my way. You'd slay me, eh? Do you really think so? Oh, I've my share of fighting to come, but not with you. What? I should fight with my own son? Never! No, I'll go forth and fight and kill like *none* before me! And I'll lust and love like twenty men, and none shall say me nay! And I'll do it to all the ends of the earth, to such excess that my name shall live forever, or be stricken forever from man's history! For what else can I do with passions such as mine, a creature such as I am, condemned to life?''

"You speak in riddles," Thibor spat on the floor. "You're a madman, crazed by your lonely life up here with nothing but wolves for company. I can't see why the Vlad fears you, one madman on his own. But I can see why he'd want you dead. You are . . . loathsome! A blemish on mankind. Misshapen, split-tongued, insane: death's the best thing for you. Or locked up where natural men won't have to look at you!"

The Ferenczy drew back a little, almost as if he were surprised at Thibor's vehemence. He hung his lantern from a bracket, seated himself on a stone bench. "Natural men, did you say? Do you talk to me of nature? Ah, but there's more in nature than meets the eye, my son! Indeed there is. And you think that I'm unnatural, eh? Well, the Wamphyri are rare, be sure, but so is the sabre-tooth. Why, I haven't seen a mountain cat with teeth like scythes in . . . three hundred years! Perhaps they are no more. Perhaps men have hunted them down to the last. Aye, and it may be that one day the Wamphyri shall be no more. But if that day should ever come, believe me it shall not be the fault of Faethor Ferenczy. No, and it shall not be yours.''

"More riddles—meaningless mouthings—madness!" Thibor spat the words out. He was helpless and he knew it. If this monstrous being wished him dead, then he was

as good as dead. And it was no use to reason with a
madman. Where is the reason in a madman? Better to
insult him face to face, enrage him and get it over with. It
would be no pleasant thing to hang here and rot, and watch
maggots crawling in the flesh of men he'd called his
comrades.

"Are you finished?" the Ferenczy asked in his deepest
voice. "Best to be done now with all hurtful ranting, for
I've much to tell you, much to show you, great knowledge
and even greater skills to impart. I'm weary of this place,
you see, but it needs a keeper. When I go out into the
world, someone must stay here to keep this place for me.
Someone strong as I myself. It is my place and these are
my mountains, my lands. One day I may wish to return.
When I do, then I shall find a Ferenczy here. Which is
why I call you my son. Here and now I adopt you, Thibor
of Wallachia. Henceforth you are Thibor Ferenczy. I give
you my name, and I give you my banner: the devil's head!
Oh, I know these honours tower above you; I know you do
not yet have my strength. But I shall *give* it to you! I shall
bestow upon you the greatest honour, a magnificent mystery. And when you are become Wamphyri, then—"

"Your name?" Thibor growled. "I don't *want* your
name. I spit on your name!" He shook his head wildly.
"As for your device: I've a banner of my own."

"Ah?" the creature stood up, flowed closer. "And what
are your signs?"

"A bat of the Wallachian plain," Thibor answered,
"astride the Christian dragon."

The Ferenczy's bottom jaw fell open. "But that is most
propitious. A bat, you say? Excellent! And riding the
dragon of the Christians? Better still! And now a third
device: let Shaitan himself surmount both."

"I don't need your blood-spewing devil." Thibor shook
his head and scowled.

The Ferenczy smiled a slow, sinister smile. "Oh, but you
will, you will." Then he laughed out loud. "Aye, and I

shall avail myself of your symbols. When I go out across the world I shall fly devil, bat, and dragon all three. There, see how I honour you! Henceforth we carry the same banner.''

Thibor narrowed his eyes. "Faethor Ferenczy, you play with me as a cat plays with a mouse. Why? You call me your son, offer me your name, your sigils. Yet here I hang in chains, with one friend dead and another dying at my feet. Say it now, you are a madman and I'm your next victim. Isn't it so?''

The other shook his wolfish head. "So little faith," he rumbled, almost sadly. "But we shall see, we shall see. Now tell me, what do you know of the Wamphyri?''

"Nothing. Or very little. A legend, a myth. Freakish men who hide in remote places and spring out on peasants and small children to frighten them. Occasionally dangerous: murderers, vampires, who suck blood in the night and swear it gives them strength. 'Viesczy,' to the Russian peasant; 'Obour,' to the Bulgar; 'Vrykoulakas' in Greekland. They are names which demented men attach to themselves. But there is something common to them in all tongues: they are liars and madmen!''

"You do not believe? You have looked upon me, seen the wolves which I command, the terror I excite in the hearts of the Vlad and his priests, but you do not believe.''

"I've said it before and I'll say it again," Thibor gave his chains a last, frustrated jerk. "The men I've killed have all stayed dead! No, I do not believe.''

The other gazed at his prisoner with burning eyes. "That is the difference between us," he said. "For the men *I* kill, if it pleases me to kill them in a certain way, do not stay dead. They become undead . . ." He stood up, stepped flowingly close. His upper lip curled back at one side, displayed a downward curving fang like a needle-sharp tusk. Thibor looked away, avoided the man's breath, which was like poison. And suddenly the Wallach felt weak, hungry, thirsty. He was sure he could sleep for a week.

"How long have I been here?" he asked.

"Four days." The Ferenczy began to pace to and fro. "Four nights gone you climbed the narrow way. Your friends were unfortunate, you remember? I fed you, gave you wine; alas, you found my wine a little strong! Then, while you, er, rested, my familiar creatures took me to the fallen ones where they lay. Faithful old Arvos, he was dead. Likewise your scrawny Wallach comrade, broken by sharp boulders. My children wanted them for themselves, but I had another use for them and so had them dragged here. This one—" he nudged the blocky Wallach with a booted foot "—he lived. He had fallen on Arvos! He was a little broken, but alive. I could see he wouldn't last till morning, and I needed him, if only to prove a point. And so, like the 'myth,' the 'legend,' I fed upon him. I drank from him, and in return gave him something back; I took of his blood, and gave a little of mine. He died. Three days and nights are passed by; that which I gave him worked in him and a certain joining has occurred. Also, a healing. His broken parts are being mended. He will soon rise up as one of the Wamphyri, to be counted in the narrow ranks of The Elite, but ever in thrall to me! He is undead." The Ferenczy paused.

"Madman!" Thibor accused again, but with something less of conviction. For the Ferenczy had spoken of these nightmares so *easily*, with no obvious effort at contrivance. He could not be what he claimed to be—no, of course not—but certainly he might believe that he was.

The Ferenczy, if he heard Thibor's renewed accusation of madness, ignored or refused to acknowledge it. " 'Unnatural,' you called me," he said. "Which is to claim that you yourself know something of nature. Am I correct? Do you understand life, the 'nature' of living, growing things?"

"My fathers were farmers, aye," Thibor grunted. "I've seen things grow."

"Good! Then you'll know that there are certain principles, and that sometimes they seem illogical. Now let me test you. How say you: if a man has a tree of favourite apples, and he fears the tree might die, how may he reproduce it and retain the flavor of the fruit?"

"Riddles?"

"Indulge me, pray."

Thibor shrugged. "Two ways: by seed and by cutting. Plant an apple, and it will grow into a tree. But for the true, original taste, take cuttings and nurture them. It is obvious: what are cuttings but continuations of the old tree?"

"Obvious?" the Ferenczy raised his eyebrows. "To you, perhaps. But it would seem obvious to me—and to most men who are not farmers—that the seed should give the true taste. For what is the seed but the egg of the tree, eh? Still, you are of course correct, the cutting gives the true taste. As for a tree grown from seed: why, it is spawned of the pollens of trees other than the original! How then may its fruit be the same? 'Obvious'—to a tree-grower."

"Where does all this lead?" Thibor was surer than ever of the Ferenczy's madness.

"In the Wamphyri," the castle's master gazed full upon him, " 'nature' requires no outside intervention, no foreign pollens. Even the tree requires a mate with which to reproduce, but the Wamphyri do not. All we require is . . . a host."

"Host?" Thibor frowned, felt a sudden tremor in his great legs—the dampness of the walls, stiffening more cramps into his limbs.

"Now tell me," Faethor went on, "what do you know of fishing?"

"Eh? Fishing? I was a farmer's son, and now I'm a warrior. What *would* I know of fishing?"

Faethor continued without answering him: "In the Bulgars and in Turkey-land, fishermen fished in the Greek Sea. For years without number they suffered a plague of starfish, in such quantities that they ruined the fishing and their great weight broke the nets. And the policy of the fishermen was this: they would cut up and kill any starfish they hauled in, and hurl it back to the fish. Alas, the true fish does not eat starfish! And worse, from every *piece* of starfish, a new one grows complete! And 'naturally,' every year there were more. Then some wise fisherman divined the truth, and they began to keep their unwanted catches, bringing them ashore, burning them and scattering their ashes in the olive groves. Lo and behold, the plague dwindled away, the fish came back, the olives grew black and juicy.''

A nervous tic jumped in Thibor's shoulder: the strain of hanging so long in chains, of course. ''Now you tell me,'' he answered, ''what starfish have to do with you and I?''

''With you, nothing, not yet. But with the Wamphyri . . . why, 'nature' has granted us the same boon! How may you cut down an enemy if each lopped portion sprouts a new body, eh?'' Faethor grinned through the yellow bone mesh of his teeth. ''And how may any mere man kill a vampire? Now see why I liked you so well, my son. For who but a hero would come up here to destroy the indestructible?''

In the eye of Thibor's memory, he heard again the words of a certain contact in the Kievan Vlad's court: *They put stakes through their hearts and cut off their heads . . . better still, they break them entirely and burn all the pieces . . . even a small part of a vampire may grow whole again in the body of an unwary man . . . like a leech, but on the inside!*

''In the bed of the forest,'' Faethor broke into his morbid thoughts, ''grow many vines. They seek the light, and climb great trees to reach the fresh, free air. Some 'foolish' vines, as it were, may even grow so thickly as to kill their trees and bring them crashing down; and so destroy themselves. You've seen that, I'm sure. But others simply use the great trunks of their hosts; they share the earth and the air and the light between them; they live out their lives together. Indeed some vines are beneficial to their host trees. Ah! But then comes the drought. The trees wither, blacken, crumble, and the forest is no more. But down in the fertile earth the vines live on, waiting. Aye, and when more trees grow in fifty, an hundred years, back come the vines to climb again towards the light. Who is the stronger: the tree for his girth and sturdy branches, or the slender, insubstantial vine for his patience? If patience is a virtue, Thibor of Wallachia, then the Wamphyri are virtuous as all the ages . . ."

"Trees, fishes, vines." Thibor shook his head. "You rave, Faethor Ferenczy!"

"All of these things I've told you," the other was undeterred, "you will understand . . . eventually. But before you can begin to understand, first you must believe in me. In what I am."

"I'll never—" Thibor began, only to be cut short.

"Oh, but you *will*!" the Ferenczy hissed, his awful tongue lashing in the cave of his mouth. "Now listen: I have willed my egg. I have brought it on and it is forming even now. Each of the Wamphyri has but one egg, one seed, in a lifetime; one chance to recreate the true fruit; one opportunity to carve his changeling 'nature' into the living being of another. You are the host I have chosen for my egg."

"Your egg?" Thibor wrinkled his nose, scowled, drew back as far as his chains would allow. "Your seed? You are beyond help, Faethor."

"Alas," said the other, lip curling and great nostrils flaring, "but you are the one who is beyond help!" His cloak belled as he flowed towards the broken body of old Arvos. He hoisted the gypsy's corpse upright in one hand, like a bundle of rags, perched it, head stiffly lolling, in a niche in the stone wall. "We have no sex as such," he said, glaring across the cell at Thibor. "Only the sex of our hosts. Ah! But we multiply their zest an hundred times! We have no lust except theirs, which we double and redouble. We may, and do, drive them to excesses—in all of their passions—but we heal their wounds, too, when the excess is too great for human flesh and blood to endure. And with long, long years, even centuries, so man and vampire grow into one creature. They become inseparable, except under extreme duress. I, who was a man, have now reached just such a maturity. So shall you, in perhaps a thousand years.''

Once more, futilely, Thibor tugged at his chains. Impossible to break or even strain them. He could put a thumb through each link!

''About the Wamphyri,'' Faethor continued. ''Just as there are in the common world widely differing sorts of the same basic creature—owl and gull and sparrow, fox and hound and wolf—so are there varying Wamphyri states and conditions. For example: we talked about taking cuttings from an apple tree. Yes, it might be easier if you think of it that way.''

He stooped, dragged the unconscious, twitching body of the squat Wallach away from the area of torn up flags, tossed old Arvos' corpse down upon the black soil. Then he tore open the old man's ragged shirt, and glanced up from where he knelt into Thibor's mystified eyes. ''Is there sufficient light, my son? Can you see?''

''I see a madman clearly enough,'' Thibor gave a brusque nod.

The Ferenczy returned his nod, and again he smiled his hideous smile, the ivory of his teeth gleaming in lantern light. ''Then see this!'' he hissed.

Kneeling beside old Arvos' crumpled form, he extended a forefinger towards the gypsy's naked chest. Thibor watched. Faethor's forearm stuck out free of his robe. Whatever the Ferenczy was up to, there could be no trickery, no sleight of hand here.

Faethor's nails were long and sharply pointed at the end of his even, slender fingers. Thibor saw the quick of the pointed finger turn red and start to drip blood. The pink nail cracked open like the brittle shell of a nut, flapped loosely like a trapdoor on a finger bloating and pulsating. Blue and grey-green veins stood out in that member, writhing under the skin; the raw tip visibly lengthened, extending itself towards the dead gypsy's cold grey flesh.

The pulsating digit was no longer a finger as such: it was a pseudopod of unflesh, a throbbing rod of living matter, a stiff snake shorn of its skin. Now twice, now three times its former length, it vibrated down at an angle to within inches of its target, which appeared to be the dead man's heart. And all of this Thibor watched with bulging eyes, bated breath and gaping mouth.

And until this moment Thibor had not really known fear, but now he did. Thibor the Wallach—warlord of however small and ragged an army, humourless, merciless killer of the Pechenegi—utterly fearless Thibor, until now. Until now he'd not met a creature he feared. In the hunt, wild boar in the forests, which had wounded men so badly as to kill them, were "piglets" to him. In the challenge: let any man only *dare* hurl down the gauntlet, Thibor would fight him any way he chose. All knew it, and none chose! And in battle: he led from the front, stood at the head of the charge, could only ever be found in the thick of the fighting. Fear? It was a word without meaning. Fear of what? When he had ridden out to battle, he'd known each day might be his last. That had not deterred him. So black was his hatred of the invaders, of all enemies, that it simply engulfed fear and put it down. No creature, or man, or threat of any device of men had ever unmanned him since . . . oh, before he could remember: since he was a child, if ever he'd been one. But Faethor Ferenczy was something other than all of these. Torture could only maim and must kill in the end, and there's no pain after death, but what the Ferenczy threatened seemed an eternity of hell. Mere moments ago it had been a strange fantasy, the dreams of a madman, but now . . . ?

Unable to tear his eyes away, Thibor groaned and grew pale at the sight of that which followed.

"A cutting, aye," Faethor's voice was low, trembling with dark passions, "to be nurtured in flesh already tainted and falling into decay. The lowest form of Wamphyri existence, it will come to nothing so long as it has no living host. But it will live, devour, grow strong—and hide! When there is nothing left of Arvos it will hide in the earth and wait. Like the vine, waiting for a tree. The cut-off leg of a starfish, which does not die but waits to grow a new body—except this thing I make waits to *inhabit* one! Mindless, unthinking, it will be a thing of the most primitive instincts. But it can nevertheless outlast the ages. Until some unwary man finds it, and it finds him . . ."

His incredible, bloody, throbbing forefinger touched Arvos' flesh . . . and leprous white rootlets sprang forth, slid like worms in earth into the gypsy's chest! Small flaps of fretted skin were laid back; the pseudopod developed tiny glistening teeth of its own; it began to gnaw its way inside. Thibor would have looked away but he could not. Faethor's "finger" broke off with a soft tearing sound and quickly burrowed its way out of sight within the corpse.

Faethor held up his hand. The severed member was shrinking back into him, pseudoflesh melting into his flesh. The cancerous colours went out of it; it assumed a more normal shape; the old fingernail fell to the floor, and right in front of Thibor's eyes a new, pink shell began to form.

"Well then, my hero son who came here to kill me," Faethor slowly stood up and held out his hand toward Thibor's bloodless face. "And could you have killed this?"

Thibor drew back his face, head and body, tried to cringe into the very stone to avoid that pointing finger. But Faethor only laughed. "What? You think that I would . . . ? But no, no, not you, my son. Oh, I could, be sure! And forever you'd be in thrall to me. But that is the second state of the Wamphyri and unworthy of you. No, for I hold you in the highest esteem. Why, you shall have my very egg!''

Thibor tried to find words but his throat lacked moisture, was dry as a desert. Faethor laughed again and drew back that threatening hand of his. He turned away and stepped to where the squat Wallach lay humped on the stone flags, gurglingly breathing, face down in a dusty corner. "He is in that second state," Thibor's tormentor explained. "I took from him and gave him something back. Flesh of my flesh is in him now, healing him, changing him. His tears and broken bones will mend and he will live—for as long as I will it. But he will always be slave to me, to do my bidding, obey my every command. You see, he *is* vampire, but without vampire mind. The mind comes only from the egg and he is not grown from a seed but is merely . . . a cutting. When he wakes, which will be soon, then you will understand.''

"Understand?" Thibor found his voice, however cracked. "But how can I understand? Why should I want to understand? You are a monster, I understand that! Arvos is dead, and yet you . . . you did *that* to him! Why? Nothing can live in him now but maggots.''

Feather shook his head. "No, his flesh is like fertile soil—or the fortile sea. I think of the starfish.''

"You will grow another . . . another *you*? Inside him?" Thibor was very nearly gibbering now.

"It will consume him," Faethor answered. "But another me—no. I have mind. It will not have mind. Arvos cannot be a host for his mind is dead, do you see? He is food, nothing more. When it grows it will not be like me. Only like . . . what you saw." He held up his pale, newly formed index finger.

"And the other?" Thibor managed to nod in the direction of the man—that which had been a man—snoring and gasping in the corner.

"When I took him he was alive," said Faethor. "His mind was alive. What I gave him is now growing in his body, and in his mind. Oh, he died, but only to make way for the life of the Wamphyri. Which is not life but undeath. He will not return to true life but to undeath.''

''Madness!'' Thibor moaned.

''As for this one—'' The Ferenczy stepped into shadows on the far side of the cell, where the light did not quite reach. The legs and one arm of Thibor's second Wallach comrade protruded from the darkness, until Faethor dragged all of him into view. ''This one will be food for both of them. Until the mindless one hides himself away, and the other takes up his duties as your servant here.''

''*My* servant?'' Thibor was bewildered. ''Here?''

''Do you hear nothing I say?'' Faethor's turn to scowl. ''For more than two hundred years I have cared for myself, protected myself, stayed alone and lonely in a world expanding, changing, full of new wonders. This I have done for my seed, which now is ready to be passed on, passed down, to you. You will stay behind and keep this place, these lands, this 'legend' of the Ferenczy alive. But I shall go out amongst men and revel! There are wars to be won, honours to be earned, history is in the making. Aye, and there are women to be spoiled!''

''Honours, you?'' Thibor had regained something of his former nerve. ''I doubt it. And for a creature 'alone and lonely,' you seem to know a great deal of what is passing in the world.''

Faethor smiled his ghastliest smile. ''Another secret art of the Wamphyri,'' he chuckled obscenely in his throat. ''One of several. Beguilement is another—which you saw at work between myself and Arvos, binding his mind to mine so that we could talk to each other over great distances—and then there is the art of the necromancer.''

Necromancy! Thibor had heard of that. The eastern barbarians had their magicians, who could open the bellies of dead men to read their lives' secrets in their smoking guts.

''Necromancy,'' Faethor nodded, seeing the look in

Thibor's eyes, "aye. I shall teach it to you soon. It has allowed me to confirm my choice of yourself as a future vessel of the Wamphyri. For who would know better of you and your deeds, your strengths and weaknesses, your travels and adventures, than a former colleague, eh?" He stopped and effortlessly flopped the body of the thin Wallach over onto its back. And Thibor saw what had been done. No wolf pack had done this, for nothing was eaten.

The thin, hunched Wallach—an aggressive man in life, who had always gone with his chin thrust forward—seemed even thinner now. His trunk had been laid open from groin to gullet, with all of his pipes and organs loose and flopping, and the heart in particular hanging by a thread, literally torn out. Thibor's sword had gutted men as thoroughly as this, and it had meant nothing. But by the Ferenczy's own account, this man had already been dead. And his enormous wound was not the work of a sword . . .

Thibor shuddered, turned his eyes away from the mutilated corpse and inadvertently found Faethor's hands. The monster's nails were sharp as knives. Worse (Thibor felt dizzy, even faint), his *teeth* were like knives.

"Why?" The word left Thibor's lips as a whisper.

"I've told you why." Faethor was growing impatient. "I wanted to know about you. In life he was your friend. You were in his blood, his lungs, his heart. In death he was loyal, too, for he would not give up his secrets easily. See how loose are his innards. Ah! How I teased them, to wrest their secrets from him."

All the strength went out of Thibor's legs and he fell in his chains like a man crucified. "If I'm to die, kill me now," he gasped. "Have done with this."

Faethor flowed close, closer, stood not an arm's length away. "The first state of being—the prime condition of the Wamphyri—does not require death. You may *think* that you are dying, when first the seed puts its rootlets into your brain and sends them groping along the marrow of your spine, but you will not die. After that . . ." he shrugged. "The transition may be laboriously slow or lightning swift, one can never tell. But of one thing be sure, it will happen."

Thibor's blood surged one last time in his veins. He could still die a man. "Then if you'll not give me a clean death, I'll give myself one!" He gritted his teeth and wrenched on his manacles until the blood flowed freely from his wrists; and still he jerked on the irons, deepening his wounds. Faethor's long drawn-out *hisssss* stopped him. He looked up from his grisly work of self-destruction into . . . into the pit, the abyss itself.

Hideous face working yet more hideously, features literally writhing in a torment of passion, the Ferenczy was so close as to be the merest breath away. His long jaws opened and a scarlet snake flickered in the darkness behind teeth which had turned to daggers in his mouth. "You dare show me your blood? The hot blood of youth, the blood which is the life?" His throat convulsed in a sudden spasm and Thibor thought he was going to be ill, but he was not. Instead he clutched at his throat, gurgled chokingly, staggered a little. When he had regained control, he said: "Ah, Thibor! But now, ready or not, you have brought on that which cannot be reversed. It is my time, and yours. The time of the egg, the seed. See! See!"

He opened his great jaws until his mouth was a cavern, and his forked, flickering tongue bent backwards like a hook into his throat. And like a hook it caught something and dragged it into view.

Gasping, again Thibor drew down into himself. He saw the vampire seed there in the fork of Faethor's tongue: a translucent, silver-grey droplet shining like a pearl, trembling in the final seconds before . . . before its seeding?

"No!" Thibor hoarsely denied the horror. But it would not be denied. He looked in Faethor's eyes for some hint of what was coming, but that was a terrible mistake. Beguilement and hypnotism were the Ferenczy's greatest accomplishment. The vampire's eyes were yellow as gold, huge and growing bigger moment by moment.

Ah, my son, those eyes seemed to say, *come, a kiss for your father.*

Then—

The pearly droplet turned scarlet, and Faethor's mouth fastened on Thibor's own, which stood open in a scream that might last forever . . .

Harry Keogh's pause had lasted for several seconds, but still Kyle and Quint sat there, wrapped in their blankets and the horror of his story.

"That is the most—" Kyle started.

Almost simultaneously, Quint said, "I've never in my life heard—"

We have to stop there, Keogh broke in on both of them, something of urgency in his telepathic voice. *My son is about to be difficult; he's going to wake up for his feed.*

"Two minds in one body," Quint mused, still awed by what he'd heard. "I mean, I'm talking about you, Harry. In a way you're not unlike—"

Don't say it. Keogh cut him off a second time. *There's no way I'm like that! Not even remotely. But listen, I have to hurry. Do you have anything to tell me?*

Kyle got a grip on his rioting thoughts, forced himself back to earth, to the present. "We're meeting Krakovitch tomorrow," he said. "But I'm annoyed. This was supposed to be exclusive, entirely an inter-branch exchange—a bit of ESP détente, as it were—but there's at least one KGB goon in on it too."

How do you know?

"We've a minder on the job—but he's strictly in the background. Their man comes close up."

The Keogh apparition seemed puzzled. *That wouldn't have happened in Borowitz's time. He hated them! And frankly, I can't see it happening now. There's no meeting ground between Andropov's sort of mind-control and ours.*

And when I say "ours" I include the Russian outfit. Don't let it develop into a shouting match, Alec. You have to work with Krakovitch. Offer your assistance.

Kyle frowned. "To do what?"

He has ground to clear. You know at least one of the sites. You can help him do it.

"Ground to clear?" Kyle got up off his bed. Hugging his blanket to him, he stepped towards the manifestation. "Harry, we still have our own ground to clear in England! While I'm out here in Italy, Yulian Bodescu is still freewheeling over there! I'm anxious about it. I keep getting this urge to turn my lot loose on him and—"

NO! Keogh was alarmed. *Not until we know everything there is to know. You daren't risk it. Right now he's at the center of a very small nest, but if he wanted he could spread this thing like a plague!*

Kyle knew he was right. "Very well," he said, "but—"

Can't stay, the other broke in. *The pull is too strong. He's waking, gathering his faculties, and he seems to include me as one of them.* His neon-etched image began to shimmer, its blue glow pulsing.

"Harry, what 'ground' were you talking about, anyway?"

The old Thing in the ground. Keogh came and went like a distorted radio signal. The hologram child superimposed over his midriff was visibly stirring, stretching.

Kyle thought: *we've had this conversation before!* "You said we know at least one of the sites. Sites? You mean Thibor's tomb? But he's dead, surely?"

The cruciform hills . . . starfish . . . vines . . . creepers in the earth, hiding . . .

Kyle drew air in a gasp. "He's still there?"

Keogh nodded, changed his mind and shook his head. He tried to speak; his outline wavered and collapsed; he disappeared in a scattering of brilliant blue motes. For a moment Kyle thought his mind still remained, but it was only Carl Quint whispering: "No, not Thibor. He's not there. Not him, but what he left behind!"

Chapter Seven

11:00 P.M., THE FIRST FRIDAY IN SEPTEMBER, 1977: IN GENOA Alec Kyle and Carl Quint were hurrying through rain-slick cobbled alleys toward their rendezvous with Felix Krakovitch at a dive called Frankie's Franchise.

But seven hundred miles away in Devon, England, the time was 10:00 P.M. on a sultry Indian summer evening. At Harkley House, Yulian Bodescu lay naked on his back on the bed in his spacious garret room and considered the events of the last few days. In many ways they had been very satisfactory days, but they had been fraught with danger, too. He had not known the extent of his influence before, for the people at school and later Georgina had all been weak and hardly provided suitable yardsticks. The Lakes had been the true test, and Yulian had sailed through that with very little difficulty.

George Lake had been the only real obstacle, but even that had been an accidental encounter, when Yulian wasn't quite ready for him. The youth smiled a slow smile and gently touched his shoulder. There was a dull ache there now, but that was all. And where was "Uncle George" now? He was down in the vaults with his wife, Anne, that's where. Down where he belonged, with Vlad standing guard on the door. Not that Yulian believed that to be absolutely necessary: it was a precaution, that's all. As for the Other: that had left its vat, gone into hiding in the earth where the cellars were darkest.

Then there was Yulian's "mother," Georgina. She was in her room, lost in self-pity, in her permanent state of terror. As she had been for the last year, since the time he did it to her. If she hadn't cut her hand that time it might never have happened. But she had, and then shown him the blood. Something had happened to him then—the same thing that happened every time he saw blood—but on this occasion it had been different. He had been unable to control it. When he had bandaged her hand, he'd deliberately let something . . . something of himself, get into the wound. Georgina hadn't seen it, but Yulian had. He had made it.

She had been ill for a long time, and when she recovered . . . well, she had never really recovered. Not fully. And Yulian had known that it had grown in her, and that he was its master. She had known it too, which was what terrified her.

His "mother," yes. Actually, Yulian had never considered her his mother at all. He had come out of her, he knew that, but he'd always felt that he was more the son of a father—but not a father in the ordinary sense of the word. The son of . . . of something else. Which was why this evening he had asked her (as he'd asked her a hundred times before) about Ilya Bodescu, and about the way he died, and where he died. And to make sure he got the entire story in every last detail, this time he'd hypnotized her into the deepest possible trance.

And as Georgina had told him how it had been, so his mind had been lured east, across oceans and mountains and plains, over fields and cities and rivers, to a place which had always existed in the innermost eye of his mind; a place of hills and woods and . . . and yes, that was it! A place of low wooded hills in the shape of a cross. The cruciform hills. A place he would have to visit. Very soon . . .

He would *have* to, for that's where the answer lay. He was in thrall to that place as much as the rest of them in the house were in thrall to him, which was to say totally. And the strength of its seduction was just as great. It was a strength he had not realized until George had come back. Back from his grave in Blagdon cemetery, back from the dead. At first that had been a shock—then an all-consuming curiosity—finally a revelation! For it had told Yulian what he was. Not who he was but what. And certainly he was more than merely the son of Ilya and Georgina Bodescu.

Yulian knew that he was not entirely human, that a large part of him was utterly *in*human, and the knowledge thrilled him. He could hypnotize people to do his will, whatever he desired. He could produce new life, of a sort, out of himself. He could change living beings, people, into creatures like himself. Oh, they did not have his strength, his weird talents, but that was all to the good. The change made them his slaves, made him their absolute master.

More, he was a necromancer: he could open up dead bodies and learn the secrets of their lives. He knew how to prowl like a cat, swim like a fish, savage like a dog. The thought had occurred to him that given wings he might even fly—like a bat. Like a vampire bat!

Beside him on a bedside table lay a hardback book titled *The Vampire in Fact and Fiction*. Now he reached out a slender hand to touch its cover, trace the figure of a bat in flight impressed into the black binding cloth. Absorbing, certainly—but the title was a lie, as were the contents. Most of the alleged fiction was fact (Yulian was the living proof), and some of the supposed fact was fiction.

Sunlight, for instance. It didn't kill. It might, if he should ever be foolish enough to stretch himself out in a sheltered cove in midsummer for more than a minute or two. It must be some sort of chemical reaction, he thought. Photophobia was common enough even among ordinary men. Mushrooms grow best under a covering of straw through foggy, late September nights. And he'd read somewhere that in Cyprus one can find the selfsame edible species, except they never break the surface. They push up the parched earth until cracks appear, which tell the locals where to find them. They didn't much care for sunlight, mushrooms, but it wouldn't kill them. No, Yulian was wary of the sun but not afraid of it. It was a question of being careful, that's all.

As for sleeping through the day in a coffin full of native soil: sheer fallacy. He did occasionally sleep during the day, but that was because he often spent much of the night deep in thought, or prowling the estate. He preferred night, true, because then, in the darkness or in the moonlight, he felt closer to his source, closer to understanding the true nature of his being.

Then there was the vampire's lust for blood: false, at least in Yulian's case. Oh, the *sight* of blood aroused him, did things to him internally, working him into a passion; but drinking it from a victim's veins was hardly the delight described in the various fictions. He did like rare meat, however, and plenty of it, and had never been much of a one for greens. On the other hand, the thing Yulian had grown in the vat in the cellar, that had thrived on blood! On blood, flesh, anything animate or ex-animate. On flesh or the red juice of flesh, alive or dead! It didn't need to eat, Yulian knew, but it would if it could. It would have absorbed George, too, if he hadn't been there to stop it.

The Other . . . Yulian shuddered deliciously. It knew him for its master, but that was its sum total of knowledge. He had grown it from himself, and remembered how that had come about:

Just after he'd been expelled from school, the first of what he had always supposed to be his adult teeth had come loose. It was a back tooth and painful. But he wouldn't see a dentist. Working and worrying at it, one night he'd broken the thread. And he'd examined the tooth closely, finding it curious that this was part of himself which had been shed. White bone and a thread of gristle, the red root. He'd put it in a saucer on the window ledge of his bedroom. But in the morning he heard it clatter to the floor. The core had put out tiny white rootlets, and the tooth was dragging itself like a hermit crab out of the morning light.

Yulian's teeth, except the back ones, had always been sharp as knives and chisel-tipped, but human teeth for all that. Certainly not animal teeth. The one which had pushed out the lost one was anything but human. It was a fang. Since then most of his teeth had been replaced, and the new ones were all fangs. Especially the eye-teeth. His jaws had changed too, to accommodate them.

Sometimes he thought: *Perhaps I'm the cause of this change in myself. Maybe I'm making it happen. Willing it. Mind over matter. Because I'm evil.*

Georgina had used to say that to him sometimes, tell him he was evil. That was when he was small and she still had a measure of control over him, when he'd done things she didn't like. When he'd first started to experiment with his necromancy. Ah, but there'd been many things she hadn't liked since then!

Georgina—"mother"—terror-stricken chicken penned with a fox cub, watching him grow sleek and strong. For as Yulian had grown older, so the element of control had changed, passed into his hands. It was his eyes; he only had to look at her with those eyes of his and . . . and she was powerless. The teachers and pupils at his school, too. And with use, so he'd become expert in hypnotism. Practice makes perfect. To that extent, at least, the book was correct: the vampire is quite capable of mesmerizing its prey.

But what about mortality—or immortality, undeath? That was still a puzzle, a mystery—but it was one he'd soon resolve. Now that he had George there was very little he couldn't resolve. For George was still in large part a man. Returned from the grave, undead, yes, but his flesh was still a man's flesh. And that which was within him couldn't have grown very large in so short a time. Unlike the Other, which had had plenty of time.

Yulian had, of course, experimented with the Other. His experiments had told him very little, but it was better than nothing. According to the fiction, vampires were supposed to succumb to the sharpened stake. The Other ignored the stake, seemed impervious to it. Trying to stake it was like trying to leave an imprint on water. The Other could be solid enough at times: it could form teeth, rudimentary hands, even eyes. But in the main its tissues were proto-plasmic, gelatinous. And as for putting a stake through its "heart" or cutting off its "head" . . .

And yet it wasn't indestructible, it wasn't immortal. It could die, could be killed. Yulian had burned part of it in an incinerator down there in the cellars. And by God—if there was a God, which Yulian doubted—it hadn't liked that! He was perfectly sure he wouldn't have liked it either. And that was a thought which occasionally worried him: if ever he were discovered, if men found out what he was, would they try to burn him? He supposed they would. But who could possibly find him out? And if someone did, who would believe it? The police weren't much likely to listen to a story about vampires, now were they? On the other hand, what with the local "satanic cult," maybe they were!

Again he smiled his awful smile. It was funny now, but it hadn't been at all funny when the police came knocking at the door the day after George came back. He had very nearly made a serious mistake then, had gone too quickly on his guard, on the defensive. But of course they'd put his nervousness down to the recent loss of his "uncle." If only they'd been able to know the truth, that in fact George Lake was right under their feet, whining and shivering in the cellars. And even so, what could they have done about it? It was hardly Yulian's fault that George wouldn't lie still, was it?

And that was another part of the legend which was a fact: that when a vampire killed a victim in a certain way, then that victim would return as one of the undead. Three nights George had lain there, and on the fourth he'd clawed his way out. A mere man buried alive could never have done it, but the vampire in him had given George all the strength he needed and more. The vampire which had been part of the Other, which had put one of its pseudohands into him and stopped George's heart. The Other which had been part of Yulian, in fact Yulian's tooth.

What a torn and bloodied state George had been in when Yulian opened the door to him that night. And how the house had rung to his demented sobbing and shrieking, until Yulian had grown angry with him, told him to be quiet and locked him in the cellar. And there he'd stayed.

Yulian watched the silver light of the moon creeping through a crack in his curtains, channelled his thoughts anew. What had he been recounting? Ah, yes, the police.

They had come to report a shocking crime, the illegal opening of George Lake's grave by person or persons unknown, and the theft of his corpse. Was Mrs. Lake still residing at Harkley House?

Why, yes she was, but she was still suffering from the shock of her husband's death. If it wasn't absolutely necessary that they see her, Yulian would prefer to break the news to her himself. But who could be responsible for so despicable a crime?

Well, sir, we do believe we've got one of them there cults at work in these here parts, despoiling graveyards and the like and holding, er, sabbats? Druids or some such. Devil worshippers, you know? But this time they've gone too far! Don't you worry, sir, we'll get 'em in the end. But do break it easy to his missus, all right?

Of course, of course. And thank you for bringing us this

news, terrible though it is. I certainly don't envy you your job.

All in a day's work, sir. Sorry we've nothing good to report, that's all. Good night to you . . .

And that was that.

But again he had strayed, and once more he was obliged to focus his thoughts back on the "legend" of the vampire. Mirrors: vampires hated mirrors because they had no reflections. False—and yet in a way true. Yulian did have a reflection; but sometimes, looking in a glass, especially at night, he saw far more than others could see. For he *knew* what he was looking at, that it was something alien to man. And he had wondered: if others saw him like that, reflected in a glass, would they too see the real thing, the monster behind the man?

And lastly there was the vampire's lust, the way he sated himself on women. Now Yulian had tasted the blood—and more than the blood—of women, and had found it rich as deep red wine. It excited him as all blood did, but not so much that he'd glut himself on it. Georgina, Anne, Helen—he'd tried the blood of all three. And certainly, in good time, he would try the blood of many more.

But his attitude toward taking blood puzzled him. If he were a true vampire, surely blood would be the driving force of his life. And yet it wasn't. Perhaps his metamorphosis wasn't yet complete. Perhaps, as the change waxed in him, so the human part would wane, disappear altogether. And then he'd become a vampire full-blown. Or full-blooded?

Lust, yes . . . but there was more to lust than mere blood-lust. Much more. And little wonder the women in the fiction succumbed so readily to the vampire's charms. Especially after the first time. Hah! What woman had ever truly felt fulfilled in the arms of a man? Not one! They only thought they had because they didn't know better. What, "fulfilled?" Filled full? By a mere man? Utterly impossible! But by a vampire . . .

Yulian turned a little to his side and gazed in the moon-pierced darkness of his room at the girl beside him. Cousin Helen. She was very beautiful and had been very innocent. Not quite pure, but very nearly. Who was it took her virginity . . . but what did that matter? In fact he had taken nothing, and he had given very little. They had been fumbling lovers for an hour.

But now? Now she knew what it was to be "fulfilled." Indeed, she knew that if Yulian willed it he could fill her to bursting—literally!

A chuckle rose in his throat, formed on his lips like a bubble of bile. Oh, yes, for the Other wasn't the only one who could put out pseudopod extensions of himself! Yulian held back the laughter he felt welling inside, reached out a hand and with a deceptive gentleness stroked Helen's cool, rounded flank.

Even deeply asleep and dreaming the dreams of the damned, still she shuddered under the touch of his hand. Gooseflesh appeared and her breathing rapidly mounted to a moaning pant. She whined in her hypnotic sleep like a thin wind through a cracked board. Her hypnotic sleep, yes. The power of hypnotism, and that of telepathy which was its kin.

Nowhere in literature—except for the occasional hint in some of the better fictions—had Yulian discovered mention of the vampire's control of others by will and the reading of minds at a distance; and yet this, too, was one of his powers. It was very inchoate as yet, as were all his talents, but it was also very real. Once touched by Yulian, once invaded by him physically, then his victim was an open book to him, even at a distance. Even now, if he reached out his mind in a certain way . . . there! Those were the dull, vacuous "thoughts" of the Other. No, not even that: he had merely touched upon the Other's instinctive sense of being, a sort of basic animal awareness. The Other was aware of himself—itself?—in much the same way as an amoeba is aware; and because it had been part of him, Yulian could sense that awareness.

Now that he had taken or used Helen, Anne, George and Georgina, why, he could sense all of them! He let his exterior thoughts leave the Other and wander, and . . . and there was Anne, asleep in some cold, damp corner down there in the dark. And there, too, was George. Except that George was not asleep.

George. Yulian knew he would soon have to do something about George. He wasn't behaving as he should. There was an obstinacy in him. Oh, he'd been completely under Yulian's control in the beginning, just like the women. But just recently . . .

Yulian focused on George's mind, wormed his way silently into his thoughts and—*a pit of black hatred shot with flashes of red rage! Lust, too—a bestial lust Yulian could scarce believe—and not only for blood but also . . . revenge?*

Frowning, Yulian withdrew his mind before George could sense him. Obviously he would have to deal with his uncle sooner than he'd thought. He had already decided to make use of him—knew *how* he would use him—but now he must set a definite date on it. Like tomorrow. He left the unsuspecting undead creature raging and prowling the cellars, and—

What was that?

Hair prickling at the nape of his neck, Yulian swung his legs down to the floor and stood up. It hadn't been one of the women, and he'd only just left George, so who had it been? Someone close by was thinking thoughts about Harkley House, thoughts about Yulian himself! He went to the curtains, opened them six inches, stared anxiously out at the night.

Out there, the estate. The old derelict buildings, gravel path, shrubbery and copse; the high perimeter wall and gate; the road beyond the gate, a ribbon of light under the moon, and beyond that a tall hedge. Yulian wrinkled his nose, sniffed suspiciously like a dog at a stranger. Oh, yes, a stranger—*there!* In the hedgerow, that glint of moonlight on glass, the dull red glow off a cigarette's tip. Someone in the shadow of the hedge, watching Harkley. Watching Yulian!

Now, knowing where to aim, he redirected his thoughts— and met the mind of the stranger! But only for a moment, the merest instant of time. Then mental shutters came down like the jaws of a steel trap. The glint of spectacles or binoculars disappeared, the cigarette's glow was extinguished, and the man himself, the merest shadow, was gone.

Vlad! Yulian commanded instinctively. *Go, find him. Whoever he is, bring him to me!*

And down in the brambles and undergrowth near the door to the vaults, where he lay half asleep, Vlad at once came alert, turned his sensitive ears towards the drive and the gate, sprang up and set off at a loping run. Deep in his throat, a growl not quite a dog's growl rumbled like dull thunder.

Darcy Clarke was doing the late shift on the Harkley place. He was a psychic sensitive with a high degree of telepathic potential. Also, he was big on self-preservation. A freakish automatic talent, over which he had no conscious control, was always on guard to keep him "safe"; he was the opposite of accident prone and led a "charmed" life. Which on this occasion was just as well.

Clarke was young, only twenty-five, but what he lacked in years he more than made up for in zeal. He would have made a perfect soldier, for his duty was his all. It was that duty which had kept him here in the vicinity of Harkley House from 5:00 till 11:00 P.M. And it was exactly on the dot of 11:00 P.M. that he saw the crack of the curtains widen a little in one of Harkley's dormer windows.

That in itself was nothing. There were five people in that house and God-knows-what else, and no reason at all why it shouldn't show signs of life. With a grimace, Clarke quickly corrected himself: sign of undeath? Fully briefed, he knew that Harkley's inhabitants were something other than they seemed. But as he adjusted his nite-lite binoculars on the window, suddenly there was something else, a realization that struck at Clarke like a bolt of lightning.

He had known, of course, that someone in there, probably the youth, was psychically endowed. That had been obvious for the last four days, ever since Clarke and the others first clapped eyes on the place. To any half-talented sensitive the old house would reek of strangeness. And not just strangeness, evil! Tonight, as darkness fell, Clarke had sensed it growing stronger, the wash of dark emanations flowing from the house right past him, without touching, but as that dark figure had come into view behind the crack in the curtains, and as he'd focussed his binoculars upon it—

—Something had been there in his head, touching on his mind. A talent at least as strong as his own, probing his thoughts! But it wasn't the talent that surprised him—that was a game he'd played before with his colleagues at INTESP, where they'd practiced constantly to break in on each other's thoughts—it was the sheer unbridled animal animosity that caused him to gasp, draw back a little, slam the doors on his ESP-endowed consciousness. The gurgling black whirlpool bog of the invading mind.

And because he had set up defences, so he failed to detect any hint of the physical threat, the orders Yulian had issued to his black Alsatian. He had failed, but his primary talent—the one no one as yet understood—was not failing him. It was 11:00 P.M. and his instructions were quite clear: he'd go back now to the temporary surveillance HQ at a hotel in Paignton and make his report. The watch on the house would begin again at 6:00 A.M. tomorrow, when a colleague of Clark's would take it up. He tossed his cigarette down, ground it out under his heel, pocketed his nite-lites.

Clarke's car was parked in a layby where the hedge and fence were cut back twenty-five yards down the road. He was on the field side of the hedge. He put his hand on the top bar preparatory to climbing over to the road, then thought better of it. Though he didn't know it, that was his hidden talent coming into play. Instead of climbing the fence, he hurried through the long grass at the edge of the field towards his car. The grass was wet where it whipped his trousers, but he ignored it. It saved time this way and he was in a hurry now, eager to be away from the place. Only natural, he supposed, considering what he'd just learned. And he hardly gave it a thought that by the time he got to his car he was almost running.

But it was then, as he fumbled the key into the lock and turned it, that he heard something else running: the faint scuff of padded feet slapping the road, the scrabble of claws as something heavy jumped the fence back there where he'd been standing. Then he was into the car, slamming the door behind him, eyes wide and heart thumping as he gazed back into the night.

And two seconds later Vlad hit the car!

He hit so hard, with forepaws, shoulder and head, that the glass of the window in Clarke's door was starred into a cobweb pattern. The impart had sounded like a hammer blow, and Clarke knew that one more charge like that would shatter the glass to fragments and leave him totally unprotected. But he'd seen who, or what, his assailant was, and he had no intention of sitting here immobile and just waiting for it to happen.

Clarke turned the key in the ignition, revved, reversed a skidding three feet to bring the bonnet free of overhanging branches. Vlad's second spring, aimed again at Clarke's window, sent the dog sprawling on the bonnet directly in front of the windscreen. And now the young esper saw just how fortunate his escape had been. Out in the open—there was little he could have done against that!

Vlad's face was a savage black mask of hatred, a contorted, snarling, saliva-flecked visage of madness! Yellow eyes spotted with crimson pupils glared through the glass at Clarke with such a burning intensity that he almost fancied he could feel their heat. Then he was into first gear and skidding out on to the road.

As the car jerked and slewed forward, so the dog's feet were jolted from under him. He crashed over on to his side on the bonnet and was sent sprawling into the darkness of the hedgerow as Clarke straightened the car up and sent it careening along the road. In his rearview mirror, he saw the dog emerge from the hedge and shake itself, glaring after the speeding car. Then Clarke was round a bend and Vlad lost to sight.

That wasn't something he felt sorry about. Indeed, he was still shaking when he switched off the car's engine in the hotel car park in Paignton. Following which . . . he flopped back in his seat and wearily lit a cigarette, which he smoked right down to the cork tip before securing the car and going in to make his report . . .

Frankie's Franchise was wall to wall sleazy. It was a place for habitual wharf-rats, prostitutes and their pimps, pushers and Genoese low-life in general. And it was noisy. An old American juke-box, back in fashion, was blasting Little Richard's raw "Tutti Frutti" across the main room like a gale force wind. There was no smallest corner of the place that escaped the music's blast, but in any one of the half-dozen arched alcoves you could at least hear yourself think. That was why Frankie's was so ideally suitable: you couldn't concentrate enough to hear anyone else think.

Alec Kyle and Carl Quint, Felix Krakovitch and Sergei Gulharov, sat at a small square table with their backs to the protective alcove walls. East and West faced each other across their drinks. Curiously, on one side Kyle and

Quint drank vodka, and on the other Krakovitch and Gulharov sipped American beers.

Identifying each other had been the easiest thing in the world: in Frankie's Franchise, no one else fitted the pre-scribed picture at all. But personal appearance wasn't the only yardstick; for of course, even in the hubbub, the three sensitives were able to detect each other's psychic auras. They had made their acknowledgement with nods of their heads, picked their way with their drinks from the bar to an empty alcove. Certain of the club's regulars had given them curious glances: the hard men a little wary, narrow-eyed, the prostitutes speculative. They had not returned them.

Seated for a few moments, finally Krakovitch had opened the discussion. "I don't suppose you speaking my lan-guage," he said, his voice heavily but not unpleasantly accented, "but I speaking yours. But badly. This my friend Sergei." He tipped his head sideways a little to indicate his companion. "He know a little, very little, English. He not have ESP."

Kyle and Quint glanced obediently at Gulharov. What they saw was a moderately handsome young man with close-cropped blond hair, grey eyes, hard-looking hands where they lay loosely crossed on the table, enclosing his drink. He seemed uneasy in his modern Western clothes, which weren't quite the right fit.

"That's true enough," Quint narrowed his eyes, turning back to Krakovitch. "He's not skilled that way, but I'm sure he has many other worthwhile talents," Krakovitch smiled thinly and nodded. He seemed a little sour.

Kyle had been studying Krakovitch, committing him to memory. The Russian head of ESPionage was in his late thirties. He had thinning black hair, piercing green eyes and an almost gaunt, hollow face. He was of medium height, slimly built. *A skinned rabbit*, thought Kyle. But his thin, pale lips were firm, and the high dome of his head spoke of a rare intelligence.

Krakovitch's impression of Kyle was much the same: a man just a few years younger than himself, intelligent, talented. It was only the physical side of Kyle that was different, which hardly mattered. Kyle's hair was brown and plentiful, naturally wavy. He was well fleshed, even a little overweight, but with his height that scarcely showed. His eyes were brown as his hair, his teeth even and white in a too-wide mouth that sloped a little from left to right. In another face that might well be mistaken for cynicism, but not in Kyle, Krakovitch thought.

Quint, on the other hand, was more aggressive, but he probably had superb self-control. He would reach conclusions quickly, right or wrong. And he would probably act on them. He would act, and hope he'd done the right thing. But he wouldn't feel guilty if it turned out wrong. Also, there wasn't much emotion in Quint. All of this showed in his face, his figure, and Krakovitch prided himself on reading character. Quint was lithe, built like a cat. In no way massive, but he had that coiled spring look about him. Not nervous tension, just a natural ability to think and act fast. He had eyes of disarming blue that took in everything, a thin, even nose, and a forehead creased from frowning. He too was in his mid-thirties, thin on top, dark featured. And he had a talent. Krakovitch could tell that Quint was extremely ESP-sensitive. He was a spotter.

"Oh, Sergei Gulharov has been trained—" Krakovitch finally answered, "—as my bodyguard. But not in your arts, or mine. He has not got that kind of mind. Indeed, of the four of us, I could argue that he is the only 'normal' man present. Which is unfortunate,"—now he stared accusingly at Kyle—"for you and I were supposed to meet as equals, without, er, backup?"

At that moment the music went quiet, the rock'n'roll replaced by an Italian ballad.

"Krakovitch," said Kyle, hard-eyed now and keeping his voice low, "we'd better be straight on this. You're right, our deal was that the two of us should meet. We could each bring along a second. But no telepaths. What we have to say to each other we'll just say, without someone picking our thoughts. Quint isn't a telepath, he's a spotter, that's all. So we weren't cheating. And as far as your man here—er, Gulharov?—is concerned: Quint says he's clean, so you aren't cheating either. Or you wouldn't appear to be—but your third man is something else!''

''My *third* man?'' Krakovitch sat up straight, seemed genuinely surprised. ''I have no—''

''But you do,'' Quint cut in. ''KGB. We've seen him. In fact, he's here in Frankie's Franchise right now.

That was news to Kyle. He looked at Quint. ''You're certain?''

Quint nodded. ''Don't look now, but he's sitting in the corner over there with a Genoese whore. He's changed his clothes, too, and looks like he's just off a ship. Not a bad cover—but I recognized him the moment we walked in here.''

Out of the corner of his eye Krakovitch looked, then slowly shook his head. ''I do not know him,'' he said. ''Not to be surprised. I do not know any of them. I dislike—strongly! But . . . you are sure? How can you be so sure?''

Kyle would have been caught on the hop, but not Quint. ''We run the same sort of branch as the one you run, Comrade,'' he stated flatly. ''Except we have the edge on you. We're better at it. He's KGB, all right.''

Krakovitch's fury was obvious. Not against Quint but the position in which he now found himself. ''Intolerable!'' he snapped. ''Why, the Party Leader himself has given me his—'' He half looked up, half turned towards the man indicated, a thick-set barrel of a man in rough and ready suit and open-necked shirt. His neck must be at least as thick as Krakovitch's thigh! Fortunately he was looking the other way, talking to the prostitute.

Before Krakovitch could carry it any further, Kyle said, ''I believe you—that you don't know him. It was done behind your back. So sit down, act naturally. Anyway, it's obvious we can't talk here. Apart from the fact that we''re being watched, it's too damned noisy. And Christ, for all we know there might even be someone listening in on us!''

Krakovitch abruptly sat down. He looked startled, glanced nervously about. "Bugged?" He remembered how his old boss, Borowitz, had had a thing about electronic surveillance.

"We could be." Quint gave a sharp nod. "This one either followed you here or he knew in advance where we were going to meet."

Krakovitch gave a snort. "This getting out of hand. I no good at this. What now?"

Kyle looked at Krakovitch and knew he wasn't faking it. He grinned. "I'm no good at it either. Listen, I'm like you, Felix. I prognosticate. I don't know your word for it. I, er, foretell the future? I occasionally get fairly accurate pictures of how things are going to be. Do you understand?"

"Of course," said Krakovitch. "My talent almost exactly. Except I usually get warnings. So?"

"So I saw us getting along OK together. How about you?"

Krakovitch heaved a sigh of relief. "I also," he shrugged. "At least, no bad warnings." Time was running out for the Russian and there were things he desperately needed to know, questions he must have answered. This Englishman might be the only one who could answer them. "So what we do about it?"

Quint said, "Wait." He got up, crossed to the bar, ordered fresh drinks. He also spoke to the bartender. Then he came back with drinks on a tray. "When we get the nod from the bloke behind the bar we pile out of here fast," he said.

"Eh?" Kyle was puzzled.

"Taxi," said Quint, smiling tightly. "I've ordered one. We'll go to . . . the airport! Why not? On the way we can talk. At the airport we find a warm, comfortable place in the arrivals lounge and carry on talking. Even if our pal

over there manages to follow us he won't dare get too
close. And if he does show up we'll take a taxi somewhere
else."

"Good!" said Krakovitch.

Five minutes later their taxi came and all four exited at
speed. Kyle was last out. Looking back, he saw the KGB
man come slowly to his feet, saw his face twisting in anger
and frustration.

In the taxi they talked, and at the airport. They started
talking at about twenty minutes before midnight and finished at 2:30 A.M. Kyle did most of it, aided by Quint,
with Krakovitch listening intently and only breaking in
here and there to confirm or ask for an explanation of
something that had been said.

Kyle started with these words:

"Harry Keogh was our best. He had talents no one ever
had before. A lot of them. He told me everything I'm
going to tell you. If you believe what I tell you, we can
help you with some big problems you've got in Russia and
Romania. In helping you, we'll also be helping ourselves,
for we'll learn by experience. Now then, do you want to
know about Borowitz and how he died? About Max Batu
and how *he* died? About the . . . the fossil men, who
wrecked the Château Bronnitsy that night? I can tell you
all of those things. More importantly, I can tell you about
Dragosani . . .".

And nearly three hours later he finished with these:
"So, Dragosani was a vampire. And there are more of
them. You have them, and we have them. We know where
at least one of yours is. Or if not a vampire, something a
vampire left behind. Which could be just as bad. Whichever, it has to be destroyed. We can help if you'll let us.
Call it what you like—détente, while we deal with a
mutual threat? But if you don't want our help, then you'll
have to do the job yourself. But we'd like to help, because
that way we might learn something. Face it, Felix, this is
bigger than East-West political squabbling. We'd work

together if it was plague, wouldn't we? Drug trafficking? Ships in trouble at sea? Of course we would. And I'm admitting right here and now, our own problem back in England might be bigger than we know. The more we learn from you, the better our chances. The better all of our chances . . ."

Krakovitch had been silent for a long time. At last he said: "You want to come to USSR with me and . . . put this thing down?"

"Not the USSR—" said Quint. "Romania. That's still your territory."

"The two of you? Both the leader, *and* a high-ranking member of your E-Branch? Is that not to be the big risks?"

Kyle shook his head. "Not from you. At least I don't think so. Anyway, we all have to start trusting someone somewhere. We've already started, so why not go all the way?"

Krakovitch nodded. "And afterwards, I perhaps come with you? See what kind problem you have?"

"If you wish."

Krakovitch pondered it. "You tell me a lot," he said. "And you solve some big problems for me, maybe. But you not say where *exactly* this thing in Romania."

"If you want to go it alone," said Kyle, "I will tell you. Not exactly, for I don't know exactly, but close enough that you'll be able to find it. Working together we might do it a lot faster, that's all."

"Also," Krakovitch was still thinking it out, "you not say how you knowing all of this. Hard to accept all I hear without I know how you know."

"Harry Keogh told me," said Kyle.

"Keogh is dead a long time now," said Krakovitch.

"Yes," Quint cut in, "but he told us everything right up to the time he died.

"Ah?" Krakovitch drew breath sharply. "He was *that* good? Such talent in a telepath must be . . . very rare."

"Unique!" said Kyle.

"And your lot killed him!" Quint accused.

Krakovitch quickly turned to him. "Dragosani killed him. And he killed Dragosani—almost."

It was Kyle's turn to gasp. "Almost? Are you saying that—?"

Krakovitch held up a hand. "I finish the job Keogh started," he said. "I tell you about that. But first: you say Keogh in contact until the end?"

Kyle wanted to say, *he still is!* But that was a secret best kept. "Yes," he answered.

"Then you can describe what happened that night?"

"In detail," said Kyle. "Would that satisfy you that the rest of what I've said is the truth?"

Krakovitch slowly nodded.

"They came out of the night and the falling snow," Kyle began. "Zombies, men dead for four hundred years, and Harry their leader. Bullets couldn't stop them, for they were already dead. Cut them down with machine-gun fire, and the bits kept right on coming. They got into your defensive positions, your pillboxes. They pulled the pins on grenades, fought with their old rusty weapons, their swords and axes. They were Tartars, fearless, and made more fearless by the fact that they couldn't die twice. Keogh wasn't just a telepath; amongst his other talents, he could also tele*port!* He did—right into Dragosani's control room. He took a couple of his Tartars with him. That was where he and Dragosani had it out, while in the rest of the Château—"

"—In the rest of the Château," Krakovitch took up the story, his face deathly white, "it was . . . *hell!* I was there. I lived through it. A few others with me. The rest died—horribly! Keogh was . . . some kind of monster. He could call up the dead!"

"Not as big a monster as Dragosani," said Kyle. "But you were going to tell me what happened after Keogh died. How you finished off the job he started. What did you mean by that?"

"Dragosani was a vampire," Krakovitch nodded, almost to himself. "Yes, you are right, of course." He got a grip on himself. "Look, Sergei here was with me when we clean up what was left of Dragosani. Let me show you what happen when I remind him about that—and when I tell to him there are more of them." He turned to his silent companion, spoke to him rapidly in Russian.

They were sitting at a scruffy bar lit by flickering neon in the airport's almost deserted night arrivals lounge. The barman had gone off duty two hours earlier and their glasses had stood empty ever since. Gulharov's reaction to what Krakovitch told him was immediate and vehement. He went white and drew back from his boss, almost falling from his barstool. And as Krakovitch finished speaking, so he slammed his empty beer glass down on the bar.

"Nyet, *nyet*!" he gasped his denial, his face working with a strange mixture of fury and loathing. And then, his voice gradually rising and growing shrill, he began a diatribe in Russian which would soon attract attention.

Krakovitch gripped his arm and shook him, and Gulharov's jabbering faded into silence. "Now I ask him if we accepting your help," Krakovitch informed. He spoke to the younger man again, and this time Gulharov nodded twice, rapidly, and his color began to return to normal.

"Da, da!" he gasped emphatically. His throat made a dry rattle as he added something else, unintelligible to the two Englishmen.

Krakovitch smiled humourlessly. "He says we should accept all the help we can get," he translated. "Because we have to kill these things—*finish* them! And I agreeing with him . . ." Then he told these strangest of allies all that had happened at the Château Bronnitsy after Harry Keogh's war.

When he'd finished there was a long silence, broken at last by Quint. "We're in agreement, then? That we'll act together on this?"

Krakovitch nodded. He shrugged, said simply, "No alternative. And no time to waste."

Quint turned to Kyle. "But how do we go about it?"

"As far as possible," Kyle answered, "we go the straightforward way. We get it all right up front, without any of the usual—" The airport tannoy broke in on him, echoing tinnily as some sleepy, unseen announcer requested in English that a Mr. A. Kyle please take a telephone call at the reception desk.

Krakovitch's face froze. Who would know that Kyle was here?

Kyle stood up, shrugged apologetically. This was very embarrassing. It could only be "Brown," and how to explain that to Krakovitch? Quint, on the other hand, was his usual ready-for-anything self. Calmly he said to Krakovitch, "Well, you have your little bloodhound following you about. And now it would seem that we have one too."

Krakovitch gave a curt, sour nod. And with an edge of sarcasm, echoing Kyle, he said, "Without any of the usual, eh? Did you know about this?"

"It's none of our doing," Quint wasn't exactly truthful. "We're in the same boat as you."

On Krakovitch's orders, Gulharov accompanied Kyle to the reception-cum-enquiries desk, leaving Quint and Krakovitch alone together. "Maybe this is all in our favour," said Quint.

"Eh?" Krakovitch had turned sour again. "We are followed, spied upon, overheard, bugged, and you say is favourable?"

"I meant you and Kyle both having shadows," Quint explained. "It evens things up. And maybe we can cancel out one with the other."

Krakovitch was alarmed. "I not being party to violence! Anything happen to that KGB dog, is possible I get the troubles."

"But if we could arrange for him to be, er, detained for

a day or two? I mean, unharmed, you understand—completely unharmed—just detained . . . ?''

"I not know . . ."

"To give you time to clear our route into Romania. You know, visas, etcetera? With a bit of luck we'll be finished there in just a day or two."

Krakovitch slowly nodded. "Maybe—but positive guarantee, no dirty work. He is KGB—*you* say—but if true, then he's Russian too. And I am Russian. If he vanish . . ."

Quint shook his head, grasped the other's thin elbow. "They *both* vanish!" he said. "But only for a few days. Then we'll be out of here and getting on with the job."

Again Krakovitch gave his slow nod. "Maybe—if it can be arranged safely."

Kyle and Gulharov returned. Kyle was careful. "That was somebody called Brown," he said. "He's been watching us, apparently." He looked at Krakovitch. "He says your KGB tail has traced us and is on his way here. By the way, this KGB fellow is well known—his name is Theo Dolgikh."

Krakovitch shook his head, shrugged, looked mystified. "I never heard of him."

"Did you get Brown's number?" Quint was eager. "I mean can we contact him again?"

Kyle raised his eyebrows. "Actually, yes," he nodded. "He said that if things were getting sticky, he might be able to help. Why do you ask?"

Quint grinned tightly, said to Krakovitch, "Comrade, it might be a good idea if you were to listen carefully. Since you're a little concerned about this, you can start working on an alibi. For from this point forward you're hand in hand with the enemy. Your only consolation is that you'll be working against a greater enemy." The grin left his face, and deadly serious he said, "OK, here's what I suggest . . ."

*　　*　　*

On Saturday morning at 8:30 Kyle phoned Krakovitch at his and Gulharov's hotel. The latter answered the call, grunted, fetched Krakovitch who came grumbling to the phone. He was just out of bed, could Kyle call later? While this brief show was going on, downstairs in the Genovese's lobby, Quint was talking to Brown. At 9:15 Kyle phoned Krakovitch again and arranged a second meeting: they would meet outside Frankie's Franchise in an hour's time and go on from there.

There was nothing new in this arrangement; it was part of the plan worked out the night before: Kyle suspected that the phone in his room was now bugged and he simply wanted to give Theo Dolgikh plenty of advance notice. If Kyle's phone wasn't bugged, then Krakovitch's surely was, which could only work out the same way. Anyway, the psychic sixth senses of both Kyle and Quint were playing up a little, which told them that something was brewing.

Sure enough, when they left the Genovese just before 10:00 A.M. and headed for the docks, they had a tail. Dolgikh was keeping well back, but it could only be him. Kyle and Quint had to admire his tenacity, for despite his rough night he was still very much the master-spy; now his attire was that of the shipyard worker, dark-blue coveralls and a heavy bag of tools, and the blue-black stubble of twenty-four hours' growth on his round, intense face.

"He must have a hell of a wardrobe, this lad," said Kyle as he and Quint approached the narrow, still slumbering streets of Genoa's dockland. "I'd hate to have to carry his luggage!"

Quint shook his head. "No," he answered, "I shouldn't think so. They'll probably have a safe house here and there's bound to be one of their ships in the harbor. Whichever, when he requires a change of clothing, they'll be the ones who'll fix it for him."

Kyle squinted at him out of the corner of his eye. "You

know," he said. "I'm sure you'd have been better off in MI5. You have a bent for it."

"It might make an interesting hobby." Quint grinned. "Mundane spying, that is—but I'm happy where I am. The real talent's with INTESP. Now if our man Dolgikh were an esper, then we could be in real trouble."

Kyle gave his companion a sharp glance, then relaxed. "But he isn't or we'd have spotted him without Brown's assistance. No, he's simply one of their surveillance types, and pretty good at his job. I've been thinking of him as something big, but this is probably the biggest assignment he's ever had."

"Which," Quint grimly added, "with any luck, is just about to terminate a mite ingloriously. But I wouldn't be too sure he's small fry, if I were you. After all, he was big enough to show up on Brown's firm's computer."

Carl Quint was right: Theo Dolgikh was not small fry, not in any sense of the word. Indeed, it was a measure of Yuri Andropov's "respect" for the Soviet E-Branch that he'd put Dolgikh on the job. For Leonid Brezhnev would likely give Andropov a hard time if Krakovitch were to report to him that the KGB were interfering again.

Dolgikh was in his early thirties, a native Siberian bred of a long line of Komsomol lumberjacks. He was the complete communist for whom little else existed but Party and State. He had trained, and later done some teaching in Berlin, Bulgaria, Palestine and Libya. He was an expert in weapons (especially Western Bloc weapons), also in terrorism, sabotage, interrogation and surveillance; as well as Russian, he could speak a broken Italian, decent German and English. But his real forte—indeed his *penchant*—lay in the field of murder. For Theo Dolgikh was a cold-blooded killer.

Because of his compressed build, Dolgikh might seem at a distance short and stubby. In fact he was five-ten and weighed in at almost sixteen stone. Heavy-boned, heavy-jowled under a moon face that supported a mop of uneven jet-black hair, Dolgikh was "heavy" in all departments. His Japanese instructor at the KGB School of Martial Arts in Moscow used to say:

"Comrade, you are too heavy for this game. Because of your bulk, you lack speed and agility. Sumo wrestling would be more your style. On the other hand, very little of your weight is fat, and muscle is most useful. Since teaching you the disciplines of self-defence is probably a great waste of time, I shall therefore concentrate my instruction on ways of killing, for which I am assured you are not only physically but mentally best suited."

Now, closing in on his quarry as they entered the winding, labyrinthine streets and alleys close to the docks, Dolgikh felt his blood rising and wished this were that sort of job. After last night's runaround he could happily murder this pair! And it would be so easy. They seemed utterly obsessed with this most seamy side of the city.

Thirty yards ahead of him, Kyle and Quint made a sudden sharp turn in a cobbled alley where the buildings loomed high, shutting out the light. Dolgikh put on a little speed, arrived at the alley's entrance, passed from gray drizzle into a steamy gloom where the refuse of four or five days stood uncollected. In many places overhead the opposing buildings were arched over. Following a frantic Friday night, this district wasn't even awake yet. If Dolgikh had been after the lives of these two, this would have been the place to do it.

Footsteps echoed back to him. The Russian agent narrowed small round eyes to gaze through the gloom of the alley at a pair of shadowy figures as they rounded a bend. He paused for a second, then started after them. But, sensing movement close by, a silent presence, he at once skidded to a halt.

From the shadows of a recessed doorway a gravelly voice said, "Hello, Theo. You don't know me, but I know you!"

Dolgikh's Japanese instructor had been right: he wasn't fast enough. At times like this his bulk got in the way. Gritting his teeth in anticipation of the dull smack of the suspected cosh and its pain, or maybe the blue glint of a silencer on the end of a gun barrel, he whirled towards the voice in the darkness, hurled his heavy bag of tools. A tall, shadowy figure caught the bag full in the chest, grunted, and lobbed it aside to clatter on the cobbles. Dolgikh's eyes were getting used to the gloom. It was still dark, but he'd seen no sign of a weapon. This was just the way he liked it.

Head down, like a human torpedo, he hurled himself into the doorway's shadows.

"Mr. Brown" hit him twice, two expertly delivered blows, not calculated to kill but simply stun. And to be doubly sure, before Dolgikh could fall, Brown slammed the Russian's head into the stout panels of the door, splintering one of them.

A moment later he stepped out of the shadows into the alley, glanced this way and that, satisfied himself that all was well. Just the drip of rain and the stinking vapours from the garbage. And now there was this extra heap of garbage. Brown grinned hugely, toed Dolgikh's crumpled figure.

That was always the way of it with big men: they tended to assume that they were the biggest, the toughest. But that wasn't always the case. Brown was about the same weight as Dolgikh, but he was three inches taller and five years younger. Ex-SAS, his training had been none too gentle. In fact, if he hadn't developed something of a kink in his mental make-up, he'd probably still be with the SAS.

He grinned again, then hunched his shoulders and shrank down into his raincoat. Hands thrust deep into his pockets, he hurried to fetch his car . . .

Chapter Eight

THAT SAME SATURDAY AT NOON, YULIAN BODESCU DECIDED he'd had enough of his "uncle" George Lake. Rather, he decided that the time had come to use Lake in his search for knowledge. His specific aim was simple: he desired to know how a vampire could be killed, how one of the undead might be made more surely dead—forever, never to return—and in this way learn how best to protect himself from any such demise.

They could die by fire, certainly, he knew that much already. But what about the other methods? Those methods specified in the so-called "fictions." George would provide the ideal test material. Better far than the Other, which was more a dull tumour than a healthy intelligence.

When a vampire comes back from the dead, the thought suddenly struck Yulian, *he comes back stronger!*

He had put something into Georgina, Anne and Helen, something of himself. But he had not killed them. Now they were his. George he had killed, or at least caused to die, and George was not his. He obeyed him, yes, or had

193

until now. But for how much longer? Now that George was over the initial shock, he was growing strong. And hungry!

Twice during the night, striving restlessly for sleep, Yulian had sprung awake feeling oppressed, menaced. And twice he had sensed Lake's skulking, furtive movements down in the cellars. The man prowled down there in the darkness, his body aching, thoughts seething. And a monstrous thirst was on him.

He had taken from the woman, from the veins of his own wife, but her blood had not been much to his taste. Oh, blood is blood—it would sustain him—but it was not the blood he craved. That blood flowed only in Yulian. And Yulian knew it. Which was the other reason he had determined to kill George. He would kill him before he himself was killed (for sooner or later George would certainly try it), and before George could drain Anne; oh yes, for if not there'd soon be two of them to deal with! It was like a plague, and Yulian thrilled to the thought that he was the source, the carrier.

And then there was a third reason why Lake must die. Somewhere out there—in the sunlight, in the woods and fields, lanes and villages—somewhere there were people who watched the house even now. Yulian's senses, his vampire powers, were weaker by day, but still he could feel the presence of the silent watchers. They *were* there, and he feared them. A little.

That man last night, for instance. Yulian had sent Vlad to fetch him, but Vlad had failed. Who had he been, that man? And why did he watch? Perhaps George's return had not gone entirely unnoticed. Was it possible that someone had seen him emerge from his grave? No, Yulian doubted that; the police, in their innocence, would have mentioned it. Or then again, perhaps the police had not been satisfied with his reaction that day they came here with their report of vile grave-robbing.

And George with his bloodlust: what if he should break

out one night? He was a vampire now, George, and grow-ing stronger. How long could Vlad contain him? No, better far if George died. Gone without a trace, leaving no shred of evidence, no jot of proof of the evil at work here. He would die a vampire's death this time, from which there'd be no returning.

At the back of the house a great stone chimney rose from earth to sky, buttressed at the bottom and flaring up through the gable end. Its source was a huge iron furnace in the cellars, a relic of older generations. Though the house was centrally heated now, a heap of dusty coke still lay in the furnace room down there, nesting place for mice and spiders. Twice, when the winters had been especially cold, Yulian had stoked up the fire and watched the iron flue glow red where its fat cylindrical conduit joined the furnace to the chimney's firebrick base. It had served to heat the back of the house admirably. Now he would go down there and sweat a little and fire the thing up again, albeit for a different purpose. But his sweat would be well worth the effort.

There was a trapdoor under one of the back rooms which, since George had been down there, Yulian had kept boarded up. That left only the entrance from the side of the house, where Vlad kept his vigil as usual. Yulian took a steak, thick and dripping blood, from the kitchen out to the dog where he guarded the cellars, left him growling and tearing at his food while he descended the narrow steps down one side of the ramp and shoved open the door.

Then, as he stepped into darkness . . . he had maybe a half-second's warning of what was waiting for him, but it was enough.

George Lake's mind was a bubbling pit of crimson hatred. Many emotions were trapped in there, controlled until that last half-second: lust, self-loathing, a hunger beyond human hunger, which was so intense it was in fact an emotion, disgust, jealousy so strong it burned, but mainly hatred. For Yulian. And in the moment before George struck, the bile of his mind touched Yulian's like acid, so that he cried out as he avoided the blow in the dark.

For darkness had been Yulian's element long before George discovered it, a fact which the new, half-mad vampire had failed to take into account. Yulian saw him crouching behind the door, saw the arc of the mattock as it swung towards him. He ducked under the rushing, rusty, vicious head of the tool, came up inside the circle of its swing and closed fingers like steel on George's throat. At the same time, with his free hand, he wrenched the mattock away from him and hurled it aside, and drove his knee again and again up into George's groin.

For any ordinary man the fight would have been over there and then, but George Lake was no longer ordinary, and no longer merely a man. Forced to his knees as Yulian's fingers tightened on his throat, he glared back at the youth through eyes like coals under a bellows' blast. A vampire, his grey undead flesh shrugged off the pain, found strength to fight back. His legs straightened against all Yulian's weight, and he smashed at Yulian's forearm to break his grip. Astonished, the youth found himself tossed back, saw the other springing at him to tear his throat out.

And again Yulian knew fear, for he saw now that his "uncle" was almost as strong as he himself. He feinted before George's charge, thrust him sprawling, snatched up the mattock from the stone floor. He hefted the tool murderously in his powerful hands, advancing on George where he came surging to his feet. At which moment Anne— Yulian's dear "Auntie" Anne—came ghosting and gibbering out of the shadows and the darkness to throw herself between Yulian and her undead husband.

"Oh, Yulian!" she wailed. "Yulian, no. Please don't kill him. Not . . . *again!*" Naked and grimy she crouched there, her eyes full of animal pleading, her hair wild.

Yulian thrust her aside just as George made his second spring.

"George," he grated through clenched teeth, "that's twice you've gone for me with this. Now let's see how you like it!"

Flakes of rust splintered from the sharp point of the mattock as it slammed into George's forehead and punched a neat hole one and a half inches square just above the triangle formed of eyes and nose. The sheer force of the blow checked George's forward impetus, snapping him upright like a puppet on a string.

"Gak!" he said, as his eyes filled with blood and his nose spurted crimson. His arms rose up at forty-five degrees, his hands fluttering as if he'd been plugged into a live electric socket. "Gug-ak-arghh!" he gurgled. Then his bottom jaw fell open and he toppled backwards like a felled tree, crashing to the floor on his back, mattock still fixed firmly in his head.

Anne came scrambling, threw herself down wailing on top of George's twitching body. She was in thrall to Yulian but George had been her husband. What he had become was Yulian's fault, not his own. "George, oh George!" she wailed. "Oh, my poor dear George!"

"Get off him!" Yulian spat at her. "Help me."

They dragged George by his ankles to the furnace room, the mattock's handle clattering on the uneven floor. In front of the cold furnace, Yulian put a foot on the vampire's throat and wrenched the mattock free of his head. Blood and greyish-yellow pulp welled up to fill the crater in his forehead and overflow the rim, but his eyes stayed open, his hands continued to flutter, and one heel thumped the floor in a continuous series of galvanic spasms..

"Oh, he'll die, he'll die!" Anne wrung her grimy hands, sobbed and cradled George's shattered head.

"No he won't." Yulian worked to get the furnace going. "That's just it, you stupid creature. He can't die—not like that, anyway. What's in him will heal him. It's working on his crushed brain even now. He could be good as new, maybe even better—except that's something I can't allow.''

The fire was set. Yulian struck a match, held it to paper, opened the iron draught grid squealingly so that the flames would draw, and closed the furnace door. As he turned from the furnace, he heard Anne gasp: "George?"

The hammering of George's spastic heel on the stone floor had been absent for some little time . . .

Yulian spun on his heel—and the *Thing* he had made crashed into him and forced him back against the furnace door! As of yet there was no heat, but the wind was driven from Yulian's lungs in a huge gasp. He drew air painfully, held the other at bay. George's feral eyes glared through blood and mucus from the hole in his head; his teeth, like small daggers, chomped in his twisted face; his hands flopped against Yulian like blind things. His ruptured brain was functioning, barely, but already the vampire in him was mending his wound. And his hatred was as strong as ever.

Yulian gathered his strength, hurled George from him. Unable to control the impaired functions of his limbs, he crashed down on to the pile of coke. Before he could rise again Yulian glared all about in the gloom, moved to take up the mattock.

"Yulian! Yulian!" Anne went to intercede.

"Get *out* of my way!" He thrust her aside.

Ignoring George where he crawled after him, hooked hands reaching, he loped to the arched entrance where the stone walls were massively thick. And there without pause he swung the shaft of the mattock against the stonework. The hardwood shaft broke, splintering diagonally across its grain, and the rusty head went clattering into darkness. Yulian's hands were left numb where they clutched a near-perfect stake: eighteen inches of hardwood, narrowing down to an uneven but deadly sharp point.

Well, and it had been his intention to discover the full range of a vampire's vitality, hadn't it?

George had somehow managed to lurch to his feet. Eyes sulphurous in the near-darkness, he came after Yulian like some demoniac robot.

Yulian glanced at the floor. Here there were thick stone paving slabs, pushed up a little in places by some force from below. The Other, of course, in its mindless burrowing. George was closer, stumbling spastically, mouthing thick, phlegmy noises unrecognizable as words. Yulian waited until the crippled vampire took another lurching pace towards him, then stepped forward and slammed the stake into George's chest slightly left of centre.

The hardwood point ripped through George's linen burial shift and grated between his ribs, shedding splinters as it went. It skewered his heart and almost severed it. George gasped like a speared fish, fumbled at the stake with useless hands. There was no way he was going to pull it out. Yulian watched him staggering there—watched in disbelief, astonishment, almost in admiration—and wondered: *would it be this hard for someone to kill me?* He supposed it would. After all, George had tried hard enough.

Then he kicked George's jelly legs out from under him and went in search of the broken mattock head. A moment later and he returned, and still George squirmed and gagged and wrestled with the stake in his chest. Yulian grabbed one of his twitching legs, dragged him to a spot where black soil showed between the broken jointing of displaced flags. He got down on his knees beside him, used the mattock head as a hammer to drive the stake right through him and into the floor. Finally, jammed between two of the flags, the stake would go no further. George was pinned like some exotic beetle on a board. Only two or three inches of the stake stood up from his chest, but there was little blood to be seen. His eyes were still open, wide as doors, and there was white froth on his lips, but no more movement in him.

Yulian stood up, wiped his hands down his trousers, went in search of Anne. He found her crouching in a dark corner, whimpering and shivering, looking for all the world like a discarded doll. He dragged her to the furnace room and pointed to a shovel. "Stoke that fire," he ordered. "I want it hotter than hell, and if you don't know now how hot hell is, I'm the one to show you! I want that flue glowing red. And whatever else you do, don't go near George. Leave him completely alone. Do you understand?"

She nodded, whimpered, shrank back away from him. "I'll be back," he told her, leaving her there by the furnace, which was now just beginning to roar.

On his way out, Yulian spoke to Vlad. "Stay, watch." Then he went back into the house. Upstairs, passing his mother's room, he heard her moving. He looked in. Georgina was pacing the floor wringing her hands and sobbing. She saw him.

"Yulian?" Her voice was a tremor. "Oh, Yulian, what's to become of you? And what's to become of me?"

"What *was* to become *has* become," he answered coldly, unemotionally. "Can I still trust you, Georgina?"

"I . . . I don't know if I trust myself," she eventually answered.

"Mother,"—he used the term without thinking—"do you want to be like George?"

"Oh, God! Yulian, please don't say . . ."

"Because if you do," he stopped her, "it can be arranged. Just remember that."

He left her and went to his own room. Helen heard him coming. She gasped at the sound of his quiet, even footfalls and threw herself on his bed. As he came in through the door she lifted her dress up to display the lower half of her body. She was naked under the dress. He saw her, the way her face worked: trying to smile through a mask of white terror. It was as if someone had thrown powdered chalk on the face of a clown.

"Cover yourself, slut!" he said.

"I thought you liked me like this!" she cried. "Oh, Yulian, don't punish me. Please don't hurt me!" She

watched him stride to a chest of drawers, take out a key
and unlock the top drawer. When he turned towards her he
was grinning his sick grin, and in his hands he weighed a
shining new cleaver. The thing had a seven inch blade and
was heavy as a small axe.

"Yulian!" Helen gasped, her mouth dry as sawdust. She
slid off the bed and shrank away from him, "Yulian, I—"

He shook his head, laughing a weird, bubbling laugh.
Then his face turned blank again. "No," he told her, "it's
not for you. You're safe as long as you're . . . *useful* to
me. And you are useful. I'd have to pay a lot to find one
as sweet and fresh as you. And even then—like all women—
she wouldn't be worth it." He walked out and closed the
door noiselessly behind him.

Downstairs, as he left the house again, Yulian noticed
the column of blue smoke rising from the chimney stack at
the back. He smiled to himself and nodded. Anne was
working hard down there. But even as he studied the
smoke, the fluffy September clouds parted a little and the
sun struck through. Struck bright, hot, searing!

The smile twisted on Yulian's face, became a snarl. He
had left his hat indoors. Even so, the sun shouldn't burn
like this. His flesh almost felt scalded! And yet, looking at
his naked forearms, he could see no blisters, no burns.

He guessed what it must mean: the change had speeded
up in him and his final metamorphosis was beginning.
Then, shrinking from the sun, gritting his teeth to keep
from crying out as the pain increased, he hurried back to
the cellars.

Down below Anne worked at the furnace. Her breasts
and buttocks were shiny with sweat and streaked with
grime. Yulian looked at her and marvelled that this had
been "a lady." As he approached, she dropped the shovel,
backing away from him. He carefully put down his cleaver,
so as not to dull its edge in any way, and advanced on her.
The sight of her like this—wild and naked, hot and per-
spiring and full of fear—had triggered his lust.

He took her on the heaped coke, filled her with himself, with the vampire thing in him, until she cried out her immeasurable horror—her unthinkable pleasure?—as his alien protoflesh surged within her . . .

Finished at last, he left her sprawling exhausted and battered on the coke and went to inspect George.

He found the Other inspecting him, too. Up from the gaps between strained flags, protoplasmic flesh had crept in doughy flaps and tendrils, binding George Lake to the floor as the Other examined him. There was no real curiosity in the thing, no hatred, no fear (except maybe an instinctive fear of even the slightest degree of light) but there was hunger. Even the amoeba, which "knows" very little, knows enough to eat. And if Yulian had not returned when he did, certainly the Other would have devoured George, absorbed him. For there was little denying that he was food.

Yulian scowled at the Other's flaccid, groping pseudopods, its quivering mouths and vacuous eyes. *No!* He sent out the sharp thought, like a drill on the creature's nerveendings. *Leave him! Begone!* And whatever else it failed to understand, definitely the Other understood Yulian.

As if seared by a blowtorch, the pseudopods and other anomalies lashed, retracted, disappeared with squelching sounds below. It took only a second or two; but this had been only part of the Other. Yulian wondered how big it had grown now, just how *much* of it filled the compacted earth under the house . . .

Yulian took his cleaver and got down beside George. He placed his hand on his midriff just under the stump of stake. Something at once moved convulsively in him. Yulian sensed it coiling itself like a prodded caterpillar. George might look dead, should *be* dead, but he wasn't. He was undead. The thing that lived in him—that which had been Yulian's, but grown now and controller of George's mind and body—merely waited. The stake alone had not been enough. But that came as no real surprise, Yulian had not been especially sure that it would be.

He took up his cleaver and wiped the shining blade on his rolled shirt sleeve. And the yellow eyes in George's grey, mutilated face moved in their blood-rimmed orbits to follow his movements. Not only was the vampire's body in George's body, but its mind was in his mind, grafted to it like a feasting leech. Good!

Yulian struck. He struck rapidly, three times: hard, chopping blows that bit into George's neck and cut through flesh and bone with perfect ease. In another moment his head rolled free.

Yulian gripped the severed head by its hair and stared into the core of the neck stump. Something green- and grey-mottled drew itself out of sight into fibrous mucus. Nothing Yulian could see looked like it should. The man-part of this thing was a mere envelope of flesh, a shell or disguise to protect the creature within. Likewise the body: when Yulian propped up the headless trunk with his knee, a sinuous something slipped quickly down into the bloody pipe of George's yawning gullet.

Perhaps in two parts the vampire would eventually die, but it was not dead yet. Which left only one sure way, one tried and true means of disposal. Fire.

Yulian kicked the head in the direction of the furnace. It rolled past Anne where she lay exhausted, barely conscious in her extremity of terror. She had seen all that Yulian had done. The head came up against the foot of the furnace, rebounded a little way and stopped. Yulian dragged the body to the furnace and threw open the door. Inside, all was an orange and yellow shimmer. Heat blasted out; a shaft of heat roared up into the flue.

Without pause Yulian picked up the head and threw it into the furnace, as far to the back as he could get it. Then he propped up George's body against the open door, and levered him shoulders first into the inferno. Last to go in were the legs and feet, which already were starting to kick.

Yulian needed all his strength to control the thrashing limbs until he at last got them up over the rim of the door and slammed it shut. The door at once banged open, impelled by a raw, steaming foot. Again Yulian thrust the member inside and slammed the door, and this time he shot the bolt. For long seconds, in addition to the roaring of the fire, there came thumping vibrations from within.

In a little while, however, the noises subsided. Then there was only a long, sustained hissing. Finally only the fire's roar could be heard. Yulian stood there for long moments with his own private thoughts, before finally turning away . . .

By 11:00 P.M. that same Saturday, Alec Kyle and Carl Quint, Felix Krakovitch and Sergei Gulharov were on a scheduled Alitalia night flight for Bucharest, which would arrive just after midnight.

Of the four, Krakovitch had spent the busiest day, arranging all the paraphernalia of entry into a Soviet satellite for the two Englishmen. He had done this the easy way: by phoning his Second in Command at the Château Bronnitsy—one Ivan Gerenko, a rarely talented "deflector"—and getting him to pass the details on to his high-powered go-between on Brezhnev's staff. He had also asked that it be arranged for him to have maximum assistance, if he should require it, from the USSR's "comrades" in puppet Romania. They were still an insular lot, the Romanians, and one could never be absolutely sure of their co-operation. . . . Thus Krakovitch's afternoon was taken up in making and answering calls between Genoa and Moscow, until all arrangements were in hand.

Not once through all of this did he mention the name of Theo Dolgikh. Ordinarily he would have taken his complaint to the very top—to Brezhnev himself, as the Party Leader had ordered—but not in the present circumstances. Krakovitch had only Kyle's word that Dolgikh was temporarily and not permanently detained. As long as he remained ostensibly in ignorance of the KGB agent and his affairs, then all would be well. And if indeed Dolgikh were safe and merely, for the moment, "secure" . . . time enough later to bring charges of interference against Yuri Andropov. Krakovitch did marvel, though, that the KGB had got on to his supposedly secret mission to Italy so quickly. It made one wonder: were E-Branch officials under KGB surveillance *all* of the time?

As for Alex Kyle: he too had made an international call, to the Duty Officer at INTESP. That had been later in the afternoon, when it had looked fairly certain that he and Quint would be accompanying the two Russians to Romania. "Is that Grieve? How are things going, John?" he asked.

"Alec?" the answer came back. "I've been expecting you to give us a ring." John Grieve had two talents; one of them "dodgy," branch parlance for an as yet undeveloped ESP ability, and the other quite remarkable and possibly unique. The first was the gift of far-seeing: he was a human crystal ball. The only trouble was he must know exactly where and what he was looking for, otherwise he could see nothing. His talent didn't work at random but must be directed: he must have a definite target.

His second string made him doubly valuable. It could well prove to be a different facet of his first talent, but on occasions like this it was a godsend. Grieve was a telepath, but one with a difference. Yet again he must "aim" his talent: he could only read a person's mind when he was face to face with that person, or when talking to him— even on the telephone, if he knew the person in question. There was no lying to John Grieve, nor any need for a mechanical scrambler. That was why Kyle had left him on permanent duty at HQ while he was away.

"John," said Kyle, "how are things are home?" And he also asked: *What's happening down on the ranch, in Devon?*

"Oh, well, you know . . ." Grieve's answer sounded iffy.

"Can you explain?" *What's up? But careful how you answer.*

"Well, see, it's young YB," came back the answer. "It seems he's cleverer than we allowed. I mean, he's inquisitive, you know? Sees and hears too much for his own good."

"Well we must give him credit for it," Kyle tried to sound casual while, in his head, he added urgently: *You mean he's talented? Telepathy?*

"I suppose so," answered Grieve, meaning probably.

Jesus Christ! Is he on to us? "Anyway, we've had tough customers before," said Kyle. "And our salesmen are in possession of the full brief . . ." *How are they armed?*

"Well, yes, they have the standard kit," said Grieve. "Still, it's a bit leery, I'll tell you! Set his dog on one of our blokes! No harm done, though. As it happens it was old DC—and you know how wary *he* is! No harm will come to that one."

Darcy Clarke? Thank God! Kyle breathed more easily. Out loud he said, "Look, John, you'd better read my file on our silent partner. You know, from eight months ago?" *The first Keogh manifestation.* "Our blokes might well need all the help they can get. And I really don't think that in this case standard kit is sufficient. It's something I should have thought of before, except I didn't anticipate young YB's foxiness." *9mm automatics might not stop him—or any of the others in that house. But there's a description in the Harry Keogh file of something that will—I think. Get the squad armed with crossbows!*

"Just as you say, Alec, I'll look into it at once," said Grieve, no sign of surprise in his voice. "And how are things with you?"

"Oh, not bad. We're thinking of moving up into the mountains—tonight, actually." *We're off to Romania with*

Krakovitch. He's OK—I hope! As soon as I've got any-thing definite I'll get back to you. Then maybe you'll be able to move in on Bodescu. But not until we know all there is to know about what we're up against.

"Lucky you!" said Grieve. "The mountains, eh? Beau-tiful at this time of year. Ah, well, some of us must work. Do drop me a card, now, won't you? And do take care."

"Same goes for you," Kyle spoke light and easy, but his thoughts were sharp with concern. *For God's sake make sure those lads down in Devon are on the ball! If anything were to happen, I—*

"—Oh, we'll do our best to keep out of trouble," Grieve cut him off. It was his way of saying, "Look, we can only do as much as we can do."

"OK, I'll be in touch." *Good luck.* And then he had broken the connection . . .

For a long time he'd stood in his room looking at the telephone and chewing his lip. Things were warming up and Alec Kyle knew it. And when Quint came in from the room next door where he'd been taking a nap . . . one look at his face told Kyle that he was right. Quint looked rough round the edges, suddenly more than a little haggard.

He tapped his temple. "Things are starting to jump," he said. "In here."

Kyle nodded. "I know," he answered. "I've a feeling they're starting to jump all over the place. . . ."

In his tiny room in what had once been Harry Keogh's Hartlepool flat, whose window looked out over a grave-yard, Harry Junior was falling asleep. His mother, Brenda Keogh, shushed the baby and lulled him with soft hum-ming sounds. He was only five weeks old, but he was clever. There were lots of things happening in the world, and he wanted in on them. He was going to make very hard work of growing up, because he wanted to be there now. She could feel it in him; his mind was like a sponge, soaking up new sensations, new impressions, thirsting to know, gazing out of his father's eyes and striving to envelop the whole wide world.

Oh, yes, this could only be Harry Keogh's baby, and Brenda was glad she'd had him. If only she could still have Harry, too. But in a way she did have him, right here in little Harry. In fact she had him in a bigger way than she might ever have suspected.

Just what the baby's father's work had been with British Intelligence (she assumed it was them) Brenda didn't know. She only knew that he had paid for it with his life. There had been no recognition of his sacrifice, not officially, anyway. But cheques arrived every month in plain envelopes, with brief little covering notes that specified the money as "widow's benefit." Brenda never failed to be surprised: they must have thought very highly of Harry. The cheques were rather large, twice as much as she could ever have earned in any mundane sort of work. And that was wonderful, for she could give all of her time to Harry.

"Poor little Harry," she crooned at him in her soft northern dialect, an old, old ditty she'd learned from her own mother, who'd probably learned it from hers. "Got no Mammy, got no Daddy, born in a coal hole."

Well, not quite as bad as all that, but bad enough, without Harry. And yet . . . occasionally Brenda felt pangs of guilt. It was less than nine months since she'd last seen him, and already she was over it. It all seemed so wrong, somehow. Wrong that she no longer cried, wrong that she never had cried a great deal, entirely wrong that he had gone to join that great majority who so loved him. The dead, long fallen into decay and dissolution.

Not necessarily morally wrong, but wrong conceptually, definitely. She didn't *feel* that he was dead. Perhaps if she'd seen his body it would be different. But she was glad that she hadn't seen it. Dead, it wouldn't have been Harry at all.

Enough of morbid thinking! She touched the baby's tiny button nose with the knuckle of her index finger. "Bonk!"

she said, but very, very softly. For little Harry Keogh was asleep . . .

Harry felt the infant's whirlpool suction ebb, felt the tiny mind relax its constraint, aimed himself into and through a trans-dimensional "door" and found himself adrift once more in the Ultimate Darkness of the Möbius continuum. Pure mind, he floated in the flux of the metaphysical, free of the distortions of mass and gravity, heat and cold. He revelled like a swimmer in that great black ocean which stretched from never to forever and nowhere to everywhere, where he could move into the past no less rapidly than into the future.

Harry could go any and everywhere—and everywhen—from here. It was simply a matter of knowing the right direction, of using the right "door." He opened a time-door and saw the blue light of all Earth's living billions streaming into unimagined, ever-expanding futures. No, not that one. Harry selected another door. This time the myriad blue life-threads streamed away from him and contracted, narrowing down to a far-distant, dazzling, single blue point. It was the door to time past, to the very beginning of human life on Earth. And that wasn't what he wanted either. Actually, he had known that neither of these doors was the right one; he was simply exercising his talents, his powers, that was all.

For the fact was that if he didn't have a mission . . . but he did have one. It was almost identical with the mission which had cost him his corporeal life, and it was still unfinished. Harry put all other thoughts and considerations aside, used his unerring intuition to point himself in the right direction, calling out to that one he knew he would find there.

"Thibor?" His call raced out into the black void. "Only answer me and I'll find you, and we can talk."

A moment passed. A second or a million years, it was

all the same in the Möbius continuum. And it made no difference at all to the dead. Then:

Ahhhh! came back the answer. *Is it you, Haarrry?*

The mental voice of the old Thing in the ground was his beacon: he homed in on it, came up against a Möbius door, and passed through it.

. . . It was midnight on the cruciform hills, and for two hundred miles in every direction, most of Romania lay asleep. No requirement for Harry and his infant simulacrum to materialize here, for there was no one to see them. But knowing that he *could* be seen there, if there were eyes to see, gave Harry a feeling of corporeality. Even as a will-o'-the-wisp he would feel that he was somebody, not merely a telepathic voice, a ghost. He hovered in the glade of stirless trees, above the tumbled slabs and close to the tottering entrance of what had been Thibor Ferenczy's tomb, and formed about his focus the merest nimbus of light. Then he turned his mind outwards, to the night and the darkness.

If he had had a body, Harry might have shivered a little. He would have felt a chill, but a purely physical chill and not one of the spirit. For the undead evil which had been buried here five hundred years ago was gone now, was no longer undead but truly dead. Which fact begged the question: had *all* of it been removed? Was it dead . . . entirely? For Harry Keogh had learned, and was learning still, of the vampire's monstrous tenacity as it clung to life.

"Thibor," said Harry, "I'm here. Against the advice of all the teeming dead, I've come again to talk to you."

Ahhhh! Haaarrry—you are a comfort, my friend. Indeed, you are my only comfort. The dead whisper in their graves, talking of this and that, but me they shun. I alone am truly . . . alone! Without you there is only oblivion . . .

Truly alone? Harry doubted it. His sensitive ESP warned him that something else was here—something that held back, biding its time—something dangerous still. But he hid his suspicions from Thibor.

"I made you a promise," he said. "You tell me the things I want to know, and I in turn will not forget you. Even if it's only for a moment or two, I'll find time now and then to come and talk to you."

Because you are good, Haaarrry. Because you are kind. While my own sort, the dead, they are unkind. They continue to hold this grudge!

Harry knew the old Thing in the ground's wiles: how he would avoid at all cost the issue of the moment, Harry's principal purpose in being here. For vampires are Satan's own kith and kin; they speak with his tongue, which speaks only lies and deceptions. Thus Thibor would attempt from the outset to turn the conversation, this time to his "unfair" treatment by the Great Majority. Harry would have none of it.

"You have no complaint," he told him. "They know you, Thibor. How many lives have you cut short in order to prolong or sustain your own? They are unforgiving, the dead, for they've lost that which was most precious to them. In your time you were the great stealer of life; not only did you bring death with you, but even on occasion undeath. You can't be surprised that they shun you."

Thibor sighed. *A soldier kills,* he answered. *But when he in turn dies, do they turn away from him? Of course not! He is welcomed into the fold. The executioner kills, also the maniac in his rage, and the cuckold when he discovers another in his bed. And are they shunned? Perhaps in life, some of them, but not after life is done. For then they move on into a new state. In my life I did what I had to do, and I paid for it in death. Must I go on paying?*

"Do you want me to plead your case for you?" Harry wasn't even half-serious.

But Thibor was quick-witted: *I had not considered that. But now that you mention it—*

"Ridiculous!" Harry cried. "You're playing with words—playing with me—and that's not why I'm here. There are a million others who genuinely desire to talk to me, and I waste my time with you. Ah, well, I've learned my lesson. I'll trouble you no more.''

Harry, wait! Panic was in Thibor Ferenczy's voice, which came to Harry quite literally from beyond the grave. *Don't go, Harry! Who will talk to me if . . . there* is *no other necroscope!*

"That's a fact you'd do well to keep in mind.''

Ahhh! Don't threaten me, Harry. What am I—what was I—after all, but an old creature entombed before his time? If I have seemed to be difficult, forgive me. Come now, tell me what it is that you want from me?

Harry allowed himself to be mollified. "Very well. It's this: I found your story very interesting.''

My story?

"Your tale of how you came to be what you were. As I recall it, you had reached that stage where Faethor had trapped you in his dungeon, and transferred or deposited in you—''

—His egg! Thibor cut him off. *The pearly seed of the Wamphyri! Your memory serves you well, Harry Keogh. And so does mine. Too well . . .* His voice was suddenly sour.

"You don't wish to continue with that story?''

I wish I had never started it! But if that is what it takes to keep you here . . . Harry said nothing, simply waited, and after a moment or two:

I see that is what it takes, the ex-vampire groaned. *Very well.*

And after a further sullen silence, Thibor continued the telling of his story . . .

Picture it, then, that strange old castle up in the mountains: its walls wreathed in mist, its central span arching over the gorge, its towers reaching like fangs for the rising moon. And picture its master: a creature who was once a man, but no longer. A Thing which called itself Faethor Ferenczy.

I have told how he . . . how he kissed me. Ah, but no son was ever kissed by his father like *that* before! He lodged his egg in me, oh yes! And if I had thought that the bruises and gouges of battle were painful . . .

To receive the seed of a vampire is to know an almost fatal agony. *Almost* fatal, but never quite. No, for the vampire chooses his egg-bearer with great care and cunning. He must be strong, that poor unfortunate; he must be keen-witted, preferably cold and callous. And I admit it, I was all of those things. Having lived a life like mine, how could I be otherwise?

And so I experienced the horror of that egg in me, which fashioned tiny pseudopods and barbs of its own to drag itself down my throat and into my body. Swift? The thing was quicksilver! Indeed, it was more than quicksilver! A vampire seed can pass through human flesh like water through sand. Faethor had not needed to terrify me with his kiss, he had simply *desired* to terrify me! And he had succeeded.

His egg passed through my flesh, from the back of my throat to the column of my spine, which it explored as a curious mouse explores a cavity in the wall—but on feet that burned like acid! And with each touch on my naked nerve endings came fresh waves of agony!

Ah! How I writhed and jerked and tossed in my chains then. But not for long. Finally the thing found a resting place. Newborn, it was easily tired. I think it settled in my bowels, which instantly knotted, causing me such pain that I cried out for the mercy of death! But then the barbs were withdrawn, the thing slept.

The agony went out of me in a moment, so swiftly indeed that the sensation was a sort of agony in itself. Then, in the sheer luxury of painlessness, I too slept . . .

When I awoke I found myself free of all manacles and chains, lying crumpled on the floor. There was no more pain. Despite my thinking that my cell should be in darkness, I found that I could see as clearly as in brightest daylight. At first I failed to understand; I sought in vain for the hole which let in the light, tried to climb the uneven walls in search of some hidden window or other outlet. To no avail.

Before that, however, before this futile attempt of mine to escape, I was confronted by the *others* who shared my dismal cell. Or by what they had become.

First there was old Arvos, who lay in a heap just as Faethor had left him—or so I thought. I went to him, observed his grey flesh, his withered chest beneath the rags of his torn, coarse shirt. And I laid my hand upon him there, perhaps in an attempt to detect the warmth of life or even a faltering heartbeat. For I had thought I saw a certain fluttering in his bony chest.

No sooner was my hand upon him than the gypsy caved in! All of him, collapsing inwards like a husk, like last year's leaves when stepped upon! Beneath the cage of ribs, which also powdered away, there was nothing. The face likewise crumbled into dust, set free by the body's avalanche; that old, grey, unlovely countenance, smoking into ruin! Limbs were last to go, deflating even as I crouched there, like ruptured wineskins! In the merest moment he was a heap of dust and small shards of bone and old leather; and all still clad in his coarse native clothes.

Fascinated, jaw lolling, I continued to stare at what had been Arvos. I remembered that worm of a finger coming loose from Faethor's hand and going into him. And was that worm responsible for this? Had that small fleshy part of Faethor eaten him away so utterly? If so, what of the worm itself? Where was it now?

My questions were answered on the instant: "Consumed, Thibor, aye," said a dull, echoing voice. "Gone to feed the one which now burrows in the earth at your feet!" Out from the dungeon's shadows stepped an old Wallach comrade of mine, a man all chest and arms, with short stumpy legs. Ehrig had been this one's name—when he was a man!

For looking at him now, I saw nothing in him that was known to me. He was like a stranger with a strange aura about him. Or maybe not so strange, for indeed I thought I knew that emanation. It was the morbid presence of the Ferenczy. Ehrig was now his!

"Traitor!" I told him, scowling. "The old Ferenczy saved your life, and now in gratitude you've given that life to him. And how many times, in how many battles, have I saved your life, Ehrig?"

"I long since lost count, Thibor," the other huskily answered, his eyes round as saucers in a gaunt, hollow face. "Enough that you must know I would never willingly turn against you."

"What? Are you saying you are still my man?" I laughed, however scathingly. "But I can *smell* the Ferenczy on you! Or perhaps you've *un*willingly turned against me, eh?" And still more harshly I added, "Why should the Ferenczy save you, eh, except to serve him?"

"Didn't he explain anything to you?" Ehrig came closer. "He didn't save me for himself. I'm to serve you—as best I may—after he departs this place."

"The Ferenczy is mad!" I accused. "He has beguiled you, can't you see? Have you forgotten why we came here? We came to kill him! But look at you now: gaunt, dazed, puny as an infant. How may one such as you serve me?"

Ehrig stepped closer still. His great eyes were very nearly vacant, unblinking. Nerves in his face and neck jumped and twitched as if they were on strings. "Puny? You misjudge the Ferenczy's powers, Thibor. What he put in me healed my flesh and bones. Aye, and it made me strong. I can serve you as well as ever, be sure. Only try me."

Now I frowned, shook my head in a sudden amaze. Certain of his words made sense, went some little way towards cooling my furious thoughts. "By now, by rights, you should indeed be dead," I agreed. "Your bones were

broken, aye, and your flesh torn. Are you saying that the
Ferenczy is truly the master of such powers? I remember
now he said that when you recovered you would be in
thrall to him. But to *him,* d'you hear? So how is it that you
stand here and tell me I am still your lord and leader?''

"He *is* the master of many powers, Thibor," he answered. "And indeed I am in thrall to him—to a point. He
is a vampire, and now I too am a vampire of sorts. And so
are you . . .''

"I?" I was outraged. "I am my own man! He did
something to me, granted—put that which was of himself
into me, which was surely poisonous—but here I stand
unchanged. You, Ehrig, my once friend and follower, may
well have succumbed, but I remain Thibor of Wallachia!''

Ehrig touched my elbow and I drew back from him.
"With me the change was swift," he said. "It was made
faster through the Ferenczy's flesh mingling with my own,
which worked to heal me. My broken parts were mended
with his flesh, and just as he has bound me together, so
has he bound me to himself. I will do his bidding, that is
true; mercifully, he demands nothing of me but that I stay
here with you.''

Meanwhile, while he spoke in his mournful fashion, I
had prowled all about the dungeon looking for an escape,
even attempted to scale the walls. "The light," I muttered. "Where does it come from? If the light finds its way
in, I can find my way out.''

"There is no light, Thibor," said Ehrig, following
behind me, his voice doleful as ever. "It is proof of the
Ferenczy's magic. Because we are his, we share his powers.
In here all is utter darkness. But like the bat of your
standard, and like the Ferenczy himself, you now see in
the night. More, you are the special one. You bear his
egg. You will become as great as, perhaps greater than the
Ferenczy himself. You are Wamphyri!''

"*I am myself!*'' I raged. And I grabbed Ehrig by the
throat.

And now as I drew him close, I noticed for the first time the yellow glow in his eyes. They were the eyes of an animal; mine, too, if he spoke the truth. Ehrig made no effort to resist me; indeed, he went to his knees as I applied greater pressure. "Well then," I cried, "why don't you fight back? Show me this wonderful strength of yours! You said I should try you, and now I take you at your word. You're going to die, Ehrig. Aye, and after you, so too your new master—the very moment he sticks his dog's nose into this dungeon! I at least have not forgotten my reason for being here."

I grabbed up a length of the chain which had bound me to the wall and looped it round his neck. He choked, gagged; his tongue lolled out; still he made no effort to resist me. "Useless, Thibor," he gasped, when I relaxed the pressure a little. "All useless. Choke me, suffocate me, break my back. I will mend. You may not kill me. You *cannot* kill me! Only the Ferenczy can do that. A fine jest, eh? For we came here to kill him!"

I tossed him aside, ran to the great oak door, raged and hammered at it. Only echoes came back to me. In desperation I turned again to Ehrig. "So then," I panted, "you are aware of the change taken place in you. Of course, for if it's plain to me it must be plainer still to you. Very well, but tell me: why then am I the same as before? I feel no different. Surely no great change is wrought in me?"

Ehrig, rubbing his throat, came easily to his feet. He had great bruises on his neck from the chains; other than this it seemed he suffered no ill effects from my manhandling; his eyes burned as before and his voice was doleful as ever. "As you say," he said, "the change in me has been wrought, as iron is wrought in the furnace. The Ferenczy's flesh has taken hold of me and bent me to its will, as iron bends in the fire's heat. But with you it is different, more subtle. The vampire's seed grows within you. It grafts itself to your mind, your heart, your very blood. You are like two creatures in one skin, but slowly you will meld, fuse into one.''

This was what Faethor had told me. I sagged against the damp wall. ''Then my destiny is no longer my own,'' I groaned.

''But it is, Thibor, it is!'' Ehrig was eager now. ''Why, now that death no longer holds any terrors, you can live forever! You have the chance to grow more powerful than any man before you! And what is that for destiny?''

I shook my head. ''Powerful? In thrall to the Ferenczy? Surely you mean powerless! For if I'm to be his man, then how may I be my own? No, that shall not be the way of it. While yet I have my will, I shall find a way.'' I prodded my chest and grimaced. ''How long before . . . before this thing within commands me? How much time do I have before the guest overpowers the host?''

Slowly, sadly I thought, he shook his head. ''You insist on making difficulties,'' he said. ''The Ferenczy told me it would be so. Because you are wild and wilful, he said. You *will be* your own man, Thibor! It shall be like this: that the thing within cannot exist without you, nor you without it. But where before you were merely a man, with a man's frailties and puny passions, now you shall be—''

''Hold!'' I told him, my memory suddenly whispering monstrous things in my mind. ''He told me . . . he said . . . that he was sexless! He said: 'The Wamphyri have no sex as such.' And you talk to me of my 'puny passions'?''

''As one of the Wamphyri,'' Ehrig patiently insisted, as doubtless the Ferenczy had ordered him to insist, ''you will have the sex of the host. And you *are* that host! You will also have your lust, your great strength and cunning— all of your passions—but magnified many times over! Picture yourself pitting your wits against your enemies, or boundlessly strong in battle, or utterly untiring in bed!''

My emotions raged within me. Ah! But could I be sure they were mine? Entirely mine? ''But—it—will—not— be—*me!*'' Emphasizing each word, I slammed my balled fist again and again into the stone wall, until blood flowed freely from my riven knuckles.

"But it *will* be you," he repeated, drawing near, staring at my bloodied hand and licking his lips. "Aye, hot blood and all. The vampire in you will heal that in a very little while. But, until then, let me tend to it." He took my hand and tried to lick the salt blood.

I hurled him away. "Keep your vampire's tongue to yourself!" I cried.

And with a sudden thrill of horror, perhaps for the first time, I began to truly understand what he had become. And what I was becoming. For I had seen that look of entirely unnatural lust on his face, and I had suddenly remembered that once there were three of us . . .

I looked all around the dungeon, into all of the corners and cobwebbed shadows, and my changeling eyes penetrated even the darkest gloom. I looked everywhere and failed to discover what I sought. Then I turned back to Ehrig. He saw my expression, began to back away from me. "Ehrig," I said, following, closing with him. "Now tell me, pray—what has become of the poor mutilated body of Vasily? Where, pray, is the corpse of our former colleague, the slender, ever aggressive . . . Vasily?"

In a corner, Ehrig had tripped on something. He stumbled, fell—amidst a small pile of bones flensed almost white. Human bones.

After long moments I found voice. "Vasily?"

Ehrig nodded, shrank back from me, scuttling like a crab on the floor. "The Ferenczy, he . . . he has not fed us!" he pleaded.

I let my head slump, turned away in disgust. Ehrig scrambled to his feet, carefully approached. "Keep well away," I warned him, my voice low and filled with loathing. "Why did you not *break* the bones, for their marrow?"

"Ah, no!" said Ehrig, as if explaining to a child. "The Ferenczy told me to leave Vasily's bones for . . . for the burrower in the earth, that which took shape in old Arvos and consumed him. It will come for them when all is quiet. When we are asleep . . .''

"Sleep?" I barked, turning on him. "You think I'll sleep? Here? With you in the same cell?"

He turned away, shoulders slumping. "Ah, you are the proud one, Thibor. As I was proud. It goes before a fall, they say. Your time is still to come. As for me, I will not harm you. Even if I dared, if my hunger was such that . . . but I would not dare. The Ferenczy would cut me into small pieces and burn each one with fire. That is his threat. Anyway, I love you as a brother."

"As you loved Vasily?" I scowled at him where he gazed at me over his hunched shoulder. He had no answer. "Leave me in peace," I growled then. "I have much to think about."

I went to one corner, Ehrig to another. There we sat in silence.

Hours passed. Finally I did sleep. In my dreams—for the most part unremembered, perhaps mercifully—I seemed to hear strange slitherings, and sucking sounds. Also a period of brittle crunching.

When I awakened, Vasily's bones had disappeared . . .

Chapter Nine

THE VOICE OF THE EXTINCT VAMPIRE FADED IN HARRY KEOGH'S incorporeal mind. For long moments nothing further was said, and they were empty seconds which Harry couldn't really afford. At any moment he could find himself recalled by his infant son, back through the maze of the Möbius continuum to the garret flat in Hartlepool. But if Harry's time was important, so too was the rest of mankind's.

"I begin to feel sorry for you, Thibor," he said, his life-force burning blue as a neon firefly in the dark glade under the trees. "I can see how you fought against it, how you did not want to become what you eventually became."

Eventually? the old Thing in the ground spoke up at last. *No eventually about it, Harry—I had become! From the moment Faethor's seed embraced my body, my brain, I was doomed. For from that moment it was growing in me, and growing quickly. First its effect became apparent in my emotions, my passions. I say "apparent," but scarcely so to me. Can you feel your body healing after a cut or a*

221

*blow? Are you aware of your hair or fingernails growing?
Does a man who gradually becomes insane* know *that he
is going mad?*

Suddenly, as the voice of the vampire faded again, there
came a rising babble in Harry's mind. A cry of frustration,
of fury! He had expected it sooner or later, for he knew
that Thibor Ferenczy was not alone here in the dark cruciform hills. And now a new voice formed words in the
necroscope's consciousness, a voice he recognized of old.

You old liar! You old devil! cried the inflamed spark, the
enraged spirit of Boris Dragosani. *Ah! And how is this for
irony? Not enough that I am dead, but to have for companion in my grave that one creature I loathed above all
others! And worse, to know that my greatest enemy in
life—the man who killed me—is now the only living man
who can ever reach me in death! Ha, ha! And to be here,
knowing once more the voices of these two—the one demand-
ing, the other wheedling, beguiling, seeking to lie as
always—and knowing the futility of it all; but yet yearn-
ing, burning to be . . . involved! Oh, God, if ever there
were a God, won't—somebody—speak—to—meeeee?!*

Pay no attention, said Thibor at once. *He raves. For, as
you well know, Harry, since you were instrumental, when
he killed me he killed himself. The thought is enough to
unhinge anyone, and poor Boris was half-mad to begin
with . . .*

I was made mad! Dragosani howled. *By a filthy, lying,
loathsome leech of a thing in the ground! Do you know
what he did to me, Harry Keogh?*

"I know of several things he did to you," Harry answered. "Mental and physical torture seems an unending
activity for creatures of your sort, alive or dead. Or undead!"

You are right, Harry! A third voice from beyond the
grave now spoke up. It was a soft, whispering voice, but
not without a certain sinister inflection. *They are cruel
beyond words, and none of them is to be trusted! I assisted
Dragosani; I was his friend; it was my finger which trig-*

gered the bolt that struck Thibor through the heart and pinned him there, half-in, half-out of his grave. Why, I was the one who handed Dragosani the scythe to cut off the monster's head! And how did he pay me, eh? Ah, Dragosani! How can you talk of lies and treachery and loathsomeness, when you yourself—

You—were—a—monster! Dragosani silenced Max Batu's accusations with one of his own. *My excuse is simple: I had Thibor's vampire seed in me. But what of you, Max? What? A man so evil he could kill with a glance?*

Batu, a Mongol esper who in life had held the secret of the Evil Eye, was outraged. *Now hear this great liar, this thief!* he hissed sibilantly. *He slit my throat, drained my blood, despoiled my corpse and tore from it my secret. He took my power for his own, to kill as I killed. Hah! Little good it did him. Now we share the same gloomy hillside. Aye, Thibor, Dragosani, and myself, and all three of us shunned by the teeming dead . . .*

"Listen to me, all of you," said Harry, before they could start again. "So you've all suffered injustices, eh? Well, maybe you have, but none so great as those you've worked. How many men did you kill with your Evil Eye, Max, stopping them dead in their tracks and crumpling their hearts like paper? And were they all bad men? Did they deserve to die? As horribly as that? No, for one at least was my friend, as good a man as you could ever wish to meet."

The head of your British E-Branch? Batu was quick off the mark. *But Dragosani ordered me to kill him!*

It was our mission!. Dragosani railed. *Don't play the innocent here, Mongol. You'd killed others before him.*

He also ordered Ladislau Giresci killed, said Batu. *One of his own countrymen, and entirely innocent! Ah, but Giresci knew Dragosani's secret—that he was a vampire!*

He was a danger to . . . to the State! Dragosani blustered. *I worked only for Mother Russia, and—*

"You worked only for yourself!" Harry stopped him.

"The truth is, you desired to be a power in the land. No, in the whole world! Lie if you must, Dragosani, for it's a trait of vampires, after all, but not to yourself. I've spoken to Gregor Borowitz, remember? And did he too die for Mother Russia? The head of your own E-branch?"

There you have it, Dragosani, said Thibor, his voice a dark chuckle. *Caught on your own barbs!*

"Don't crow, Thibor," Harry's voice was lower still. "You were as bad and probably worse than both of them."

I? Why, I have—or I had—lain here in the earth for five hundred years! What harm can a poor thing in the ground do, alone with the worms in the cold hard earth?

"And what of the five hundred years before that?" said Harry. "You know as well as I that Wallachia trembled to your tread for centuries! The earth itself is soaked black with the blood you spilled. And don't lay it all at Faethor Ferenczy's feet. He's not entirely to blame. He knew what you were, else he wouldn't have chosen you . . ."

And is that why you've come? Thibor asked after a moment. *To harangue and accuse and denounce?*

"No, I came to learn," said Harry. "Now look, I can't lie as well as you do. I was never much of a liar at the best of times. So I'm sure you'd see through me if I tried any sort of subterfuge. That's why I'll come straight out with it . . ."

Well then? said Dragosani. *Out with it, if you will.*

Harry ignored him, was silent for a few seconds. "Thibor," he said at last, "a moment ago you asked what harm you'd done, buried here these last five hundred years."

I can tell you what harm he did! Dragosani would not be ignored. *Only look at me! I was an innocent child and he taught me the arts of necromancy. Later, as a youth, he beguiled me with his hypnotism and his lies. As a man he put his vampire egg in me, and when it had matured, he—*

"Your history concerns me not at all!" Harry stopped him. "Neither that nor any calumny of charges you bring against Thibor or anyone else."

Calumny? Dragosani was furious.

"Be quiet!" Harry's patience had broken. "Be quiet now, or I leave you at once, immediately, to wait out all the ages in your loneliness. All three of you."

There was a sullen silence.

"Very well," said Harry. "Now, as I was saying, I'm not greatly concerned with Thibor's crimes or supposed crimes against you, Boris Dragosani. No, but I am concerned to know about what he did to another. I refer to a woman, Georgina Bodescu, who came here with her husband one winter. There was an accident and the man died.He died here, on this very spot. She was pregnant and fainted at the sight of his blood. And afterwards . . ."

Ah? said Thibor, his interest quickening. *But I've already told you that story. Are you telling me now that . . . are you saying it took effect?*

Beware, Harry Keogh! Dragosani interrupted. *Tell him no more. I heard the tale, too, when the old liar told it to you. If that unborn child as was is now a man, he'll be in thrall to Thibor! Aye, even though his master's dead! Can't you see? This devil would see himself alive again—in the body and mind of this new disciple!*

You . . . dog! Thibor howled. *You are Wamphyri! Does that mean nothing to you? We may fight among ourselves, but we do not divulge our secrets to others! You are damned for all time, Dragosani!*

Old fool, I'm that already! Dragosani snarled.

"Very well then," Harry sighed. "I can see I'm wasting precious time. That being the case, I'll bid you—"

Wait! Thibor's voice was all burning anguish. *You can't tell me just so much and leave it at that. That's . . . inhuman!*

"Hah!" Harry snorted.

A trade, then. I shall finish my story, and you shall tell me if the child was born and lives. And . . . how he lives. Agreed?

Harry guessed he'd said too much already, which in

itself might be as good a reason as any for going on. There were now four principal things he must try to discover. One: the full range of a vampire's powers. Two: how, exactly, Thibor might try to use Yulian Bodescu. For Dragosani seemed to think it was possible for Thibor to resurrect himself, in Bodescu. Three: the rest of Thibor's story concerning the occurrences a thousand years ago at the castle of Faethor Ferenczy, so that he might know if anything of evil yet remained in that place. And four: how to kill a vampire, but definitely!

As to the last: Harry had *thought* he knew that much eight months ago, when he'd waged war on the Château Bronnitsy. But looking back now he saw that Dragosani's death had only come about through a fortunate combination of events. For one thing Dragosani had been blinded: his eyes had been ruined by a reflected mind-bolt when Max Batu's stolen talent had rebounded on him from one of Harry's zombies; for of course Harry had had his zombie Tartars, his shock troops, for back-up in that affray. It had been one of them, called up from the preserving peat, who'd hacked Dragosani's head from his shoulders; and another who'd pinned his parasite vampire to his chest with a wooden stake when it deserted his shattered body. Harry couldn't have done all of these things, maybe not any of them, on his own. In fact, Harry's only real ace had been his mastery of the Möbius continuum: when he'd been very nearly cut in half by machinegun fire, he'd fled his dying body and dragged Dragosani's mind in there with him. In the Möbius continuum he'd hurled Dragosani through a past-time door, which had led the necromancer back to Thibor in his grave. And there an "earlier" Dragosani had lured up and killed Thibor, never dreaming that with the same stroke he had also determined his own fate. As for Harry's incorporeal mind: he'd gone forward, found his son's life-thread and joined with it, lay with it in the womb of Brenda waiting to be born. She had been his lover, his wife, and now, in a way, might even be considered his mother. His second mother.

But what if he had left Dragosani's mind in his corpse back at the Château? How long would that broken body have *stayed* a corpse? That was conjectural . . .

And Harry wondered: how had the surviving Russian E-Branch members dealt with what remained when all the fighting stopped? What had they made of his zombies? It must have seemed utter madness, an absolute nightmare! Harry supposed that after he left the Château along the Möbius way, the Tartars had fallen once more into quiescence . . .

Perhaps by now Alec Kyle had the answers to these questions, learned from Felix Krakovitch. Harry would find out eventually, but for now there were fresh problems. Foremost among them: how much dare he tell Thibor about Yulian Bodescu? Very little, he supposed. But, on the other hand, by now the extinct vampire had probably guessed all of it for himself. Which made any continued secrecy pointless.

"Very well," said Harry, finally, "we trade."

Fool! Dragosani cut in at once. *I had given you some credit, Harry Keogh—I thought you were cleverer than that. And yet here you are attempting to bargain with the devil himself! I see now that I was unlucky in our little contest. You are as big a fool as I was!*

Harry ignored him. "The rest of your story then, Thibor, and quickly. For I don't know how much time I have . . ."

The first time the old Ferenczy came, I was not ready for him. I was asleep; but exhausted, half-starved, it's unlikely I could have done anything anyway. The first I knew of his visit was when I heard the heavy oaken door slam, and a bar was dropped into place outside. Four trussed chickens, alive, full-feathered, squawked and fluttered in a basket just inside the door. As I roused myself and went to the door, Ehrig was a pace ahead of me.

I caught him by the shoulder, threw him aside, got to the basket first. "What's this, Faethor?" I cried. "Chickens? I thought we vampires supped on richer meat!"

"We sup on blood!" he called back, chuckling a little beyond the door. "On coarse meat if and when we must, but the blood is the true life. The fowl are for you, Thibor. Tear out their throats and drink well. Squeeze them dry. Give the carcasses to Ehrig, if it please you, and what's left goes to your 'cousin' under the flags."

I heard him starting up stone steps, called out: "Faethor, when do I take up my duties? Or perhaps you've changed your mind and deem it too dangerous to let me out?"

His footsteps paused. "I'll let you out when I'm ready," his muffled voice came back. "And when *you* are ready . . ." He chuckled again, but more deeply in his throat this time.

"Ready? I'm ready for better treatment than this!" I told him. "You should have brought me a girl. You can do more with a girl than just eat her!"

For a moment there was silence, then he said, "When you are your own master you may take what you like." His voice was colder. "But I am not some mother cat to fetch fat mice for her kittens. A girl, a boy, a goat—blood is blood, Thibor. As for lust: you'll have time for that later, when you understand the real meaning of the word. For now . . . save your strength." And then he moved on.

Ehrig had meanwhile taken hold of the basket, was sidling off with it. I gave him a clout which knocked him protesting to the floor. Then I looked at the terrified birds and scowled. But . . . I was hungry and meat is meat. I had never been a squeamish one, and these birds were plump. And anyway, the vampire in me was taking the edge off all points of mannered custom and nicety and civilized behaviour. As for civilization: what was that to me? A Wallach warrior, I had always been two-thirds barbarian!

I ate, and so did the dog Ehrig. Aye, and later, when next we slept, so did my "cousin" . . .

The next time I came awake—more strongly, surging awake, refreshed from my meal—I saw the Thing, that mindless being of vampire flesh which hid in the dark earth under the floor. I do not know what I had expected. Faethor had mentioned vines, creepers in the earth. That is what it was like. Partly, anyway.

If you have seen a squashy octopus from the sea, then you have seen something like the creature spawned of the finger which Faethor shed, fattened on the flesh of Arvos the gypsy. The one thing I cannot comment upon was its size; however, if a man's body were flattened to a doughy mass . . . it would spread a long way. The matter of Arvos had been reshaped.

Certainly the groping "hands" which the being put up were stretchy things. There were also many of them, and they were not lacking in strength. Its eyes were *very* strange: they formed and unformed, came and went; they ogled and blinked; but in all truth I cannot say that they saw. Indeed, I had the feeling they were blind. Or perhaps they saw in the way a newborn infant sees, without understanding.

When one of the thing's hands came up from the soil close to where I lay, I cursed out loud and kicked it away—and how it shot down out of sight then! How well another might fare I could not say, but the vampire thing was certainly wary of me. Perhaps it sensed that I was a higher form—of itself! I remember how at the time, that was a very shuddersome thought . . .

Faethor had this way with him: he was devious, sly as a fox, slippery as an eel. That was how I considered him, feelings brought on by sheer frustration. Of course he was that way: he was of the Wamphyri! I should not have expected him to be any other way. But quite simply, he would not be ambushed. I spent hours waiting for him behind the oak door, chains in my hands, hardly daring to breathe lest he hear me. But let hell freeze over, he would not come. Ah! But only let me fall asleep . . . a squealing piglet would wake me, or the fluttering of a tethered pigeon. And so the days, probably weeks, passed . . .

I will give him his due: after that first time the old devil didn't let me get too hungry. I think to myself now that the initial period of starvation was to let the vampire in me take hold. It had nothing else to feed on and so must rely on my stored fats, must become more fully a part of me. Similarly, I was obliged to draw on its strength. But as soon as the bond was properly formed, then Faethor could begin to fatten us up again. And I use that phrase advisedly.

Along with the food, there would be the occasional jug of red wine. At first, remembering how the Ferenczy had drugged me, I was careful. I would let Ehrig drink first, then watch for his reaction. But apart from a loosening of his tongue, there was nothing. And so I too drank. Later I would give Ehrig none of the wine but consume it myself. That, too, was exactly the way the old devil had planned it.

Came the time when, after a meal, I was thirsty and quaffed a jug at one swig—then staggered this way and that before collapsing. Poisoned again! Faethor had made a fool of me at every turn. But this time my vampire strength buoyed me up; I held fast to my consciousness, and sprawling there in my fever I wondered: now what is the purpose of this? *Hah!* Only listen, and I'll explain Faethor's purpose.

"A girl, a boy, a goat—blood is blood," he'd told me that time. "The blood is the life." Indeed, but what he had *not* told me was this: that of all pulses of delight, of all founts of immortality, of all nectar-bearing flowers, that one source from which a vampire would most prefer to sip is the throbbing red rush of another vampire's blood! And so, when I had succumbed more fully to his wine, then Faethor came to me again.

"Two purposes are served here," he told me, crouching over me. "One: it is long and long since I took from one of my own, and a great thirst is on me. Two: you are a hard one and will not submit to thraldom without a fight. So be it, this should take all of the sting out of you."

"What . . . what are you doing?" I croaked the question, tried to will my leaden arms to rise up and fend him off. It was useless; I was weak as a kitten; even my throat found the greatest difficulty simply forming words.

"Doing? Why, I sit me down to my evening meal!" he answered, gleefully. "And such a menu! Blood of a strong man—spiced with the blood of the fledgling vampire within him!"

"You . . . you'll drink from . . . from *my* throat?" I stared up at him aghast, my vision swimming.

He merely smiled—but a smile hideous as any I ever saw him make—and tore my clothes. Then he put his terrible tapering hands on me and felt my flesh all over, frowning a little as he searched for something. He turned me on my side, touched my spine, pressed it again, harder, and said, "Ah! The very gobbet, the prize itself!"

I would have cringed away from him but could not. Inside I cringed—perhaps that child of his within me cringed, too—but externally my skin merely shivered. I tried to speak, but that also had grown too difficult. My lips only trembled and I made a moaning sound.

"Thibor," the old devil said, his voice level as if in polite conversation, "you've much to learn, my son. About me, about yourself, about the Wamphyri. You are not yet aware, you fail to perceive all the mysteries I have bestowed upon you. But what I am, you shall be. And the powers I possess, they too shall be yours. You have seen and learned a little, now see and experience more!"

He continued to balance me on my side, but propped up my head a little so that I could see his face. His magnetic eyes held me, a fish, speared on their pupils. My blurred sight cleared; the picture sharpened; I saw more clearly than ever before. My body and limbs might well be made of lead, but my mind was sharp as a knife, my awareness so keen that I could almost *feel* the change taking place in the creature who leaned over me. Faethor had somehow, for some reason, heightened my perceptions, increased my sensitivity.

"Now watch," he hissed. "Observe!"

The skin of Faethor's face, large-pored and grainy at best, underwent a swift metamorphosis. Watching it I thought: *I have never known what he looks like. And even now I won't know. He is how he wants me to see him!*

The pores of his face opened up more yet, pockmarks cratering his flesh. His jaws, enormous already, elongated with a sound like gradually tearing cloth, and his leathery lips rolled back until his mouth was all bulging, crimson gums and jagged, dripping teeth. I had seen Faethor's teeth before, but never displayed like this. Nor was the metamorphosis complete.

It was all in the jaws, in the teeth, in the nightmarish contours of the face. Faethor already resembled a great bat—or perhaps a wolf, or both—but now it rapidly grew into more than a resemblance. He was not a bat, neither bat nor wolf, but a creature somewhere between; and Faethor the man was only the shell, like the chrysalis covering some monstrous grub. Except that now the chrysalis had cracked wide open.

His teeth were like slender, crooked icebergs grinding together in the red ocean of his raw gums. His mouth bled, flesh erupting as those terrible teeth sprouted, cutting upwards like serrated knives from jawbones that broke through torn flesh to form gaping ridges of glistening gristle like a bony beartrap. Looking into that maw, which dwarfed the rest of his face, I knew he could close it on *my* face and strip my flesh to the bone. But that wasn't his purpose.

Yellow eyes burning above the flattened, convoluted ridges of his flaring nostrils, he laughed a gurgling laugh as his upper eye-teeth elongated more yet, like bloody tusks emerging to almost overshoot his great lower jaw. A sabretooth, now Faethor was finally ready. Before he toppled me facedown, I saw that his incredible fangs were hollow at their tips—siphons for my blood!

Paralyzed, I could do nothing. Not even scream. The worst of it was that I could no longer see him! But I felt his knowing hands examining my back, felt the suddenly fearful squirming of something inside, something Faethor had discovered clamped to my spine. Aye, and then I felt the monster's great teeth punching through my flesh like hammered nails, pinning my immature parasite where it writhed in its own agony. But its agony was mine and mine was its, and neither one of us could bear it. Faethor had made me more sensitive in order that I might know the most exquisite pain! And damn his rotten heart, how I knew it! Darkness came down on me.

Then, for a long time, I knew no more.

For which, as you might suppose, I was not unthankful . . .

At first, when I regained consciousness, I thought that I was alone. But then I heard Ehrig whimpering in a shadowed corner—heard him and remembered. I remembered the comradeship we'd shared, all the bloody battles we'd been through together. Remembered how he had been my true friend, who would gladly lay down his life for me—and I mine for him.

Perhaps he remembered, too, and that was why he whimpered. I did not know. I only knew that when the Ferenczy had fastened his teeth in my spine, Ehrig was nowhere to be seen . . .

To say that I beat him would not do his punishment justice, but without Faethor's vampire stuff in him he would certainly have died. It could be that I consciously tried to kill him; I can't say about that, either, for the episode is no longer clear in my mind. I only know that when I was done with him he no longer felt my blows, and that I myself was completely exhausted. But he healed, of course, and so did I. And I conceived a new strategy.

After that . . . there were times of sleeping, of waking, of eating. Outwardly, life consisted of little more. But for me these were also times of waiting, and of patient, silent scheming. As for the Ferenczy: he tried to train me like a wild dog.

It started like this: he would come silently to the door and listen. Strangely, I knew when he was there. I would feel fear! And when I became afraid, then he would be there. At times I could feel him groping at the edges of my mind, slyly attempting to insinuate himself into my very thoughts. I remembered how he had communicated with old Arvos over a distance and did what I could to close my mind to him. I think I succeeded greatly, for after that I could sense a frustration other than my own.

He used a system of rewards: if I was "good" and obeyed him, there would be food. He would call through the door: "Thibor, I have a pair of fine piglets here!"

If I answered: "Aha! Your parents have come visiting!" he would simply take the food away. But if I said: "Faethor, my father, I am starving! Feed me, pray, for if not then I shall be obliged to eat this dog you've locked in with me down here. And who will serve me then, when you are out in the world and I am left in charge of your lands and castle?" Then he would open the door a crack and place the food inside. But only let me stand too close to the door and I would see neither Faethor nor food for three or four days.

And so I "weakened"; I grew less and less abusive; I began to plead. For food, for the freedom of the castle, for fresh air and light, and water to bathe myself—but most of all for separation, however brief, from Ehrig whom I now detested as a man detests his own wastes. Moreover, I made out that I was growing physically weaker. I spent more time "asleep", and came less readily awake.

Finally came the time when Ehrig could not wake me, and how the dog battered on the door and screamed for his true master then! Faethor came; they carried me up, up to the battlements above the covered hall where it spanned the gorge. There they laid me down in the clean air under the first stars of night, pale spectres in a sky I had not seen for far too long. The sun was a dull blister on the hills, casting its last rays over the spires of rock behind the castle's towers.

"He is likely starved for air," said Faethor, "and maybe simply starved a little, too! But you are right, Ehrig—he seems weaker than he should be. I desired only to break his will a little, not the man himself. I have powders and salts that sting, which should stir him up. Wait here and I'll fetch them. And watch him!"

He descended through a trapdoor out of sight, leaving Ehrig to hunch down to his vigil. All of this I saw through eyes three-quarters shuttered. But the moment Ehrig allowed his attention to wander I was on him in a trice! Closing off his windpipe with one hand, I snatched from my pocket a leather thong which I'd earlier removed from my boot. I had intended it for the Ferenczy's neck, but no matter. Wrapping my legs round Ehrig to stop him kicking, I looped the thong round his neck and yanked it tight, then made a second loop and tied it off. Choking, he tried to lurch to his feet, but I slammed his head so hard against the stone parapet that I felt his skull shatter. He went limp and I lowered him to the timbered floor.

At that moment my back was to the trapdoor, and of course that was when the Ferenczy chose to return. Hissing his fury, he came leaping up light as a youth—but his hands were iron on me where he took hold of my hair and grasped the flesh between my neck and shoulder. Ah, but strong though he was, old Faethor was out of practice! And my own fighting skills were as fresh in my mind as my last battle with the Pechenegi.

I kneed him in the groin and drove my head up under his great jaw so hard that I heard his teeth crunching. He released me, fell to the planking where I leaped astride him; but as his fury waxed, so waxed his strength. Calling on the vampire within, he tossed me aside as easily as a

bale of straw! And in a moment he was on his feet,
spitting shattered teeth, blood and curses as he came glid-
ing after me.

I knew then that I couldn't beat him, not unarmed, and I
cast all about in the eerie twilight for a weapon. And found
several.

Suspended from the high rear battlements, a row of
circular bronze mirrors hung at different angles, two or
three of them just catching the last faint rays of sunlight
and reflecting them away down the valley. The Ferenczy's
signalling devices. Arvos the gypsy had said that the old
Ferengi didn't have much use for mirrors, or for sunlight. I
wasn't exactly sure what he'd meant, but I seemed to
remember something of the sort from old campfire legends. In any case I didn't have a lot of choice. If Faethor
was vulnerable, then there was only one sure way to find
out.

Before he could close with me, and avoiding places
where the timbers seemed suspect, I ran across the roof.
He came after me like a great loping wolf, but pulled up
short when I tore down a mirror from its fastenings and
turned to face him. His yellow eyes went very wide and he
bared bloodied teeth at me like rows of shattered spires.
He hissed and his forked tongue flickered like crimson
lightning between his jaws.

I held the "mirror" in my hands and knew at once what
it was: a sturdy bronze shield, possibly old Varyagi. It had
a grip at the back for my hand. Aye, and I knew how to
use it—but if only it were spiked in the centre of its face!
Then, unwitting, the burnished bronze caught a stray ray
from the scythe of sun setting on the hills—caught it and
hurled it straight into Faethor's snarling visage. And now I
knew old Arvos's meaning.

The vampire cringed before that blaze of sunlight. He
shrank down into himself, threw up spider hands before
his face, backed off a pace. I was never one to waste an
opportunity. I pursued, drove the buckler clanging into his

face, kicked at his loins again and again as I forced him back. And whenever he'd make to advance on me, then I'd catch the sun and throw it in his teeth, so that he had no chance to gather his reserves.

In this way I beat him back across the roof, with kicks and blows and blinding rays of sunlight. Once his leg went through the rotten roof, but he dragged it out and continued to retreat before me, frothing and cursing his fury. And so at last he came up against the parapet wall. Beyond that parapet was eighty feet of thin air, then the rim of the gorge and three hundred feet of almost sheer slope clad in close-packed, spiky pines. Down at the bottom was the bed of a rivulet. In short, a nightmare of vertigo.

He looked over the rim, glanced at me with eyes of fire—eyes of fear? At which precise moment the sun dipped down out of sight.

The change in Faethor was instantaneous. The twilight deepened, and the Ferenczy swelled up like some great bloating toadstool! His face split open in the most soul-wrenching smile of triumph—which I at once crushed under one last battering blow of my buckler.

And over he went.

I couldn't believe that I'd got him. It seemed a fantasy. But even as he toppled so I clung to the parapet wall and peered after him. Then . . . the strangest thing! I saw him like a dark blot falling towards the greater darkness. But in another moment the shape of the blot changed. I thought I heard a sound like a vast stretching, like giant knuckles cracking, and the shape hurtling towards the trees and the gorge seemed to unfurl like a huge blanket. It no longer fell so swiftly, nor even vertically. Instead it seemed to glide like a leaf, away from the castle's walls, out a little way over the gorge.

It dawned on me then that in the fullness of his powers Faethor might indeed have flown, in a fashion, from these battlements. But I had taken him by surprise, and in the shock of falling he had lost precious moments. Too late, he'd wrought a great change in himself, flattening himself like a sail to trap the rushing air. Too late, because even as I stared in fascination, so he struck a high branch. Then, in a dark whirling and a snapping of branches, the blot was gone. There followed from below a series of crashes, a shriek, a final, distant thud. And silence . . .

I listened for long moments in the rapidly deepening gloom. Nothing.

And then I laughed. Oh, how I laughed! I stamped my feet and thumped the top of the parapet wall. I'd got the old bastard, the old devil. I'd really *got* him!

I stopped laughing. True, I had thrown him down from the wall. But . . . was he dead?

Panic gripped me. Of all men, I knew how difficult it was to kill a vampire. Proof of that was right here on the roof with me, in the shape of the gurgling, fitfully twitching Ehrig. I hurried to him. His face was blue and the thong had buried itself in the flesh of his neck. His skull, which had been soft at the back where I'd crashed it against the wall, was already hard. How long before he awakened? In any case, I couldn't trust him. Not to do what must now be done. No, I was on my own.

Quickly I carried Ehrig back down into the bowels of the castle, to our cell in the roots of one of the towers. There I dumped him and barred the door. Perhaps the vampire filth under the earth would find him and devour him before he recovered fully. I didn't know and cared much less.

Then I hurried through the castle, lighting lamps and candles wherever I found them, illuminating the place as it had not been lit in a hundred years. Perhaps it had never known such light as I now brought into being in it.

There were two entrances: one was across the draw-bridge and through the door I'd used when first I arrived here escorted by Faethor's wolves, which I now barred; the other was from a narrow ledge in the cliff at the rear, where a roofed over causeway of doubtful timbers formed a bridge from the ledge to a window in the wall of the second tower. Doubtless this had been the Ferenczy's bolthole, which he'd never had cause to use. But if he could get out that way, so could he get in. I found oil, drenched the planking, set fire to the causeway and stayed long enough to ensure that it was well ablaze.

I paused periodically at other embrasures to gaze out on the night. At first there were only the moon and stars, stray wisps of cloud, the valley, silvered, touched occasionally by fleeting shadows. But as I proceeded with my task of lighting and securing the castle, so I was aware that things were beginning to stir. A wolf howled mournfully afar, then closer, then many wolves. The trees in the gorge were inky now, ominous as the gates to the underworld.

In the first tower I found a barred, bolted room. A treasure house, maybe? I threw back the bolts, lifted the bar, put my shoulder to the door. But the key had been turned in the great lock and removed. I leaned my ear to the oak panels and listened: there was sly movement in there, and . . . whispering?

Perhaps it was as well the door was locked. Perhaps it had been locked not to keep thieves out but something in!

I climbed to the hall where Faethor had poisoned me, and there found my weapons where I had last seen them. More, I took down from the wall a mighty long-handled axe. Then, armed to the teeth, I returned to the locked room. There I loaded my crossbow and placed it close to hand, stuck my sword point-down in a crack in the floor, ready for grasping, and took both hands to the axe in a huge swing at the door. I succeeded with that blow in caving in a narrow panel, but at the same time I dislodged from its hiding place atop the lintel a rusty iron key.

The key fitted the lock. I was on the point of turning it to enter, when—

Such a clamouring from the wolves! So loud I could hear its doomful dinning even down here! Something was afoot . . .

I left the door unopened, took up my weapons and raced up winding stairs to the upper levels. Wolves howled all around the castle now, but they were loudest at the rear. In a very little while I traced the uproar to the burning causeway, and arrived in time to see the bridge go crashing down, blazing into the back chasm. And there across the gap were Faethor's wolves in a pack, crowding the narrow ledge.

Behind them in the shadow of the cliff . . . was that the Ferenczy himself? The hairs on my neck stood erect. If it was him, he stood crookedly, like a queer bent shadow. Broken from his fall? I took up my crossbow but when I looked again—gone! Or perhaps he'd never been there. The wolves were real enough, however, and now the leader, a giant of a beast, stood at the rim measuring the gap.

It would be a leap of all of thirty feet, possible only if he had a clear run along the ledge. And even as I thought it, so the lesser wolves made way, shrank back into shadows, left the ledge clear. He ran back, turned, made his loping run and leaped—and mid-flight met my bolt, which sank directly into his heart. Dead, but still snarling his last snarl, he hit the rim of the opening and went tumbling into oblivion. And when I looked up, the rest of the pack had melted away.

But I knew that the Ferenczy would not give up that easily.

I went up onto the battlements, found jars up there full of oil and cauldrons seated on tilting gear. Setting fires in braziers under the cauldrons, I half-filled each one with oil and left them to simmer. And only then did I return to the locked room.

As I approached a hand, slender, female, wriggled in the hole in the panelling, tried desperately to reach and take hold of the key in the lock. What? A prisoner? A woman? But then I remembered what old Arvos had said about the Ferenczy's household: "Retainers? Serfs? He has none. A woman or two, perhaps, but no men." Here was a seeming contradiction: if this woman was his servant, why was she locked in? For her safety while there was a stranger in the house? That seemed unlikely in a house like this.

For *my* safety?

An eye peered out at me; I heard a gasp and the hand was withdrawn. Without further pause I turned the key, kicked open the door.

There were two of 'em, aye. And they'd been handsome enough women in their time.

"Who . . . who are you?" One of them approached me with a curious half-smile. "Faethor did not tell us that there would be . . ." She floated closer, gazed upon me in open fascination. I stared back. She was wan as a ghost, but there was a fire in her sunken eyes. I looked about the room.

The floor had a covering of local weave; ancient and wormy tapestries hung on the walls; there were couches and a table. But there were no windows, and no light other than the yellow aura from a silver candelabrum on the table. The room was sparse, but sumptuous by comparison with the rest of the place. Safe, too.

The second woman was sprawled somewhat wantonly on one of the couches. She stared sulphurously upon me but I ignored her. The first drifted closer still. Stirring myself, I held her at bay with the point of my sword. "Move not at all, lady, or I'll spit you here and now!"

She turned wild in a moment, glowered at me and hissed between her needle teeth; and now the second woman rose like a cat from her couch. They faced me menacingly, but both were wary of my sword.

Then the first one spoke again, her voice hard and cold as ice: "What of Faethor? Where is he?"

"Your master?" I backed out of the door. They were vampires, obviously. "He's gone. You've a new master now—me!"

Without warning, the first one sprang at me. I let her

come, then drove the pommel of my sword against the side of her head. She collapsed in my arms and I threw her aside, then yanked shut the door in the face of the second. I barred it, locked it and pocketed the key. Inside the room, the trapped vampire hissed and raged. I picked up her stunned sister, carried her to the dungeon and tossed her inside.

Ehrig came crawling. He had managed somehow to remove the thong from his neck, which was white and puffy and looked sliced as if by a knife around its entire circumference. Similarly, his head at the back was strangely lumpy, deformed like a freak's or a cretin's. He could hardly speak and his manner was childlike in the way of simpletons. Perhaps I had damaged his brain, and the vampire in him had not yet corrected it.

"Thibor!" he husked his amazement. "My friend, Thibor! The Ferenczy—did you kill him?"

"Treacherous dog!" I kicked at him. "Here, amuse yourself with this."

He fell upon the woman where she lay moaning. "You've forgiven me!" he cried.

"Not now, not ever!" I answered. "I leave her here because she's one too many. Enjoy yourself while you may." As I barred the door he had already begun to rip his filthy clothes off, hers too.

Now, climbing the spiralling steps, I heard the wolves again. Their song had a triumphant note to it. What now?

Like a madman I raced through the castle. The massive door in the foot of the tower was secure, and the causeway burned down—where would Faethor attempt his next assault? I went to the battlements—only just in time!

The air over the castle was full of tiny bats. I saw them against the moon, flitting in their myriads, their concerted voices shrill and piercing. Was that how the Ferenczy would come: flitting like a great bat, a stretchy blanket of flesh falling out of the night to smother me? I shrank down, gazed fearfully up into the vault of the night sky.

But no, surely not; his fall had injured him and he would not yet be ready to tax himself so greatly; there must be some other route with which I was not familiar.

Ignoring the bats, which came down at me in waves, but not so close as to strike or interfere with me, I went to the perimeter wall and looked over. Why I did this I can't say, for it would take more than any mere man to climb walls as sheer as these. Fool that I was—the Ferenczy was no mere man!

And there he was: flat to the wall, making his way agonizingly slowly, like a great lizard, up the stonework. A lizard, aye, for his hands and feet were huge as banquet platters and sucked where they slapped the walls! Horrified to my roots, I stared harder in the dark. He had not yet seen me. He grunted quietly and his huge disc of a hand made a quagmire sound where it left the wall and groped upward. His fingers were long as daggers and webbed between. Hands like that would pull a man's flesh from his bones as if they were plucking a chicken!

I looked wildly about. The bubbling cauldrons of oil were positioned at the ends of the span, where the great hall joined the towers. Rightly so, for who would suppose that a man could crawl *under* the flying buttresses and come up that way, with nothing but the gorge and certain death beneath him?

I flew to the closest cauldron, laid my hands on its rim. *Agony!* The metal was hot as hell.

I took my sword belt and passed it through the metal framework of the tilting engine, then dragged device and cauldron and all back the way I had come. Oil splashed and drenched my boot; one foot of the tilting bench went through a rotten plank and I must pause to free it; the entire contraption jerked and shuddered through friction with the planking, so that I knew Faethor must hear me and guess what I was about. But finally I had the cauldron above the spot where I had seen him.

I glanced fearfully over the parapet—and a great groping sucker hand came up over the rim, missed my face by inches, slapped down and gripped the coping of the wall!

How I gibbered then! I threw myself on to the tilting device, turned the handle furiously, and saw the cauldron bearing over towards the wall. Oil spilled and ran down the cauldron's side. It met the hot brazier and caught fire; my boot went up in flames. The Ferenczy's face came up over the rim of the parapet. His eyes reflected the leaping flames. His teeth, whole again, were gleaming white slivers of bone in his gaping jaws, with that flickering abomination of a tongue slithering over them.

Shrieking, I worked at the handle. The cauldron tilted, slopped a sea of blazing oil towards him.

"NO!" he croaked, his voice a broken bell. "NO—NO— NOOOOOO!"

The blue and yellow fire paid him no heed, ignored his cry of terror. It washed over him, lit him like a torch. He wrenched his hands from the wall and reached for me, but I fell back out of harm's way. Then he screamed again, and launched himself from the wall into space.

I watched the fireball curving down into darkness and turning it day bright, and all the while the Ferenczy's scream echoed back up to me. His myriad minion bats flocked to him mid-flight, dashing their soft bodies against him to quell the flames, but the rush of air thwarted them. A torch, he fell, and his scream was a rusty blade on the ends of my nerves. Even blazing, he tried to form a wing shape, and I heard again that rending and crackling sound. Ah, what sweet agony *that* must have caused him, with his crisp skin splitting instead of stretching, and the burning oil getting into the cracks!

Even so, he half-succeeded, began to glide as before, and as before struck a tree and so went spinning and crashing through the pines and out of sight.

He left a few sparks and scraps of fire drifting on the air, and a host of scorched bats skittering crippled against the moon, and a lingering odour of roasted flesh. And that was all.

Still I wasn't satisfied that he was dead, but I was satisfied that he wouldn't be back that night. It was now time to celebrate my triumph.

I doused the fire where it had taken hold of dry timbers, shut down the burning braziers, and went wearily to Faethor's living quarters. There was good wine there which I sipped warily, then gulped heartily. I spitted pheasants, sliced an onion, nibbled on dry bread and swilled wine until the birds were done. And then I dined royally. It was a good meal, aye, and my first in a long time, and yet . . . it lacked something. I couldn't say just what. Fool, I still thought of myself as a man. In other ways, however, I still *was* a man!

I took a stone jar of proven wine with me and went unsteadily to the lady in the locked room. She did not desire to receive me, but I was in no mood for arguments. I took her again and again; in as many ways as entered my head, so I entered her. Only when she was exhausted and slept did I, too, sleep.

And so the castle of Faethor Ferenczy became mine . . .

Chapter Ten

HARRY KEOGH'S NIMBUS OF BLUE FIRE BURNED BRIGHT IN THE stirless glade over Thibor's tumbled mausoleum, and Keogh's incorporeal mind was aware of the passage of time. In the Möbius continuum time was a very nearly meaningless concept, but here in the first low foothills of the Carpatii Meridionali it was very real, and still the dead vampire's tale was not completely told. The important part—for Harry, and for Alec Kyle and INTESP—was still to come, but Harry knew better than to ask directly for the information he desired. He could only press Thibor to the bitter end.

"Go on," he urged, when the vampire's pause threatened to stretch indefinitely.

What? Go on? Thibor seemed mildly surprised. *But what more is there? My tale is told.*

"Still, I'd like to hear the rest of it. Did you stay in the castle as Faethor had commanded, or did you return to Kiev? You ended your days in Wallachia, right here, in these cruciform hills. How did that come about?"

Thibor sighed. *Surely it is now time for you to tell me certain things. We made a bargain, Harry.*

I warned you, Harry Keogh! the spirit of Boris Dragosani joined in, sharper than that of Thibor. *Never bargain with a vampire. For there's always the devil to pay . . .*

Dragosani was right, Harry knew. He'd heard of Thibor's cunning from the very horse's mouth: it had taken no small amount of guile to defeat Faethor Ferenczy. "A deal is a deal," he said. "When Thibor has delivered, so shall I. Now come on, Thibor, let's have the rest of the story."

So be it, he said. *This is how it was . . .*

Something brought me awake. I thought I heard the rending of timber. My mind and body were dull from the night's excesses—all of the night's excesses, of which Faethor had only been the first—but nevertheless I stirred myself up. I lay naked on the lady's couch. Smiling strangely, she approached from the direction of the locked door, her hands clasped behind her back. My dull mind saw nothing to fear. If she had sought to escape she could easily have taken the key from my clothes. But as I made to sit up her expression changed, became charged with hatred and lust. Not the human lust of last night but the inhuman lust of the vampire. Her hands came into view, and clasped in one of them was a splinter of oak ripped from the shattered door panel. A sharp knife of hardwood!

"You'll put no stake through my heart, lady," I told her, knocking the splinter from her hand and sending her flying. While she hissed and snarled at me from a corner I dressed, went out, and locked the door behind me. I must be more careful in future. She could easily have slipped away and unbarred the castle's door for Faethor—if he still lived. Obviously she'd been more intent on putting an end to me than on seeing to his well-being. Her master he may have been, but that wasn't to say she'd relished it!

I checked the castle's security. All stood as before. I

looked in on Ehrig and the other woman. At first I thought they were fighting, but they were not . . .

Then I want up onto the battlements. A weak sun peered through dark, drifting clouds heavy with rain. I thought the sun frowned on me. Certainly I did not enjoy the sensation of its feeble rays on my naked arms and neck, and in a very little while I was glad to return indoors. And now I found myself with time on my hands, which I put to use exploring the castle more fully than before.

I searched for loot and found it: some gold, very ancient, in plate and goblets; a pouch of gems; a small chest of rings, necklaces, bangles and such in precious metals. Enough to keep me in style for an entire lifetime. A normal lifetime, anyway. As for the rest: empty rooms, rotten hangings and wormy furniture, a general air of gloom and decay. It was oppressive, and I determined to be on my way as soon as possible. But first I would like to be sure that the Ferenczy was not lying in wait.

In the evening I dined and drowsed in front of a fire in Faethor's quarters. But as night drew on it brought thoughts to disturb and niggle in the back of my mind, disquieting ideas which would not surface. The wolves were aprowl again, but their howling seemed dismal, distant. There were no bats. The fire lulled me . . .

Thibor, my son, said a voice. *Be on your guard!*

I started awake, leaped to my feet, snatched up my sword.

Oh? Ha, ha, ha! that same voice laughed—but no one was there!

"Who is it?" I cried, knowing who it was. "Come out, Faethor, for I know you're here!"

You know nothing. Go to the window.

I stared wildly all about. The room was full of shadows, leaping in the fire's flicker, but plainly I was alone. Then it came to me that while I had heard the Ferenczy's voice, I had not "heard" it. It had been like a thought in my head, but not *my* thought.

Go to the window, fool! the voice came again, and again I started.

Shaken, I went to the window, tore aside the hangings. Outside the stars were coming out, a moon was rising, and the eerie crying of wolves floated down from distant peaks.

Look! said the voice. *Look!*

My head turned as if directed by some other's will. I looked up, away to the ultimate range, a black silhouette against the sunken sun's fast fading glow. Up there, a far weary distance, something glinted, caught the rays of the sun, aimed them at me. Blinded by that effulgence, I threw up an arm and staggered back.

Ah! Ah! See how it hurts, Thibor. A taste of your own medicine! The sun, which once was your friend. But no more.

"It didn't hurt!" I shouted at no one, stepping to the window again and shaking my fist at the mountains. "It merely startled me. Is that really you, Faethor?"

Who else? Did you think me dead?

"I willed you dead!"

Then you are weak willed.

"Who travels with you?" I asked, surrendering to the strangeness of it. "Not your women, for I have them. Who signals with your mirrors now, Faethor? It isn't you who casts the sun about."

The mirror flashed at me again but I stepped aside.

My own go where I go, came his voice in answer. *They carry my scorched and blackened body until it is whole again. You have won this round, Thibor, but the battle is undecided.*

"Old bastard, you were lucky!" I boasted. "You'll not be so fortunate next time."

Now listen. He ignored my bluster. *You have incurred my wrath. You will be punished. The degree of punishment is up to you. Stay and guard my lands and castle and all that is mine while I'm gone, and I may be merciful. Desert me—*

"And what?"

And you shall know hell's torment for eternity. This I, Faethor Ferenczy, swear!

"Faethor, I'm my own man. Even if it were in me to serve, I could never call you master. You must know that, for I did my best to destroy you."

Thibor, you do not yet understand, but I have given you many things, great powers. Ah, but I've also given you several great weaknesses. Common men, when they die, lie in peace. Most of them . . .

That last was some sort of threat and I knew it. It was in his voice, a DOOM delivered in a whisper. "What do you mean?" I asked.

Only defy me and you shall find out. I have sworn. And for now, farewell!

And he was gone.

The mirror twinkled once more, like a brilliant star on the far ridge, and then it too was gone . . .

I had had enough of vampires, male and female. I locked my bedmate of last night in the dungeon with her sister, Ehrig and the burrowing thing, and slept in a chair in front of the fire in Faethor's apartments. Come daybreak and there was nothing to hold up my departure. Except . . . yes, there were certain things I must do before leaving. The Ferenczy had made threats, and I was never one to suffer threats lightly.

I went out of the castle, shot two fat rabbits with my crossbow, and took them down to the dungeon. I showed them to Ehrig, told him what I wanted and that he must help me. Together we tightly bound and gagged the women, dumping them in one corner of the dungeon. Then, though he protested loudly, I also bound and gagged Ehrig and put him with the women. Finally, I cut open the rabbits and threw their crimson carcasses down on the black soil where the flags were torn up.

Then it was a matter of waiting, but not for long. In a

little while a tentacle of leprous flesh came to explore the
source of the fresh blood; came groping up through the
crumbly soil, pushing it aside, and in a trice I took what I
wanted. I left Ehrig and the women tied up, barred the
door on them, and went up into the base of the tower.
Above the dungeon the steps wound about a central stone
pillar. I broke up furniture, piled the pieces around this
pillar. I scavenged through the castle, breaking furniture
wherever I found it and sharing the wood between the
towers. Then I poured oil on all the timbers of the battlements, in the hall and rooms where they spanned the
gorge, down all the stairwells. At last I was done, and the
work had taken me half-way through the morning.

I left the castle with my loot, walked out a little way
from it and looked at it again, one last time, then returned
and set a fire in the open door and on the drawbridge. And
never looking back, I started out to retrace my steps to
Moupho Alde Ferenc Yaborov.

At midday I met my five remaining Wallachs come to
find me. They saw me coming down the cliff-hugging path
and waited for me in the stony depression at its base.
"Hallo, Thibor!" the senior man greeted me when I joined
them. He looked beyond me. "Ehrig and Vasily, they are
not with you?"

"They are dead." I jerked my head towards the peaks.
"Back there." They looked, saw the column of white
smoke reaching like some strange mushroom into the sky.
"The house of the Ferenczy," I told them, "which I have
burned."

Then I looked at them more sternly. "Why did you wait
so long before coming to look for me? How long has it
been, five, six weeks?"

"Those damned gypsies, the Szgany!" their spokesman
growled. "When we awoke, the morning after the three of
you left, the village was all but deserted. Only women and
children left. We tried to find out what was happening; no
one seemed to know, or they weren't saying. We waited

two days, then set out after you. But the missing Szgany menfolk were waiting along the way. Five of us and more than fifty of them. They blocked the way, and they had the advantage of good positions in the rocks." He shrugged uncomfortably, tried not to look embarrassed. "Thibor, we'd have been of use to no one dead!"

I nodded, spoke quietly: "And yet now you have come?"

"Because they are gone." He shrugged again. "When they stopped us, we went back down to their so-called 'village.' Yesterday morning, the women and kids started to drift off in ones and twos, small parties here and there. They wouldn't speak and looked miserable as sin, as if they were in mourning, or something! At sun-up today the place was empty, except for one old grandad chief—a 'prince,' he calls himself—his crone and a couple of grand-children. He wasn't saying anything, and anyway he looks half simple. So, I came up the trail alone, sticking close to cover, and discovered that all the men had gone, too. Then I called up these lads to come and look for you. Truth to tell, we'd long thought you were a goner!"

"I might well have been," I answered, "but I'm not. Here—" I tossed him a small leather sack, "carry this. And you—" I gave my loot to another, "you burden yourself with this. It's heavy and I've carried it far enough. As for the job we came to do: it's done. Tonight we stay in the village; tomorrow it's back to Kiev to see a lying, cheating, scheming Prince Vladimir Svyatoslavich!"

"Ugh!" The spokesman held out his sack at arm's length. "There's a creature in here. It moves!"

I chuckled darkly. "Aye, handle it carefully—and to-night put it in a box, sack and all. But don't sleep with it next to you . . ."

Then we went down to the village. On the way down I heard them talking among themselves, mainly of the trouble the Szgany had given them. They mentioned putting the village to the torch. I wouldn't hear of it. "No," I said. "The Szgany are loyal in their way. Loyal to their own. Anyway, they've moved on, gone for good. What profit in burning an empty village?"

And so they said no more about it . . .

That evening I went to the ancient Szgany prince in his hut and called him out. He came out into the coolness of the clearing and saluted me. I stepped close to him and he looked hard at me, and I heard him gasp. "Old chief," I said, "my men said burn this place, but I stopped them. I've no quarrel with you or the Szgany."

He was brown and wrinkled as a log, toothless, hunched. His dark eyes were all aslant and seemed not to see too clearly, but I was sure they saw me. He touched me with a hand that trembled, gripped my arm hard above the elbow. "Wallach?" he inquired.

"That I am, and I'll return there soon," I answered.

He nodded, said, "Ferengi!—you." It was not a question.

"Thibor's my name," I told him. And on impulse: "Thibor . . . Ferenczy, aye."

Again he nodded. "You—*Wamphyri!*"

I began to shake my head in denial, then stopped. His eyes were boring into mine. He knew. And so did I, for certain now. "Yes," I said. "Wamphyri."

He drew breath sharply, let it out slow. Then: "Where will you go, Thibor the Wallach, son of Old One?"

"Tomorrow I go to Kiev," I answered grimly. "I've business there. After that, home."

"Business?" He laughed a cackling laugh. "Ah, business!"

He released my arm, grew serious. "I too go Wallachia. Many Szgany there. You need Szgany. I find you there."

"Good!" I said.

He backed away, turned and went back into his hut . . .

We came out of the forest into Kiev in the evening, and I found a place on the outskirts to rest and buy a skin of wine. I sent four of my five into the city. Soon they began to return, bringing with them prominent members of my peasant army—what was left of it. Half had been lured away by Vladimir and were off campaigning against the Pechenegi, the rest remained faithful; they had gone into hiding and waited for me.

There were only a handful of the Vlad's soldiers in the city; even the palace guard were away fighting. The prince had only a score of men, his personal bodyguard, at court. That was part of the news, and this was the rest: that tonight there was to be a small banquet at the palace in honour of some boot-licking Boyar. I invited myself along.

I arrived at the palace alone, or that is the way it must have appeared. I strode through the gardens to the sound of laughter and merrymaking from the great hall. Men at arms barred my way, and I paused and looked at them. "Who goes there?" a Guardsmaster challenged me.

I showed myself. "Thibor of Wallachia, the Prince's Voevod. He sent me on a mission, and now I am returned." Along the way I had walked in mire, deliberately. The last time I was here, the Vlad had commanded that I come in my finery, unweaponed, all bathed and shining. Now I was weighed down with arms; I was unshaven, dirty, and my forelocks all awry. I stank worse than a peasant, and was glad of it.

"You'd go in there like that?" The Guardsmaster was astonished. He wrinkled his nose. "Man, wash yourself, put on fresh robes, cast off your weapons!"

I glowered at him. "Your name?"

"What?" He stepped a pace to the rear.

"For the Prince. He'll have the balls of any man who impedes me this night. And if you've none of those, he'll have your head instead! Don't you remember me? Last time I came it was to a church, and I brought a sack of thumbs." I showed him my leather sack.

He went pale. "I remember now. I . . . I'll announce you. Wait here."

I grabbed his arm, dragged him close. I showed him my

teeth in a wolf's grin and hissed through them. "No, *you* wait here!"

A dozen of my men stepped out of the trees, held cautionary fingers to their lips, and bundled the Guardsmaster and his men away.

I went on, entering the palace and the great hall unimpeded. Oh, true, a pair of royal bully-boy bodyguards closed on me at the door, but I thrust them aside so hard they almost fell, and by the time they were organized I was among the revellers. I strode to the centre of the floor. I stood stock still, then slowly turned and gazed all about from under lowered brows. The noise subsided. There came an uneasy silence. Somewhere a lady laughed, a titter which was quickly stilled.

Then the crowd fell away from me. Several ladies looked fit to faint. I smelled of ordure, which to my nostrils was fresh and clean compared to the scents of this court.

The crowd parted, and there sat the Prince at a table laden with food and drink. His face wore a frozen smile, which fell from it like a leaden mask when he saw me. And at last he recognized me. He straightened to his feet. "You!"

"None other, my Prince." I bowed, then stood straight.

He couldn't speak. Slowly his face went purple. Finally he said, "Is this your idea of a joke? Get out—*out!*" He pointed a trembling finger at the door. Men were closing on me, hands on their sword hilts. I rushed the Vlad's table, sprang up onto it, drew my sword and held it on his breast.

"Tell them to come no closer!" I snarled.

He held up his hands and his bodyguard fell back. I kicked aside platters and goblets and made a space before him, throwing down my sack. "Are your Greek Christian priests here?"

He nodded, beckoned. In their priestly robes, they came, hands fluttering, jabbering in their foreign tongue. Four of them.

At last it got through to the prince that he was in danger of his life. He glanced at my sword's point lying lightly on his breast, looked at me, gritted his teeth and sat down. My sword followed him. Pale now, he controlled himself, gulped, and said, "Thibor, what is all of this? Would you stand accused of treason? Now put up your sword and we'll talk."

"My sword stays where it is, and we've time only for what *I* have to say!" I told him.

"But—"

"Now listen, Prince of Kiev. You sent me on a hopeless quest and you know it. What? Me and my seven against Faethor Ferenczy and his Szgany? What a joke! But while I was away you could steal my good men, and if I were so lucky as to succeed . . . that would be even better. If I failed—and you believed I would—it would be no great loss." I glared at him. "It was *treachery!*"

"But—" he said again, his lips trembling.

"But here I am, alive and well, and if I leaned a little on my sword and killed you it would be my right. Not according to your laws but according to mine. Ah, don't panic, I won't kill you. Let it suffice that all gathered here know your treachery. As for my 'mission': do you remember what you commanded me to do? You said, 'Fetch me the Ferenczy's head, his heart, and his standard.' Well, at this very moment his standard flies atop the palace wall. His and mine, for I've taken it for my own. As for his head and heart: I've done better. I've brought you the very essence of the Ferenczy!"

Prince Vladimir's eyes went to the sack before him and his mouth twitched at one corner.

"Open it," I told him. "Tip it out. And you priests, come closer. See what I've brought you."

Among the thronging courtiers and guests, I spied grim-faced men edging closer. This couldn't last much longer. Close by, a high-arched window looked out on a balcony and the gardens beyond. Vladimir's hands trembled towards the sack.

"Open it!" I snapped, prodding him. He took up the sack, tugged at its thong, tipped the contents onto the table. All stared, aghast.

"The very *essence* of the Ferenczy!" I hissed.

The part was big as a puppy, but it had the colour of disease and the shape of nightmare. Which is no shape at all but a morbid suggestion. It could be a slug, a foetus, some strange worm. It writhed in the light, put out fumbling fingers and formed an eye. A mouth came next, with curving dagger teeth. The eye was soft and mucous damp. It stared about while the mouth chomped vacuously.

The Vlad sat there white as death, his face twisting grotesquely. I laughed as the vampire stuff wriggled closer to him, and he gave a cry and toppled himself over backwards in his chair. The thing had intended no harm; it *had* no intent. Larger and hungry it might be dangerous, or if it were alone with a sleeping man in a dark room, but not here in the light. I knew this, but Vladimir and the court didn't.

"Vrykoulakas, vrykoulakas!" the Greek priests began to scream. And at that, though few could have known what the word meant, the great hall became the scene of furious chaos. Ladies cried out and fainted; everyone drew back from the huge table; guests crushed together at the door. To give the Greeks their due, they were the only ones who had any idea what to do. One of them took a dagger and pinned the thing to the table. It at once split open, slipped free of the blade like water. The priest pinned it again, cried, "Bring fire, *burn* it!"

In the pandemonium now reigning, I jumped down from the table, up into the window embrasure, and so on to the low balcony. As I vaulted the balcony wall into the garden, a pair of angry faces appeared at the window behind me. The Vlad's bodyguard, all brave and bristling now that the danger was past. Except that for them it wasn't yet past. I glanced back. The two were now out onto the balcony.

They shouted and waved swords, and I ducked low. Bolts whistled overhead out of the dark garden; one pursuer was taken in the throat, the other in the forehead. The noise from the hall was an uproar, but there were no more pursuers. I grinned, made away . . .

We camped that night in the woods on the outskirts. All of my men slept, for I posted no guards. No one came near.

In the morning light we sauntered our horses through the city, then turned and headed west for Wallachia. My new standard still fluttered from its pole over the palace wall. Apparently no one had dared remove it while we were near. I left it there as a reminder: the dragon, and riding its back the bat, and surmounting them both the livid red devil's head of the Ferenczy. For the next five hundred years those arms would be mine . . .

My tale's at an end, said Thibor. *Your turn, Harry Keogh.*

Harry had got something of what he wanted, but not everything. "You left Ehrig and the women to burn," he voiced his disgust. "The women—vampire women—I think I can understand that. But would it have been so hard to give them a decent death? I mean, did they have to burn . . . like that? You could have made it easier for them. You could have—"

Beheaded them? Thibor seemed unconcerned, gave a mental shrug.

"And as for Ehrig: he had been your friend!"

Had been, yes. But it was a hard world a thousand years ago, Harry. And anyway, you are mistaken—I didn't leave them to burn. They were deep down under the tower. The broken furniture I piled around the central pillar was to shatter it, bring the stone steps down into the stairwell and block it forever. Burn them, no—I simply buried them!

Harry recoiled from Thibor's morbid, darkly sinister tone. "That's even worse," he said.

You mean better, the monster contradicted him, chuckling. *But better far than even I guessed. For I didn't know then that they'd live down there forever. Ha, ha! And how's that for horror, Harry? They're down there even now. Mummied, aye—but still "alive" in their way. Dry and desiccated as old bones, bits of leather and gristle and—*

Thibor came to an abrupt halt. He had sensed Harry's keen interest, the intense, calculating way in which he seized on all of this and analysed it. Harry tried to back off a little, tried to close his mind to the other. Thibor sensed that, too.

I suddenly have this feeling, he very slowly said, *that I may have said too much. It comes as something of a shock to learn that even a dead creature must guard its thoughts. Your interest in all of these matters is more than merely casual, Harry. I wonder why?*

Dragosani, for so long silent, broke in with a burst of laughter. *Isn't it obvious, old devil?* he said. *He's outsmarted you! Why is he so interested? Because there are vampires in the world—in* his *world—right now! It's the only answer. And Harry Keogh came here to find out about them, from you. He needs to find out about them for the sake of his intelligence organization, and for the sake of the world. Now tell me: does he really* need *to tell you the present circumstances of that innocent you corrupted while he was still in his mother's womb? He has* already *told you! The boy lives—and yes, he is a vampire!* Dragosani's voice died away . . .

There was silence in the motionless glade, where only Harry's neon nimbus lit the darkness to give any indication of the drama enacted there. And finally Thibor spoke again. *Is it true? Does he live? Is he—?*

"Yes," Harry told him. "He lives—as a vampire—for now."

Thibor ignored the implications of that last. *But how do you know he is . . . Wamphyri?*

"Because already he works his evil. That's why we have to put him down—myself and others who work for the same cause. And certainly we must destroy him before he 'remembers' you and comes to seek you out. Dragosani has said that you would rise up again, Thibor. Now how would you set about that?"

Dragosani is a brash fool who knows nothing. I fooled him, you fooled him—so well, indeed, that you helped him destroy himself—why, any child could make a fool of Dragosani! Take no notice of him.

Hah! cried Dragosani. *A fool, am I? Listen to me, Harry Keogh, and I'll tell you exactly how this devious old devil will use what he has made. First—*

BE SILENT! Thibor was outraged.

I will not! Dragosani cried. *Because of you, I am here, a ghost, nothing! Should I lie still while you prepare to be up and about? Listen to me, Harry. When that youth—*

But that was as much as Thibor was willing to let him say. A hideous mental babble started up—such a blast of telepathic howling that Harry could unscramble no single word of it—and not only from Thibor but also Max Batu. Understandably, the dead Mongol sided with Thibor against his murderer.

"I can hear nothing," Harry tried to break into the din and through it to Dragosani. "Absolutely nothing!"

The telepathic cacophony went on unabated, louder if anything, more insistent than ever. In life Max Batu had been able to concentrate hatred into a glare that could kill; in death his concentration hadn't failed him; if anything the mental din he created was greater than Thibor's. And since there was no physical effort involved, they could probably keep it up indefinitely. Quite literally, Dragosani was being shouted down.

Harry attempted to lift his voice above all three: "If I leave you now, be sure I won't be back!" But even as he issued his threat he realized that it no longer carried any weight. Thibor was shouting for his life, the sort of life he had not known since the day they buried him here five hundred years ago. Even if the others did quieten down, he would go right on bellowing.

Stalemate. And too late, anyway.

Harry felt the first tug of a force he couldn't resist, a force that drew him as a compass is drawn northwards. Harry Jr. was stirring again, coming awake for his scheduled feed. For the next hour or so the father must merge again with the id of his infant son.

The tugging strengthened, an undertow that began to draw Harry along with it. He searched for a Möbius door, found one and started towards it.

In that same instant of time, as he made to enter the Möbius continuum, something other than Harry Jr. stirred, something in the earth where the rubble of Thibor's tomb lay scattered. Perhaps the concentrated mental uproar had disturbed it. Maybe it had sensed events of moment. Anyway, it moved, and Harry Keogh saw it.

Great stone slabs were shoved aside; tree roots snapped loudly where something massive heaved its bulk beneath them; the earth erupted in a black spray as a pseudopod thick as a barrel uncoiled itself and lashed upwards almost as high as the trees. It swayed there among the treetops, then was drawn down again.

Harry saw this—and then he was through the door and into the Möbius continuum. And incorporeal as he was, still he shuddered as he sped across hitherto hypothetical spaces towards the mind of his infant son. And uppermost in his own mind this single thought: *"Ground to clear,"* indeed!

Sunday, 10:00 A.M. Bucharest. The Office of Cultural and Scientific Exchanges (USSR), housed in a converted museum of many domes, standing conveniently close to the Russian University. The wrought-iron gates being opened by a yawning, uniformed attendant and a black Volkswagen Variant accelerating out into the quiet streets and heading for the motorway to Pitesti.

Inside the car Sergei Gulharov was driving, with Felix Krakovitch as front-seat passenger, and Alec Kyle, Carl Quint and an extremely thin, hawk-faced, bespectacled, middle-aged Romanian woman in the back. She was Irma Dobresti, a high-ranking official with the Ministry of Lands and Properties and a true disciple of Mother Russia.

Because Dobresti spoke English, Kyle and Quint were a little more careful than usual how they spoke to each other and what they said. It was not that they feared they'd let something slip about their mission, for she would see more than enough of that, but simply that they might err and make some comment about the woman herself. Not that they were especially rude or churlish men, but Irma Dobresti *was* a very different sort of woman.

She wore her black hair in a bun; her clothes were almost a uniform: dark grey shoes, skirt, blouse and coat. She wore no make-up or jewellery at all and her features were sharp and mannish. Where womanly curves and other feminine charms were concerned, Nature seemed to have forgotten Irma Dobresti entirely. Her smile, showing yellow teeth, was something she switched on and off like a dim light, and on those few occasions when she spoke her voice was deep as any man's, her words blunt and always to the point.

"If I were not thinly," she said, making a common enough mistake in her attempt at casual conversation, "this long ride is most uncomfortable." She sat on the extreme left, Quint in the middle and then Kyle.

The two Englishmen glanced at each other. Then Quint smiled obligingly. "Er, true," he said. "Your thinlyness is most accommodating."

"Good." She gave a curt nod.

The car sped on out of the city, picked up the motorway . . .

Kyle and Quint had spent the night at the Dunarea Hotel in the city centre, while Krakovitch had spent most of it up and about making connections and arrangements. This morning, looking haggard and hollow-eyed, he'd joined them for breakfast. Gulharov had picked them up and they'd driven to the Office of Cultural and Scientific Exchanges where Dobresti had been getting her instructions from a Soviet liaison officer. She had met Krakovitch the night before. Now they were on their way into the Romanian countryside, following a route Krakovitch knew fairly well.

"Actually," he said, stifling a yawn, "this not too surprising. Coming here, I mean." He turned to look at his guests. "I know this place. After that business at Château Bronnitsy, when Party Leader Brezhnev give me my appointment, he ordered me to find out everything I could about . . . about what happened. I suspected Dragosani was at root of it. So I came here."

"You followed his old tracks, you mean?" said Kyle.

Krakovitch nodded. "When Dragosani have holiday, he always come here, to Romania. No family, no friends, but he come here."

Quint nodded. "He was born here. Romania was home to him."

"And he did have one friend here," Kyle quietly added.

Krakovitch yawned again, peered at Kyle through eyes which were a little red in their corners. "So it would seem. Anyway, he used to call this place Wallachia, not Romania. Wallachia is a country long gone and forgotten, but not by Dragosani."

"Where exactly are we going?" Kyle asked.

"I was hoping you could tell me!" said Krakovitch. "You said Romania, a place in the foothills where Dragosani was a boy. So that is where we are going. We'll stay at a little village he liked off the Corabia-Calinesti highway. We should be there in maybe two hours. After that," he shrugged, "your guess is as good as mine."

"Oh, we can do better than that," said Kyle. "How far is Slatina from this place where we're staying?"

"Slatina? Oh, about—"

"One hundred twenty kilometers," said Irma Dobresti. Krakovitch had earlier told her the name of the place they were staying—a difficult and meaningless name to the two Englishmen—but she had known it fairly well. A cousin of hers had lived there once. "About an hour and half to travelling."

"Do you want to go straight to Slatina?" Krakovitch asked. "What's in Slatina, anyway?"

"Tomorrow will do," said Kyle. "We can spend tonight making plans. As for what's in Slatina—"

"Records," Quint cut in. "There'll be a local registrar, won't there?"

"Pardon?" Krakovitch didn't know the word.

"A person who registers marriages and births," Kyle explained.

"And deaths," Quint added.

"Ah! I begin to see," said Krakovitch. "But you are mistaken if you think a small town's records will go back five hundred years to Thibor Ferenczy."

Kyle shook his head. "That's not it. We have our own vampire, remember? We know he, er, got started out here. And we more or less know how. We want to find out where Ilya Bodescu died. The Bodescus were staying in Slatina when he had some sort of skiing accident in the hills. If we can trace someone who was involved in the recovery of his body, we'll be within an ace of finding Thibor's tomb. Where Ilya Bodescu died, that's where the old vampire was buried."

"Good!" said Krakovitch. "There should be a police report, statements—perhaps even a coroner's report."

"Doubting," said Irma Dobresti, shaking her head. "How long ago this man die?"

"Eighteen, nineteen years," Kyle answered.

"Simple death—accident." Dobresti shrugged. "Not

suspicious—no coroner's report. But police report, yes. Also, ambulance recovery. They make report, too.''

Kyle began to warm towards her. ''That's good reasoning,'' he said. ''As for getting hold of those reports through the local authorities, that's your job, Mrs. er—?''

''Not Mrs. Never had time. Just call me Irma, please.'' She smiled her yellow-toothed smile.

Her attitude in all of this puzzled Quint a little. ''You don't think it's a bit odd that we're here hunting for a vampire, er, Irma?''

She looked at him, raised an eyebrow. ''My parents come from the mountains,'' she said. ''When I am little they sometimes talk about *wampir*. Up there in Carpatii Meridionali, old people still believe. Once there were great bears up there. And sabretooth tigers. Before that, big lizards—er, dinosaurs? Yes. They are no more—but they *were*. Later, there was plague that swept the world. All of these things, gone. Now you tell me that my parents were right, there were vampires, too. Odd? No, I not think so. If you want hunt vampires, where better than Romania, eh?''

Krakovitch smiled. ''Romania,'' he said, ''has always been something of an island.''

''True,'' Dobresti agreed. ''But that not always good. World is big. No strength in being small. Also, being cut off means stagnation. Nothing new ever comes in.''

Kyle nodded, thinking to himself, *and some of the old things are things you can well do without . . .*

It had been a rough night for Brenda Keogh.

When Harry Jr. had finished his small hours feed, he hadn't wanted to go back to sleep again. He wasn't bad about it, just wouldn't sleep.

After an hour or two of rocking him, then cradling and crooning to him, she'd finally put the baby down and gone back to bed herself.

But at 6:00 A.M. he'd been right on time again, crying for his change and another feed. And she'd known from the way he twisted his little face and clenched his fists that he was tired: he'd been awake right through the night, from no cause that Brenda could discover. But good? What a *good* little chap he was! He hadn't cried at all until he was hungry and uncomfortable, just lay there in his cot through the night doing his own thing—whatever that might be.

Even now his will to stay awake and be a part of the world was strong, but his yawning told his mother that he couldn't. With dawn an hour away, Harry was going to have to go to sleep. The world would have to wait. No matter how fast your mind grows up, your body goes more slowly . . .

As his baby son went to sleep, Harry Sr. found himself free and was struck with a thought as strange as any he'd ever had, even in his thoroughly strange existence.

He's leeching on me! he thought. *The little rascal's into my mind, into my experiences. He can explore my stuff because there's lots of it, but I can't touch him because there's nothing in there—yet!*

He put the extraordinary idea to the back of his mind. Now that Harry Jr. had released him he had places to go, people—dead people—to talk to. There were things he knew which he was unique in knowing. He knew, for instance, that the dead inhabit another sphere; also that in their lonely nether-existence they go on doing all the things they've done in life.

The writers write masterpieces they can never publish, each line perfectly composed, each paragraph polished, every story a gem. Where time isn't a problem and deadlines don't exist, things get done right. The architects plot their cities of the mind, beautiful aerial constructs flung across fantastic worlds and spanning sculpted oceans and continents, each brick and spire and sky-riding highway immaculately positioned, no smallest detail missing or botched. The mathematicians continue to explore the Formulae of the Universe, reducing THE ALL to symbols they can never put on paper, for which men in the corporeal world should be grateful. And the Great Thinkers carry on thinking their great thoughts, which far outweigh any they thought in life.

That had been the way of it with the Great Majority. Then Harry Keogh, Necroscope, had come along.

The dead had taken to Harry at once; he had given their existence new meaning. Before Harry, each one of them had inhabited a world consisting of his own incorporeal thoughts, without contact with the rest. They had been like houses with no doors or windows, no telephones. But Harry had connected them up. It made no difference to the living (who simply weren't aware) but it made a great deal of difference to the dead.

Möbius had been one such, mathematician and thinker both, and he had shown Harry Keogh how to use his Möbius continuum. He'd done so gladly, for like all of the dead he'd quickly come to love the Necroscope. And the Möbius continuum had given Harry access to times and places and minds beyond the reach of any other intelligence in all of man's history.

Now Harry knew of a man whose one obsession in life had been the myths and legends and lore of the vampire. His name was Ladislau Giresci. How was it going for him now, Harry wondered, in the aftermath of his murder? Max Batu had killed him with his evil eye, for no good reason other than that Dragosani had ordered it. Killed *him,* yes, but not Giresci's life-long *penchant* for the legend of the vampire. What had been an obsession in life must certainly have continued afterwards.

Harry could no longer make any headway with Thibor, and Thibor would not let him get through to Dragosani. His next best bet had to be Ladislau Giresci. How to reach him, however, was a different matter. Harry had never met the Romanian in life; he did not know the ground where

Giresci's spirit lay; he must rely on the dead to supply him with directions, see him on his way.

Across the road from Brenda's flat—once Harry and Brenda's flat—there sprawled a graveyard hundreds of years old, containing a large number of Harry's friends. He knew most of them personally from previous conversations. Now he drifted towards the lines of markers and occasionally leaning tombstones, his mind drawn by the minds of the dead where they lay in their graves communing. They sensed him at once, knew that it was him. Who else could it be?

Harry! said their spokesman, an ex-railway engineer who'd lived all his life in Stockton, until he died in 1938. *It's good to talk to you again. Nice to know you haven't forgotten us.*

"How are things with you?" Harry inquired. "Still designing your trains?"

The other came aglow in a moment. *I have designed* the *train!* he answered. *Do you want to hear about it?*

"Unfortunately I can't." Harry was genuinely sorry. "My visit is purely business, I'm afraid."

Well, spit it out, Harry! someone else exclaimed, an ex-bobby of Harry's acquaintance, late of Sir Robert Peel's time. *How can we help you, sir?*

"There are some hundreds of you here," Harry answered. "But is there anyone from Romania? I want to go there, and I need directions and an introduction. The only people I know there are . . . bad people."

Voices rose in something of a babble, but one of them cut through, speaking directly to Harry. It was a girl's voice, sweet and small. *I know Romania,* it said. *Something of it, anyway. I came here from Romania after the war. There were troubles and oppressions, and so my elder brothers sent me away to an aunt who lived here. Strange, but I came all this way, then caught a cold and died! I was very young.*

"And do you know someone I can seek out, who can

perhaps help me on my way?'' Harry didn't like to seem too eager to be off, but he really couldn't help himself. ''It's very important, I assure you.''

But my brothers will be delighted to guide you, Harry! she said at once. *It's only since you came that we've all been able to . . . well, get together again. We all owe you so much. . . .*

''If I may,'' Harry answered, ''I'll come back and talk to you again some time. Meanwhile, I'm afraid I've no time to spare. What are your brothers called?''

They are Jahn and Dmitri Syzestu, she said. *Wait and I'll call them for you.* She called, and in a moment her brothers answered. They were very faint, like voices on a telephone from the other side of the world. Harry was introduced.

''Just keep talking to me,'' he told the brothers, ''and I'll find my way to you.''

He excused himself from the company of his friends in the Hartlepool cemetery, found a space-time door and passed through it into the Möbius continuum. ''Jahn, Dmitri? Are you still there?''

We're here, Harry, and we're honoured to be able to help you like this.

He homed in on them, emerged through another door into the grey Romanian dawn. He found himself in a field of grass beside a pock-marked wall fast crumbling into ruins. There were ponies in the field but of course they couldn't see him; they just stood still, shivering a little, their coats shining with drops of dew. Plumes of warm air came snorting from their nostrils like smoke. In the distance, the last lights of a town were blinking out as the sun rose on the eastern horizon.

''Where is this place?'' Harry asked the brothers Syzestu.

The town is Cluj, said Jahn, who was the oldest. *This place is just a field. We were in prison—political prisoners— and we ran away. They came after us with guns and*

*caught us here, trying to climb this wall. Now tell us,
Harry Keogh, how we can help you?*

"Cluj?" said Harry, a little disappointed. "I need to be
south, I think, and east—across the mountains."

This is easy! The younger brother, Dmitri, was excited.
*Our father and mother lie side by side in the grave-
yard in Pitesti. Only a little while ago we were talking
to them!*

Indeed they were, a deeper, sterner voice joined in,
from some distance away. *You're welcome to come and
visit, Harry, if you can find your way here.*

Harry excused himself—a little hastily but with many
apologies—and re-entered the Möbius continuum. In a
little while he was in a misted graveyard in Pitesti. *Who is
it you're seeking?* inquired Franz Syzestu.

"His name is Ladislau Giresci," said Harry. "All I can
tell you is that he died some little time ago at his home
near a town called Titu."

Titu? Anna Syzestu repeated. *Why that's nought but fifty
kilometres or so away! What's more, we've friends buried
there!* She was plainly proud to be of assistance to the
Necroscope. *Greta, can you hear?*

Indeed I can! A new voice, sharp and shrewish, answered. *And I've the very man right here.*

There you are! said Anna Syzestu, in a told-you-so
tone. *If you want to meet someone in Titu, ask Greta
Mirnosti. She knows everyone!*

Harry Keogh? A male voice now came to the fore. *I'm
Ladislau Giresci. Do you want to come closer or will this
do?*

"I'm on my way!" said Harry. He thanked the Syzestus
and went to Giresci's plot in Titu. And finally, at last in
the presence of the vampire expert himself, he asked,
"Sir, I believe you can help me—if you will?"

Young man, said Giresci, *unless I'm very much mistaken
I know why you're here. Last time someone came to me
inquiring about vampires, it cost me my life! But if there's*

*any way I can help you, Harry Keogh, any way at all, just
ask it!*

"That was Boris Dragosani who came to see you, right?"
said Harry. He sensed the other's shudder. Giresci might
have no body, but at the mention of Dragosani's name he
shuddered.

That one, yes, Giresci answered at last. *Dragosani.
When first I met him I didn't know it, but he was already
one of them. Or as good as. He didn't know it himself, not
quite, but the evil was in him.*

"He sent Max Batu to kill you with his evil eye."

*Yes, because by then I knew what he was. That's the
thing a vampire fears most: that people will discover what
he is. Anyone who suspects . . . he has to die. So the little
Mongol killed me, and he stole my crossbow.*

"That was for Dragosani. He used it to kill Thibor
Ferenczy in the cruciform hills."

*Then at least it was put to good use! Ah, but when you
talk about Thibor, you're talking about a* real *vampire!*
said Giresci. *If Dragosani, with all of his potential for
evil, had lived—alive or undead—as long as that one, then
the world would have an incurable illness!*

"I'm sorry," said Harry, "but I can find nothing to
admire in such monsters. And in any case, there was one
greater than Thibor, who came before him, and outlasted
him. His name was Faethor, and Thibor took his second
name from him. Rightly so, for it was Faethor who made
him a vampire. I'm speaking of Faethor Ferenczy, of
course."

Ladislau Giresci's voice was the merest whisper now as
he answered: *Indeed, and that was where my interest in
the undead really began. For I was with Faethor when he
died. Imagine that, and him a creature at least thirteen
hundred years old!*

"These are the ones I want to know about." Harry was
eager. "Thibor and Faethor. In your life you were a
vampire expert; however people might scorn your obses-

sion or look upon you as an eccentric, you studied the vampire's myths, his legends, his lore. You were still studying them when you died, and it's my guess that dying didn't stop you. So where's your research led you now, Ladislau? How did Thibor end up buried there on the cruciform hills? And what of Faethor between the tenth and twentieth centuries? It's important that I know these things, for they relate to what I'm doing now. And what I'm doing relates to the safety and sanity of the whole world.''

I understand, said Giresci, soberly. *But Harry, don't you think you should speak to someone with even more authority? I believe it can be arranged . . .*

''What?'' Harry was taken aback. ''Someone with more authority than you? Is there such a person?''

Ahhh! said a new voice, a powerful voice. It was black as the night itself and deep as the roots of hell, and it seemed to come from everywhere and nowhere at the same time. *Oh, yesss, Haarrry, there is—or was—just such a one. And I am he. No one knows as much about the Wamphyri as I do, for no one has or ever will live so long. So very long, indeed, that when I died I was ready for it. Oh, I fought against it, be sure, but in the end it was for the best. Now I have peace. And I have Ladislau Giresci to thank for giving me that final, merciful release. Since he obviously holds you in the greatest esteem—as do all the dead, apparently—then so must I. So come to me, Harry Keogh, and let a real expert answer your questions.*

It was an offer Harry couldn't refuse. He knew who it must be at once, of course, and he wondered why he hadn't thought of it himself. It was, after all, the obvious answer.

''I'm coming, Faethor,'' he said. ''Just give me a moment and I'll be right there . . .''

Chapter Eleven

TO THIS DAY, ON THE OUTSKIRTS OF PLOIESTI, TOWARDS
Bucharest, there stand gutted ruins, reminders of the
mundane horrors of war. The burned-out shells lie like
half-buried stony corpses in open countryside, strangely
gorgeous in the summer when the old bomb craters are full
of flowers and brambles and wildlife, and ivy climbs
shattered walls to turn them green. But it takes the winter
and the snow to make the devastation visible, to bring into
monochrome perspective the gaunt reality of the region.
The Romanians have never rebuilt in or near these ruins.

This was where Faethor Ferenczy had finally met his
death at the hands of Ladislau Giresci during a Second
World War bombing raid on Bucharest and Ploiesti. Pinned
to the floor of his study by a splintered ceiling beam when
his home was hit, he had feared the encroaching flames
because alive, vampires burn very slowly. Giresci, working for the Civil Defence, had seen the house bombed,
entered the blazing ruin and tried to free Faethor—to no
avail. It was hopeless.

275

The vampire had known that he was finished. With a superhuman effort of will he had commanded Giresci to make a quick end of it. The old way was still the only way. Since Faethor was already staked, Giresci need only behead him. The flames would do the rest, and the ancient monster would burn along with his house.

The things he experienced in that house of horror stayed with Giresci for the rest of his life. They were what had made him an authority on vampirism. Now Ladislau Giresci was dead along with Faethor, but still the vampire stood in his debt. Which was why he would give Harry Keogh whatever assistance he could; at least, that was part of the reason. The rest of it was that Keogh was up against Thibor the Wallach.

It wasn't yet winter when Harry Keogh homed in on Faethor's incorporeal thoughts and emerged from the Möbius continuum into the creeper- and bramble-grown ruin which had been the vampire's final refuge on earth. Indeed, the summer was barely turning to autumn, the trees still green, but the chill Harry felt might have suggested winter to the bones of any ordinary man. Harry was least of all ordinary. He knew it was a chill of the spirit, a wintry blast blowing on the soul. A psychic chill, which is only felt in the presence of a supernatural Power. Faethor Ferenczy had been such, and Harry recognized that fact. But just as surely Faethor, too, knew when he was face to face with a Power.

The dead speak well of you, Harry, the vampire opened, his mental voice sepulchral. *Indeed, they love you! That is hard for one who was never loved to understand. You are not one of them, and yet they love you. Perhaps it is because you too, like them, are without body.* The voice took on a grimly humorous note. *Why! It might even be said that you are . . . undead?*

"If there's one thing I've learned about vampires," Harry answered evenly, "it's that they love riddles and word games. But I'm not here to play. Still, I'll answer your questions. Why do the dead love me? Because I bring them hope. Because I intend no harm but only good. Because through me they are something more than memories."

In other words, because you are "pure?" The vampire's words dripped with sarcasm.

"I was never pure," said Harry, "but I understand your meaning and I suppose you're near enough right. Which might also explain why they'll have nothing to do with you. There's no life in you, only death. You were dead even in life. You *were* death! And death walked with you wherever you walked. Don't compare my condition with undeath—I'm more alive now than you ever were. When I arrived here and before you spoke, I noticed something. Do you know what it was?

The silence.

"Exactly. No cock crowing. No birdsong. Even the droning of bees is absent here. The brambles are lush and green but they bear no fruit. Nothing, no one will come near you, not even now. The things of Nature sense your presence. They can't speak to you like I can, but they know you're here. And they shun you. Because you were evil. Because even dead, you're still evil. So don't sneer at my 'pureness,' Faethor. I shall never be alone."

And after a moment's silence, Faethor said thoughtfully, *For one who seeks my help, you don't much hide your feelings . . .*

"We are poles apart," Harry told him, "but we do have a mutual enemy."

Thibor? Why then have you spent time with him?

"Thibor is the source of the trouble," Harry answered. "He is, or was, your enemy, and what he left behind is my enemy. I hoped to learn things from him and was partially successful. Now he'll tell me no more. You offered help, and here I am to accept your offer. But we don't have to pretend friendship."

Guileless, Faethor said. *That is why they love you. But you are right: Thibor was and is my enemy. However much I've punished him, I can never punish him enough. So ask what you will of me, and I'll answer all.*

"Then tell me this," said Harry, eager once more. "After he hurled you from your castle in flames, what became of you then?"

I shall be brief, Faethor answered, *because I sense that this is only part of what you desire to know. Cast your mind back then, if you will, one thousand years into the past . . .*

Thibor the Wallach, whom I had called son—to whom I had given my name and banner, and into whose hands I had bequeathed my castle, lands and Wamphyri power—had injured me sorely. More sorely than even he suspected. That cursed ingrate!

Thrown down from the walls of my castle in flames, I was burned and blinded. Myriad minion bats fluttered to me as I fell, were scorched and died, but dampened the flames not at all. I crashed through trees and shrubs, tumbled in a thousand agonies down the steep side of the gorge, was torn by trees and boulders alike before striking bottom. But my fall was broken in part by the foliage, and I fell in a shallow pool which put out the flames that threatened to melt my Wamphyri flesh.

Stunned, as close to true death as a vampire might come and remain undead, still I put out a call to my faithful gypsies down in the valley. I know you will understand what I mean, Harry Keogh. We share the power to speak with others at a distance. To speak with the mind alone, as we do now. And the Szgany came.

They took out my body from the still, salving water and cared for it. They carried me west over the mountains into the Hungarian Kingdom. They protected me from jars and jolts, hid me from potential enemies, kept me from the sun's searing rays. And at last they brought me to a place of rest. Ah! And that was a long rest: for recuperation, for reshaping, a time of enforced retirement.

I have said Thibor had hurt me. But *how* he had hurt me! I was sorely damaged. All bones broken: back and neck, skull and limbs. Chest staved in, heart and lungs a mangle. Skin flayed by fire, torn by sharp branches and boulders. Even the vampire in me, which occupied most parts and portions, was battered, torn and scorched. A week in the healing? A month? A year? Nay, an *hundred* years! A century, in which to dream my dreams of red—or night-black—revenge!

My long convalescence was spent in an inaccessible mountain retreat, but a place more a cavern than a castle; and all the while my Szgany tended me, and their sons, and *their* sons. And their daughters, too. Slowly I became whole again; the vampire in me healed itself, and then healed me; Wamphyri, I walked again, practised my arts, made myself wiser, stronger, more terrible than ever before. I went abroad from my aerie, made plans for my life's adventure as if Thibor's treachery had been but yesterday and all my wounds no more than a stiffness of the joints.

And it was a terrible world in which I emerged, with wars everywhere and great suffering, and famines, and pestilence. Terrible, aye, but the very stuff of life to me! For I was Wamphyri . . .

I builded me a small castle in the border with Wallachia, almost impregnable, and there set myself up as a Boyar of some means. I led a mixed body of Szgany, Hungarians and local Wallachs, paid them well, housed and fed them, was accepted as a landowner and leader. The Szgany, of course, would have followed me to the ends of the earth— and they did, they did!—not out of love but some strange emotion which is in the wild breast of all the Szgany. Simply say that I was a Power, and that they associated with me. As for my name: I became Stefan Ferrenzig, common enough in those parts. But that was only the first of my names. Thirty years after my full recovery I became the "son" of Stefan, called Peter, and thirty years later

Karl, then Grigor. A man must not be seen to live too long, and certainly not for centuries. You understand?

As for Wallachia: I avoided crossing the border, mainly. For there was one in Wallachia whose strength and cruelty were already renowned: a mysterious mercenary Voevod named Thibor, who commanded a small army for the Wallach princelings. And I did not wish to meet him, who should now be guarding my lands and properties in the Khorvaty! No, I would not meet him now, not yet. Oh, I doubted that he would recognize me, for I was changed beyond measure. But if I saw him I might not be able to contain myself. That could well prove fatal, for in the years of my healing he had been active and was grown strong; indeed, he was in large part the power behind the throne of Wallachia. He had his own Szgany, but well disciplined, and he also commanded the army of a prince; while I merely led an untrained rabble of gypsies and peasants. No, my revenge could wait. What is time to the Wamphyri, eh?

For a further sixty years I bided my time, contained my activities, was subdued, covert. By now I had access to a worthy force of fighters for payment, fierce mercenaries, and I considered how best to use them. I was tempted to take on Thibor and the Wallachs, but any sort of even fight was not to my liking. I wanted the dog on his knees before me, to do with him as I desired. I did *not* want a battlefield confrontation, for I had learned at first hand his wiles and his strength. By now he possibly considered me dead; it were best I continued to let him think it; my time would still come.

But meanwhile I was restless, confined, pent up. Here was I, lusty, strong, something of a power, and I had nowhere to channel my energies. It was time I went further abroad in the roiling world.

Then I heard of a great Crusade by the Franks against the Moslems. The world was two years into its thirteenth Christian century, and even now a fleet was sailing against

Zara. Originally the Crusaders had intended to attack Egypt, then the centre of Moslem power, but their armies were heirs to a long hostility towards Byzantium. The old Doge of Venice, who provided their fleet, and who was himself an enemy of Byzantium, had diverted them first to Hungary. Zara, only recently won by the Hungarians, was retaken and sacked by Venetians and Crusaders alike in November 1202; by which time I was on my way to that key city with a select company of my own supporters. The Hungarian King, "my master," believing I was acting for him against the Crusaders, put no obstacle in my way. When I reached Zara, however, I sold myself into mercenary service and took the Cross, which had been my intention all along.

It seemed to me that the best way to venture out across the world would be with the Crusaders; but if I had hoped for instant action, then it was a vain hope. The Venetians and Franks had already divided the city's spoils—they had argued and fought over them, too, but their quarreling was soon over—and now the Doge and Boniface of Montferrat, who led the expedition, decided to winter at Zara.

Now, the original intention, the prime purpose of this Fourth Crusade, had been of course to destroy the Moslems. But many Crusaders believed that Byzantium had been a traitor to Christendom throughout all the Holy Wars. And suddenly Constantinople was within grasp, or at least within reach, of vengeful Crusader passions. Moreover, Constantinople was rich—wildly rich! Madly rich! The prospect of loot such as Constantinople offered settled the matter. Egypt could wait—the very world could wait—for the target was now the Imperial Capital itself!

I shall be brief. We set sail for Constantinople in the spring, stopped off at several places to do various things, and late in June arrived before the Imperial Capital. I will assume you know something of history. For months running to years there were objections, moral, religious and political, to the city's sack; avarice and lust eventually won the day. All schemes of going on from there to fight the infidel were finally abandoned. Pope Innocent III, who had been in large part responsible for calling the Crusade, had already excommunicated the Venetians for sacking Zara; now he was once more aghast, but both news—and intervention—travelled slowly in those days. And in the eyes of the Crusaders Constantinople had become a jewel, their quest's end, and every man of us lusted after it. Agreement was reached on the division of spoils, and then—

—Early in April 1204, we commenced the attack! All political scheming and pious talk were put aside at last, for *this* was why we were here.

Ah! And how my fierce heart rejoiced. Every fibre of my being thrilled. Gold is one thing, but blood is another. Blood spilled, blood drunk, blood coursing through veins of fire!

I will tell you what we came up against. First of all, the Greeks had ships on the Golden Horn to keep us from landing below the walls. They fought hard but in vain, though their efforts were not entirely wasted. Greek fire is a terrible thing—it ignites and burns in water! Their catapults hurled it among our ships, and men blazed in the sea itself. I was scalded, my right shoulder, chest and back burned near to the bone. Ah! But I had been burned before, and by an expert. A mere scorching could not keep me out of it. My pain served only to spur me on. For this was my day.

You might wonder about the sun: how could I, Wamphyri, fight under its searing ray? I wore a flowing black cloak in the fashion of Moslem chiefs, and a helm of leather and iron to guard my head. Also, I fought wherever possible with the sun at my back. When I was not fighting—and believe me there were other things to do as well as fight— then of course I kept out of it. But the Crusaders, when they saw me and my Szgany in battle—ah, they were awed! Ignored hitherto, considered a rabble to bulk out the ranks and go down as fodder to fire and sword, now we were regarded by Frank and Venetian alike as demons, as fighting hell-fiends. How glad they must have been to have us on their side. So I thought . . .

But let me not stray. A breach was made in the wall guarding the Blachernae quarter of the city. Simultaneously a fire broke out in the city in that quarter. The defenders were confused; they panicked; we crushed them and poured over them into the mainly empty streets, where the fighting was nothing much to mention.

For after all, what we were up against? Greeks with all of the wind knocked out of them; an ill-disciplined army, mainly mercenary, still suffering from years of misman-agement. Slav and Pechenegi units which would fight only so long as their chances were good and the payment better; Frankish units whose members were torn, obviously, two ways; the Varangian Guard, a company composed of Danes and Englishmen who knew their Emperor Alexius III for a usurper with merit neither as a fighting man nor as a man of state. What work there was for us was slaughter. Those who were not willing to die at once fled. There was no other choice. In a few hours the Doge and Frankish and Venetian Lords occupied the Great Palace itself.

From there they issued their orders: the war- and loot-crazed Crusaders were told that Constantinople was theirs and they had three days in which to complete the city's sack. They were the victors; there was no crime they could commit. They could do with the capital, its people and possessions whatever they wished. Can you imagine what such orders conveyed?

For nine hundred years Constantinople had been the centre of Christian civilization, and now for three days it became the sinkhole of hell! The Venetians, who appreci-ated great works, carried off Grecian masterpieces and other works of art and beauty by the ton, and treasures in precious metals near enough to sink their ships. As for the French, the Flemings and various mercenary Crusaders, including me and mine: they desired only to destroy. And destroy we did!

However precious, if something could not be carried or hauled away it was reduced to wreckage on the spot. We fuelled our madness from rich wine-cellars, paused only to drink, rape or murder, then returned to the sack. Nothing, no one was spared. No virgin came out of it intact, and few came out alive. If a woman was too old to be stabbed with flesh she was stabbed with steel, and no female was too young. Convents were sacked and nuns used as whores— Christian nuns, mind!

Men who had not fled but stayed to protect their homes and families were slit up their bellies and left clutching their steaming guts to die in the streets. The city's gardens and squares were full of its dead inhabitants, mainly women and children. And I, Faethor Ferenczy—known to the Franks as the Black One, or Black Grigor, the Hungarian Devil—I was ever in the thick of it. The thickest of it. For three days I glutted myself as if there were no end to my lust.

I did not know it but the end—my end, the end of glory, of power, of notoriety—was already looming. For I had forgotten the prime rule of the Wamphyri: do not be seen to be too different. Be strong, but not overpowering. Be lustful, but not a legendary satyr. Command respect, but not devotion. And above all do nothing to cause your peers, or those who have the power to consider themselves your superiors, to become afraid of you.

But I had been burned by Greek fire and it had merely infuriated me. And rapacious? For every man I had killed I had taken a woman, as many as thirty in a day and a night! My Szgany looked to me as a sort of god—or devil. And finally . . . finally, of course, the Crusaders proper had come to fear me. More than all matters of "conscience," more than all the murder and rape and blasphemies *they* had committed, *my* deeds had given them bad dreams.

Aye, and they were sore in need of a scapegoat.

I believe that even without Innocent's pious protestations and hand-flutterings and cries of horror, still I would have been persecuted. Anyway, this was the way of it. The Pope had been enraged by the sack of Zara, at first delighted by Constantinople, then aghast when he heard of the atrocities. He now washed his hands of the crusade in its entirety. Far from helping true Christian soldiers in their fight against Islam, it seemed its only aim had been to conquer Christian territories. And as for the blasphemies and generally atrocious behaviour of the Crusaders in Constantinople's holy places . . .

I say again: they needed a scapegoat, and no need to look too far for one. A certain "bloodthirsty mercenary recruited in Zara" would fit the bill nicely. In secret communiqués Innocent had ordered that those directly responsible for "gross acts of excessive and unnatural cruelty" must gain "neither glory nor rich rewards nor lands" for their barbarism. Their names should no more be spoken by good men and true but "struck forever out of the records." All such great sinners were to be offered "neither respect nor high regard," for by their acts they had shown that they were "worthy only of contempt." *Hah!* It was more than excommunication—it was a death warrant!

Excommunication . . . I had taken the Cross in Zara as a matter of expediency. It meant nothing. A cross is a symbol, nothing more. Soon, however, I would come to hate that symbol.

We had a large house on the outskirts of the sacked city, my Szgany and I. It had been a palace or some such, was now filled with wine and loot and prostitutes. The other mercenary groups had turned over their plunder to their Crusader masters for the prearranged split, but I had not. For we had not yet been paid! Perhaps I was in error there. Certainly our loot was an extra incentive for Crusader treachery.

They came at night, which was their mistake. I am—or was—Wamphyri; night was my element. Some vampire premonition had warned me that all was not well. I was awake and on the prowl when the attack came. I roused up my men and they set to. But it was no good; we were heavily outnumbered and, taken by surprise, my men were still half-asleep. When the place began to burn I saw that I couldn't win. Even if I beat off all of these Crusaders, they formed only a fraction of the total body. They had probably diced with ten other equal parties for the privilege of killing and robbing me. Also, if they had guessed what I was—and the fire suggested that they had—quite obviously my situation was untenable.

I took gold and a great many gemstones and fled into the darkness. On my way I carried off one of my attackers with me. He was a Frenchman, only a lad, and I made a quick end of it, for I had not time to tarry. Before he died, though, he told me what it was all about. From that day to this I have loathed the cross and all who wear it, or live in its shadow or under its influence.

Of my Szgany, not a man of them survived to follow me out of that place; but I later learned that two captives had been taken for questioning. As it was I stood off and watched the blaze from afar. And since the inferno was ringed about by Crusaders, I could only suppose that *they* assumed I had died in the flames. So be it—I would not disillusion them.

And now I was alone and a long way from home. Well, hadn't I desired to see the world?

Now, I have said I was a long way from home. In miles on the ground this statement is seen to be far from accurate. But where indeed *was* my home? I could hardly return to Hungary, not for some little time. Wallachia was no place for me, and my old castle in the Khorvaty, looking down on Russia, was in ruins. What, then, was I to do? Where to go? Ah, but the world is a wide place!

To detail my adventures from that time forward would take too long. I shall merely outline my deeds and travels, and you must forgive or fill in for yourself any great gaps or leaps in time.

North was out of the question; likewise west; I headed east. It was 1204. Need I remind you of a singular emergence in Mongolia just two years later? Of course not, his name was Temujin—later Genghis Khan! With a party of Uighurs I joined him and helped subdue and unite the last of the rowdy Mongol tribes, until all Mongolia was finally united. I proved myself a capable warlord and he showed me some respect. With some small effort I was able to change my features until I looked the part; that is to say I willed my vampire flesh into a new mould. The Khan knew that I was not a Mongol, of course, but at least I was acceptable. And later he would have many mercenaries in his command, so that my participation was in no way a rare thing.

I was with him against the Chin, when we penetrated that Great Wall, and after his death I was there to see the total obliteration of the Chin Empire. I passed my "loyalty" down to Genghis's grandson, Batu. I could have offered my services to other Mongol Khans, but Batu's objective was Europe! It was one thing to return a man alone, but another to go back as a general in a Mongol army!

In the winter of 1237–8, in a lightning campaign, we smashed the Russian principalities. In 1240 we took Kiev by storm and burned it to ashes. From there we struck at Poland and Hungary. Only the death of the Great Khan Ogedei in 1241 saved Europe in its entirety; there were disputes about the succession and the westward campaigns were stalled.

Later, it was time for The Fereng, as I was known, to "die" again. I obtained permission to journey to an ambiguous homeland far in the West; my "son" would join Húlegú in his push against the Assassins and the Caliphate. As Fereng the Black, Son of The Fereng, under Húlegú, I assisted in the extermination of the Assassins and was there at the fall of Baghdad in 1258. Ah, but a little more than two years later, at Ain Jalut in the so-called Holy Land, we were delivered a crushing defeat by the Mamelukes; the turning point for the Mongols had come.

In Russia Mongol rule would continue to the end of the fourteenth century, but "rule' implies peace and my taste for war had grown insatiable. I stuck it out forty years more, then parted company with the Mongols and sought action elsewhere . . .

I fought for Islam! I was now an Ottoman, a Turk! Aha! What it is to be a mercenary, eh? Yes, I become a *ghazi*, a Moslem Warrior, fighting against the polytheists, and for nearly two centuries my life was one great unending river of blood and death! Under Bayezid, Wallachia became a vassal state which the Turks called Eflak. I could have returned then and sought out Thibor, who had moved with his Szekely into the mountains of Transylvania, but I was busy campaigning elsewhere. By the middle of the fifteenth century my chance had passed me by; the boundaries of the Ottoman state at the accession of Mehemmed II were shrinking. In 1431 Sigismund the Holy Roman Emperor had invested Vlad II of Wallachia with the Order of the Dragon—licence to destroy the infidel Turk. And who was Vlad's instrument in his "holy" work? Who was his war-weapon? Thibor, of course!

Of Thibor's deeds, strangely, I heard with no small measure of pride. He butchered not only the infidel Turk but Hungarians, Germans, and other Christians in their thousands. Ah, he was a true son of his father! If only he had not been disobedient. Alas (for him) but disobedience to me was not his only failing; like myself at the end of my Crusader adventure, he had not practised the caution of the Wamphyri. He was adored by the Szekely but set himself on a level with his superiors, the Wallachian princes, and his excesses had made him notorious. He was feared throughout the land. In short, he had in every way brought himself into prominence. A vampire may *not* be prominent, not if he values his longevity.

But Thibor was wild, demented in his cruelties! Vlad the (so called) Impaler, Radu the Handsome, and Mircea the Monk (whose reign was so short) had all tasked him with the protection of Wallachia and the chastisement of its enemies; tasks in which he delighted, at which he excelled. Indeed, the Impaler, one of history's favourite villains, suffers undeservedly: he was cruel, aye, but in fact he has been named for Thibor's deeds! Like my name, Thibor's has been struck, but the stark terror of his deeds will live forever.

Now let me get on. When I had lived too long with the Turks, finally I deserted their cause—which was crumbling, as all causes must in the end—and returned to Wallachia. The time was well chosen. Thibor had gone too far; Mircea had recently acceded to the throne and he feared his demon Voevod mightily. This was the moment I had so long awaited.

Crossing the Danube, I put out Wamphyri thoughts ahead of me. Where were my gypsies now? Did they still remember me? Three hundred years is a long time. But it was night, and I was night's master. My thoughts were carried on the dark winds' all across Wallachia and into the shadowed mountains. Romany dreamers where they lay about their campfires heard me and started awake, gazing at each other in wonder. For they had heard a legend from their grandfathers, who had heard it from their grandfathers, that one day I would return.

In 1206 two of my mercenary Szgany had come home—the same two taken for questioning on the night of Crusader cowardice and treachery, whose lives had been spared—and they had returned to foster an awesome myth. But now I was here, a myth no longer. "Father, what shall we do?" they whispered into the night. "Shall we come to meet you, master?"

"No," I told them across all the rivers and forests and

miles. ''I have work to finish, and I alone must see to it.
Go into the Carpatii Meridionali and put my house in
order, so that I may have my own place when my work is
done.'' And I knew that they would do it.

Then . . . I went to Mircea in Targoviste. Thibor was
campaigning on the Hungarian border, a good safe way
away. I showed the Prince living vampire flesh taken from
my own body, telling him that it was flesh of Thibor.
Then, because he was close to fainting, I burned it. This
showed him one way in which a vampire may be killed. I
told him the other way, too: the stake and decapitation.
Then I questioned him about his Voevod's longevity: did
he not deem it strange that Thibor must be at least three
hundred years old? No, he answered, for it was not one
man but several. They were all part of the same legend,
they all took the same name, Thibor. All of them, down
through the years, had fought under the devil-bat-dragon
banner.

I laughed at him. What? But I had studied Russian
records and knew for a fact that this selfsame man—this
one man—had been a Boyar in Kiev three hundred years
ago! At that time it had been rumored that he was Wamphyri.
The fact that he still lived gave the rumour ample founda-
tion. He *was* a lustful vampire—and now it seemed he
lusted after the throne of Wallachia!

Did I have any proof at all in support of my accusations,
the Prince asked me.

I told him: you have seen his vampire flesh.

It could have been the loathsome flesh of any vampire,
he said.

But I had dedicated myself to seek out vampires and
destroy them wherever I found them, I told him. In pursuit
of such creatures I had been in China, Mongolia, Turkey-
land, Russia—and I spoke many languages to prove it.
When Thibor had been wounded in battle, I had been there
to take and keep a piece of his flesh, which had grown into
what the Prince had seen. What more proof did he need?

None. He too had heard rumours, had his suspicions, his doubts . . .

The Prince already feared Thibor, but what I had told him—mostly the truth, except perhaps concerning Thibor's ambition—had utterly terrified him. How could he deal with this monster?

I told him how. He must send for Thibor on some pretext or other—to bestow upon him a great honour! Yes, that would do it. Vampires are often prideful; flattery, carefully applied, can win them over. Mircea must tell Thibor that he desired to make him Voevod in Chief over all Wallachia, with powers second only to Mircea himself.

"Power? He has that already!"

"Then tell him that eventually succession to the throne will not be out of the question."

"What?" The Prince pondered. "I must take advice."

"Ridiculous!" I was forceful. "He may have allies among your advisors. Don't you know his strength?"

"Say on . . ."

"When he comes, I shall be here. He must be told to come alone, his army staying on the Hungarian border to continue the skirmishing. Orders can be sent to them later, dispersing them to lesser, more trusted generals. You shall receive him alone—at night."

"Alone? At night?" Mircea the Monk was sore afraid.

"You must drink with him. I shall give you wine with which to drug him. He is strong, however, and no amount of wine will kill him. It may not even render him unconscious. But it will rob him of his senses, make him clumsy, stupid, like a man drunk.

"I shall be close at hand with four or five of the most trusted members of your guard. We'll confine him, naked, in a place you shall nominate. A special place, somewhere in the grounds of the palace. Then, when the sun rises, you will know you have trapped a vampire. The sun's rays on his flesh will be a torture to him! But that in itself will not be sufficient proof. No, for above all else we must be just.

Bound, his jaws will be forced open. You shall see his tongue, O Prince—forked like a snake's, and red with blood!

"At once a stake of hard wood shall be driven through his heart. This, for the greater part, will immobilize him. Then into a coffin with him, and off to a secret place. He shall be buried where no one should ever find him, a place forbidden to men from this time forward."

"Will it work?"

I gave the Prince my guarantee that it would work. And it did! Exactly as I have stated.

From Targoviste to the cruciform hills is perhaps one hundred miles. Thibor was carried there at all speed. Holy men came with us all the way, with exorcisms ringing until I thought I would be sick. I was dressed in the plain black habit of a monk, with the hood thrown up. None had seen my face except Mircea and a handful of officials at the palace, all of whom I had beguiled, or hypnotized as you now have it, to a degree.

There in the hills a rude mausoleum was hastily constructed of local stone; it bore no name or title, no special marks; standing low to the ground and ominous in a gloomy glade, as you have seen it, it would in itself suffice to keep away the merely curious. Years later someone cut Thibor's emblem into the stone—as an additional warning, perhaps. Or it could be that some Szgany or Szekely follower found him and marked the place, but feared to bring him up or lacked the wit.

I have gone ahead of myself.

We took him there, to the foothills of the Carpatii, and there he was lowered into his hole four or five feet deep in the dark earth. Wrapped in massy chains of silver and iron, he was, and the stake still in him and nailing him secure in his box. He lay pale as death, his eyes closed, for all the world a corpse. But I knew that he was not.

Night was falling. I told the soldiers and priests that I would climb down and behead Thibor, and set a fire of branches in his grave to burn him, and when the fire was dead fill in the hole. It was dangerous, witchcrafty work, I said, which could only be done by the light of the moon. They should now retreat, if they valued their souls. They went, stood off, and waited for me on the plain.

The moon, thin-horned, rose up. I looked down on Thibor and spoke to him in the manner of the Wamphyri. "Ah, my son, and so it is come to this. Sad, sad day for a fond father, who bestowed upon an ingrate son mighty powers to be wasted. A son who would not honour his father's ordinances, and is therefore fallen in the world. Wake up, Thibor, and let that also which is in you waken, for I know that you are not dead."

His eyes opened a crack as my words sank in, then gaped wide in sudden understanding. I threw back my cowl so that he might see me, and smiled in a manner he must surely remember. He marked me and gave a great start. Then he marked his whereabouts—and screamed! Ah, how he screamed!

I threw earth down upon him.

"Mercy!" he cried out loud.

"Mercy? But are you not Thibor the Wallach, given the name Ferenczy and commanded to tend in his absence the lands of Faethor of the Wamphyri? And if you are, what do you here, so far from your place of duty?"

"Mercy! Mercy! Leave me my head, Faethor."

"I intend to!" I tossed in more dirt.

He saw my meaning, my intention, and went mad, shaking and vibrating and generally threatening to tear himself loose from his stake. I put down a long, stout pole into the grave and tapped home the stake more firmly, driving it through the bottom of the coffin itself. As for the coffin's lid, I merely let it stand there on its side in the bottom of the hole. What? Cover him up and lose sight of that frantic, fear-filled face? "But I am Wamphyri!" he screamed.

"You could have been," I told him. "Ah, you *could* have been! Now you are nothing."

"Old bastard! How I hate you!" he raved, blood in his eyes, his nostrils, the writhing gape of his mouth.

"Mutual, my son."

"You are afraid. You fear me. *That* is the reason!"

"Reason? You desire to know the reason? How fares my castle in the Khorvaty? What of my mountains, my dark forests, my lands? I will tell you: the Khans have held them for more than a century. And where were you, Thibor?"

"It's true!" he screamed, through the earth I threw in his face. "You *do* fear me!"

"If that were true, then I should most certainly behead you," I smiled. "No, I merely hate you above all others. Do you remember how you burned me? I cursed you for a hundred years, Thibor. Now it is your turn to curse me—for the rest of time. Or until you stiffen into a stone in the dark earth."

And without further ado I filled in his grave.

When he could no longer scream with his mouth he screamed with his mind. I relished each and every yelp. Then I built a small fire to fool the soldiers and the priests, and warmed myself before it for an hour, for the night was chill. And eventually I went down to the plain.

"Farewell, my son," I told Thibor. And then I shut him out of my mind, as I had shut him out of the world, forever . . .

"And so you took your revenge on Thibor," said Harry when Faethor paused. "You buried him alive—or undead—forever. Well, that might have suited your cruel purpose, Faethor Ferenczy, but you certainly weren't doing the world at large any favours by letting him keep his head. He corrupted Dragosani and planted his vampire seed in him, and between times infected the unborn Yulian Bodescu, who is now a vampire in his own right. Did you know these things?

Harry, said Faethor, *in my life I was a master of telepathy, and in death . . .? Oh, the dead won't talk to me, and I can't blame them—but there is nothing to keep me from listening in on their conversations. In a way, it could even be argued that I'm a Necroscope, like you. Oh, I've read the thoughts of many. And there have been certain thoughts which interested me greatly—especially those of that dog Thibor. Yes, since my death, I have renewed my interest in his affairs. I know about Boris Dragosani and Yulian Bodescu.*

"Dragosani is dead," Harry told him, albeit unnecessarily, "but I've spoken to him and he tells me Thibor will try to come back, through Bodescu. Now, how can this be? I mean, Thibor *is* dead—no longer merely undead but utterly dead, dissolved, finished."

Something of him remains even now.

"Vampire matter, you mean? Mindless protoplasm hiding in the earth, shunning the light, devoid of conscious will? How may Thibor use that when he no longer commands it?"

An interesting question, Faethor answered. *Thibor's root— his creeper of flesh, a stray pseudopod detached and left behind—would seem to be the exact opposite of you and me. We are incorporeal: living minds without material bodies. And it is . . . what? A living body without a mind?*

"I've no time for riddles and word games, Faethor," Harry reminded him.

I was not playing but answering your question, said Faethor. *In part, anyway. You are an intelligent man. Can't you work it out for yourself?*

That got Harry thinking. About opposite poles. Was that what Faethor meant: that Thibor would make a new home for himself in a composite being? A thing formed of Yulian's physical shape and Thibor's vampire spirit? While he worried at the problem, Faethor was not excluded from Harry's thoughts.

Bravo! said the vampire.

"Your confidence is misplaced," Harry told him. "I still don't have the answer. Or if I do then I don't understand it. I can't see how Thibor's mentality can govern Yulian's body. Not while it's controlled by Yulian's own mind, anyway."

Bravo! said Faethor again; but Harry remained in the dark.

"Explain," said the Necroscope, admitting defeat.

If Thibor can lure Yulian Bodescu to the cruciform hills, said Faethor, *and there cause his surviving creeper—the protoflesh he shed, perhaps for this very purpose—to join with Bodescu . . .*

"He can form a hybrid?"

Why not? Bodescu already has something of Thibor in him. He already is influenced by him. The only obstacle, as you point out, will be the youth's mind. Answer: Thibor's vampire tissue, once it is in him, will simply eat Yulian's mind away, to make room for Thibor's!

"Eat it away?" Harry felt a dizzy nausea.

Literally!

"But . . . a body without a mind must quickly die."

A human body, yes, if it is not kept alive artificially. But Bodescu's body is no longer human. Surely that is the essence of your problem? He is a vampire. And in any case, Thibor's transition would take the merest moment of time. Yulian Bodescu would go up into the cruciform hills, and he would appear to come down again from them. But in fact—

"It would be Thibor!"

Bravo! said Faethor a third time, however caustically.

"Thank you," said Harry, ignoring the other's sarcasm, "for now I know that I'm on the right track, and that the course of action chosen by certain friends of mine is the right one. Which leaves only one last question unanswered."

Oh? Black humour had returned to Faethor's voice, a certain sly note of innuendo. *Let me see if I can guess it. You desire to know if I, Faethor Ferenczy—like Thibor the*

Wallach—have left anything of myself behind to fester in the dark earth. Am I right?

"You know you are," said Harry. "For all I know it's a precaution all the Wamphyri take—against the chance that death will find them out."

Harry, you have been straightforward with me, and I like you for it. Now I too shall be forthright. No, this thing is of Thibor's invention. However, I would add that I wish I had thought of it first! As for my "vampire remains": yes, I believe there is such a revenant. If not several. Except "revenant" is perhaps the wrong word, for we both know there will be no return.

"And it—they, whatever—is in your castle in the Khorvaty, which Thibor razed?"

A simple enough deduction.

"But have you no desire to use such remains, like Thibor, to raise yourself up again?"

You are naïve, Harry. If I could, I probably would. But how? I died here and may not depart this spot. And anyway, I know that you will destroy whatever Thibor left buried in that castle a thousand years ago—if it has survived. But a thousand years, Harry—think of it! Even I do not know if vampire protoplasm can live that long, in those circumstances.

"But it might have survived. Doesn't that . . . interest you?"

Harry detected something like a sigh. *Harry, I will tell you something. Believe me if you like, or disbelieve, but I am at peace. With myself, anyway. I have had my day and I am satisfied. If you had lived for thirteen hundred years then you might understand. Perhaps you will believe me if I say that even you have been a disturbance. But you must disturb me no longer. My debt to Ladislau Giresci is paid in full. Farewell . . .*

Harry waited a moment, then said, "Goodbye, Faethor."

And tired now, strangely weary, he found a space-time door and returned to the Möbius continuum . . .

* * *

Harry Keogh's conversation with Faethor Ferenczy had ended none too soon; Harry Jr. was awake and calling his father's mind home. Snatched from the Möbius continuum into the infant's increasingly powerful id, Harry was obliged to wait out his son's period of wakefulness, which continued into Sunday evening. It was 7:30 P.M. in England when finally Harry Jr. went back to sleep, but in Romania it was two hours later and darkness had already fallen.

The vampire-hunters had a suite of rooms in an old world inn on the outskirts of Ionesti. There in a comfortable pine-panelled lounge they finalized their plans for Monday and enjoyed drinks before making an early night of it. That at least was their intention. Only Irma Dobresti was absent, having gone into Pitesti to make final arrangements for certain ordnance supplies. She had wanted to be sure the requisition was ready. All of the men were agreed that whatever she lacked in looks and personal charm, Irma certain made up for in efficiency.

Harry Keogh, when he materialized, found them with drinks in their hands around a log fire. The only warning of his coming was when Carl Quint suddenly sat bolt upright in his easy chair, spilling his slivovitz into his lap. Visibly paling, staring all about the room with eyes round as saucers, Quint stood up; but even standing it was as if he had shrunk down into himself. "Oh-oh!" he managed to gasp.

Gulharov was plainly puzzled but Krakovitch, too, felt something. He shivered and said, "What? What? I think there is some—"

"You're right," Alec Kyle cut him off, hurrying to the main door of the suite and locking it, then turning off all the lights except one. "There *is* something. Take it easy, all of you. He's coming."

"What?" Krakovitch said again, his breath pluming as the temperature plummeted. "Who is . . . coming?"

Quint took a deep breath. "Felix," he said, his voice

shivery, "you'd better tell Sergei not to panic. This is a friend of ours—but at first meeting he may come as a bit of a shock!"

Krakovitch spoke to Gulharov in Russian, and the young soldier put down his glass and slowly got to his feet. And right then, at that very moment, suddenly Harry was there.

He took his usual form, except that now the infant was no longer foetal but seated in his mid-section, and it no longer turned aimlessly on its own axis but seemed to recline against Harry, eyes closed, in an attitude almost of meditation. Also, the Keogh manifestation seemed paler, had less luminosity, while the image of the child was definitely brighter.

Krakovitch, after the initial shock, recognized Keogh at once. "My God!" he blurted. "A ghost—two ghosts! Yes, and I know one of them. That thing is Harry Keogh!"

"Not a ghost, Felix," said Kyle as he took the Russian's arm. "It's something rather more than a ghost—but nothing to be afraid of, I assure you. Is Sergei all right?"

Gullharov's Adam's apple bobbed frantically; his hands shook and his eyes bulged; if he could have run he probably would have, but the strength had gone out of his legs. Krakovitch spoke to him sharply in Russian, told him to sit, that everything was in order. Sergei didn't believe him but he sat anyway, almost collapsing into his chair.

"The floor's yours, Harry," said Kyle.

"For the sake of goodness!" said Krakovitch, feeling a growing hysteria, but trying to stay calm for Gullharov's sake. "Won't someone explain?"

Keogh looked at him, at Gulharov, too. *You are Krakovitch,* he said to the former. *You have psychic awareness, which makes it easier. But your friend doesn't. I'm getting through to him, but it's an effort.*

Krakovitch opened and closed his mouth like a fish, saying nothing, then thumped down into his chair beside Gulharov. He licked dry lips, glanced at Kyle. "Not . . . not a ghost?"

No, I'm not, Harry answered. *But I suppose it's an understandable mistake. Look, I haven't time to explain my circumstances. Now that you've seen me, maybe Kyle will do that for me? But later. Right now I'm short of time again, and what I have to say is rather important.*

"Felix," said Kyle, "try to put your astonishment behind you. Just accept that this is happening and try to take in what he's saying. I'll tell you all about it just as soon as I have the chance."

The Russian nodded, got a grip of himself, said, "Very well."

Harry told all that he'd learned since the last time he and Kyle had spoken. His terms of expression were very abbreviated; he brought the INTESP men up to date in less than half an hour. Finally he was done, and looked to Kyle for his response. *How are things in England?*

"I contact our people tomorrow at noon," Kyle told him.

And the house in Devon?

"I think the time has come to order them in."

Keogh nodded. *So do I. When do you make your move in the cruciform hills?*

"We finally get to see the place tomorrow," Kyle answered. "After that . . . Tuesday, in daylight!"

Well, remember what I've told you. What Thibor left behind is—big!

"But it lacks intelligence. And as I said, we'll be working in daylight."

Again the Keogh apparition nodded. *I suggest you move in on Harkley House and Bodescu at the same time. By now he has to be pretty sure what he is and he's probably explored his vampire powers, though from what we know of him he doesn't have Thibor's or Faethor's cunning or insularity. They guarded their Wamphyri identities—jealously! They didn't go around making more vampires unnecessarily. On the other hand Yulian Bodescu, perhaps because he's had no instruction, is a time-bomb! Frighten him, then make a mistake and let him go free, and he'll go like wildfire, a vile cancer in the guts of all humanity . . .*

Kyle knew he was right. "I agree with you on the timing," he said, "but are you sure you're not just worrying about Bodescu getting to Thibor before we can act against him?"

I might be, the apparition frowned. *But as far as we know Bodescu isn't even aware of the cruciform hills and what's buried there. But put that aside for now. Tell me, do your men in England know what has to be done? It isn't every man who'd have the stomach for it. It's rough work. The old methods—the stake, decapitation, fire—there are no other ways. Nothing else will work. It can't be done with kid gloves. The fire at Harkley will have to be a big one. A bonfire! Because of the cellars . . .*

"Because we don't know what's down there? I agree. When I speak to my men tomorrow, I'll make sure they fully understand. They already do, I'm sure, but I'll make absolutely certain. The whole house has to go—from the cellars up! Yes, and maybe down a little, too."

Good, said Keogh. For a moment he stood silent, a hologram of thin blue neon wires. He seemed a little uncertain about something, like an actor needing a prompt. Then he said: *Look, I've things to do. There are people— dead people—I need to thank properly for their help. And I've not yet worked out how to break my baby son's hold on me. That's becoming a problem. So if you'll excuse me . . .*

Kyle stepped forward. There seemed some sort of air of finality about Harry Keogh. Kyle wanted to hold out his hand but knew there was nothing there. Nothing of any substance, anyway. "Harry," he said. "Er, give them our thanks, too. Your friends, I mean."

I will, said the other. He smiled a wan smile and disappeared in a rapidly dispersing burst of foxfire.

For long moments there was a breathless silence. Then Kyle turned the light up and Krakovitch drew a massive breath of air. Finally he expelled it, and said: "And now—now I hope you'll agree that you owe me something of an explanation!"

Which was something Kyle could only go along with . . .

Harry Keogh had done all he could. The rest of it lay in the hands of the physically alive, or at least with people who still had hands to accept it.

In the Möbius continuum Harry felt a mental tugging; even sleeping, his baby son's attraction was still enormous. Harry Jr. was tightening his grip, and Harry Sr. was sure that he had been right about the infant: he *was* drawing on his mind, leeching his knowledge, absorbing the substance of his id. Soon Harry must make a permanent break. But how? To where? What would be left of him, he wondered, if he were completely absorbed? Would there be anything left at all?

Or would he simply cease to be except as the future esoteric talent of his own son?

Using the Möbius continuum, Harry could always plumb the future to find the answers to these questions. He preferred not to know all of the answers, however, for the future seemed somehow inviolable. It wasn't that he would feel a cheat but rather that he doubted the wisdom of knowing the future.

For like the past, the future was fixed; if Harry saw something he didn't like, would he try to avoid it? Of course he would, even knowing it was unavoidable. Which could only complicate his weird existence more yet!

The one single glimpse he would allow himself would be to discover if indeed he had any future at all. Which for Harry Keogh was the very simplest of exercises.

Still fighting his son's attraction, he found a future door and opened it, gazed out upon the ever expanding future. Against the subtly shifting darkness of the fourth dimension, Earth's myriad human life-lines of neon blue shot away into a sapphire haze, defining the length of lives that were and lives still to come. Harry's line sped out from his own incorporeal being—from his mind, he supposed—and wound away apparently interminably. But he saw that just beyond the Möbius door it took on a course lying parallel to a second thread, like the twin strips of a motorway with a central verge or barrier. And this second life-line, Harry supposed, must belong to Harry Jr.

He launched himself from the door and traversed future time, following his own and the infant Harry's threads. Faster than the life-lines themselves, he propelled himself into the near future. He witnessed and was saddened by the termination of many blue threads, which simply dimmed and went out, for he knew that these were deaths; and he saw others burst brightly into existence like stars, then extend themselves into brilliant neon filaments, and knew that these were births, new lives. And so he forged a little way forward. Time was briefly furrowed in his wake like the sea behind a forging ship, before closing in and sealing itself once more.

Suddenly, despite the fact that Harry was without body, he felt an icy blast blowing on him from the side. It could hardly be a physical chill and must therefore be of the psyche. Sure enough, away out across the panorama of speeding life-lines, he spied one that was as different as a shark in a school of tuna. For this one was scarlet—the mark of a vampire!

And quite deliberately, it was angling in towards his and Harry Jr.'s threads! Harry knew panic. The scarlet life-line drifted closer; at any moment it must converge with his and the infant's. Then—

Harry Jr.'s life-thread abruptly veered away from his father's, raced off at a tangent on its own amidst an ocean of weaving blue lines. And the thread of Harry Sr. followed suit, avoiding the vampire thread's thrust and turning desperately away. The action had looked for all the world like the manoeuvring of drivers on some other-worldly race track. But the last move had been blind, almost instinctive, and Harry's life-thread seemed now to careen, out of control, across the skein of future time.

Then, in another moment, Harry witnessed and indeed was party to the impossible—a collision! Another blue life-thread, dimming, crumbling, disintegrating, converged with his out of nowhere. The two seemed to bend towards each other as by some mutual attraction, before slamming together in a neon blaze that was much brighter and speeding on as one thread. Briefly Harry felt the presence—or the faint, fading echo—of another mind superimposed on his own. Then it was gone, extinct, and his thread rushed on alone.

He had seen enough. The future must go its own way. (Which it surely would.) He cast about, found a door and side-stepped out of time into the Möbius continuum. At once the infant Harry's tractor id put a grapple on him and began to reel him in. Harry didn't fight it but merely let himself drift home. Home to his son's mind in Hartlepool, on a Sunday night early in the autumn of 1977.

He had intended to talk to certain new friends in Romania, but that would have to wait. As for his "collision" with the future of some other person: he hardly knew what to make of that. But in the brief moment before its expiry, he was sure that he had *recognized* that fading echo of a mind.

And that was the most puzzling thing of all . . .

Chapter Twelve

GENOA IS A CITY OF CONTRASTS. FROM THE LOW-LEVEL POVERTY in the cobbled alleys and sleazy bars of its waterfront areas, to its high-rise luxury apartments looking down on the streets from broad windows and spacious sun-balconies; from the immaculate swimming pools of the rich to the dirty, oil-blackened beaches; from the shadowy, claustrophobic labyrinthine alleys down in the guts of the city to the airy, hugely proportioned stradas and piazzas—contrast is everywhere evident. Gracious gardens give way to chasms of concrete, the comparative silence of select residential suburbs is torn cityward by blasts of traffic noise which lessen not at all through the night, and the sweet air of the higher levels gives way to dust and blue exhaust fumes in the congested, sunless slums. Built on a mountainside, Genoa's levels are many and dizzying.

British Intelligence's safe house there was an enormous top-floor flat in a towering block overlooking the Corso Aurelio Saffi. To the front, facing the ocean, the block rose five high-ceilinged storeys above the road; at the rear, because its foundations were sunk into the summit of a fang of rock, with the building perched on its rim, there was a second level three floors deeper. The aspect from the stubby, low-walled rear balconies was vertiginous, and especially so to Jason Cornwell, alias "Mr. Brown."

Genoa, Sunday, 9:00 P.M.—but in Romania Harry Keogh was still talking to the vampire-hunters in their suite of rooms in Ionesti, and would soon set off to follow his life-thread into the near future; and in Devon, Yulian Bodescu continued to worry about the men who were watching him and worked out a plan to discover who they were and what their interest was. But here in Genoa Jason Cornwell sat thin-lipped and stiffly erect in his chair and watched Theo Dolgikh using a kitchen knife to pick the rotten mortar out of the stonework of the balcony's already dangerous wall. And the sweat on Cornwell's upper lip and in his armpits had little or nothing to do with Genoa's sticky, sultry Indian summer atmosphere.

But it did have to do with the fact that Dolgikh had caught him out, trapped the British spider in his own web, right here in this safe house. Normally the flat would be occupied by a staff of two or three other secret service agents, but because Cornwell (or "Brown") was busy with stuff beyond the scope of ordinary espionage—a specialist job, as it were—the regular occupiers had been "called away" on other work, leaving the premises suitably empty and accessible to Brown alone.

Brown had taken Dolgikh on Saturday, but only a little more than twenty-four hours later the Russian had managed to turn the tables. Feigning sleep, Dolgikh had waited until Sunday noon when Brown went out for a glass of beer and a sandwich, then had worked frenziedly to free himself from the ropes that bound him. When Brown returned fifty minutes later, Dolgikh had taken him completely by surprise. Later . . . Brown had come to with a start, mind and flesh simultaneously assaulted by smelling salts squirted into his nostrils and sharp kicks in his sensi-

tive places. He'd found their positions reversed, for now
he was tied in the chair while Dolgikh was the one with
the smile. Except that the Russian's smile was that of a
hyena.

There had been one thing—really only one—that Dolgikh
wanted to know: where were Krakovitch, Kyle and co.
now? It was quite obvious to the Russian that he'd been
taken out of the game deliberately, which might possibly
mean that it was being played for high stakes. Now it was
his intention to get back in.

"I don't know where they are," Brown had told him.
"I'm just a minder. I mind people and I mind my own
business."

Dolgikh, whose English was good however guttural,
wasn't having any. If he couldn't find out where the espers
were, that was the end of his mission. His next job would
likely be in Siberia! "How did they get on to me?"

"*I* got on to you. Recognized your ugly face—details of
which I've already passed on to London. As for them
recognizing you: without me they wouldn't have been able
to spot you in a monkey-house at the zoo! Not that that
would mean a lot . . ."

"If you told them about me, they must have told you
why they wanted me stopped. And they probably told you
where they were going. Now you'll tell me."

"I can't do that."

At that Dolgikh had come very close, no longer smiling.
"Mr. Secret Agent, minder, or whatever you are, you are
in a lot of trouble. The trouble is this: that unless you
cooperate I will surely kill you. Krakovitch and his soldier
friend are traitors, for they must at least have knowledge
of this. You told them I was here; they gave you your
orders, or at least went along with those orders. I am a
field agent outside my country, working against my country's enemies. I will not hesitate to kill you if you are
obstinate, but things will get very unpleasant before you
die. Do you understand me?"

Brown had understood well enough. "All this talk of killing," he tut-tutted. "I could have killed you many times over, but those weren't my instructions. I was to delay you, that's all. Why blow it up bigger than it is?"

"Why are the British espers working with Krakovitch? What are they doing? The trouble with this psychic gang is this: both sides think they're bigger than the rest of us. They think mind should rule the world and not muscle. But you and me and the others like us, we know that's not the way it is. The strongest always wins. The great warrior triumphs while the great thinker is still thinking about it. Like you and me. You do what they tell you and I work from instinct. And I'm the one on top."

"Are you? Is that why you use the threat of death?"

"Last chance, Mr. Minder. Where are they?"

Still Brown wasn't saying anything. He merely smiled and gritted his teeth.

Dolgikh had no more time to waste. He was an expert in interrogation, which on this occasion meant torture. Basically, there are two types of torture: mental and physical. Just looking at Brown, Dolgikh guessed that pain alone wouldn't crack him. Not in the short term. Anyway, Dolgikh wasn't carrying the rather special tools he'd require. He could always improvise but . . it wouldn't be the same. Also, he didn't wish to mark Brown; not initially, anyway. It must, therefore, be psychological—fear!

And the Russian had discovered Brown's weakness at the very first pass. "You'll notice," he told the British agent conversationally, "that while you are securely trussed, a far better job than you did on me, I have not in fact bound you to the chair." Then he had opened tall louvre doors leading out onto a shallow rear balcony. "I assume you've been out here to admire the view?"

Brown had gone pale in a moment.

"Oh?" Dolgikh was onto him in a flash. "Something about heights, my friend?" He had dragged Brown's chair out onto the balcony, then swung it sharply round so that

Brown was thrown against the wall. Six inches of brick and mortar and a crumbling plaster finish saved him from space and gravity. And his face told the whole story.

Dolgikh had left him there, hurried through the flat and checked out his suspicion. Sure enough, he found every window and balcony door shuttered, closing off not only the light but the height. Especially the height! Mr. Brown suffered from vertigo.

And after that it had been a different game entirely.

The Russian had dragged Brown back inside and positioned him in his chair six feet from the balcony. Then he'd taken a kitchen knife and started to loosen the masonry of the wall, in plain view of the helpless agent. As he'd worked, so he'd explained what he was about.

"Now we're going to start again and I will ask you certain questions. If you answer correctly—which is to say truthfully and without obstruction—then you stay right where you are. Better still, you stay alive. But every time you fail to answer or tell a lie I shall move you a little closer to the balcony and loosen more of the mortar. Naturally, I'll become frustrated if you don't play the game my way. Indeed, I shall probably lose my temper. In which case I may be tempted to throw you against the wall again. Except that the next time I do that, the wall will be so much weaker . . ."

And so the game had begun.

That had been about 7:00 P.M. and it was now 9:00 P.M.; the face of the balcony wall, which had become the focus of Brown's entire being, was now thoroughly defaced and many of the bricks were visibly loose. Worse, Brown's chair now stood with its front legs on the balcony itself, no more than three feet from the wall. Beyond that wall the city's silhouette and the mountains behind it were sprinkled with twinkling lights.

Dolgikh stood up from his handiwork, scuffed at the rubble with his feet, sadly shook his head. "Well, Mr. Minder, you have done quite well—but not quite well

enough. Now, as I suspected might be the case, I am tired
and a little frustrated. You have told me many things,
some important and others unimportant, but you have not
yet told me what I most want to know. My patience is at
an end.''

He moved to stand behind Brown, and pushed the chair
gratingly forward, right up to the wall. Brown's chin came
level with the top, which faced him only eighteen inches
away. ''Do you want to live, Mr. Minder?'' Dolgikh's
voice was soft and deadly.

In fact the Russian fully intended to kill Brown, if only
to pay him back for yesterday. From Brown's point of
view, Dolgikh had no need to kill him; it would be a
pointless exercise and could only queer it for Dolgikh with
British Intelligence, who would doubtless place him on
their ''long overdue'' list. But from the Russian's view-
point . . . he was already on several lists. And in any case,
murder was something he enjoyed. Brown couldn't be
absolutely sure of Dolgikh's intentions, however, and where
there's life there's always hope.

The trussed agent looked across the top of the wall at
Genoa's myriad lights. ''London will know who did it if
you—'' he started to say, then gave a small shriek as
Dolgikh jerked the chair violently. Brown opened his eyes,
drew breath raggedly, sat gulping, trembling, close to
fainting. There was really only one thing in the world that
he feared, and here it was right in front of him. The reason
he'd become useless to the SAS. He could feel the empti-
ness underneath him as if he were already falling.

''Well,'' said the Russian, sighing, ''I can't say it was a
pleasure knowing you—but I'm sure it will be a great
pleasure not knowing you! And so—''

''*Wait!*'' Brown gasped. ''Promise me you'll take me
back inside if I tell you.''

Dolgikh shrugged. ''I shall only kill you if you make
me. Not answering will be more suicide than murder.''

Brown licked his lips. Hell, it was his life! Kyle and the

others had their head start. He'd done enough. "Romania, Bucharest!" he blurted. "They took a plane last night, to get into Bucharest around midnight."

Dolgikh stepped beside him, cocked his head on one side and looked down at his sweating, upturned face. "You know that I only have to telephone the airport and check?"

"Of course." Brown sobbed. His tears were open and unashamed. His nerve had gone entirely. "Now get me inside."

The Russian smiled. "I shall be delighted." He stepped out of Brown's view. The agent felt him sawing with his knife at the ropes where they bound his wrists behind him. The ropes parted, and Brown groaned as he brought his arms around in front of him. Stiff with cramp, he could hardly move them. Dolgikh cut his feet free and collected up the short lengths of rope. Brown made an effort, started to rise unsteadily to his feet—

—And without warning the Russian put both hands on his back and used all his strength to push him forward. Brown cried out, sprawled forward, went crashing over and through the wall into space. Fancy brickwork, fragments of plaster and mortar fell with him.

Dolgikh hawked and spat after him, then wiped his mouth with the back of his hand. From far below there came a single heavy thud and the crashing of fallen masonry.

Moments later the Russian put on Brown's lightweight overcoat, left the flat and wiped the doorknob behind him. He took the lift to the ground floor and left the building, walking unhurriedly. Fifty yards down the road he stopped a taxi and asked to be taken to the airport. On the way he wound down the window, tossed out a few short lengths of rope. The driver, busy with the traffic, didn't see him . . .

By 11:00 that night, Theo Dolgikh had been in touch with his immediate superior in Moscow and was already on his way to Bucharest. If Dolgikh hadn't been incapacitated for the past twenty-four hours—if he'd had the chance to contact his controller earlier—he would have discovered where Kyle, Krakovitch and the others had gone without killing Mr. Brown for that information. Not that it mattered greatly, for he knew he would have killed him anyway.

Moreover, he could have learned something of what the espers were doing there in Romania, that in fact they were searching for . . . something in the ground? Dolgikh's controller hadn't waited to be more specific than that. Treasure, maybe? Dolgikh couldn't imagine, and he wasn't really interested. He put the question out of his mind. Whatever they were doing, it wasn't good for Russia, and that was enough for him.

Now, crammed in the tiny seat of the passenger aircraft as it sped across the northern Adriatic, he tilted himself backwards a little and relaxed, allowing his mind to drift with the hum of the engines . . .

Romania. The region around Ionesti. Something in the ground. It was all very strange.

Strangest of all, Dolgikh's "controller" was one of them—one of these damned psychic spies, whom Andropov so heartily detested! The KGB man closed his eyes and chuckled. What would Krakovitch's reaction be, he wondered, when he eventually discovered that the traitor in his precious E-Branch was his own Second in Command, a man called Ivan Gerenko?

Yulian Bodescu had not spent a pleasant night. Even the presence of his beautiful cousin in his bed—her lovely body his to use in whichever way amused him—had not compensated for his nightmares and fantasies and frustrated half-memories out of a past not entirely his own.

It was all down to the watchers, Yulian supposed, those damned busybodies whose spying (For what purpose? What did they know? What were they trying to find out?) over the last forty-eight hours had become an almost unbearable irritation. Oh, he no longer had any real cause to fear them—George Lake was fine ashes, and the three women would never dare go against Yulian—but still the men were there! Like an itch you can't scratch. Or one you aren't able to reach—for the moment. Yes, it was down to them.

They had brought on Yulian's nightmares, his dreams of wooden stakes, steel swords and bright, searing flames. As for those other dreams: of low hills in the shape of a cross, tall dark trees, and of a Thing in the ground that called and called to him, beckoning with fingers that dripped blood . . . Yulian was not quite sure what he should make of them.

For he had been there—actually *there,* on the cruciform hills—the night his father died. He had been a mere foetus in his mother's womb when it had happened, he knew that, but what *else* had happened that time? His roots were there, anyway, Yulian felt sure of that. But the fact remained that there was only one way he could ever be absolutely sure, and that would be to answer the call and go there. Indeed a trip to Romania might well be useful in solving two problems at once; for with the secret watchers out there in the fields and lanes around Harkley, now was probably as good a time as any to make himself scarce for a while.

Except . . . first he would like to know what the real purpose of those watchers was. Were they merely suspicious, or did they actually know something? And if so, what did they intend to do about it? Yulian had already developed a plan to get those questions answered. It was just a matter of getting it right, that was all . . .

The sky was cloudy and the morning dull that Monday when Yulian rose up from his bed. He told Helen to bathe, dress herself prettily, go about the house and grounds just as if her life were completely normal, unchanged. He dressed and went down to the cellars, where he gave the same instructions to Anne. Likewise his mother in her room. Just act naturally and let nothing appear suspicious;

indeed, Helen could even drive him into Torquay for an hour or two.

They were followed into Torquay but Yulian was not aware of it. He was distracted by the sun, which kept breaking through the clouds and reflecting off mirrors, windows and chrome. He still affected his broad-brimmed hat and sunglasses, but his hatred of the sun—and its effect on him—were much stronger now. The car's mirrors irritated him; his reflection in the windows and other bright surfaces disturbed him; his vampire "awareness" was playing hell with his nerves. He felt closed in. Danger threatened and he knew it—but from which quarter? What sort of danger?

While Helen waited in the car, three storeys up in a municipal car park, he went to a travel agency and made inquiries, then gave instructions. This took a little time, for the holiday he had chosen was outside the usual scope of the agency. He wanted to spend a week in Romania. Yulian might simply have phoned one of London's airports and made a booking, but he preferred to let an authorized agency advise him on restrictions, visas, etc. This way there would be no errors, no last minute holdups. Also, Yulian couldn't stay penned up in Harkley House forever; driving into town had at least given him a break from routine, from his watchers, and from the increasing pressures of being a creature alone. What was more, the drive had let him keep up appearances: Helen was his pretty cousin down from London, and he and she were simply out for a drive, enjoying what was left of the good weather. So it would appear.

After making his travel arrangements (the agency would ring him within forty-eight hours and let him have all the details) Yulian took Helen for lunch. While she ate listlessly and tried desperately hard not to look fearful of him, he sipped a glass of red wine and smoked a cigarette. He might have tried a steak, rare, but food—ordinary food—no longer appealed. Instead he found himself watching Helen's throat. He was aware of the danger in that, however, and so concentrated his mind on the details of his plan for tonight instead. Certainly he did not intend to stay hungry for very long.

By 1:30 P.M. they had driven back to Harkley; and then, too, Yulian had briefly picked up the thoughts of another watcher. He'd tried to infiltrate the stranger's mind but it immediately shut him out. They were clever, these watchers! Furious, he raged inwardly through the afternoon and could scarcely contain himself until the fall of night.

Peter Keen was a comparatively recent recruit to INTESP's team of parapsychologists. A sporadic telepath, (his talent, as yet untrained, came in uncontrolled, unannounced bursts, and was wont to depart just as quickly and mysteriously) he'd been recruited after tipping off the police on a murder-to-be. He had accidentally scanned the mind—the dark intention—of the would-be rapist and murderer. When it happened just as he'd said it would, a high-ranking policeman, a friend of the branch, had passed details on to the INTESP. The job in Devon was Keen's first field assignment, for until now all of his time had been spent with his instructors.

Yulian Bodescu was under full twenty-four hour surveillance now, and Keen had the mid-morning shift, 8:00 A.M. till 2:00 P.M. At 1:30 when the girl had driven Bodescu back through Harkley's gates and up to the house, Keen had been only two hundred yards behind in his red Capri. Driving straight past Harkley, he'd stopped at the first telephone kiosk and phoned headquarters, passing on details of Bodescu's outing.

At the hotel in Paignton, Darcy Clarke took Keen's call and passed the telephone to the man in charge of the operation, a jolly, fat, middle-aged chain-smoking "scryer" called Guy Roberts. Normally Roberts would be in London, employing his scrying to track Russian submarines, terrorist bomb squads and the like, but now he was here as head of operations, keeping his mental eye on Yulian Bodescu.

Roberts had found the task not at all to his liking and far from easy. The vampire is a solitary creature whose nature it is to be secretive. There is that in a vampire's mental makeup which shields him as effectively as the night screens his physical being. Roberts could see Harkley House only as a vague, shadowy place, as a scene viewed through dense, weaving mist. When Bodescu was there this mental miasma rolled that much more densely, making it difficult for Roberts to pinpoint any specific person or object.

Practice makes perfect, however, and the longer Roberts stayed with it the clearer his pictures were coming. He could now state for certain, for instance, that Harkley House was occupied by only four people: Bodescu, his mother, his aunt and her daughter. But there was something else there, too. Two somethings, in fact. One of them was Bodescu's dog, but obscured by the same aura, which was very strange. And the other was—simply "the Other." Like Yulian himself, Roberts thought of it only that way. But whatever it was—in all likelihood the thing in the cellars which Alec Kyle had warned about—it was certainly there and it was alive . . .

"Roberts here," the scryer spoke into the telephone. "What is it, Peter?"

Keen passed his message.

"Travel agency?" Roberts frowned. "Yes, we'll get on to it at once. Your relief? He's on his way right now. Trevor Jordan, yes. See you later, Peter." Roberts put down the telephone and picked up a directory. Moments later he was phoning the travel agency in Torquay, whose name and address Keen had given him.

When he got an answer, Roberts held a handkerchief to his mouth, contrived a young voice. "Hello? Er, hello?"

"Hello?" came back the answer. "Sunsea Travel, here—

who's calling, please?" It was a male voice, deep and smooth.

"Seem to have a bad line," Roberts replied, keeping his voice to a medium pitch. "Can you hear me? I was in, oh, an hour ago. Mr. Bodescu?"

"Ah, yes, sir!" The booking agent raised his voice. "Your Romanian inquiry. Bucharest, any time in the next two weeks. Right?"

Roberts gave a start, made an effort to keep his muffled voice even. "Er, Romania, yes, that's right." He thought fast—furiously fast. "Er, look, I'm sorry to be a nuisance, but—"

"Yes?"

"Well, I've decided I can't make it after all. Maybe next year, eh?"

"Ah!" There was some disappointment in the other's tone. "Well, that's the way it goes. Thanks for calling, sir. So you're definitely cancelling, right?"

"Yes." Roberts jiggled the phone a bit. "I'm afraid I have to . . . Damn bad line, this! Anyway, something's come up, and—"

"Well, don't worry about it, Mr. Bodescu," the travel agent cut him off. "It happens all the time. And anyway, I haven't yet found the time to make any real inquiries. So no harm done. But do let me know if you change your mind again, won't you?"

"Oh, indeed! I will, I will. Most helpful of you. Sorry to have been such a nuisance."

"Not at all, sir. Bye now."

"Er, goodbye!" Roberts put the phone down.

Darcy Clarke, who had been party to this exchange, said, "Sheer genius! Well done, Chief!"

Roberts looked up but didn't smile. "Romania!" he repeated, ominously. "Things are hotting up, Darcy. I'll be glad when Kyle gets his call through. He's two hours overdue."

At that very moment the phone rang again.

Clarke inclined his head knowingly. "Now that's what I call a talent. If it doesn't happen—make it!"

Roberts pictured Romania in his mind's eye—his own interpretation, for he'd never been there—then superimposed an image of Alec Kyle over a rugged Romanian countryside. He closed his eyes and Kyle's picture came up in photographic—no, live—detail.

"Roberts here."

"Guy?" Kyle's voice came back, crisp with static. "Listen, I intended to route this through London, John Grieve, but I couldn't get him." Roberts knew what he meant: obviously he would have liked the call to be one hundred per cent secure.

"I can't help you there," he answered. "There's no one that special around right now. Are there problems, then?"

"Shouldn't think so." In the eye of Roberts's mind, Kyle was frowning. "We lacked a bit of privacy in Genoa, but that cleared up. As for why I'm late; it's like contacting Mars getting through from here! Talk about antiquated systems. If I didn't have local help . . . anyway, have you got anything for me?"

"Can we talk straight?"

"We'll have to."

Roberts quickly brought him up to date, finishing with Bodescu's thwarted trip to Romania. In his mind's eye he saw, as well as physically hearing, Kyle's gasp of horror. Then the head of INTESP got hold of his emotions; even if Bodescu's plans to come over here hadn't been foiled, still it would have been too late for him.

"By the time we've finished over here," he grimly told Roberts, "there'll be nothing left for him anyway. And by the time you've finished over there . . . he won't be able to go anywhere." Then he told Roberts in detail exactly what he wanted done. It took him a good fifteen minutes to make sure he covered everything.

"When?" Roberts asked him when he was finished.

Kyle was cautious. "Are you part of the surveillance

team? I mean, do you physically go out to the house and watch him?''

"No. I co-ordinate. I'm always here at the HQ. But I do want to be in on the kill."

"Very well, I'll tell you when it's to be," said Kyle. "But you're *not* to pass it on to the others! Not until as close as possible to zero hour itself. I don't want Bodescu picking it out of someone's mind."

"That makes sense. Wait—" Roberts sent Clarke into the next room, out of earshot, "OK, when?"

"Tomorrow—in daylight. Let's settle for 5:00 P.M. your time. By then we'll have done our bit, just an hour or so earlier. There are certain obvious reasons why daylight will be best, and on your side of the job one not so obvious reason. When Harkley goes up, it'll make a big blaze. You'll need to make sure local fire services don't get there too soon and put it out. If it was at night, the flames would be visible for miles. Anyway, that's for you to work on. But the last thing you want is outside interference, OK?''

"Got it," said Roberts.

"That's it, then," said Kyle. "We probably won't be talking again until it's all finished. So good luck!"

"Good luck," Roberts answered, letting Kyle's face fade in his mind as he replaced the receiver in its cradle . . .

Most of Monday found Harry Keogh trying without success to break the magnetic attraction of his son's psyche. There was no way. The child fought him, clung to both Harry and the waking world alike with an incredible tenacity, would *not* go to sleep. Brenda Keogh marked the baby's fever, thought to call a doctor, then changed her mind; but she determined that if the baby stayed as bad tempered through the night, and if in the morning his temperature was still on the high side, then she'd get advice.

She couldn't know that Harry Jr.'s fever resulted from the mental contest he waged with his father, a fight the infant was winning hands down. But Harry Sr. knew it well enough. The baby's will—and his strength—both were enormous! The child's mind was a black hole whose gravity must surely pull Harry in entirely. And Harry had discovered something: that indeed a mind without a body can grow weary, and just like flesh be worn down. So that when he could no longer fight he gave in and retreated into himself, glad that for now his vain striving and struggling were over.

Like a game fish on the end of a line, he allowed himself to be reeled in, close to the boat. But he knew he must fight again when he sensed the gaff poised to strike. Incorporeal, it would be Harry's last chance to retain an individual identity. That was why *he* would fight, for the continuation of his existence, but he couldn't help wondering: what did all of this mean to his son? *Why* did Harry Jr. want him? Was it simply the terrific greed of any healthy infant, or was it something else entirely?

As for the baby himself: he recognized his father's partial surrender, accepted the fact that for now the fight was over. And he had no means by which to tell this fantastic adult that it wasn't a fight at all, not really, but simply a desperate desire to know, to learn. Father and son, two minds in one small, fragile—defenseless?—body, both of them took the welcome opportunity to sleep.

And at 5:00 P.M. when Brenda Keogh looked in on her baby son, she was pleased to note that he lay still and at peace in his cot, and that his temperature was down again . . .

About 4:30 P.M. that same Monday afternoon, in Ionesti: Irma Dobresti had just answered a telephone call from Bucharest. The telephone conversation had grown sufficiently heated to cause the rest of the party to listen in. Krakovitch's face had fallen, telling Kyle and Quint that something was amiss. When Irma was through and after she'd hurled the phone down, Krakovitch spoke up.

"Despite the fact that all of this should have been

cleared, now there is a problem from the Lands Ministry. Some idiot is questioning our authority. You are remembering, this Romania—not Russia! The land we want to burn is common land and has belonged to the people since time—how do you say?—immemorial. If it was just some farmer's property we could buy him off, but—'' He shrugged helplessly.

"This is correct," Irma spoke up. "Men from the Ministry, from Ploiesti, will be coming here to talk to us later tonight. I don't knowing how this leaked out, but this is officially their area and under their, er, jurisdiction? Yes. It could be big problems. Questions and answers. Not everyone believe in vampires!''

"But aren't you from the Ministry?" Kyle was alarmed. "I mean, we have to get the job done!"

They had driven out early that morning to the spot where almost two decades ago Ilya Bodescu's body had been recovered from a tangle of undergrowth and densely grown firs on a steep south-facing slope of the cruciform hills. And when they had climbed higher, then they'd come across Thibor's mausoleum. There, where lichen-covered slabs had leaned like menhirs under the motion-less trees, all three psychics—Kyle, Quint and Krakovitch alike— had felt the still extant menace of the place. They had left quickly.

Wasting no time, Irma had called up her team of civil engineers, a foreman and five men, based in Pitesti. Through Krakovitch, Kyle had put a question to the hardhat boss.

"Are you and your men used to handling this stuff?"

"Thermite? Oh, yes. Sometimes we blast, and sometimes we burn. I've worked for you Russians before, up north in Berezov. We used it all the time—to soften up the permafrost. Can't see the point of it here, though . . .''

"Plague," said Krakovitch at once, by way of explanation. It was an invention of his own. "We've come across old records that tell of a mass burial of plague victims right here. Although it was three hundred years ago, the soil deep down is still likely to be infected. These hills have been redesignated arable land. Before we let any unsuspecting farmer start ploughing it up, or terracing the hillside, we want to make sure it's safe. Right down to the bedrock!''

Irma Dobresti had caught all of this. She had raised an eyebrow at Krakovitch but said nothing.

''And how did you Soviets get involved?'' the hard-hat had wanted to know.

Krakovitch had anticipated that one. ''We dealt with a similar case in Moscow just a year ago,'' he had answered. Which was more or less the truth.

Still the hard-hat had been curious. ''And the British?''

Now Irma stepped in. ''Because they may have a similar problem in England,'' she snapped. ''And so they're here to see how we deal with it, right?''

The ganger hadn't minded facing up to Krakovitch, but he wasn't going to go against Irma Dobresti. ''Where do you want your holes?'' he'd asked. ''And how deep?''

By just after midday the preparations were completed. All that remained was the detonators to be wired up to a plunger, a ten minute job which for safety's sake could wait until tomorrow.

Carl Quint had suggested. ''We could finish it now . . .''

But Kyle had decided against it. ''We don't really know what we're playing with here,'' he'd answered. ''Also, when the job's done, I don't want to hang about but get straight on with the next phase—Faethor's castle in the Khorvaty. I imagine that after we've burned this hillside there'll be all kinds of people coming up here to see what we've been up to. So I'd prefer to be out of it the same day. This afternoon Felix has travel arrangements to see to, and I've a call to make to our friends in Devon. By the time that's done the light will be failing, and I'd prefer to work in daylight after a good night's sleep. So—''

''Sometime tomorrow?''

"In the afternoon, while the sun's still slanting onto that hillside."

Then he'd turned to Krakovitch. "Felix, are these men going back to Pitesti today?"

"They will be," Krakovitch answered, "if there is nothing else for them to do until tomorrow afternoon. Why are you asking this?"

Kyle had shrugged. "Just a feeling," he said. "I would have liked them to be closer at hand. But—"

"I, too, have had a feeling," the Russian answered, frowning. "I am thinking, nerves—perhaps?"

"That makes all three of us then," Carl Quint had added. "So let's hope that it is just nerves and nothing else, right?"

All of that had been mid-morning, and everything had appeared to be going smoothly. And now suddenly there was this threat of outside interference. Between times Kyle had made his call to Devon, taking two hours to get through, and had arranged for the strike against Harkley House. "Damn it!" he snapped now. "It *has* to be tomorrow. Ministry or none, we've got to go ahead with this."

"We should have done it this morning," said Quint, "when we were right on top of it . . ."

Irma Dobresti stepped in. She narrowed her eyes and said, "Listen. These local bureaucrats are annoying me. Why don't you four just drive back to the site? Right now, I mean! See, I was perhaps alone when that call came in—you men were all out there in the foothills, doing your job. I'll telephone Pitesti, get Chevenu and those rough men of his back up there to meet you at the site. You can do the job—I mean finish it—tonight."

Kyle stared at her. "That's a good idea, Irma—but what about you? Won't you be setting yourself up? Won't they give you a hard time?"

"What?" She looked surprised at the suggestion. "Is it my fault I was alone here when I took that telephone call? Is it me for blaming that my taxi took a wrong turning and

I couldn't find you to stop you from burning the hills? All these country tracks looking the same to me!''

Krakovitch, Kyle and Quint, all three grinned at each other. Sergei Gullharov was mainly out of it, but he sensed the excitement of the others and stood up, nodding his head as if in agreement. "Da, da!''

"Right,'' said Kyle, "let's do it!'' And on impulse, he grabbed Irma Dobresti, pulled her close and kissed her soundly . . .

Monday night.

9:30 middle-European time, and in England 7:30 P.M.

There was fire and nightmare on the cruciform hills under the moon and stars and the looming Carpatii Meridionali, and the nightmare transferred itself westward across mountains and rivers and oceans to Yulian Bodescu where he tossed on his bed and sweated the chill, rank sweat of fear in his garret room at Harkley House.

Exhausted by the unspecified fears of the day, he now suffered the telepathic torments of Thibor the Wallach, the vampire whose last physical vestiges were finally being consumed. There was no way back for the vampire now; but unlike Faethor, Thibor's spirit was unquiet, restless, malignant. And it ached for revenge!

Yuliaannn! Ah, my son, my one true son! See what is become of your father now . . .

"What?'' Yulian talked in his sleep, imagined a blistering heat, flames that crept ever closer. And in the heart of the fire, a figure beckoning. "Who . . . who are you?''

Ah, you know me, my son. We met but briefly, and you were still unborn at the meeting, but you can remember if you try.

"Where am I?''

For the moment, with me. Ask not where you are, but where I am. These are the cruciform hills—where it started for you, and where it now ends for me. For you this is merely a dream, while for me it is reality.

"You! Now Yulian knew him. The voice that called in the night, unremembered until now. The Thing in the ground. The source. "You? My . . . father?"

Indeed! Oh, not through any lover's tryst with your mother. Not through the lust or love of a man for a woman. No, but your father nevertheless. Through blood, Yulian, through blood!

Yulian fought down his fear of the flames. He sensed that he only dreamed—however real and immediate the dream—and knew he would not be hurt. He advanced into the inferno of fire and drew close to the figure there. Black billowing smoke and crimson flames obscured his view and the heat was a furnace all around, but there were questions Yulian must ask, and the burning Thing was the only one who could answer them.

"You have asked me to come and seek you out, and I will come. But why? What is it you want of me?"

Too late! Too late! the flame-wreathed apparition cried out in anguish. And Yulian knew that his pain was not born of the consuming fire but bitter frustration. *I would have been your teacher, my son. Yes, and you would have learned all the many secrets of the Wamphyri. In return . . . I can't deny that there would have been a reward in it for me. I would have walked again in the world of men, known again the unbearable pleasures of my youth! But too late. All dreams and schemes to no avail. Ashes to ashes, dust to dust . . .*

The figure was slowly melting, its outline gradually changing, rendering down into itself.

Yulian must know more, must see more clearly. He penetrated the very heart of the inferno, came close up to the burning Thing. "I already know the secrets of the Wamphyri!" he cried above the crackle of blazing trees and the hiss of molten earth. "I learned them for myself!"

Can you put on the shapes of lesser creatures?

"I can go on all fours like a great dog," Yulian answered. "And in the night, people would swear I *was* a dog!"

Hah! A dog! A man who would be a dog! What is that for an ambition? It is nothing! Can you form wings, glide like a bat?

"I . . . haven't tried."

You know nothing.

"I can make others like myself!"

Fool! That is the simplest of things. Not to make them is much harder!

"When harmful men are nearby, I sense their minds . . ."

That is instinct, which you got from me. Indeed, everything you have you got from me! So you read minds, eh? But can you bend those minds to your will?

"With my eyes, yes."

Beguilement, hypnotism, a stage magician's trick! You are an innocent.

"Damn you!" Yulian's pride was hurt at last, his patience all used up. "What are you anyway but a dead thing? I'll tell you what I've learned: I can take a dead creature and draw out its secrets, and know all that it knew in life!"

Necromancy? It is so? And no one to show you how? That is an achievement! There is hope for you yet.

"I can heal my own wounds as though they never were, and I've the strength of any two men. I could lie with a woman and love her—to death, if I desired—and not even weary myself. And only anger me, dear father, and then I could kill, kill, *kill!* But not you, for you're already dead. Hope for me? I'll say there is. But what hope is there for you?"

For a moment there was no answer from the melting Thing. Then—

Ahhh! And indeed you are my son, Yuliaannn! Closer, come closer still.

Yulian moved to less than arm's length from the Thing, facing it squarely. The stench of its burning was monstrous. Its blackened outer shell began to crumble, rapidly disintegrated and fell away. The flames immediately attacked the inner image, which Yulian now saw almost as a reflection of himself. It had the same features, the same bone structure, the same dark attraction. The face of a fallen angel. They could be peas from the same pod.

"You . . . you *are* my father!" he gasped.

I was, the other groaned. *Now I am nothing. I am burning away, as you see. Not the real me but something I left behind. It was my last hope, and through it—and with your help—I might have been a power in the world once again. But it's too late now.*

"Then why do you concern yourself with me?" Yulian tried to understand. "Why have you come to me—or drawn me to you? If I can't help you, what's the point of this?"

Revenge! The burning Thing's voice was suddenly sharp as a knife in Yulian's dreaming mind. *Through you!*

"I should avenge you? Against whom?"

Against the ones who found me here. The ones who even now destroy my last chance for a future. Against Harry Keogh and his pack of white magicians!

"You're not making sense." Yulian shook his head, gazed in morbid fascination as the Thing continued to melt. He saw his own features liquefying, streaming away and falling from the burning creature in molten tatters. "What white magicians? Harry Keogh? I don't know anyone of that name."

But he knows you! First me, Yulian, and then you! Harry Keogh knows us—and he knows the way: the stake, the sword, and the fire! You tell me you can sense the presence of enemies—and have you not sensed just such enemies close to you even now? They are one and the same. First me, and then you!

Even dreaming, Yulian felt his scalp crawling. The secret watchers, of course! "What must I do?"

Avenge me, and save yourself. That, too, is one and the same. For they know what we are, Yulian, and they cannot abide us. You must kill them, for if you don't they'll surely kill you!

The last scrap of human flesh fell from the nightmarish entity, revealing at last its true, inner reality. Yulian hissed his horror, drew back a little way, gazed upon the face of all evil. He saw Thibor's bat's snout, his convoluted ears, long jaws, crimson eyes. The vampire laughed at him—the bass booming of a great hound—and a split tongue flickered redly in a cave of teeth. Then, as if someone had applied a giant's bellows to the task, the flames roared up higher still and rushed in, and the image blackened at once and turned to glowing cinders.

Trembling violently, running with sweat, Yulian came awake, sat bolt upright in his bed. And as from a million miles away he heard again, one last time, Thibor's far, faint voice: *Avenge me, Yuliaannn* . . .

He stood up in the dark room, went shakily to the window, looked out on the night. Out there, a mind. A man. Watching. Waiting.

Sweat quickly dried on Yulian and his flesh turned cold, but still he stood there. Panic receded, was replaced by rage, hatred. "Avenge you, father?" he finally breathed. "Oh, I will. I will!"

In the window's luminous, night-dark pane his reflection was an echo from the dream. But Yulian was neither shocked nor surprised. It simply meant that his metamorphosis was now complete. He looked through the reflection at the dark, furtive shadow there in the hedgerow . . . and grinned.

And his grin was like an invitation to step in through the gates of hell . . .

At the foot of the cruciform hills, Kyle and Quint, Krakovitch and Gulharov waited close together in a small group. It wasn't cold but they stood together, as if for warmth.

The fire was dying down now; the wind which had

earlier sprung up out of nowhere had quickly blown itself out, like the dying breath of some unseen Gargantuan. Human figures, half hidden in the trees and the billowing black smoke, toiled above and to the east of the devastated area, containing the fire and beating it down. A grimy, coveralled hulk of a man came stumbling from the trees at the foot of the slope toward the vampire hunters where they huddled. It was the Romanian ganger, Janni Chevenu.

"You!" He grabbed Krakovitch's arm. "Plague, you said! But did you *see* it? Did you see that . . . that *thing* before it burned? It had eyes, mouths! It lashed, writhed . . . it . . . it . . . my God! My *God!*"

Under the soot and sweat, Chevenu's face was chalk. Slowly his glazed eyes cleared. He looked from Krakovitch to the others. The gaunt faces that looked back seemed carved of the same emotion: a horror, no less than Chevenu's own.

"Plague, you said," he dazedly repeated. "But that wasn't any kind of plague I ever heard of."

Krakovitch shook himself loose. "Oh yes it was, Janni," he finally answered. "It was the very worst kind. Just consider yourself lucky you were able to destroy it. We're in your debt. All of us. Everywhere . . ."

Darcy Clarke should have had the 8:00 P.M.–2:00 A.M. shift; instead he was bedded down at the hotel in Paignton—something he'd eaten, apparently. Stomach cramps and violent diarrhoea.

Peter Keen had taken the shift in Clarke's place, driving out to Harkley House and relieving Trevor Jordan of the job of keeping Bodescu under observation.

"Nothing's happening up there," Jordan had whispered, leaning in through the open window of his car, handing Keen a powerful crossbow with a hardwood bolt. "There's a light on downstairs, but that's all. They're all in there, or if not then they didn't come out through the gate! The light did come on in Bodescu's attic room for a few minutes, then went out again. That was probably him getting his head down. Also, I felt that there just might be someone probing for my thoughts—but that lasted for only a moment. Since when it's been quiet as the proverbial tomb.''

Keen had grinned, however nervously. "Except we know that not every tomb is quiet, eh?''

Jordan hadn't found it funny. "Peter, that's a really weird sense of humour you've got there.'' He nodded at the crossbow in Keen's hand. "Do you know how to use that? Here, I'll load it for you.''

"That's OK,'' Keen nodded affably. "I'll manage it all right. But if you want to do me a real favour, just make sure my relief's on time at two in the morning!''

Jordan got into his car and started it, trying not to rev the engine. "This makes twelve hours out of twenty-four for you doesn't it? Son, you're a glutton for punishment. Keen by name, and all that. You should go far—if you don't kill yourself first. Have a nice night!'' And he'd pulled carefully away in his car, only turning on the lights when he was a hundred yards down the road.

That had been only half an hour ago but already Keen was cursing himself for his big mouth. His old man had been a soldier. "Peter,'' he'd once told him, "never volunteer. If they need volunteers, that's because nobody wants the job.'' And on a night like this it was easy to understand why.

There was something of a ground mist and the air was laden with moisture. The atmosphere felt greasy, and heavy as a tangible weight on Keen's shoulders. He turned up his collar, lifted infra-red binoculars to his eyes. For the tenth time in thirty minutes he scanned the house. Nothing. The house was warm, which showed clearly enough, but nothing moved in there. Or the movement was too slight to detect.

He scanned what could be seen of the grounds. Again, nothing—or rather, something! Keen's sweep had passed over a hazy blue blur of warmth, just a blob of body heat which his special nite-lites had picked up. It could be a fox, badger, dog—or a man? He tried to find it again, failed. So . . . had he seen something, or hadn't he?

Something buzzed and tingled in Keen's head, like a sudden burst of electrical current, making him start . . . *Slimy gibber-gobble spying babble-gabble bastard!*

Keen froze stiff as a board. What was that? What the *hell* was that?

You're going to die, die, die! Ha, ha, ha! Gibber-jabber, gobble-gabble . . . And then some more of the electrical tingling. And silence.

Jesus Christ! But Keen knew without further inquiry what it was: his unruly talent. For a moment then, just for a few seconds, he'd picked up another mind. A mind full of hate!

"Who?" Keen said out loud, staring all about, ankle-deep in swirling mist. "What . . . ?" Suddenly the night was full of menace.

He'd left the crossbow in his car, loaded and lying on the front seat. The red Capri was parked with its nose in a field, about twenty-five yards away along the road. Keen was on the verge, his shoes, socks and feet already soaking from walking in the grass. He looked at Harkley House, standing sinister in its misty grounds, then started to back off towards the car. In the grounds of the old house, something loped towards the open gate. Keen saw it for a moment, then lost it in the shadows and the mist.

A dog? A large dog? Darcy Clarke had had trouble with a dog, hadn't he?

Keen backed faster, stumbled and almost fell. An owl hooted somewhere in the night. Other than that there was only silence. And a soft, deliberate padding—and a panting? —from beyond the gate just across the road. Keen backed faster yet, all his senses alert, his nerves starting to jump. Something was coming, he could feel it. And not just a dog.

He slammed backwards into the side of his car, drew breath in an audible, grateful gasp. He half turned, reached in through the open window, groped with his hand on the front seat. He found something, drew it into view . . .

The lignum vitae bolt—broken in two halves—hanging together by a mere splinter of wood! Keen shook his head in dumb disbelief, reached into the car again. This time he found the crossbow, unloaded, its tough metal wings bent back and twisted out of shape.

Something tall and black flowed out of the shadows right up to him. It wore a cape which, at the last moment, it threw back. Keen looked into a face which wasn't nearly human. He tried to scream but his throat felt like sandpaper.

The thing in black glared at Keen and its lips drew back. Its teeth were hooked together, meshing like the teeth of a shark. Keen tried to run, leap, move, but couldn't; his feet were rooted to the spot. The thing in black raised its arm in a swift movement and something gleamed a wet, silvery gleam in the night.

A cleaver!

Chapter Thirteen

WHEN KYLE AND HIS COMPANIONS GOT BACK TO IONESTI AND the inn, they found Irma Dobresti pacing the floor of their suite, nervously massaging her long hands. Her relief when she saw them was obvious. Likewise her delight when they told her the operation had been a complete success. They weren't eager, however, to detail much of what had happened in the foothills; looking at their drawn faces, she was wise enough not to pry. They might tell her later, in their own time.

"So," she said, after they'd had a drink, "the job is done here. We are not needing to stay any longer in Ionesti. It is ten-thirty—late, I know, but I am suggesting we go now. These red tape dolts will arrive soon. Is better if we are not here."

"Red tape?" Quint looked surprised. "I didn't know you used that term, er, over here!"

"Oh, yes," she answered, unsmiling. "Also 'Commie,' and 'Zurich Gnome,' and 'Capitalist dog!' "

"I agree with Irma," said Kyle. "If we wait we'll only

be obliged to brazen it out—or tell the truth. And the truth, while it is verifiable in the long term, isn't immediately believable. No, I can see all kinds of problems coming up if we stay here.''

''All true.'' She nodded, sighing her relief that the Englishman was of a like mind. ''Later, if they are determined to talk about this, they can contact me in Bucharest. There I am on my own ground, with the backing of my superiors. I am not for blaming. This was a matter of national security, a liaison of a scientific, preventative nature between three great countries, Romania, Russia, and Great Britain. I am secure. But right now, here in Ionesti, I do not feel secure.''

''So let's get to it,'' said Quint, with his usual efficiency.

Irma showed her yellow teeth in one of her infrequent smiles. ''No need for getting to it,'' she informed. ''Nothing to get to. I took the liberty of packing your bags! Can we go now, please?''

Without more ado, they paid the bill and left.

Krakovitch opted to drive, giving Sergei Gulharov a break. As they sped back towards Bucharest on the night roads, Gulharov sat beside Irma in the back of the car and quietly filled her in as best he could on the story of what had happened in the hills, the monstrous thing they had burned there.

When he was finished she said simply, ''Your faces told me it must have been like that. I am glad I am not seeing it . . .''

After his last painful visit, at about 10:00 P.M., Darcy Clarke had slept like a log in his hotel bedroom for nearly three hours solid. When he woke up he felt fighting fit. All very mysterious; he'd never known an attack of gastroenteritis to come and go so quickly (not that he was sorry it had gone) and he had no idea what he could have eaten to cause it. Whatever it had been, the rest of the team had felt no ill effects. It was because he didn't want to let that team down that Clarke dressed quickly and went to report himself fit for duty.

In the control room (the living area of their main suite of rooms), he found Guy Roberts slumped in his swivel chair, head on his folded arms where he sprawled across his "desk": a dining table, cluttered with notes, a log book and a telephone. He was fast asleep with an ashtray piled full of dog-ends right under his nose. A tobacco addict, he probably wouldn't be able to sleep comfortably without it!

Trevor Jordan snoozed in a deep armchair while Ken Layard and Simon Gower quietly played their own version of Chinese Patience at a small green-baize card table. Gower, a prognosticator or augur of some talent, played badly, making too many mistakes. "Can't concentrate!" he growlingly complained. "I have this feeling of bad stuff coming—lots of it!"

"Stop making excuses!" said Layard. "Hell, we *know* bad stuff is coming! And we know where from. We don't know when, that's all."

"No" Gower frowned, tossed in his hand, "I mean not of our making. When we go against Harkley and Bodescu, that will be different. This thing I'm feeling is—" he shrugged uneasily, "something else."

"So maybe we should wake up the Fat Man there and tell him?" Layard suggested.

Gower shook his head. "I've been telling him for the last three days. It isn't specific—it never is—but it's there. You could be right: I'm probably feeling the ding-dong coming up at Harkley House. If so, then believe me it's going to be a good one! Anyway, let old Roberts kip. He's tired—and when he's awake the place stinks of bloody weed! I've seen him with three going at once! God, you need a respirator!"

Clarke stepped around Roberts's snoring form to check the roster. Roberts had only mapped it out until the end of the afternoon shift. Keen was on now, to be relieved by

Layard, a locator or finder, who in turn would watch Harkley till 8:00 A.M. Then it would be Gower's turn until 2:00 P.M., followed by Trevor Jordan. The roster went no farther than that. Clarke wondered if that was significant . . .

Maybe that was what Gower was feeling: a ding-dong, as he had it, but a little closer than he thought.

Layard cocked his head on one side, looked at Clarke where he studied the roster. "What's up, old son? Still got the runs? You can stop worrying about shift work at Harkley. Guy has pulled you off it."

Gower looked up and managed a grin. "He doesn't want you polluting the bushes out there!"

"Ha-ha!" said Clarke, his face blank. "Actually, I'm fine now. And I'm starving! Ken, you can go and jump in your bed if you like. I'll take the next shift. That'll adjust the roster back to normal."

"What a hero!" Layard gave a soft whistle. "Great! Six hours in bed will suit me just fine." He stood up, stretched. "Did you say you were hungry? There are sandwiches under the plate on the table there. A bit curly by now, but still edible."

Clarke started to munch on a sandwich, glancing at his watch. It was 1:15 P.M. "I'll have a quick shower and get on my way. When Roberts wakes up, tell him I'm on, right?"

Gower stood up, went to Clarke and stared hard at him. "Darcy, is there something on your mind?"

"No," Clarke shook his head, then changed his mind. "Yes . . . I don't know! I just want to get out to Harkley, that's all. Do my bit."

Twenty-five minutes later he was on his way . . .

Shortly before 2:00 A.M. Clark parked his car on the hard shoulder of the road maybe a quarter of a mile from Harkley House and walked the rest of the way. The mist had thinned out and the night was starting to look fine. Stars lit his

way, and the hedgerows had a nimbus of foxfire to sharpen
their silhouettes.

Oddly enough, and for all his terrifying confrontation
with Bodescu's dog. Clarke felt no fear. He put it down to
the fact that he carried a loaded gun, and that back there
in the boot of his car was a small but quite deadly metal
crossbow. After he had seen Peter Keen off duty, he'd
bring up his car and park it in Keen's spot.

On his way he met no one, but he heard a dog yapping
across the fields, and another answering bark for bark,
apparently from miles away. A handful of hazy lights
shone softly on the hills, and just as he came in sight of
Harkley's gates a distant church clock dutifully gonged out
the hour.

Two o'clock and all's well, thought Clarke—except he
saw that it wasn't. There was no sign of Keen's unmistakeable
red Capri, for one thing. And for another there was no sign
of Keen.

Clarke scratched his head, scuffed the grass where Keen's
car should be parked. The wet grass gave up a broken
branch, and . . . no, it wasn't a branch. Clarke stooped,
picked up the snapped crossbow bolt in fingers that were
suddenly tingling. Something was very, very wrong here!

He looked up, staring at Harkley House standing there
like a squat sentient creature in the night. Its eyes were
closed now, but what was hiding behind the lowered lids
of its dark windows?

All of Clarke's senses were operating at maximum efficiency: his ears picked up the rustle of a mouse, his eyes
glared to penetrate the darkness, he could taste, almost *feel*
the evil in the night air, and—and something stank. Literally. The stink of a slaughterhouse.

Clarke took out a pencil-slim torch and flashed it on the
grass—which was red and wet and sticky! The cuffs of his
trousers were stained a dark crimson with blood. Someone
(God, let it *not* be Peter Keen!) had spilled pints of the
stuff right here. Clarke's legs trembled and he felt faint,

but he forced himself to follow a track, a bloody swath, to a spot behind the hedgerow, hidden from the road. And there it was much worse. Did one man *have* that much blood!

Clarke wanted to be sick, but that would incapacitate him and right now he *dare not be* incapacitated. But the grass . . . it was strewn with clots of blood, shreds of skin and gobbets of . . . of meat! Human flesh! And under the narrow beam of his torch there was something else, something which might just be—God, a kidney!

Clarke ran—or rather floated, fought, swam, drifted, as in a dream or nightmare—back to his car, drove like a madman back to Paignton, hurled himself into INTESP's suite of rooms. He was in shock, remembered nothing of the drive, nothing at all except what he'd seen, which had seared itself onto his mind. He fell into a chair and lolled there, gasping, trembling: his mouth, face, all of his limbs, even his mind, trembling.

Guy Roberts had come half-awake when Clarke rushed in. He saw him, the state of his trousers, the dead white slackness of his face, and was fully alert in an instant. He dragged Clarke to his feet and slapped him twice, ringing blows that brought the colour back to Clarke's cheeks— and blood to his previously blank eyes. Clarke drew himself up and glared; he growled and showed his gritted teeth, went for Roberts like a madman.

Trevor Jordan and Simon Gower dragged him off Roberts, held him tight—and at last he broke down. Sobbing like a child, finally he told the whole story. The only thing he didn't tell was the one which must be perfectly obvious: why it had affected him so very badly.

"Obvious, yes," said Roberts to the others, cradling Clarke's head and rocking him like a child. "You know what Darcy's talent is, don't you? That's right: he has this thing that looks after him. What? He could walk through a minefield and come out unscathed! So you see, Darcy's blaming himself for what happened. He had the

shits tonight and couldn't go on duty. But it wasn't anything he ate that queered his guts—it was his damned
talent! Or else it would be Darcy himself minced out there
and not Peter Keen . . ."

Tuesday, 6:00 A.M.: Alex Kyle was shaken rudely awake
by Carl Quint. Krakovitch was with Quint, both of them
hollow-eyed through travel and lack of sleep. They had
stayed overnight at the Dunarea, where they'd checked in
just before 1:00 A.M. They had had maybe four hours'
sleep; Krakovitch had been roused by night staff to answer
a call from England on behalf of his English guests; Quint,
knowing by means of his talent that something was in the
air, had been awake anyway.

"I've had the call transferred to my room," said
Krakovitch to Kyle, who was still gathering his senses. "It
is someone called Roberts. He is wishing to speak to you.
Most important."

Kyle shook himself awake, glanced at Quint.

"Something's up," Quint said. "I've suspected it for a
couple of hours. I tossed and turned, sleep all broken
up—but too tired to respond properly."

All three in pyjamas, they went quickly to Krakovitch's
room. On the way the Russian inquired, "How do they
know where you are, your people? It is them, yes? I mean,
we had not planned to be here tonight."

Quint raised an eyebrow in his fashion. "We're in the
same business as you, Felix, remember?"

Krakovitch was impressed. "A finder? Very accurate!"

Quint didn't bother to put him right. Ken Layard was
good, all right, but not that good. The better he knew a
person or thing the easier he could find him or it. He'd
have located Kyle in Bucharest; they'd have systematically
checked out the major hotels. Since the Dunarea was one
of the biggest, it must have come up high on the list.

In Krakovitch's room Kyle took the call. "Guy? Alec
here."

"Alec? We have a big problem. It's bad, I'm afraid. Can we talk?"

"Can't it go through London?" Kyle was fully awake now.

"That'll take time," Roberts answered, "and time's important."

"Wait," said Kyle. He said to Krakovitch: "What are the odds this is being monitored?"

The Russian shrugged, shook his head. "None at all, that I can see." He stepped to the window, opened the curtains. It would soon be dawn.

"OK, Guy," Kyle spoke into the phone. "Let's have it."

"Right," said Roberts. "It's just about four A.M. here. Now go back two hours . . ." He told Kyle the entire story, then detailed the action he'd taken since Clarke's hag-ridden drive back to the hotel in Paignton.

"I got Ken Layard in on it. He was great. He fixed Keen's location somewhere on the road between Brixham and Newton Abbot. Keen and his car, smashed up, burned out. I scried out Layard's fix and he was right, of course; we were able to say quite definitely that Peter was . . . that he was dead.

"I contacted the police in Paignton, told them I was waiting for a friend who was a little overdue, gave them his name, description, a description of his car. They said there'd been an accident; he was being cut out of the car; they could tell me no more, but an ambulance was on the scene and the driver of the car would be taken to the emergency hospital in Torquay. For me that was a ten minute drive. I was there when he was brought in. I identified him . . ." He paused.

"Go on," said Kyle, knowing there must be worse to come.

"Alec, I feel responsible. We should have been tighter. The trouble with this game is that we rely on our talents too damned much! We've almost forgotten how to use simple technology. We should have had walkie-talkies, better contact. We should have given this damned monster more credit for mayhem! I mean, Christ, how could I let this happen? We're espers; we have special talents; Bodescu is only one man and we're—''

"He's not just a man!" Kyle snapped. "And we don't have a monopoly on talent. He has it, too. It's not your fault. Now please tell me the rest of it."

"He . . . Peter was . . . hell, he didn't get those injuries in any car smash! He'd been opened up . . . gutted! Everything was exposed. His head was . . . God *it was in two halves!*"

Despite the horror conjured by Roberts's description, Kyle tried to think dispassionately. He'd known Peter Keen well and liked him. But now he must put that aside and think only of the job. "Why the car smash? What did that bastard hope to get out of it?"

"The way I see it," Roberts answered, "he was just covering up the murder, and what he'd *done* to Peter's poor body. The police said there was a strong petrol smell all around and inside the car. I reckon Bodescu drove Peter out there, put the car in top gear, pointed it downhill and let it roll. Being what he is, a few grazes and cuts wouldn't matter much when he jumped for it. And he probably splashed a lot of petrol around inside the car first, so as to burn the evidence. But the way he'd cut that poor lad up was . . . Jesus, it was horrible! I mean, *why?* Peter must have been dead long before that ghoul was finished. If he was torturing him at least there'd be some sense in it. I mean, however horrible, at least I could understand it. But you can't learn anything from a dead man, now can you?"

Kyle almost dropped the telephone. "Oh, my God!" he whispered.

"Eh?"

Kyle said nothing, stood frozen in sudden shock.

"Alec?"

"Yes you can," Kyle finally answered. "You can learn

an awful lot from a dead man—everything, in fact—if you're a necromancer!''

Roberts had had access to the Keogh file. Now it all came back to mind and he saw Kyle's meaning. ''You mean like Dragosani?''

''I mean *exactly* like Dragosani!''

Quint had caught most of this. ''Good Lord!'' He grabbed Kyle's elbow. ''He knows all about us. He knows—''

''Everything!'' Kyle said, to Quint and to Roberts. ''He knows the lot. He dragged it out of Keen's guts, out of his brains, his blood, his poor violated organs! Guy, now listen, this is important. Did Keen know when you plan to move in on Harkley House?''

''No. I'm the only one who knows that. Those were your instructions.''

''That's right. Good! Well, we can thank God we got that right, anyway. Now listen: I'm coming home. Tonight— I mean today! On the first possible flight. Carl Quint will stay out here and see this end sewn up, but I'm coming back. Don't wait for me if I can't get down to Devon in time. Go in as planned. Have you got that?''

''Yes.'' The other's voice was grim. ''Oh, yes, I've got that! Christ, and I'm looking forward to it!''

Kyle's eyes narrowed, grew very bright and fierce. ''Have Peter's body burned,'' he said, ''just in case . . . And then burn Bodescu. Burn all the blood-sucking bastards!''

Quint gently took the phone from him and said, ''Guy, Carl here. Listen, this is top priority. Get a couple of our best men up to Hartlepool A.S.A.P. Darcy Clarke especially. Do it now, even before you move on Harkley.''

''Right,'' Roberts answered. ''I'll do it.'' Then he got the point. His gasp was perfectly audible, even over the none too clear connection. ''Hell, of course I'll do it— right now!''

Wide-eyed and pale, Kyle and Quint stared at each other. There was no need to give voice to what was on their minds. Yulian Bodescu had learned almost everything there was to know about them. Keen had access, as had they all, to the Keogh file. A vampire's greatest fear is to be discovered for what he is. He will try to destroy anyone who even suspects him.

INTESP knew what he was, and the focus—the *jinni loci*—of INTESP was someone called Harry Keogh . . .

Darcy Clarke had swallowed two double brandies in quick succession before insisting on going back on duty. That had been shortly before Roberts's call to the Hotel Dunarea in Bucharest. Roberts, at first dubious, had finally let Clarke go back to Harkley, but with this warning: "Darcy, stay in your car. Don't leave it, no matter what. I know you have your juju working, but in this case it mightn't be enough. But we do need someone watching that hell-house, at least until we can get fully mobilized, and so if you're volunteering . . ."

Clarke had driven carefully, coldly back to Harkley House and parked on the stiff black grass close to where Keen's car had stood. He tried not to think about the ground where his car stood, or what had happened there. He was aware of it—would never forget it—but he kept it on the periphery of his consciousness, didn't let it interfere. And so with his gun and loaded crossbow beside him he'd sat there watching the house, never taking his eyes off it for a moment.

Fear had turned to hatred in Clarke's heart; he was here as a duty, yes, but it was more than that. Bodescu might just come out, might just show his face, and if he did . . . Clarke needed desperately to kill him.

In the house Yulian sat in darkness by his garret window. He, too, had known a little fear, something of panic. But now, like Clarke, he was cold, calm, calculating. For now, with one very important exception, he knew all there was to know about the watchers. The one thing he didn't know was when. But certainly it would be soon.

He gazed out into the darkness and could sense the approaching dawn. Down there, beyond the gate, in a car in the field across the road someone else watched. Ah, but this one would be better prepared. Yulian sent his vampire senses reaching into the cold and misty pre-dawn gloom, touched lightly upon a mind. Hatred lashed out at him before the mind closed itself—but not before he recognized it. Yulian merely grinned.

He sent his telepathic thoughts down to the vaulted cellars: *Vlad, an old friend of yours is keeping a vigil on the house. I want you to watch him. But don't let him see you, and don't try to hurt him. They are wary now, these watchers, and coiled like springs. If you are seen it may not go well for you. So just watch him, and let me know if he moves or does anything other than watch us! Now go . . .*

A huge black shadow, slope-eared, feral-eyed, padded silently up the narrow steps in the small building standing towards the rear of the house. It came out into the grounds, turned towards the gates, kept to the darker areas of trees and shrubbery. Tongue lolling, Vlad hastened to obey . . .

Yulian called the women down into the main living room on the ground floor. It was totally dark in that room, but each present could see the others perfectly well. Like it or not, night was now their element. When they were assembled, Yulian seated himself beside Helen on a couch, waited a moment to be sure he had the full attention of the women, then spoke.

"Ladies," he commenced, mockingly, his voice low and sinister, "it will soon be dawn. I can't be certain but I rather fancy that it will be one of the last dawns you ever see. Men will come and they will try to kill you. That may not be easy, but they're determined and they'll try very hard."

"Yulian!" His mother at once stood up, her voice shocked, fearful. "What have you done?"

"Sit down!" he commanded, glaring at her. She obeyed, but reluctantly. And when she was perched again on the

edge of her chair, he said, "I have done what I must do to protect myself. And you—all of you—shall be obliged to do likewise, or die. Soon."

Helen, simultaneously fascinated and horrified by Yulian, her skin crawling with her fear of him, timorously touched his arm. "I shall do whatever you ask of me, Yulian."

He thrust her away, almost hurled her from the couch. "Fight for yourself, slut! That is all I ask. Not for me but for yourself—if you desire to live!"

Helen cringed away from him. "I only—"

"Only be quiet!" he snarled. "You *must* fight for yourselves, for I shall not be here. I'm leaving with the dawn, when they'd least expect me to leave. But you three will remain. While you are here they may be fooled into thinking that I am still here." He nodded and smiled.

"Yulian, look at you!" his mother suddenly hissed, her voice venomous. "You were always a monster inside, and now you're a monster outside, too! I don't want to die for you, for even this half-life is better than none, but I don't intend to fight for it. Nothing you can say or do shall make me kill to preserve what you've made of me!"

He shrugged. "Then you'll die very quickly." He turned his eyes on Anne Lake. "And you, Auntie dear? Will you go to your maker so passively?"

Anne was wild-eyed, dishevelled. She looked mad. "George is dead!" she babbled, her hands flying to her hair. "And Helen is . . . changed. My life is finished." She stopped fussing, leaned forward in her chair and glowered at Yulian. "I hate you!"

"Oh, I know you do," he nodded. "But will you let them kill you?"

"I'd be better off dead," she answered.

"Ah, but *such* a death!" he said. "You saw George go, Auntie dear, and so you know how hard it was. The stake, the cleaver, and the fire."

She sprang to her feet, shook her head wildly. "They wouldn't! People . . . don't!"

"But *these* people do," he gazed at her wide-eyed, almost innocently, aping her expression. "They will, for they know what you are. They know that you're Wamphyri!"

"We can leave this place!" Anne cried. "Come on, Georgina, Helen—we'll leave right now!"

"Yes, go!" Yulian snapped, as if done with them, utterly sick of them. "Do go, all of you. Leave me—go now . . ."

They looked at him uncertainly, blinking their yellow eyes in unison. "I won't stop you," he told them with a shrug. He got to his feet, made to leave the room. "No, not I. But *they* will! They'll stop you dead! They're out there now, watching—and waiting."

"Yulian, where are you going?" His mother stood up, looked as if she might even try to take hold of him, detain him. He forced her back with nothing but a growl of warning, swept by her.

"I have preparations to make," he said, "for my departure. I imagine that you, too, will have certain final things you want to do. Prayers to some non-existent god, perhaps? Cherished photographs to look at? Old friends and lovers to remember, while you may?" And sneering, he left them to their own devices . . .

Tuesday, 8:40 A.M. middle-European time, the airport in Bucharest.

Alec Kyle's flight was due to leave in twenty-five minutes and the passengers had just been called forward. Kyle would be in Rome in two-and-a-half hours; given that there would be no problems with his connection, he'd be into Heathrow around 2:00 P.M. local time. With a bit of luck he would reach his destination in Devon with half an hour to spare before Guy Roberts and his team went in and "cleaned up" at Harkley House. Even if his timings were wrong, Roberts should still be in situ at the house when finally he did arrive. The last stages of his journey would be by MOD helicopter from Heathrow down to Torquay, and on to Paignton in an air-sea rescue chopper courtesy of the Torquay coastguard.

Kyle had made these final arrangements by telephone from the airport via John Grieve in London as soon as he'd discovered that he couldn't get a flight until now. And mercifully, for once, he'd got the call through without too much difficulty.

On hearing the call for embarkation, Felix Krakovitch stepped forward and took Kyle's hand. "A lot has happened in short time," the Russian psychic said. "But to know you has been . . . my pleasure." They shook hands awkwardly but both men meant it. Sergei Gulharov was much more open: he hugged Kyle close and kissed his cheeks. Kyle shrugged and grinned, he hoped not too sheepishly. He was only glad he'd said his farewells to Irma Dobresti the previous night. Carl Quint nodded and gave him a thumbs-up signal.

Krakovitch carried Kyle's hand luggage to the departure gate. From there Kyle went on alone, through the gates and out onto the asphalt, finding a space in the jostling line of passengers. He looked back once, waved, turned and hurried on.

Quint, Krakovitch and Gulharov watched him go, waiting until he rounded the corner of the massive air control tower and so out of sight. Then they quickly left the airport. Now they were ready to commence their own journey: up into old Moldavia, where they'd cross the Russian border by car over the River Prut. Krakovitch had already made the necessary arrangements—through his Second in Command, of course, at the Château Bronnitsy.

Out on the airfield, Kyle approached his plane. Close to the foot of the mobile boarding stairway, uniformed aircrew saluted him and checked his boarding pass one last time. A smiling official stepped forward, glanced at Kyle's boarding pass. "Mr. Kyle? One moment please." His voice was bland, conveyed nothing. Nor did Kyle's inbuilt warning system. Why should it? There was nothing

outside of nature here. On the contrary, what was coming
was very down-to-earth—but terrifying for all that.

As the last of the passengers disappeared into the body
of the aircraft, three men emerged from behind the stairs.
They wore lightweight overcoats and dark grey felt hats.
Though their clothes were intended to lend anonymity,
they were almost a uniform in their own right, an
unmistakeable mode of identification. Even if Kyle hadn't
known them, he would have recognized the cases one of
them was carrying. His cases.

Two of the KGB men, unsmiling, restrained him while
the third moved up very close, put down his suitcases and
took his cabin luggage. Kyle felt a stab of fear, a moment
of panic.

"Need I introduce myself?" The Russian agent's eyes
bored into Kyle's.

Kyle found his nerve, shook his head and managed a
rueful smile. "I think not," he answered. "How are you
this morning, Mr. Dolgikh? Or should I simply call you
Theo?"

"Try 'Comrade,' " said Dolgikh without humour. "That
will suffice . . ."

Whatever Yulian Bodescu's intentions had been, he had not
left Harkley House at dawn.

At 5:00 A.M. Ken Layard and Simon Gower arrived to
relieve Darcy Clarke, who then returned to Paignton. At
6:00 A.M. Trevor Jordan joined Layard and Gower; the
three split up, formed points of triangulation. An hour later
there were two more men, reinforcements Roberts had
earlier called down from London. All of these arrivals
were dutifully reported by Vlad, until Yulian cautioned the
huge dog and ordered him down to the cellars. It was
broad daylight now and Vlad would be seen coming and
going. The Alsatian was Yulian's rearguard and no harm
must come to him just yet.

The enemy's numbers had penned Yulian in; but just as

bad from his point of view was the fact that the day was cloudless, the risen sun bright and strong. The mists of the night had soon been steamed away, and the air was clear and smelled fresh. Behind the house, beyond the wall that marked the boundary of the grounds, woods rose to the top of a low hill. There was a track through the woods and one of the watchers had somehow managed to get his vehicle up there. He sat there now, watching the house through binoculars. Yulian could easy have seen him through one of the upper storey rear windows, but he didn't need to. He sensed that he was there.

At the front of the house were two more watchers: one not far from the gate, standing beside his car, the other fifty yards away. Their weapons were not visible but Yulian knew they had crossbows. And he knew the agony a hardwood bolt would cause him. Two more men guarded the flanks, one at each side of the house, where they could look into the grounds across the walls.

Yulian was trapped—for the moment.

Fight? He couldn't even leave the house without them seeing him. And those crossbows of theirs would be deadly accurate. The day wore on through midday and into the afternoon, and Yulian began to sweat. At 3:00 P.M. a sixth man came on the scene—driving a truck. Yulian watched carefully from behind the curtains at his garret window.

The driver of the truck must be the leader of these damned psychic spies. The leader of this group, anyway. He was fat, but in no way clumsy; his mind would be hard and clear, except he guarded his thoughts like gold. He began to distribute indeterminate items of heavy equipment in canvas containers, also jerrycans, food and drink, to the other men. He spent a little time with each of them, talking to them, demonstrated with certain pieces of equipment, gave instructions. Yulian sweated more yet. He knew now it would be this evening. Traffic rolled as usual on the autumn road; couples walked together in the sunshine hand in hand; birds sang in the woods. The world looked the same as it always looked—but those men out there had determined that this would be Yulian Bodescu's last day.

Using what cover he could find, the vampire risked his neck making excursions outside the house. He used a rear ground floor window where it was shrouded by shrubbery, also the cellar exit through the out-building. Twice, if he'd been fully prepared, he might have made a break for it, when the watchers to the rear and at one side of the house went down to the road for their supplies; on both occasions they returned while he was still calculating the odds. Yulian grew still more nervous, his thinking becoming very erratic.

Back in the house, whenever he crossed tracks with one of the women, he would lash out, shout, curse. His nervousness transferred itself to Vlad and the great dog prowled the empty cellars to and fro, to and fro.

Then, about 4:00 P.M., suddenly Yulian was aware of a weird psychic stillness, the mental lull before the storm. He strained his vampire senses to their fullest extent and could detect . . . nothing! The watchers had screened their minds, so that not even a trace of their thoughts—their intentions—could escape. In so doing they gave away their final secret, they told Yulian the time they had planned for his death.

It was to be now, within the hour, and the light only just beginning to fade as the sun lowered itself towards the horizon.

Yulian put fear aside. He was Wamphyri! These men had powers, yes, and they were strong. But he had powers too. And he might yet prove to be stronger.

He went down into the cellars and spoke to Vlad: *You've been faithful to me as only a dog can be*, he said, facing the great beast, their yellow eyes locked, *but you are more than a dog. Those men out there might suspect that, and they might not. Whichever, when they come, you go out first to meet them. Give no quarter. If you survive, seek me out . . .*

And then he "spoke" to the Other, that loathsome extrusion of himself. It was the implanting of suggestions in a blank space, the imprinting of an idea upon a void, the burning of a brand into a beast's hide. Floor flags buckled in one dark corner, the ground underfoot shifted and dust fell in rills from the low vaulting. That was all. Perhaps it had understood, and perhaps not . . .

Finally Yulian returned to his room. He changed his clothes, put on a neutral grey track-suit and shoved his wide-brimmed hat into the waistband. He neatly folded a suit of clothes into a small travelling case, along with a wallet containing a good deal of money in large notes. That was that; he needed nothing more.

Then, as the minutes ticked by, he sat down, closed his eyes and pitted his own dark nature against the great Mother Nature herself in one final test of his now mature vampire powers. He willed a mist, called up a wreathing white screen from the earth and the streams and the woods, a clinging fog down from the hillsides.

The watchers, tense now and taut as the strings of their crossbows, scarcely noticed the sun slipping behind the clouds and the ground mist creeping at their ankles; as a man, their attention was riveted on the house.

And time moved inexorably towards the appointed hour . . .

Darcy Clarke drove furiously north. He had cursed aloud until his throat was raw and then silently until his cursing had come down to one four-letter word repeated over and over again in his fuming mind. What his fury amounted to was this: he wouldn't be in on the kill. He was out of the attack on Harkley. Now, instead, he was to be minder-in-chief to a . . . a tiny infant!

Clarke was well aware of the importance of his new task and understood the purpose of it: with his talent it was unlikely that any harm would come to him. And so, if he was shielding the young Harry Keogh, the baby should likewise be safe. But to Darcy's way of thinking, prevention was better then cure. Stop Bodescu dead at Harkley House, and you wouldn't have to worry about the baby at all. And if he, Darcy Clarke, was at Harkley—if *only* he was there—then guarantee Bodescu would be stopped!

But he wasn't there, he was here, driving north for that godforsaken hole Hartlepool . . .

On the other hand, he knew that every single man of them back there was equally dedicated to Bodescu's destruction. Which helped a little.

Clarke had got back to Paignton before 6:00 A.M. and Roberts had ordered him straight into bed. Later, he said, he would have a big job for him and wanted him to get at least six hours' sleep. Finally Clarke had dozed off, and though he'd feared the very worst dreams none had come. At noon Roberts had shaken him awake, told him what his new job was. Since when Clarke had been driving, and cursing.

He had joined the M1 at Leicester, then picked up the A19 at Thirsk. He was now something less than an hour from his destination, and the time was (he glanced at his watch)—4:50 P.M.

Clarke stopped cursing. God! What would it be like right now, down there?

"Where the hell did this mist *spring* from?" Trevor Jordan shivered, turning up the collar of his coat. "Hell, it was a nice day, from the weather point of view, anyway." For all his vehemence, Jordan had spoken in a whisper.

All of the INTESP agents, at their various stations around Harkley House, had been speaking in whispers for the last twenty minutes. At 4:30, working to Roberts's instructions, they'd formed pairs—which was as well, for the mist had thickened up and started to threaten their individual security. It felt nice to have someone really close to you.

Jordan's "buddy" in the system was Ken Layard the

locator. He was shivering, too, despite the fact that he carried seventy-eight pounds of Brissom Mark III flame-thrower on his back. "I'm not sure," he finally answered Jordan's question, "but I think it's from him." He nodded towards the house where it stood swathed in mist.

They were just inside the north wall, at a place where they'd found a gap in the stonework. Just a minute ago, at 4:50, they'd checked their watches and squeezed through, and Jordan had helped Layard into his asbestos leggings and jacket. Then they'd strapped the tank on his back and he'd checked the valve on the hose and trigger mechanism. With the valve open, all he had to do was squeeze the trigger and he could conjure up an inferno. And he fully intended to.

"Him?" Jordan frowned. He looked around at the mist: It crept everywhere. From here the rear wall up the hillside was invisible; likewise the wall fronting onto the road. Harvey Newton and Simon Gower would be making their way down from the hill, Ben Trask and Guy Roberts coming up the drive from the gate. They would all converge on the house together, at 5:00 P.M. sharp. "Who do you mean, 'him?' Bodescu?" Jordan led the way through shrubbery towards the dimly looming mass of the house.

"Bodescu, yes," Layard answered. "I'm a locator, remember? It's my thing."

"What's that got to do with the mist?" Jordan's nerves were starting to jump. He was a telepath of uncertain skill, but Roberts had warned him not to try it on Bodescu—and certainly not at this crucial stage of play.

"When I try to find him in my mind's eye," Layard attempted to explain, "inside the house there, I can't zero in on him. It's as if he were part of the mist. That's why I think he's somehow behind it. I sense him as a huge amorphous cloud of fog!"

"Jesus!" Jordan whispered, shivering again. In utter, eerie silence they moved towards the small outbuilding, whose open door led down to the cellars . . .

* * *

Simon Gower and Harvey Newton approached the house from the gently sloping field of shrubs at its rear. There wasn't too much cover so the mist was a boon to them. So they thought. Newton was a telepath, called down from London along with Ben Trask as reinforcements. Newton and Trask weren't quite as *au fait* with the situation as the rest, which was why they'd been split up.

"What a team we make, eh?" said Newton nervously as the ground levelled out and the mist billowed up more yet. "You with that bloody great torch on your back—and me with a crossbow? You know, if this stake-out is a dud, we're going to look awfully—"

"*God!*" Gower cut him short, dropped to one knee and worked furiously at the valve on his hose.

"What?" Newton gave a massive start, glared all about, held his loaded crossbow out in front of him like a shield. "What?" He couldn't see anything, but he knew Gower's talent lay in reading the future—especially the immediate future!

"It's coming!" Gower no longer whispered. In fact, he was shouting. "It's coming—NOW!"

At the front of the house, where Guy Roberts and Ben Trask pulled up in Roberts's truck, Gower's shouting wasn't heard over the throbbing of the vehicle's engine. But on the north-facing side of the house it was. Trevor Jordan instinctively crouched down, then began to run at an angle towards the rear of the building. Ken Layard, hampered by his flame-thrower load, was slower off the mark.

Layard, stumbling through damp shrubbery, saw Jordan's figure swallowed into a rolling bank of mist where he ran past the open door in the small outbuilding—then saw something *erupt* from that door in a snarling, slavering frenzy! Bodescu's great dog! Without pause the flame-eyed brute hurled itself into the mist after Jordan.

"Trevor, behind you!" Layard yelled at the top of his

voice. He yanked open the valve on his hose, jerked the trigger, prayed: *God, please don't let me burn Trevor!*

A roaring, gouting stream of yellow fire tore open the curtain of mist like a blowtorch through cobwebs. Jordan was already round the corner of the house, but Vlad was still in view, bounding purposefully after him. The expanding, blistering "V" of heat reached after the dog, touched him, enveloped him—but briefly. Then he, too, was round the corner.

By now, at the front of the house, Guy Roberts and Ben Trask were down from the truck. Roberts heard shouting, the roar of a flame-thrower. It was still a minute or two to five but the attack had started—which probably meant that the other side had started it. Roberts put a police whistle to his lips, gave one short blast. Now, whatever else was happening, all six INTESP agents would move on the house together.

Roberts had the third flame-thrower; he headed straight for the main door of the house where it stood ajar in the shadow of a columned portico. Trask followed. He was a human lie-detector; his talent had no application here, but he was also young, quick-thinking and he knew how to look after himself. As he made to follow Roberts something caught his attention: a furtive movement glimpsed in the very corner of his eye.

Twenty-five yards away between billowing banks of mist, a flowing figure had passed swiftly, silently inside the shell of the old barn. Who or whatever had gone in there, there would be nothing to stop it from clearing off out of the grounds once Roberts and Trask were inside the house. "Oh no you *don't!*" Trask grunted. And raising his voice: "Guy, in the barn there."

Roberts, at the door of the house, turned to see Trask running at a crouch towards the barn. Cursing under his breath, he strode after him.

At the back of Harkley House, Vlad came coughing and mewling out of the mist and attempted to spring at the

three men he found there. The dog was a blackened silhouette sheathed in smoke and flame, burning even as he
launched himself lopsidedly at Jordan's back.

As Jordan had come running round the corner of the
building, Gower had very nearly triggered his flame-thrower;
he'd recognized Jordan only at the last possible moment.
Harvey Newton, on the other hand, had actually drawn a
bead on the misted figure and was in the act of firing his
bolt when Gower cried a warning and shouldered him
aside. The bolt flashed harmlessly off at a tangent and
disappeared in mist and distance. Fortunately Jordan had
seen the two men—saw them apparently aiming at him—
and thrown himself flat. He hadn't seen what pursued him,
however, which even now overshot his sprawled body and
arced overhead in a cloud of sparks and smoulder. Vlad
landed awkwardly, gathered himself to spring at Newton
and Gower, and discovered himself forging head-on into a
withering jet of flame from Gower's torch. The dog crumpled to earth, a blazing, crackling, screaming ball of fire
that tried to run in all directions at once and ran nowhere.

Jordan got to his feet and the three men stood panting,
watching Vlad burn. Newton had fumblingly reloaded his
crossbow; he thought he saw something move in the mist
and turned in that direction. What was *that?* A loping
shape? Or . . . just his imagination? The others didn't
seem to have noticed; they were watching Vlad.

"Oh my God!" Jordan gasped. Newton saw the look on
Jordan's face, forgot the thing he thought he had seen,
turned to watch the death agonies of the incandescent dog.

Vlad's blackened body throbbed and vibrated, burst open,
put up a nest of tentacles that twined like alien fingers four
or five feet into the air. Mouthing obscenities, eyes bulging, Gower hosed the thing down with fire. The tentacles
steamed, blistered and collapsed but the dog's body continued to pulsate.

"Jesus Christ!" Jordan moaned his horror. "He changed
the dog too!" He unhooked a cleaver form his belt, moved

forward, shielded his eyes against the blaze and severed
Vlad's head from his body with one single clean stroke.

Jordan backed off, shouted at Gower: "You finish it—
make *sure* you finish it! I heard Roberts's whistle just
now. Harvey and me will go on in."

As Gower continued to burn the remains of the dog-
thing, Jordan and Newton went stumbling through smoke
and reek to the rear wall of the house, where they found an
open window. They looked at each other, then licked their
lips nervously in unison. Both of them were breathing
raggedly of the sodden, stinking air.

"Come on," said Jordan. "Cover me." He aimed his
crossbow in front of him, swung his leg across the window
sill . . .

In the barn Ben Trask pulled up short, his square face
alert, ears attentive to the silence. The silence said there
was no one here, but it was lying. Trask knew it as surely
as if he sat behind a one-way window and listened in on an
important interrogation by police of big-time criminals.
The picture here was false, a lie.

Old farm implements were strewn everywhere. The mist,
billowing in through the open ends of the building, had
turned old steel slick with a sort of metallic sweat; chains
and worn tyres hung from hooks in the walls; a stack of
tongue-and-groove boards teetered uncertainly, as if recently disturbed. Then Trask saw the wooden steps as-
cending into gloom, and at the same time a single stem of
straw where it came drifting down.

He drew air in a sharp gasp, turned his face and crossbow up towards the badly gapped boarding overhead—and
was just in time to see a woman's insanely working face
framed there, and hear her *hiss* of triumph as she launched
a pitchfork at him! Trask had no time to aim but simply
pulled the trigger.

The pitchfork's sharp offside tine missed him but its
twin scraped under his collar bone and passed through his

right shoulder, driving him down and backwards. At the same time there came a mad, babbling shriek to end all shrieks, and Anne Lake crashed through rotten boards in a cloud of dust and powdery straw. She landed square on her back, with Trask's bolt sticking out of her chest dead centre. The bolt alone should have done for her, and the fall certainly, but she was no longer entirely human.

Trask lay against the side wall and tried to pull the pitchfork out of his shoulder. There was no strength in him; he couldn't do it; pain and shock had left him weak as a kitten. He could only watch and try to keep from blacking out as Yulian Bodescu's "auntie" crept towards him on all fours, grabbed the pitchfork and yanked it viciously free. And then Trask *did* black out.

Anne Lake drew back the pitchfork, growling like a big cat as she aimed it at Trask's heart. Behind her, Guy Roberts grabbed the fork's wooden handle, hauled on it and threw her off balance. She howled her frustration, fell on her back again, grasped the bolt in her chest with both hands and tried to draw it out. Roberts, impeded by the apparatus on his back, lumbered by her, took hold of Trask by the front of his jacket and somehow managed to drag him clear of the barn. Then he turned back, aimed his hose, and applied a firm and steady pressure to the trigger.

The barn was at once transformed into a gigantic oven; heat and fire and smoke filled it floor to tiled roof, spilling out of its open ends. And in the middle of it all something screamed and screamed, a wildly hissing, rising scream that finally shut itself off as the upper floor collapsed and tipped blazing hay down into the roaring inferno. And still Roberts kept his finger on the trigger, until he knew that nothing—*nothing*—could have survived in there . . .

At the back of the house Ken Layard found Gower burning Vlad. Jordan had just stepped in through the open window and Newton was about to follow him. "Hold it!" Layard shouted. "You can't work two crossbows together!" He came forward. "I'll go in this way," he told Newton, "with Jordan. You stick with Gower and go round the front. Go now!"

As Layard clambered awkwardly in through the window, Newton dragged Gower away from the cindered, smoking thing that had been Vlad and jerked his thumb towards the far corner of the house. "That thing's finished," he shouted, "so now get a grip of yourself! Come on—the others will be inside by now."

They quickly made their way through the mist-wreathed gardens on the south side of the house, and saw Roberts turn away from the blazing barn and drag Trask out of the danger area. Roberts saw them, yelled: "What the hell's going on?"

"Gower burned the dog," Newton yelled back. "Except it wasn't . . . wasn't a dog—not any more!"

Roberts's lips drew back from his teeth in a half-snarl, half-grimace. "We got Anne Lake," he said, as Newton and Gower came closer. "And, of course, *she* wasn't all woman! Where're Layard and Jordan?"

"Inside," said Gower. He was shaking, rivered in sweat. "And it's not finished yet, Guy. Not yet. There's more to come!"

"I've tried scanning the house," Roberts said. "Nothing! Just a fog in there. A mental fucking fog! Pointless trying, anyway. Too damned much going on!" He grabbed Gower. "You OK?"

Gower nodded. "I think so."

"Right. Now listen. Thermite bombs in the truck; plastic explosive, too, in haversacks. Dump 'em in the cellars. Spread 'em out. Try to take 'em all down in one go. And no torching while you're holding the stuff! In fact get out of that kit and take a crossbow like Newton. The stuff's all set to go off from excessive heat or naked flame. Plant it and get out—and then stay out! Three of us in the house itself should be enough. If not—the fire will be."

"You're going in there?" Gower looked at the house, licked his lips.

"I'm going in, yes," Roberts nodded. "There's still Bodescu, his mother and the girl to account for. And don't worry about me. Worry about yourself. The cellars could be far worse than the house." He headed for the open door under the columned portico . . .

Chapter Fourteen

INSIDE THE HOUSE, LAYARD AND JORDAN HAD CAREFULLY, systematically searched the ground floor and now approached the main staircase to the upper levels. They'd switched on dim lights as they went, compensating a little for the gloom. At the foot of the stairs they paused.

"Where the hell is Roberts?" Layard whispered. "We could use some instructions."

"Why?" Jordan glanced at him out of the corner of his eye. "We know what we're up against—mainly. And we know what to do."

"But there should be four of us in here."

Jordan gritted his teeth. "There was something of a row out front. Trouble, obviously. Anyway, by now someone should be planting charges in the cellars. So let's not waste time. We can ask questions later."

On a narrow landing where the stairs turned through a right angle, a large, built-in cupboard faced them squarely, its door a little ajar. Jordan kept his crossbow lined up on the large-panelled door, sidled past and continued up the

stairs. He wasn't passing the buck; it was simply that if
there was anything nasty in there, he knew Layard could
stop it with a single burst of liquid fire.

Layard checked that the valve on his hose was open,
rested his finger on the trigger, toed the door open. In
there . . . darkness.

He waited until his eyes were growing accustomed to
the dimness, then spotted a light switch on the wall just
inside the door. He reached out his hand, then drew it
back. He stepped forward a pace, used the nozzle of his
hose to trip the switch. A light came on, throwing the
interior of the cupboard into sharp relief. At the back—a
tall figure! Layard drew breath sharply; his jaw fell partly
open and the corners of his mouth drew back in a half-rictus
of fear. He was a breath from squeezing the trigger—but then
his eyes focussed and he saw only an old raincoat, hanging
on a peg.

Layard gulped, filled his lungs, quietly closed the door.

Jordan was up on the first floor landing. He saw two
alcoves, arched over, with closed doors set centrally. There
was also a passage, with two more doors that he could see
before the corridor turned a corner. The closest door was
maybe eight paces away, the furthest twelve. He turned
back to the doors in the alcoves, approached the first of
them, turned the doorknob and kicked it open, it was a
toilet with a high window, letting in grey light.

Jordan turned to the second door, dealt with it as with
the first. Inside was an extensive library, the whole room
visible at a glance. Then, aware that Layard was coming
up the stairs, he started down the corridor—and at once
paused. His ears pricked up. He heard . . . water? The hiss
and gurgle of a tap?

A shower! The water sounds were coming from the
second room—a bathroom?—down the corridor. Jordan
looked back. Layard was at the top of the stairs. Their
eyes met. Jordan pointed to the first door, then at Layard.

Layard was to deal with it. Then Jordan thumbed his own chest, pointed along the corridor to the second door.

He went on, but cautiously, crossbow held chest high and pointed dead ahead. The water sounds were louder, and—a voice? A girl's voice—singing? Humming, anyway. Some utterly tuneless melody . . .

In *this* house at *this* time, a girl humming to herself in a shower? Or was it a trap?

Jordan took a tighter grip on his crossbow, turned the knob and kicked in the door. No trap! Not that he could see. In fact the completely natural scene beyond the bathroom door left him at a total loss. All of the tension went out of him in a moment, and he was left feeling . . . like some gross intruder!

The girl (Helen Lake, surely?) was beautiful, and quite naked. Water streamed down on her, setting her lovely body gleaming. She stood sideways on, picked out in clear definition against blue ceramic tiles, in the shower's shallow well. As the door slammed open she jerked her head round to stare at Jordan, her eyes opening wide in terror. Then she gasped, crumpled back against the shower's wall, looking as if she were about to faint. One hand flew to her breasts and her eyelids fluttered as her knees began to give way.

Jordan half-lowered his crossbow, said to himself: *Sweet Jesus! But this is just a frightened girl!* He began to reach out his free hand—to steady her—but then other thoughts, her thoughts, abruptly printed themselves on his telepathic mind.

Come on my sweet! come help me! Ah, just touch me, hold me! Just a little closer, my sweet . . . there! And now—

Jordan jerked back as she turned more fully towards him. Her eyes were wide, triangular, demonic! Her face had been instantly transformed into that of a beast! And in her right hand, invisible until now, was a carving knife. The knife rose as she reached out and grasped Jordan's jacket. Her grip was iron! She drew him effortlessly towards her—and he fired his bolt into her breast point-blank.

Slammed back against the rear wall of the shower, pinned there by the bolt, she dropped her knife and began to issue peal after ringing peal of soul-searing screams. Blood gushed from where the bolt was bedded in her with little more than its flight protruding. She grasped it, and still screaming jerked her body this way and that. The bolt came loose from the wall in a crunching of tiles and plaster and she staggered to and fro in the shower, yanking on the bolt and screaming endlessly.

"God, God, oh *God!*" Jordan cried, riveted to the spot.

Layard shouldered him aside, squeezed the trigger on his flame-thrower, turned the entire shower unit into a blistering, steaming pressure-cooker. After several seconds he stopped hosing, and stared with Jordan at the result. Black smoke and steam cleared and the water continued to hiss, spurting from half-a-dozen places now in the molten plastic tubing of the shower's system. In the shallow well, Helen Lake's body slumped, features bubbling, hair like smouldering stubble, every inch of her skin peeling from her in great raw strips.

"God help us!" Jordan gasped, turned away to be sick.

"God?" the thing in the shower croaked, like a voice from the abyss. "What god? *You bloody black bastards!*"

Impossibly she came erect, took a blind, stumbling, groping step forward.

Layard torched her again, but more out of mercy than from fear. He let his flame-thrower roar until fire belched out of the shower and threatened to burn him, too. Then he switched off, backed away down the corridor to where Jordan stood retching over the stair's balustrade.

From below, Roberts's voice reached anxiously up to them: "Ken? Trevor? What is it?"

Layard wiped his forehead. "We . . . we got the girl," he whispered, then shouted. "We got the girl!"

"We got her mother," Roberts answered, "and Bodescu's dog. That leaves Bodescu himself, and his mother."

"There's a door up here, locked," Layard called back. "I thought I heard someone in there."

"Can't you break it in?"

"No, it's oak, old and heavy. I could burn it . . ."

"No time for that. And if there is anyone in there, they're finished anyway. The cellars are mined by now. You'd better come down—and quickly! We have to get out of here."

Layard dragged Jordan after him down the stairs, calling ahead. "Guy, where the hell have you been?"

"I'm on my own," Roberts responded. "Trask's out of it for now—but he's OK. Where've I been? I've been checking this place through downstairs."

"A waste of time," Jordan groaned, half to himself.

"What?" Roberts raised his voice more yet.

"I said, we'd already done it!" Jordan yelled, but needlessly for they were down the stairs, with Roberts propelling them towards the entrance hall and the open door . . .

Simon Gower and Harvey Newton had gone down into the cellars via the outbuilding with its narrow steps and central ramp. Loaded down with almost two hundred pounds of explosives between them, they had found the lights out of order, and so been obliged to use pocket torches. The vaults under the house were black and silent as a tomb, seemed extensive as a catacomb. They stuck close together, dumping thermite and plastic explosive packages wherever they found support walls or buttressed archways, and even though they went with something of caution, still they managed rapidly to fairly well saturate the place with their load. Newton carried a small can of petrol with which he left a trail from one dump to the next, until the whole place reeked of highly volatile fuel.

Finally they were satisfied that they'd explored and mined every part—and likewise pleased that they'd come across nothing dangerous—and so turned back and retraced their tracks to the exit. At a place they both agreed to be approximately central under the house, they set down the last of their load. Then Newton splashed what was left of his petrol all the way to the foot of the outbuilding steps, while Gower double-checked the charges they'd planted, making sure they were all amply primed.

At the steps Newton tossed down his empty can, turned and looked back into the gloom. From a little way back, round a corner, he could hear Gower's hoarse breathing and he knew that the other man worked furiously at his task. Gower's torch made flickering patches of light back there, its beam swinging this way and that as he worked.

Roberts appeared at the top of the steps, called down, "Newton, Gower? You can come up out of there as quick as you like. We're all set if you are. The others are spread out round the house, just waiting. The mist has cleared. So if anything tries to break loose, we'll—"

"Harvey?" Gower's tremulous voice came out of the darkness, several notes higher up the scale than it should be. "Harvey, was that you just then?"

Newton called back, "No, it's Roberts. Hurry up, will you?"

"No, not Roberts," Gower was breathless, almost whispering. "Something else . . ."

Roberts and Newton looked at each other round-eyed. The ground gave itself a shake, a very definite tremor. From inside the cellars, Gower screamed.

Roberts came half-way down the steps, stumbling and yelling: "Simon, get out of there! Hurry, man!"

Gower screamed again, the cry of a trapped animal. "It's here, Guy! Oh, God—it's here! *Under the ground!*"

Newton made to go in after him but Roberts reached down and grabbed his collar. The ground was shaking now, dust billowing out of the yawning mouth of the old cellars. There were rending sounds, and other noises which might or might not be Gower choking his life out. Bricks started to slide loose from rotten mortar in the retaining walls, spilling down the sides of the ramp.

Newton started to back up the trembling steps, with Roberts dragging him from above. When they were almost at the top, they saw a cloud of dust and debris suddenly expelled forcefully from the entrance to the cellar—and then the door itself was lifted off its rusty hinges and hurled down at the foot of the ramp, a mass of splintered boards.

Something was framed in the dusty gap of the entrance. It was Gower, and it was more than Gower. He hung for a moment suspended in the otherwise empty doorway, swaying left and right. Then he emerged more fully and the watchers saw the huge, leprous trunk which propelled him. The thing—indeed "the Other"—had entered his back in a solid shaft of matter, but inside Gower its massive pseudo-pod of vampire flesh had branched, following his pipes and conduits to several exits. Tentacles writhed from his gaping mouth and nostrils, the sockets of his dislocated eyes, his ruptured ears. And even as Roberts and Newton clambered in a frenzy of terror up the last few steps from the ramp, so Gower's entire front burst open, revealing a lashing nest of crimson, groping worms!

"Jesus!" Guy Roberts shouted then, his voice a sandpapered howl of horror and hatred. "Sweet *J-e-s-u-s!*"

He aimed his hose down the ramp. "Goodbye, Simon. God grant you peace!"

Liquid fire roared its rage, ran like a flood down the ramp, hurled itself in a fireball at the suspended man and the beat-thing holding him upright. The great pseudopod was instantly retracted—Gower with it, snatched back like a rag doll—and Roberts aimed his hose directly at the doorway at the foot of the steps. He turned the valve up full, and a shimmering jet of heat blasted its way into the cellar, fanning out inside the labyrinth of vaults into every niche and corner. For a count of five Roberts held it. Then came the first explosion.

Down went the entrance in a massive shuddering of earth. A shockwave of lashing heat hurled dirt and pebbles up the ramp, knocking Roberts and Newton off their feet. Roberts's finger automatically came off the trigger. His weapon smoked hot but silent in his hands. And *crump! crump! crump!* came evenly spaced, muffled concussions from deep in the earth, each one shaking the ground with pile-driver power.

Faster came the underground explosions, occurring in sporadic bursts, occasionally twinned, as the planted charges reacted to the heat and added to the unseen inferno. Newton got up and helped Roberts to his feet. They stumbled clear of the house, took up positions with Layard and Jordan, a man to each of the four corners but standing well back. The old barn, still blazing, began to vibrate as if itself alive and suffering its death agonies. Finally it shook itself to pieces and slid down into the suddenly seething earth. For a moment a lashing tentacle reached up from the shuddering foundations to a height of some twenty feet, then collapsed and was sucked back down into the quaking, liquefying quag of earth and fire.

Ken Layard was closest to that area. He ran raggedly away from the house, put distance between himself and the barn, too, before stumbling to a halt and staring with wide eyes and gaping mouth at the upstairs windows of the main building. Then he beckoned to Roberts to come and join him.

"Look!" Layard yelled, over the sound of subterranean thunder and the hiss and crackle of fire. They both stared at the house.

Framed in a second-floor window, the figure of a mature woman stood with her arms held high, almost in an attitude of supplication. "Bodescu's mother," Roberts said. "It can only be her: Georgina Bodescu—God help her!"

A corner of the house collapsed, sank into the earth in ruins. Where it went down, a geyser of fire spouted high as the roof, hurling broken bricks and mortar with it.

There were more explosions and the entire house shuddered. It was visibly settling on its foundations, cracks spreading across its walls, chimneys tottering. The four watchers backed off further yet, Layard dragging Ben Trask with him. Then Layard noticed the truck where it stood on the drive, jolting about on its own suspension.

He went to get it, but Guy Roberts stayed where he was, stood over Trask and continued to watch the figure of the woman at the window.

She hadn't changed her position. She stumbled a little now and then as the house settled, but always regained her pose, arms raised on high and head thrown back, so that it seemed to Roberts that indeed she talked to God. Telling Him what? Asking for what? Forgiveness for her son? A merciful release for herself?

Newton and Jordan left their positions at the rear of the house and came round to the front. It was clear that nothing was going to escape from that inferno now. They helped Layard get Trask into the truck; and while they busied themselves with preparations for their leaving, still Roberts watched the house burn, and so was witness to the end of it.

The thermite had done its job and the earth itself was on fire. The house no longer had foundations on which to stand. It slumped down, leaned first one way and then the other. Old brickwork groaned as timbers sheared, chimney stacks toppled and windows shivered into fragments in their twisting frames. And as the house sank in leaping flames and molten earth, so its substance became fuel for the fire.

Fire raced up walls inside and out; great red and yellow gouts of flame spurted from broken windows, bursting upward through a rent and sagging roof. For a single instant longer Georgina Bodescu was silhouetted against a background of crimson, searing heat, and then Harkley House gave up the ghost. It went down groaning into a scar of bubbling earth that resembled nothing so much as the mouth of a small volcano. For a little while longer the peaked gable ends and parts of the roof were visible, and then they too were consumed in vengeful fire and smoke.

Through all of this the reek had been terrible. Judging by the stench, it might well have been that fifty men had died and been burned in that house; but as Roberts climbed up into the passenger seat of the truck and Layard headed the vehicle down the drive towards the gates, all five survivors, including Trask who was now mainly conscious, knew that the stench came from nothing human. It was partly thermite, partly earth and timber and old brick, but mainly it was the death smell of that rendered down, gigantic monstrosity under the cellars, that "Other" which had taken poor Gower.

The mist had almost completely cleared now, and cars were beginning to pull up along the verges of the road, their drivers attracted by the flames and smoke rising high into the air where Harkley House had stood. As the truck rolled out of the gates onto the road, a red-faced driver leaned out of his car's window, yelled, "What is it? That's Harkley House, isn't it?"

"It was," Roberts yelled back, offering what he hoped looked like a helpless shrug. "Gone, I'm afraid. Burned down."

"Good Lord!" The red-faced man was aghast. "Has the fire service been informed?"

"We're off to do that now," Roberts answered. "Little good that'll do, though. We've been in to have a look, but there's nothing left to see, I'm afraid." They drove on.

A mile towards Paignton, a clattering fire engine came tearing from the other direction. Layard drew dutifully in towards the side of the road to give the fire engine room. He grinned tiredly, without humour. "Too late, my lads," he commented under his breath. "Much too late—thank all that's merciful!"

*   *   *

They dropped Trask off at the hospital in Torquay (with a story about an accident he'd suffered in a friend's garden) and after seeing him comfortable went back to the hotel HQ in Paignton to debrief.

Roberts enumerated their successes. "We got all three women, anyway. But as for Bodescu himself, I have my doubts about him. Serious doubts, and when we're finished here I'll pass them on to London, also to Darcy Clarke and our people up in Hartlepool. These will be simply precautionary measures, of course, for even if we did miss Bodescu we've no way of knowing what he'll do next or where he'll go. Anyway, Alec Kyle will be back in control shortly. In fact it's queer he hasn't shown up yet. Actually, I'm not looking forward to seeing him: he's going to be furious when he learns that Bodescu probably got out of that lot."

"Bodescu *and* that other dog," Harvey Newton put in, almost as an afterthought. He shrugged. "Still, I reckon it was just a stray that got into . . . the grounds . . . somehow?" He stopped, looked from face to face. All were staring back at him in astonishment, almost disbelief. It was the first they'd heard of it.

Roberts couldn't restrain himself from grabbing Newton's jacket front. "Tell it now!" he grated through clenched teeth. "*Exactly* as it happened, Harvey." Newton, dazed, told it, concluding:

"So while Gower was burning that . . . that bloody thing which *wasn't* a dog—not all of it, anyway—this other dog went by in the mist. But I can't even swear that I saw it at all! I mean, there was so much going on. It could have been just the mist, or my imagination, or . . . anything! I thought it loped, but sort of upright in an impossible forward crouch. And its head wasn't just the right shape. It had to be my imagination, a curl of mist, something like that. Imagination, yes—especially with Gower standing there burning that godawful dog! Christ, I'll dream of dogs like that for the rest of my life!"

Roberts released him violently, almost tossed him across the room. The fat man wasn't just fat; he was heavy, too, and very strong. He looked at Newton in disgust. "Idiot!" he rumbled. He lit a cigarette, despite the fact that he already had one going.

"I couldn't have done anything anyway!" Newton protested. "I'd shot my bolt, hadn't reloaded yet . . ."

"Shot your bloody bolt?" Roberts glared. Then he calmed himself. "I'd like to say it's not your fault," he told Newton then. "And maybe it isn't your fault. Maybe he was just too damned clever for us."

"What now?" said Layard. He felt a little sorry for Newton, tried to take attention away from him.

Roberts looked at Layard. "Now? Well, when I've calmed down a little you and me will have to try and find the bastard, that's what now!"

"Find him?" Newton licked dry lips. "How?" He was confused, wasn't thinking clearly.

Roberts at once tapped the side of his head with huge white knuckles. "With *this!*" he shouted. "It's what I do. I'm a 'scryer,' remember?" He glared again at Newton. "So what's your fucking talent? Other than screwing things up, I mean . . ."

Newton found a chair and fell into it. "I . . I saw him, and yet convinced myself that I hadn't seen him. What the hell's *wrong* with me? We went there to trap him—to trap *anything* coming out of that house—so why didn't I react more posit—"

Jordan drew air sharply and made a conclusive, snapping sound with his fingers. He gave a sharp nod, said, "Of course!"

They all looked at him.

"Of *course!*" he said again, spitting the words out. "He's talented too, remember? Too bloody talented by a mile! Harvey, he got to you. Telepathically, I mean. Hell, he got to me too! Convinced us he wasn't there, that we couldn't see him. And I really *didn't* see him, not a hair of

him. I was there, too, remember, when Simon was burning that thing. But I saw nothing. So don't feel too bad
about it, Harvey—at least you actually *saw* the bastard!"

"You're right," Roberts nodded after a moment. "You
have to be. So now we know for sure; Bodescu is loose,
angry and—God, dangerous! Yes, and he's more powerful, far more powerful, than anyone has yet given him
credit for . . ."

Wednesday, 12:30 A.M. middle-European time, the border
crossing-point near Siret in Moldavia.

Krakovitch and Gulharov had shared the driving between them, though Carl Quint would have been only too
happy to drive if they had let him. At least that might have
relieved some of his boredom. Quint hadn't found the
Romanian countryside along their route— railway depots
standing forlorn and desolate as scarecrows, dingy industrial sites, fouled rivers and the like—especially romantic.
But even without him, and despite the often dilapidated
condition of the roads, still the Russians had made fairly
good time. Or at least they'd made good time until they
arrived here; but "here" was the middle of nowhere, and
for some as yet unexplained reason they'd been held up
"here" for the last four hours.

Earlier their route out of Bucharest had taken them
through Buzau, Focsani and Bacau along the banks of the
Siretul, and so into Moldavia. In Roman they'd crossed the
river, then continued up through Botosani where they'd
paused to eat, and so into and through Siret. Now, on the
northern extreme of the town, the border crossing-point
blocked their way, with Chernovtsy and the Prut some
twenty miles to the north. By now Krakovitch had planned
on being through Chernovtsy and into Kolomyya under the
old mountains—the old Carpathians—for the night, but . . .

"But!" he raged now in the paraffin lamplight glare of
the border post. "But, but, *but!*" He slammed his fist
down on the counter-top which kept staff a little apart from

travellers; he spoke, or shouted, in Russian so explosive that Quint and Gulharov winced and gritted their teeth where they sat in the car outside the wooden chalet-styled building. The border post sat centrally between the incoming and outgoing lanes, with barrier arms extending on both sides. Uniformed guards manned sentry boxes, a Romanian for incoming traffic, a Russian for outgoing. The senior officer was, of course, Russian. And right now he was under pressure from Felix Krakovitch.

"Four hours!" Krakovitch raved. "Four bloody hours sitting here at the end of the world, waiting for you to make up your mind! I've told you who I am and proved it. Are my documents in order?"

The round-faced, overweight Russian official shrugged helplessly. "Of course, comrade, but—"

"No, no, *no!*" Krakovitch shouted. "No more buts, just yes or no. And Comrade Gulharov's documents, are they in order?"

The Russian customs man bobbed uncomfortably this way and that, shrugged again. "Yes."

Krakovitch leaned over the counter, shoved his face close to that of the other. "And do you believe that I have the ear of the Party Leader himself? Are you sure that you're aware that if your bloody telephone was working, by now I'd be speaking to Brezhnev himself in Moscow, and that next week you'd be manning a crossing-point into Manchuria?"

"If you say so, Comrade Krakovitch," the other sighed. He struggled for words, a way to begin a sentence with something other than "but." "Alas, I am also aware that the other gentleman in your car is *not* a Soviet citizen, and that his documents are *not* in order! If I were to let you through without the proper authorization, next week I could well be a lumberjack in Omsk! I don't have the build for it, Comrade."

"What sort of a bloody control point is this, anyway?" Krakovitch was in full flood. "No telephone, no electric light? I suppose we must thank God you have toilets! Now listen to me—''

"—I *have* listened, Comrade,'' at least the officer's guts weren't all sagging inside his belly, "to threats and vitriolic raving, for at least three-and-a-half hours, but—''

"BUT?'' Krakovitch couldn't believe it; this couldn't be happening to him. He shook his fist at the other. "Idiot! I've counted eleven cars and twenty-seven lorries through here towards Kolomyya since our arrival. Your man out there didn't even check the papers of half of them!''

"Because we know them. They travel through here regularly. Many of them live in or close to Kolomyya. I have explained this a hundred times.

"Think on *this!*'' Krakovitch snapped. "Tomorrow you could be explaining it to the KGB!''

"More threats.'' The other gave another shrug. "One stops worrying.''

"Total inefficiency!'' Krakovitch snarled. "Three hours ago you said that the telephones would be working in a few minutes. Likewise two hours ago, and one hour ago— and the time now is fast approaching one in the morning!''

"I know the time, Comrade. There is a fault in the electricity supply. It is being dealt with. What more can I say?'' He sat down on a padded chair behind the counter.

Krakovitch almost leaped over the counter to get at him. "Don't you *dare* sit down! Not while I am on my feet!''

The other wiped his forehead, stood up again, prepared himself for another tirade . . .

Outside in the car, Sergei Gulharov had restlessly turned this way and that, peering first out of one window, then another. Carl Quint sensed problems, trouble, danger ahead. In fact he'd been on edge since seeing Kyle off at the airport in Bucharest. But worrying about it would get him nowhere, and anyway he felt too banged-about to pursue it. If anything, not being allowed to drive—being obliged to simply sit there, with the drab country-side slipping endlessly by outside—had made him more weary yet. Now he felt that he could sleep for a week, and it might as well be here as anywhere.

Gulharov's attention had now fastened on something outside the car. He grew still, thoughtful. Quint looked at him: "silent, Sergei," as he and Kyle had privately named him. It wasn't his fault he spoke no English; in fact he did speak it, but very little, and with many errors. Now he answered Quint's glance, nodded his short-cropped head, and pointed through the open window of the car at something. "Look," he softly said. Quint looked.

Silhouetted against a low, distant haze of blue light—the lights of Kolomyya, Quint supposed—black cables snaked between poles over the border check point, with one section of cable descending into the building itself. The power supply. Now Gulharov turned and pointed off to the west, where the cable ran back in the direction of Siret. A hundred yards away, the loop of cable between two of the poles dipped right down under the night horizon. It had been grounded.

"Excusing," said Gulharov. He eased himself out of the car, walked back along the central reservation, and disappeared into darkness. Quint considered going after him, but decided against it. He felt very vulnerable, and outside the car would feel even more so. At least the car's interior was familiar to him. He tuned himself again to Krakovitch's raving, coming loud and clear through the night from the border post. Quint couldn't understand what was being said, but someone was getting a hard time . . .

"An end to all foolishness!" Krakovitch shouted. "Now I will tell you what I am going to do. I shall drive back into Siret to the police station and phone Moscow from there."

"Good," said the fat official. "And providing that Moscow can send the correct documentation for the Englishman, down the telephone wire, then I shall let you through!"

"Dolt!" Krakovitch sneered. "You, of course, shall

come with me to Siret, where you'll receive your instructions direct from the Kremlin!''

How dearly the other would have loved to tell him that he had already received his instructions from Moscow, but . . . he'd been warned against that. Instead he slowly shook his head. "Unfortunately, Comrade, I can't leave my post. Dereliction of duty is a very serious matter. Nothing you or anyone else could say could force me from my place of duty.''

Krakovitch saw from the official's red face that he'd pushed him too far. Now he would probably be more stubborn than ever, even to the point of deliberate obstruction.

That was a thought which made Krakovitch frown. For what if all of this trouble had been "deliberate obstruction" right from the start? Was that possible? "Then the solution is simple," he said. "I assume that Siret does have a twenty-four hour police station—with telephones that work?''

His opponent chewed his lip. "Of course," he finally answered.

"Then I shall simply telephone ahead to Kolomyya and have a unit of the nearest military force here within the hour. How will it feel, Comrade, to be a Russian, commanded by some Russian army officer to stand aside, while I and my friends are escorted through your stupid little checkpoint? And to know that tomorrow all hell is going to descend on you because *you* will have been the focus of what could well be a serious international incident?''

At which precise moment, out in the field to the west of the road and back a little way towards Siret, Sergei Gulharov stooped and picked up the two uncoupled halves, male and female, of a heavy electrical connection. Taped to the main supply cable was a much thinner telephone wire. Its connection, also broken, was a simple, slender plug-and-socket affair. He connected the telephone cable first, then without pause screwed the heavier couplings together. There

came a sputter and crackle of current, a flash of blue
sparks, and—

The lights came on in the border post. Krakovitch, on
the point of leaving to carry out his threat, stopped at the
door, turned back and saw the look of confusion on the
official's face. "I suppose," Krakovitch said, "this means
your telephone is also working again?"

"I . . . I suppose so," said the other.

Krakovitch came back to the counter. "Which means,"
his tone was icy, "that from now on we might just start to
get somewhere . . ."

1:00 A.M. in Moscow. At the Château Bronnitsy, some
miles out of the city along the Serpukhov Road, Ivan
Gerenko and Theo Dolgikh stood at an oval observation
port of one-way glass and stared into the room beyond at a
scene like something out of a science fiction nightmare.

Inside the "operating theatre," Alec Kyle lay unconscious on his back, strapped to a padded table. His head
was slightly elevated by means of a rubber cushion, and a
bulky stainless-steel helmet covered his head and eyes in a
half dome, leaving his nose and mouth free for breathing.
Hundreds of hair-fine wires cased in coloured plastic sleeves
shimmered like a rainbow from the helmet to a computer
where three operators worked frantically, following thought
sequences from beginning to end and erasing them at the
point of resolution. Inside the helmet, many tiny sensor
electrodes had been clamped to Kyle's skull; others, along
with batteries of micro-monitors, were secured by tape to
his chest, wrists, stomach and throat. Four more men,
telepaths, sat paired on each side of Kyle on stainless-steel
chairs, scribbling in notebooks in their laps, each with one
hand resting lightly on Kyle's naked body. A master
telepathist—Zek Föener, E-Branch's best—sat alone in
one corner of the room. Föener was a beautiful young
woman in her mid-twenties, an East German recruited by
Gregor Borowitz during his last days as head of the branch.

She sat with her elbows on her knees, one hand to her brow, utterly motionless, totally intent upon absorbing Kyle's thoughts as quickly as they were stimulated and generated.

Dolgikh was full of morbid fascination. He had arrived with Kyle at the château about 11:00 A.M. Their flight from Bucharest had been made in a military transport aircraft to an airbase in Smolensk, then to the Château in E-Branch's own helicopter. All of this had been achieved in absolute secrecy; KGB cover had been tight as a drum. Not even Brezhnev—*especially* Brezhnev—knew what was happening here.

At the Château Kyle had been injected with a truth serum—not to loosen his tongue but his mind—which had rendered him unconscious. And for the last twelve hours, with booster shots of the serum at regular intervals, he had been giving up all the secrets of INTESP to the Soviet espers. Theo Dolgikh, however, was a very mundane man. His ideas of interrogation, or "truth gathering," were far removed from anything he saw here.

"What *exactly* are they doing to him? How does this work, Comrade?" he asked.

Without looking at Dolgikh, with his faded hazel eyes following every slightest movement in the room beyond the screen, Gerenko answered, "You, of all people, have surely heard of brainwashing, Theo? Well, that is what we are doing: washing Alec Kyle's brain. So thoroughly, in fact, that it will come out of the wash bleached!"

Ivan Gerenko was slight, and so small as to be almost childlike in stature; but his wrinkled skin, faded eyes and generally sallow appearance were those of an old man. And yet he was only thirty-seven. A rare disease had stunted him physically, aged him prematurely, and a contrary Nature had made up the deficiency by giving him a supplementary "talent." He was a "deflector."

Like Darcy Clarke in many ways, he was the opposite of accident-prone. But where Clarke's talent avoided danger, Gerenko actually deflected it. A well-aimed blow would not strike him; the shaft of an axe would break before the blade could touch his flesh. The advantage was enormous, immeasurable: he feared nothing and was almost scornful of physical danger. And it accounted for his totally disdainful manner where people such as Theo Dolgikh were concerned. Why should he afford them any sort of respect? They might dislike him, but they could never hurt him. No man was capable of bringing physical harm to Ivan Gerenko.

"Brainwashing?" Dolgikh repeated him. "I had thought some sort of interrogation, surely?"

"Both," Gerenko nodded, talking rather to himself than by way of answering Dolgikh. "We use science, psychology, parapsychology. The three Ts: technology, terror, telepathy. The drug we've put in his blood stimulates memory. It works by making him feel alone—utterly alone. He feels that no one else exists in all the universe—even his own existence is in doubt! He wants to 'talk' about all of his experiences, everything he ever did or saw or said, because that way he will know that he is real, that he has existence. But if he physically tried to do it at the speed his mind is working, he would rapidly dehydrate and burn himself out; especially if he were awake, conscious. Also, we are not interested in the accumulation of all of that information, we do not wish to know 'everything.' His life in general holds little of interest to us, but of course we are completely fascinated with details of his work for INTESP."

Dolgikh shook his head in bewilderment. "You are stealing his thoughts?"

"Oh yes! It's an idea we borrowed from Boris Dragosani. He was a necromancer: he could steal the thoughts of the dead! We can only do it to the living, but when we're finished they're as good as dead . . ."

"But . . . I mean, *how?*" The concept was over Dolgikh's head.

Gerenko glanced at him, just a glance, a twitch of the eyes in his wizened head. "I can't explain 'how'—not to you—only 'what.' When he touches upon a mundane matter, the entire subject is drawn from him swiftly—and erased. This saves time, for he can't return to that subject again. But when we are interested in his subject, then the telepaths absorb the content of his thoughts as best they can. If what they learn is difficult to remember or understand, they make a note, a jotting which can be studied later. And as soon as that line of inquiry is exhausted, then that subject, too, is erased."

Dolgikh had taken most of this in, but his interest now centred on Zek Föener. "That girl, she is very beautiful." His gaze was openly lecherous. "Now if only *she* were a subject for interrogation. My sort of interrogation, of course." He gave a coarse chuckle.

At that exact moment the girl looked up. Her bright blue eyes blazed with fury. She looked directly at the one-way glass, as if . . .

"Ah!" said Dolgikh, the word a small gasp. "Impossible! She looks through the glass at us!"

"No," Gerenko shook his head. "She *thinks* through it—at you, if I'm not mistaken!"

Föener stood up, strode purposefully to a side door and left the room, emerging into the rubber-floored corridor where the observers stood. She came straight up to them, glanced once at Dolgikh and showed him her perfect, sharp white teeth, then turned to Gerenko. "Ivan, take this . . . this ape away from here. He's inside my radius, and his mind's like a sewer!"

"Of course, my dear," Gerenko smiled and nodded his wrinkled walnut head. He turned away, taking Dolgikh's elbow. "Come, Theo."

Dolgikh shook himself loose, scowled at the girl. "You are very free with your insults."

"That is the correct way." She spoke curtly. "Face to face and out with it. But *your* insults crawl like worms, and you keep them in the slime in your head!'' And to Gerenko she added: "I can't work with him here.''

Gerenko looked at Dolgikh. "Well?''

Dolgikh's expression was ugly, but slowly he relaxed, shrugged. "Very well, my apologies, Fräulein Föener.'' He deliberately avoided use of his customary "Comrade''; and when he looked her up and down one last time, that too was quite deliberate. "It's simply that I've always considered my thoughts private. And anyway, I'm only human.''

"Barely!'' she snapped, and at once returned to her work.

As Dolgikh followed Gerenko to his office, the Second in Command of E-Branch said, "That one's mind is very finely tuned, finely balanced. We must be careful not to disturb it. However distasteful this may seem, Theo, you should never forget that any one of the espers here is worth ten of you.''

Dolgikh had pride. "Oh?'' he growled. "Then why didn't Andropov ask you to send one of them to Italy, eh? Maybe you yourself, eh, Comrade?''

Gerenko smiled thinly. "Muscle occasionally has its advantages. That's why you went to Genoa, and it's why you're here now. I expect to have more work for you very soon. Work to your liking. But, Theo, be warned: so far you've done very well, so don't spoil it now. Our mutual, er, shall we say 'superior,' will be well pleased with you. But he would *not* be pleased if he thought you'd tried to impose your matter over our mind. Here at the Château Bronnitsy, it's always the other way around—mind over matter!''

They climbed spiralling stone stairs in one of the Château's towers, and arrived at Gerenko's office. Before Gerenko it had housed Gregor Borowitz, and it was now Felix Krakovitch's seat of control; but Krakovitch was temporarily absent, and both Ivan Gerenko and Yuri Andropov intended that his absence should become permanent. This, too, puzzled Dolgikh.

"In my time," he said, taking a seat opposite Gerenko's desk, "I've been quite close to Comrade Andropov—or as close as a man can get. I've watched him rise, followed his rising star, you might say. In my experience, since the early days of E-Branch, there has been friction between the KGB and you espers. Yet now, with you, things are changing. What has Andropov got on you, Ivan?"

Gerenko's grin was that of a weasel. "He has nothing on me," he answered. "But he does have something *for* me. You see, I have been cheated, Theo. Nature has robbed me. I would like to be a man of heroic proportions— perhaps a man like you. But I'm stuck in this feeble shell. Women are not interested in me; men, while they cannot hurt me, consider me a freak. Only my mind has value, and my talent. The first has been useful to Felix Krakovitch; I've taken a great deal of the branch's burden off his shoulders. And the second is a subject for intense study by the parapsychologists here—they would all like to have my, shall we say, guardian angel? Why, an army of men with my talent would be quite invulnerable!"

"So you see how important I am. And yet what am I but a shrunken little man, whose lifespan is destined to be short? And so while I live I want power. I want to be great, for however short a span. "And because it *will* be short, I want it now."

"And with Krakovitch gone, you'll be the boss here." Dolgikh nodded.

Gerenko smiled his withered smile. "That for a start. But then comes the integration of E-Branch and the KGB. Brezhnev would be against it, of course, but alas the Party Leader is rapidly becoming a mumbling, crumbling cretin. He can't last long. And Andropov, because he *is* strong, has many enemies. How long will he last, do you think? Which means that eventually, possibly, even probably—"

"You'll have it all!" Dolgikh could see the logic of it.

"But by then, surely, you too will have made enemies. Leaders always climb to the top over the bodies of dead leaders."

"Ah!" Gerenko's smile was sly, cold, and not entirely sane. "But this time it will be different. What do I care for enemies? Sticks and stones will *not* break my bones! And I shall weed them out, one by one, until there are no more. And I shall die small and wrinkled, but also great and very powerful. So whatever you do, Theo Dolgikh, make sure you're my friend, not my enemy . . ."

Dolgikh said nothing for a moment but let all that Gerenko had said sink in. The man was obviously a megalomaniac! Tactfully, Dolgikh changed the subject. "You said there'd likely be more work for me. What sort of work?"

"As soon as we are sure that we can learn everything we desire to know from Alec Kyle, then Krakovitch, his man Gulharov, and the other British agent, Quint, will become quite expendable. At the moment, when Krakovitch wants something done, he speaks to me and I in turn pass on his request to Brezhnev. Not directly to Brezhnev but through one of his men—a mere lackey, but a powerful lackey. The Party Leader is keen on E-Branch and so Krakovitch usually gets what he wants. Witness this unheard of liaison between British and Soviet espers!

"But of course I'm also working for Andropov. He, too, knows everything that is happening. And he has already instructed me that when the time comes you are the tool I shall throw into Krakovitch's machinery. E-Branch has been soundly beaten, almost destroyed, by INTESP once before. Brezhnev wants to know how and why, and so does Andropov. We had a mighty weapon in Boris Dragosani, but their weapon, a youth called Harry Keogh, was mightier. What gave him his power? What *were* his powers? And right now; we know that with the aid of INTESP Krakovitch has destroyed something in Romania. I have been through Krakovitch's files and I think I know what he destroyed: the same thing which gave Dragosani *his* powers! Krakovitch sees it as a great evil, but I see it only as another tool. A powerful weapon. That is why the British are so eager to help Krakovitch: the fool is systematically destroying a possible route for future Soviet supremacy!''

"Then he's a traitor?" Dolgikh's eyes narrowed. The Soviet Union was all. Power struggles within the structure were only to be expected, but treachery of this sort was something else.

"No." Gerenko shook his head. "He's a dupe. Now listen: At this very moment Krakovitch, Gulharov and Quint are stalled at a crossing-point on the Moldavian border. I organized that through Andropov. I know where they want to go, and very shortly I'll be sending you to deal with them there. When exactly rather depends on how much we get from Kyle. But in any case we must stop them from doing any more damage. Which means that time is of the essence; they can't be stalled forever, and soon must be allowed to proceed. Also, they know the location of whatever it is they're seeking, and we do not. Not yet. Tomorrow morning you will be there to follow them to their destination, their ultimate destination. At least I hope so . . ."

Dolgikh frowned. "They've destroyed something, you say? And they'll do it again? What sort of something?"

"If you had been in time to follow them into the Romanian hills, you'd probably have seen for yourself. But don't worry about it. Let it suffice that this time they mustn't succeed."

As Gerenko finished speaking his telephone rang. He lifted it to his ear—and his expression at once became wary, alert. "Comrade Krakovitch!" he said. "I was beginning to worry about you. I had expected to hear from you before now. Are you in Chernovtsy?" He looked pointedly across his desk at Dolgikh.

Even from where he sat, Dolgikh could hear the angry,

tinny clatter of Krakovitch's distant voice. Gerenko began to blink rapidly and a nervous tic jerked the corner of his mouth.

Finally, when Krakovitch was finished, he said, "Listen, Comrade. Ignore that stupid frontier guard. He isn't worth losing your temper over. Just stay exactly where you are and in a few minutes I shall have full authorization phoned through. But first let me speak to that idiot."

He waited a moment, until he heard the slightly tremulous, inquiring voice of the border official, and then very quietly said, "Listen. Do you recognize my voice? Good! In approximately ten minutes I shall phone again and tell you I am the commissioner for Frontier Control in Moscow. Ensure that you and you alone answer the phone, and that you can't be overheard. I will order you to let comrade Krakovitch and his friends through, and you will do so. Do you understand?"

"Oh, yes, Comrade!"

"If Krakovitch should ask you what I have just said, tell him I was shouting at you and calling you a fool."

"Yes, of course, Comrade."

"Good!" Gerenko put the phone down. He looked at Dolgikh. "As I was saying, I couldn't hold them up forever. Already this affair is growing clumsy, becoming embarrassing. But even though they'll now go through to Chernovtsy, they can do nothing tonight. And tomorrow you'll be there to stop them doing anything."

Dolgikh nodded. "Do you have any suggestions?"

"In what respect?"

"About how it should be done? If Krakovitch is a traitor, it seems to me that the easiest way of dealing with this would be— "

"No!" Gerenko cut him off. "That would be hard to prove. And he has the ear of the Party Leader, remember? We must never leave ourselves open to question in this matter." He tapped a finger on his desk, gave the problem a moment's thought. "Ah! I think I may have it. I have called Krakovitch a dupe—so let it appear. Let Carl Quint be the guilty party! Arrange it so that he can be blamed. Let it be seen that the British espers came into Russia to discover what they could of E-Branch, and to kill its head. Why not? They've damaged the branch before, haven't they? But on this occasion Quint will err and become a fatality of his own strategy."

"Good!" said Dolgikh. "I'm sure I'll work something out along those lines. And of course I'll be the only witness . . ."

Light footsteps sounded and Zek Föener appeared on the office threshold. She merely glanced coldly at Dolgikh, then fixed her gaze on Gerenko. 'Kyle is a goldmine—the sane part of him, anyway! There is nothing he doesn't know, and he's releasing it in a flood. He even knows a good many—too many—things about us. Things *I* didn't know. Fantastic things . . ." Suddenly she looked tired.

Gerenko nodded. "Fantastic things? I had supposed that they would be. Is that why you think he's partly insane? That his mind is playing him tricks? Believe me, it isn't! Do you know what they destroyed in Romania?"

She nodded. "Yes, but . . . it's hard to believe. I—"

Gerenko held up a warning hand. She understood, felt caution emanating from him. Theo Dolgikh was not to know. Like most of the other espers at the Château, Föener hated the KGB. She nodded, and kept her silence.

Gerenko spoke again. "And is it the same sort of thing that lies hidden in the mountains beyond Chernovtsy?"

Again she nodded.

"Very well." Gerenko smiled without emotion. "And now, my dear, you must return to your work. Give it total priority."

"Of course," she answered. "I only came away while they were dosing him again. And because I need a break from . . ." She shook her head dazedly. Her eyes were wide, bright with strange new knowledge. "Comrade, this thing is utterly—"

Again Gerenko held up his child's hand in warning. "I know."

She nodded, turned and left, her footsteps a little uncertain on the descending stone stairs.

"What was that all about?" Dolgikh was mystified.

"That was the joint death certificate of Krakovitch, Gulharov and Quint," Gerenko answered. "Actually, Quint was the only one who might have been useful—but no longer. Now you can get on your way. Is the branch helicopter ready for you?"

Dolgikh nodded. He began to stand up, then frowned and said, "First tell me, what will happen to Kyle when you are finished with him? I mean, I'll take care of that other pair of traitors, and the British esper, Quint, but what of Kyle? What will become of him?"

Gerenko raised his eyebrows. "I thought that was obvious. When we have what we want, everything we want, then we'll dump him in the British zone in Berlin. There he'll simply die, and their best doctors won't know why."

"But why will he die? And what of that drug you're pumping into him? Surely their doctors will pick up traces?"

Gerenko shook his walnut head. "It leaves no trace. It completely voids itself in a few hours. That is why we have to keep dosing him. A clever lot, our Bulgarian friends. He's not the first one we've drained in this fashion, and the results have always been the same. As to why he will die: he will have no incentive for life. Less than a cabbage, he will not retain sufficient knowledge or instinct even to move his body. There will be no control—none! His vital organs will not function. He might survive longer on a life-support machine, but . . ." And he shrugged.

"Brain-death." Dolgikh nodded and grinned.

"But there you have it in a nutshell." Gerenko emotionlessly clapped his child's hands. "Bravo! For what is an entirely empty brain if not dead, eh? And now, if you'll excuse me, I have a telephone call to make."

Dolgikh stood up. "I'll be on my way," he said. Already he was looking forward to the task in hand.

"Theo," said Gerenko. "Krakovitch and his friends—they should be killed with despatch. Don't linger over it. And one last thing: do not be too curious about what they are trying to do up there in the mountains. Do not concern yourself with it. Believe me, too much curiosity could be very, very dangerous!"

In answer to which Dolgikh could only nod. Then he turned and left the room . . .

As their car drew away from the checkpoint towards Chernovtsy, Quint might have expected Krakovitch to carry on raging. But he didn't. Instead the head of the Soviet E-Branch was quiet and thoughtful, and even more so after Gulharov quickly told him about the disconnected cable.

"There are several things I not liking here," Krakovitch told Quint in a little while. "At first I am thinking that fat man back there is simply stupid, but now not being so sure. And this business with the electricity—all very strange. Sergei finds and fixes that which they could not—and he does it quickly and without difficulty. Which would seem to make our fat friend at the checkpoint not only stupid but incompetent!"

"You think we were deliberately delayed?" Quint felt an uneasy, dark oppressiveness settling all around him, like a positive weight on his head and shoulders.

"That telephone call he got just now," Krakovitch mused. "The Commissioner for Frontier Control, in Moscow? I never heard of him! But I suppose he must exist. Or must he? One commissioner, controlling all of the thousands of crossing points into the Soviet Union? So, I assume he exists. Which is meaning that Ivan Gerenko got in touch with him, in the dead of night, and that he then personally called up this little fat official in his stupid sentry-box of a control hut—all in ten minutes!"

"Who knew we were coming through here tonight?"

Quint, in his way of going to the root of things, asked the most obvious questions.

"Eh?" Krakovitch scratched behind his ear. "We knew it, of course, and—"

"And?"

"And my Second in Command at the Château Bronnitsy, Ivan Gerenko." Krakovitch turned to Quint and stared hard at him.

"Then, while I dislike saying it," said Quint, "if there _is_ something funny going on, Gerenko has to be your man."

Krakovitch gave a disbelieving snort, shook his head. "But why? What reason?"

Quint shrugged. "You have to know him better than I do. Is he ambitious? Could he have been got at—and by whom? But remember, we did have that trouble in Genoa, and didn't you remark how surprised you were that the KGB were trailing you? Your explanation was that they'd probably had you under constant surveillance—until we put a stop to it, anyway. But just let's suppose there is an enemy in your camp. Did Gerenko know you were meeting us in Italy?"

"Apart from Brezhnev himself—through an intermediary who cannot be brought into question—Gerenko is the _only_ one who knew!" Krakovitch answered.

Quint said nothing, merely shrugged again and raised an eyebrow.

"I am thinking," said Krakovitch slowly, "that from now on I tell no one how I moving until after the move is completed!" He looked at Quint, saw his troubled frown. "Is there something else?"

Quint pursed his lips. "'Let's just say this Gerenko fellow is a plant, a spy in your organization. Am I right in thinking he can only be working for the KGB?"

"For Andropov, yes. Almost certainly."

"Then Gerenko must think you're a complete fool!"

"Oh? Why do you say so? In fact he thinks most men

are fools. He fears no one, Gerenko, and so can afford to think so. But I? No, I believe I am one of the few men who he respects—or used to.''

''Used to,'' Quint nodded. ''But no more. Surely he must know you'll work all of this out for yourself given a little time? Theo Dolgikh in Genoa, and now this shambles at the Romano-Soviet border? Unless he himself is an idiot, Gerenko must know he's for the high-jump as soon as you get back to Moscow!''

Sergei Gulharov had managed to understand most of this. Now he spoke to Krakovitch in a soft, rapid burst of Russian.

''*Hah!*'' Krakovitch's shoulders jerked in a humourless chuckle. For a moment he was silent, then he said, ''Perhaps Sergei is smarter than all of us. And if he is, then we're in for trouble.''

''Oh?'' said Quint. ''What did Sergei say?''

''He said, perhaps Comrade Gerenko feels that he can now afford to be a little slipshod. Perhaps he isn't expecting to see me again in Moscow! And as for you, Carl—we just crossed the border and you're in Russia.''

''I know,'' Quint quietly answered. ''And I must say, I don't exactly feel at home.''

''Strangely,'' Krakovitch nodded, ''neither do I!''

Nothing more was said until they reached Chernovtsy . . .

Chapter Fifteen

BACK IN LONDON AT **INTESP** HQ, GUY ROBERTS AND KEN Layard had traced Alec Kyle, Carl Quint and Yulian Bodescu. The Devon-based team of espers had travelled back to the capital by train, leaving Ben Trask to mend in the Torquay hospital. Having used the journey to catch up on some sleep, they'd got into HQ just before midnight. Layard had roughly "located" the three figures in question, and Roberts had attempted to scry their whereabouts a little more precisely. Desperation had seemingly honed their talents and the familiarity of their surroundings had helped them to get results—of a sort.

Now Roberts held a briefing: in attendance were Layard, John Grieve, Harvey Newton, Trevor Jordan, and three others who were permanent members of the HQ's staff. Roberts was red-eyed, unshaven and itchy; his breath reeked of an endless chain of cigarettes. He glanced around the table and nodded to each man in turn, then got straight into it.

"We've been trimmed back a bit," he said, untypically

phlegmatic. "Kyle and Quint are out of it, perhaps permanently; Trask is banged up a bit; Darcy Clarke's up north, and . . . and then there's poor Simon Gower. And the result of our outing? Our job isn't only that much harder, it's that much more important! Yes, and we've less men to do it. We could certainly use Harry Keogh now—but Alec Kyle was Keogh's main man, and Alec's not here. And as well as the danger we *know* exists—out there, loose—there's now a second problem which could be just as big. Namely, the espers of the Soviet E-Branch have got Kyle on ice at the Château Bronnitsy."

This was news to everyone except Layard. Lips tightened and heartbeats stepped up. Ken Layard took up the briefing. "We're pretty sure he's there," he said. "I located him—I think—but only with the greatest difficulty. They've got espers blocking everything in there, far more concentrated than we've ever known it before. The place is a mental miasma!"

"That's a fact," Roberts nodded. "I tried to pin-point him, get a picture of him—and failed miserably! Just a general mind-smog. Which doesn't bode at all well for Alec. If his being there was all above board, they'd have nothing to hide. Also, he's not supposed to be there at all but here. My guess is, they'll be milking him for all he's worth. And for all we're worth. If I'm cold-blooded about it, believe me it's only to save time."

"What about Carl Quint?" John Grieve put the question. "How's he faring?"

"Carl's where he should be," Layard said. "Near as I can make out, in a place called Chernovtsy under the Carpathians. Whether he's there willingly is another matter."

"But we think willingly," Roberts added. "I've managed to reach and see him, however briefly, and I *think* he's with Krakovitch. Which only serves to confuse things further. If Krakovitch is straight up, then why is Kyle in trouble?"

"And Bodescu?" Newton asked. He now felt he had a personal vendetta with the vampire.

"That bastard is heading north," Roberts grimly answered. "It could be coincidence, but we don't think so. Ultimately, we think he's after the Keogh child. He knows everything, knows the guiding force behind our organization. Bodescu has been hit, and now he wants to hit back. The one mind in this entire world which is an authority on vampires—particularly Yulian Bodescu—is housed in that child. That has to be his target."

"We don't know how he's travelling," Layard carried on. "Public transport? Could be. He could even be thumbing lifts! But he's certainly not in any sort of hurry. He's just taking it easy, taking his time. He got into Birmingham an hour ago, since when he's been static. We think he's put up for the night. But it's the same story as before: he exudes this mental swamp. That's what it's like: groping around in the heart of a foggy swamp. You can't pinpoint him at all, but you know there's a crocodile in there somewhere. At the moment, Birmingham is the centre of it . . ."

"But do we have any plans?" Jordan couldn't stand the inactivity. "I mean, are we going to do something? Or do we just sit here playing with ourselves while everything goes to hell?"

"There are jobs for everybody." Roberts held up a huge, controlling hand. "First I need a volunteer to go up and help Darcy Clarke in Hartlepool. Apart from a couple of Special Branch men—who are good blokes but simply can't be expected to know what they're on—Darcy's on his own. The ideal thing would be to send a spotter, except we don't have one right now. So it will have to be a telepath." He looked pointedly at Jordan.

Harvey Newton got in first, however, saying: "That's me! I owe Bodescu that much. He got by me last time, but he won't do it again."

Jordan shrugged and no one else objected. Roberts nod-

ded. ''OK—but stay sharp! Go now, by car. The roads will
be empty, so you should be able to go flat out. Depending
on how things go at this end, I'll probably be joining you
sometime tomorrow.''

That was all Newton had wanted. He stood up, nodded
once to all in general, got on his way. ''Take a crossbow,'' Roberts called after him. ''And Harvey, next time
you 'shoot your bolt' make sure you hit the target!''

''What's my job?'' Jordan asked.

''You'll work with Mike Carson,'' Roberts told him.
''And with me and Layard. We'll try to locate Quint
again, and you telepaths can take a stab at sending to him.
It's a long shot, but Quint's a spotter, he's a psychic
sensitive; he might just feel you. Your message to him will
be simple: if he can he's to get in touch with us. If we can
get him on the phone, we can perhaps find out about Kyle.
And if he doesn't know about Kyle—well, that in itself
will answer one question. Also, if we do manage to contact him, it might be a good idea to tell Quint to get the
hell out of there—if and while he can! So that's the four of
us tied up for the night.'' He looked round the table.

''The rest of you can concentrate on the proper running
of this place before it comes apart at the seams. Every man
Jack is on duty full time as of now. Right, are there any
questions?''

''Are we the only ones in on this?'' John Grieve asked.
''I mean, are the public, the authorities, still entirely in the
dark?''

''Totally. What do we tell them—that we're chasing a
vampire through the countryside from Devon to British
West Hartlepool? Listen, even the people who fund us and
know we exist don't wholly believe in us! How do you
think they'd react to the facts about Yulian Bodescu? And
as for Harry Keogh . . . of course the public is in the dark
about it.''

''With a single exception, anyway,'' said Layard. ''We've
had the police alerted to the fact that there's a mad killer

on the loose—Bodescu's description, of course. We've told them he's heading north, possible destination the Hartlepool area. They've been warned that if he's spotted they're not to apprehend him but get in touch with us first, then the Special Branch lads who are up there on the job. As and when Bodescu gets closer to his target, then we'll be more specific. That's as much as we dare do for now."

Roberts looked from face to face. "Any more questions?" he asked. There were none . . .

3:30 A.M. at Brenda Keogh's tiny but immaculate garret flat overlooking the main road through the town and, across the road, an old, old cemetery. Harry Jr. lay in his cot sleeping and dreaming baby dreams, and his father's mind slept with him exhausted from a struggle he now knew he had no hope of winning. The child had him, it was as simple as that. Harry was the baby's sixth sense.

In the wee small hours of the misty morning, with dawn still half an hour away, a thicker mist was forming in slumbering minds bringing horror as it swirled and eddied in subconscious caverns of dream. And out of nowhere, telepathic fingers were reaching, probing, discovering!

Ahhh! came that gurgling, clotted mental voice in the two Harrys' minds. *Is that you, Haarrryyy? Yesss, I see it is! Well, I'm coming for you, Haarrrryyy—I'm coming . . . for . . . you!"*

The baby's scream of terror ripped his mother from her bed as if it were the hand of some cruel giant. She stumbled to his tiny room, shook herself awake as she entered and went to him. And how he cried, cried, *cried* when she took him in her arms, cried like she'd never heard before. But he wasn't wet, and no nappy pins were sticking in him. Was he hungry? No, it wasn't that either.

She rocked him in her arms, but still he sobbed, and his little eyes wide and wild and full of fear. A dream, maybe? "But you're too tiny, Harry," she told him, kissing his hot little head. "Far too tiny and sweet and so very, very young to be dreaming naughty dreams! That's all it was, baby, a naughty dream.''

She carried him back to her own bed, thinking: *Yes, and I must have been dreaming too!* She must have been, for the baby's scream when it woke her hadn't sounded like the scream of a child at all but that of a terrified man . . .

It was 3:30 in London, where Guy Roberts and Ken Layard, assisted by the telepaths Trevor Jordan and Mike Carson, had spent the last ninety minutes trying to "get through" to Carl Quint—without any success that they could measure.

They were working in Layard's private locations room, an office or study set by solely for his use. Wall racks carried maps and charts of the entire world, without which Layard's work for INTESP would be almost impossible. The map which had been spread on his desk for the last two hours was a blown-up aerial recce photograph of the Russo-Moldavian border, with Chernovtsy circled in red felt-tip.

The air was blue and acrid from Roberts's endless chain-smoking, and steam whistled from an electric kettle in one corner where Carson was making yet another cup of instant coffee. "I'm knackered," Roberts admitted, stubbing out his half-smoked cigarette and lighting another. "We'll take a break, find somewhere quiet and try to snatch forty winks. Start up again in an hour's time." He stood up, stretched, said to Carson, "Stow the coffee for me, Mike. One addiction's enough, thanks!"

Trevor Jordan pushed his chair away from the desk, went over to the room's small window and opened it as far as possible. He lowered himself into a chair beside it and hung his head out into the night.

Layard yawned, rolled up the map and pigeon-holed it in a rack behind him. In doing so he exposed the huge 1:625,000 scale map of England which they had worked on earlier. At ten miles to an inch the thing covered the desk. He glanced at it, at Birmingham's grey blot, let his talent reach out and touch that sleeping city—and . . .

"Guy!" Layard's whisper stopped Roberts half-way out of the door.

He looked back. "Eh?"

Layard jerked stiffly to his feet, crouched over the map. His eyes searched frantically and he licked suddenly dry lips. "Guy," he said again, "we thought he was down for the night, but he's not! He's off and running again—and for all we know he's been on the move for the last hour and a half!"

"What the hell . . .?" Roberts's tired mind could barely grasp it. He came lurching back to the desk, Jordan too. "What are you talking about? Bodescu?"

"Right," said Layard, "that bloody thing! Bodescu! He's cleared off out of Birmingham!"

Grey as death, Roberts slumped down into his chair as before. He put a meaty hand over Birmingham on the map, closed his eyes, forced his talent into action. But no use, there was nothing; no mind-smog, no slightest suggestion that the vampire was there at all. "Oh, *Christ!*" Roberts hissed through grating teeth.

Jordan looked across the room at Carson where he was stirring sugar into three cups of coffee. "Square one, Mike," he said. "You'd better make it four after all . . ."

It had been Harvey Newton's first choice to take the A1 north, but in the end he'd settled for the motorway. What he lost in actual distance he'd get back in speed, comfort, three-lane running, and M1's ruler-straight road.

At Leicester Forest East he stopped for a coffee break, answered the call of nature, picked up a can of Coke and a wrapped sandwich. And breathing the cool, moist night air he turned up his coat collar and made his way back across the almost deserted car park to his car. He had left the door open but had taken his keys with him. The whole

stop had taken no more than ten minutes. Now he'd top up
with petrol and get on his way again.

But as he approached his car he slowed down, stopped.
His footsteps, echoing back to him, seemed to pause just a
moment too late. Something niggled at the back of Newton's mind. He turned, looked back towards the friendly
lights of the all-night eater. For some reason he was
holding his breath, and maybe it was a very good reason.
He turned in a slow circle, took in the entire car park, the
squat, hulking snail-shapes of parked cars. A heavy vehicle, turning off the motorway, lit him up in the glare of its
thousand watt eyes. He was dazzled, and after the lorry
angled away the night was that much darker.

Then he remembered the upright, forward-leaning
dog-thing he thought he'd seen—no, which he *had* seen—at
Harkley House, and that brought his mission back into
focus. He shook off his nameless fears, got into his car
and started the engine.

Something closed on Newton's brain like a clamp, a
mind warped and powerful and growing ever *more* powerful! He knew it was reading him like a stolen book, reading
his identity, divining his purpose. "Good evening," said a
voice like hot tar in Newton's ear. He gave a gasp of
shock and terror combined, an inarticulate cry, and turning
looked into the back of the car. Feral eyes fixed him in a
glare far more penetrating, far worse than the lorry's lamps.
Beneath them, the darkness was agleam with twin rows of
white daggers.

"Wha—!?" Newton started to say. But there was no
need even to ask. He *knew* that his vendetta with the
monster had run its course.

Yulian Bodescu lifted Newton's crossbow, aimed it directly into his gaping, gasping mouth—and pulled the
trigger.

It had been Felix Krakovitch's plan to stay overnight in
Chernovtsy; in the event, however, he had ordered Sergei

Gulharov to drive straight on to Kolomyya. Since Ivan
Gerenko had known that Krakovitch's party was scheduled
to stop over in Chernovtsy, it had seemed a very good idea
not to. Thus, after Theo Dolgikh got into Chernovtsy at
about 5:00 A.M. it had taken him a futile and frustrating two
hours simply to discover that the men he sought were not
there. After another delay while he contacted the Château
Bronnitsy, Gerenko had finally suggested that he go on to
Kolomyya and try again.

Dolgikh had been flown from Moscow to a military
airport in Skala-podolskaya where he'd been required to
sign for a KGB Fiat. Now, in the somewhat battered but
unobtrusive car, he drove to Kolomyya and arrived there
just before 8:00 A.M. Discreetly checking out the hotels, it
was a case of third time lucky— and also unlucky. They
had put up at the Hotel Carpatii, but they had been up and
on their way again by 7:30. He had missed them by half an
hour. The proprietor was only able to tell him that before
leaving they'd inquired the address of the town's library
and museum.

Dolgikh obtained the same address and followed after
them. At the museum he found the curator, a bustling,
beaming little Russian in thick-lensed spectacles, in the act
of opening the place up. Following him inside the old
cupolaed building, where their footsteps echoed in musty
air, Dolgikh said, "Might I enquire if you've had three
men in to see you this morning? I was supposed to meet
them here, but as you see I'm late."

"They were fortunate to find me working so early," the
other replied. "And luckier still that I let them in. The
museum doesn't really open until 8:30, you see. But since
they were obviously in a hurry . . ." He smiled and
shrugged.

"So I've missed them by . . . how much?" Dolgikh put
on a disappointed expression.

The curator shrugged again. "Oh, ten minutes, maybe.
But at least I can tell you where they went."

"I would be very grateful, Comrade," Dolgikh told him, following him into his private rooms.

"Comrade?" The curator glanced at him, his eyes bright and seeming to bulge behind the dense glass of his spectacles. "We don't hear that term too much down here—on the border, so to speak. Might I inquire who you are?"

Dolgikh presented his KGB identification and said, "That makes it official. Now then, I've no more time to waste. So if you'll just tell me what they were looking for and where they went . . ."

The curator no longer beamed, no longer seemed happy. "Are they wanted, those men?"

"No, just under observation."

"A shame. They seemed pleasant enough."

"One can't be too careful these days," said Dolgikh. "What did they want?"

"A location. They sought a place at the foot of the mountains called Moupho Alde Ferenc Yaborov."

"A mouthful!" Dolgikh commented. "And you told them where to find it?"

"No," the other shook his head. "Only where it used to be—and even then I can't be sure. Look here." He showed Dolgikh a set of antique maps spread on a table. "Not accurate, by any means. The oldest is about four hundred and fifty years old. Copies, obviously, not the originals. But if you look there"—he put his finger on one of the maps—"you'll see Kolomyya. And here—"

"Ferengi?"

The curator nodded. "One of the three—English, I believe—seemed to know exactly where to look. When he saw that ancient name on the map, 'Ferengi,' he grew very excited. And shortly after that they left."

Dolgikh nodded, studied the old map very carefully. "It's west of here," he mused, "and a little north. Scale?"

"Roughly one centimetre to five kilometres. But as I've said, the accuracy is very suspect."

"Something less than seventy kilometres, then," Dolgikh

frowned. "At the foot of the mountains. Do you have a modern map?"

"Oh, yes," the curator sighed. "If you'll just come this way . . ."

Fifteen miles out of Kolomyya a new highway, still under construction, sped north for Ivano-Frankovsk, its tarmac surface making for a smooth ride. Certainly to Krakovitch, Quint and Gulharov the ride was a delightful respite, following in the wake of their bumpy, bruising journey from Bucharest, through Romania and Moldavia. To the west rose the Carpathians, dark, forested and brooding even in the morning sunlight, while to the east the plain fell gently away into grey-green distance and a far, hazy horizon.

Eighteen miles along this road, in the direction of Ivano-Frankovsk, they passed a fork off to the left which inclined upwards directly into misty foothills. Quint asked Gulharov to slow down and traced a line on a rough map he'd copied at the museum. "That could be our best route," he said.

"The road has a barrier," Krakovitch pointed out, "and a sign forbidding entry. It's disused, a dead end."

"And yet I sense that's the way to go," Quint insisted.

Krakovitch could feel it too: something inside which warned that this was *not* the way to go, which probably meant that Quint was right and it was. "There's grave danger there," he said.

"Which is more or less what we expected," said Quint. "It's what we're here for."

"Very well." Krakovitch pursed his lips and nodded. He spoke to Gulharov, but the latter was already slowing down. Up ahead the twin lanes narrowed into one where a construction gang worked to widen the road. A steam roller flattened smoking tarmac in the wake of a tar-spraying lorry. Gulharov turned the car about-face and, at Krakovitch's command brought it to a halt.

Krakovitch got out, went to find the ganger and speak to him. Quint called after him, "What's up?"

"Up? Oh! I mean to see if these people know anything about this area. Also, perhaps I am able to enlist their aid. Remember, when we find what we're looking for, we still have to destroy it!"

Quint stayed in the car and watched Krakovitch stride towards the workmen and speak to them. They pointed along the deserted road to a construction shack. Krakovitch went that way. Ten minutes later he came back with a bearded giant of a man in faded overalls.

"This is Mikhail Volkonsky," he said, by way of introduction. Quint and Gulharov nodded. "Apparently you are right, Carl," Krakovitch continued. "He says that back there, up in the mountains, that's the place of the gypsies."

"Da, da!" Volkonsky growled and nodded his concurrence. He pointed westward. Quint got out of the car, Gulharov too. They looked where the ganger pointed. "Szgany!" Volkonsky insisted. "Szgany Ferengi!"

Beyond the foothills, rising out of the thin morning mist, the blue smoke of a wood fire climbed almost vertically into the still air. "Their camp," said Krakovitch.

"They . . . they still come." Quint shook his head in disbelief. "They *still* come!"

"Their homage," Krakovitch nodded.

"What now?" asked Quint, after a moment's silence.

"Now Mikhail Volkonsky will show us the place," said Krakovitch. "That blocked off road we passed back there goes to within half a mile of the castle's site. Volkonsky has actually seen the place."

All three searchers got back into the car, the huge foreman with them, and Gulharov began to drive back the way they'd come.

Quint asked, "But where does the road go?"

"Nowhere!" Krakovitch answered. "It was meant to cut through the mountains to the railhead at Khust. But a year ago the pass was declared unworkable because of shale, sliding scree and badly fractured rock. To force it through would constitute a major engineering feat, and there'd be little real benefit to show from it. As an alternative, and to save face, the road will be driven through to Ivano-Frankovsk instead; that is, the existing road will be widened and improved. All on this side of the mountains. There is already a railway route, however tortuous, from Ivano-Frankovsk through the mountains. As for the fifteen miles of new road already built''—he shrugged—''eventually there may be a town out there, industrial sites. It won't have been a total waste. Very little is wasted in the Soviet Union.''

Quint smiled, however warily.

Krakovitch saw it, said, ''Yes, I know—dogma. It's a disease we all seem to catch sooner or later. Now it appears I have it too. There *is* great waste, not least in the mass of words from which we build our excuses . . .''

Gulharov stopped the car at the new road's barrier; Volkonsky got out, swivelled the barrier to one side, waved them through. They picked him up again and headed up into the mountains.

No one noticed the battered old Fiat parked a half-mile down the road back towards Kolomyya, or the blue exhaust fumes and cloud of dust as it rumbled into life and followed in their tracks . . .

Guy Roberts had eaten two British Rail breakfasts, washed down with pints of coffee, and by the time his train pulled out of Grantham he was half-way through the day's first packet of Marlborough Kings. He was huge, red-eyed and whiskery, and no one bothered him much. He had his corner of the carriage all to himself. No one looking at him would ever have guessed he possessed the talent of some primal wizard, or that his mission was to slay a twentieth-century vampire. Indeed the thought might be amusing—if it wasn't so very desperate. There were too many desperate things, too much to do, and no time to do it all. It was so very tiring.

Thinking back on the events of last night, he lay back in his seat and closed his eyes. He and Layard had stayed with it right through the night, and it had been one strange, strange night for both of them. Kyle, for instance, at the Château Bronnitsy. As the sky had brightened into dawn, so Layard had found it increasingly difficult to locate Alec Kyle. In his own words it had been like "the difference between finding a live man and a dead one, with Kyle somewhere in between." That didn't bode at all well for INTESP's Number One.

Roberts, too, had been unable to penetrate the Château's mind blocks. He should have been able to "scry" Kyle, but all he'd got on those few occasions when he had actually penetrated the mental defences of Bronnitsy's espers had been . . . well, an *echo* of Kyle. A fast-fading image. Roberts didn't know for sure what E-Branch was doing to Kyle, and he didn't much care to guess.

Then there'd been Yulian Bodescu; or rather, there hadn't been him. For try as they might, Layard and Roberts hadn't been able to relocate the vampire. It was as if he'd simply vanished off the face of the map. There was no "mind-smog" in or around Birmingham, none anywhere in the whole country, so far as the British espers were able to discover. But after they'd thought about it for a little while, then the answer had seemed obvious. Bodescu knew they were tracking him, and he had talents, too. Somehow he was screening himself, making himself "disappear" out of mindscan.

But at 6:30 in the morning, Layard had picked him up again. Very briefly he'd made contact with a reeking, writhing mind-smog, an evil *something* that had sensed him at once, snarling its mental defiance before disappearing once more. And Layard had located it somewhere in the vicinity of York.

That had been enough for Roberts. It had seemed to him

that if there'd ever been any doubt as to where Bodescu was heading, his destination was now confirmed. Leaving INTESP HQ once more in the capable hands of John Grieve, the permanent Duty Officer, he'd prepared to head north.

It was only as he was actually making his exit from the HQ that word of Harvey Newton came in: how his car had been discovered in an overgrown ditch just off the motorway at Doncaster, and how his mutilated body had been found in the boot with a crossbow bolt transfixing the head. That had clinched it, not only for Roberts but for everyone else involved. They didn't even consider that there might be some other explanation apart from Bodescu. From now on it would be outright warfare—no quarter asked and none given—until the fiend was staked, decapitated, burned and definitely dead!

At this juncture of Roberts's reflections, someone "ahemmed" and stepped over his outstretched feet. He opened his eyes briefly, saw a slim man in a hat and overcoat claiming the seat beside him. The stranger took off his hat, shrugged out of his coat and sat down. He produced a paperback book and Roberts saw that it was *Dracula,* by Bram Stoker. He couldn't help but grimace.

The stranger saw his expression, shrugged almost apologetically. "A little fantasy doesn't hurt," he said, in a thin, reedy voice.

"No," Roberts growled his agreement before closing his eyes again. "Fantasy doesn't hurt anyone." And to himself: *But the real thing is something else entirely!*

It was 4:00 P.M., on the Russian side of the Carpathians, and Theo Dolgikh was weary as a man could be, but he drew strength from the sure knowledge that his job was almost done. After this he'd sleep for a week, then indulge himself in as many pleasurable diversions as he could manage before seeking a new assignment. Assuming, that was, that he hadn't already been assigned some new task.

But pleasure can take many forms, depending on the man, and Dolgikh's work had its moments. His missions were often very . . . satisfying? Certainly he was going to enjoy the end of this one.

He looked out and down from his vantage point in a clump of pines on the north face of the mountainside where it wound back into the gorge, and trained his binoculars on the four men who climbed carefully along the last hundred yards of boulder- and scree-littered ledge weathered into the sheer cliff which formed the south face. They were less than three hundred yards away, but Dolgikh used his binoculars anyway.

He enjoyed close-up the strain in their sweating faces, imagined he could feel their aching muscles, tried to picture their thoughts as they headed one last time for the old creeper-grown ruins up there where the ravine bottle-necked and the stream rushed and gurgled unseen in the depths of the gorge. They'd be congratulating themselves that their quest—their mission—was almost concluded; ah, but they could hardly imagine that they themselves were also at an end!

This was the part that Dolgikh was going to enjoy: bringing them to their conclusion, and letting them know that he was their executioner.

Most of the time the four moved in clear light, free of shadows; Krakovitch and his man, the British esper, and the big construction boss. But where the cliff overhung, there they merged with brown and green shade and black darkness. Dolgikh squinted into the sky. The sun was well past its zenith, sinking slowly beyond the looming mass of the Carpathians. In just two more hours it would be twilight, the Carpathians twilight, when the sun would abruptly slip down behind the peaks and ridges. And that was when the "accident" would happen.

He trained his binoculars on them again. The huge Russian foreman carried a haversack with its strap across one shoulder. A T-shaped metal handle protruded: the firing box for gelignite charges. Dolgikh nodded to himself. Earlier in the day he'd watched them lay charges in and around the old ruins; now they were going to blow the place and whatever it contained—a fabulous weapon according to that twisted dwarf Ivan Gerenko—to hell! So they thought, but that was what Dolgikh was here to prevent.

He put his binoculars away, waited impatiently until they were safely off the ledge and into the woods of the overgrown slope beyond, then quickly moved in pursuit— for the last time. The cat and mouse game was over and it was time for the kill. They were out of sight in the trees now, with perhaps a mile to go to the ruins, and so Dolgikh must make haste.

He checked his blunt, blued-steel, standard issue Tokarev automatic, shoved home the clip of snub-nosed rounds and reholstered the heavy weapon under his arm. Then he stepped out from cover. Directly opposite his position, across the narrow gorge, the new road came to an abrupt end. This was the point at which someone had decided it wouldn't be cost effective to proceed further. Rubble from the blasted cliff filled the depression, forming a dam for the mountain stream. A small lake lay smooth as a mirror behind it. Beneath the dam the water had forced a route, erupting in a torrent where the much reduced stream continued its course down towards the plain.

Dolgikh scrambled down to the jumbled debris which formed the bridge of the dam and nimbly made his way across and up on to the road. A minute more and he'd left the tarmac behind for the narrow, treacherous surface of the scree-littered ledge. And without further pause he followed in the tracks of his quarry. As he went, he thought back on the events of the day . . .

This morning he'd followed them when they first came up here. Finding their car parked on the road, he'd hidden his Fiat in a dense clump of bushes and tracked them on foot along this very ledge. Then, at the apex of the gorge

where the two sides almost came together, they'd entered
crumbling old ruins and searched through them. Dolgikh
had observed, keeping well back. For maybe two hours
they'd busied themselves digging in the ruins. By the time
they were ready to leave they all seemed much subdued.
Dolgikh didn't know what they'd found, or failed to find,
but in any case he'd been told that it was probably dangerous and warned to steer clear.

Seeing them about to leave, he'd quickly hurried back to
his car, waited for them to show up. And in passing, so as
to be on the safe side, he'd fitted their vehicle with a
magnetic bug. They'd driven back into Kolomyya then,
with Dolgikh close behind but keeping just out of sight.
He'd almost caught up with them where they stopped,
half-way back along the new road, to talk with a party of
gypsies in their encampment. But in a few minutes they'd
been on their way again, and still they hadn't seen him.

Kolomyya was a railhead and meeting point for four
tracks, from Khust, Ivano-Frankovsk, Chernovtsy and
Gorodenka; every other building seemed to be a warehouse
or storage depot. It wasn't hard to find one's way about;
the industrial and commercial sides of the town were
distinctly separate. The four men Dolgikh followed had
driven to the town's main telephone exchange, parked
outside and gone in.

Dolgikh parked his Fiat, stopped a passerby and asked
about public call boxes. "Three!" the man told him,
obviously disgusted. "Only three public telephones in a
town as big as this! And all of them constantly in use. So
if you're in a hurry you'd best make your call here, at the
exchange. They'll put you through quick as a flash."

In about ten minutes Krakovitch and his party had left
the exchange, got into their car and driven off. Their
tracker had been torn two ways: to follow them, or find
out who they'd contacted and why. Since their car was
bugged and he could always find them later, he'd decided
on the latter course. Inside the small but busy exchange

he'd wasted no time but asked for the manager. His KGB ID had guaranteed immediate co-operation. It turned out that Krakovitch had called Moscow—but not a number Dolgikh was familiar with. It seemed that the head of E-Branch had required higher authorization for something or other; there had been some talk of blasting, and the big man in overalls had been very much involved. Krakovitch had allowed him also to use the phone. That was as much as anyone at the exchange knew of the matter. Dolgikh had then asked to be put through to Gerenko at the Château Bronnitsy, to whom he'd passed on all that he had learned.

At first Gerenko had seemed confused, but then: "They're working directly through Brezhnev's contact!" he'd snapped. "Not through me. Which can only mean that they suspect! Theo, make sure you get them all. Yes, including that construction foreman. And when it's done let me know at once."

Tracking the bug he'd planted, Dolgikh had arrived at the depot of a local civil engineering firm in the town just in time to see Gulharov and Volkonsky loading a box of explosives into the boot of their car while Krakovitch and Quint looked on. Obviously the big Russian foreman was now a member of their team. Equally obvious, their contact in Moscow had cleared the use of materials for blasting. While Dolgikh still did not know *what* they intended to destroy, he did have an idea *where* it was. And what was more, that was as good a place as any for them to die . . .

While Theo Dolgikh was thinking back on the day's events, Carl Quint's mind was similarly engaged; and now that the broken fangs of Faethor Ferenczy's castle once more appeared through the dark, motionless pines, so his memory instinctively homed in on what he and Felix Krakovitch had found there during their first visit this morning. All four of them had been present, but only he and Krakovitch had known where to look.

The place had been almost magnetic in their psychically

enhanced minds; the *exact spot* had drawn them like iron filings to a magnet. Except they were not filings, and it was not their intention to get stuck here. Quint remembered now how it had been . . .

"Faethor's castle," he'd breathed, as they came to a halt at the very rim of the ruins. "The mountain fastness of a vampire!" And in the eye of his mind he'd seen it again as it must have been a thousand years ago.

Volkonsky would have gone clambering into and amongst the crumbling stone blocks, but Krakovitch had stopped him. The ganger knew nothing at all of what was buried here, and Krakovitch didn't intend to tell him. Volkonsky was down to earth as any man could be. At the moment he was committed to assist them, but that might change if they tried to tell him what they were doing here. And so Krakovitch had simply warned, "Be careful! Try not to disturb anything . . ." And the big Russian had shrugged and climbed down again from the tumbled mass of the decaying old pile.

Then Quint and Krakovitch together had simply stared at the place and touched its stones, and let the aura of its antiquity and its immemorial evil wash over them. They'd breathed its essence, tasted of its mystery and let their talents lead them to its innermost secret. As they had picked their way carefully, almost timidly through the fallen rubble of ancient masonry, suddenly Quint had come to an abrupt halt and said huskily, "Oh, yes, it was here all right. It still *is* here! This is the place!"

And Krakovitch had agreed: "Yes, I sense it too. But I *only* sense it—I don't fear it. There's no warning to bar me from this place. I'm sure that there was a great evil here, but it's gone now, extinct, utterly lifeless."

Quint had nodded, sighed his relief. "That's my feeling, too; still here, but no longer active. It's been too long. There was nothing to sustain it."

Then they had stared at each other, both of them thinking the identical thought. Finally Krakovitch had given it voice. "Dare we try to find it, perhaps disturb it?"

For a moment Quint had known fear, but then he'd answered, "If I don't at least discover what it was like—at the end, I mean—then I'll wonder about it for the rest of my life. And since we're both agreed that it's harmless now . . . ?"

And so they had called up Gulharov and Volkonsky to the place where they stood, and all four of them had set to work. At first the going was easy and they used makeshift implements and their bare hands to clear away masses of loose dirt and rubble. Soon they'd revealed the inner core of an ancient stone staircase, with the steps winding on the outside. The stone had been scorched black with fire and was scarred by jagged cracks as from great heat. Apparently Thibor's plan had worked: the spiral stairwell leading downstairs had been blocked by blazing debris, burying the vampire women and the unfortunate Ehrig alive. Yes, and the burrowing proto-thing too. All of them, buried alive—or undead. But a thousand years is a long time, in which even the undead might truly die.

Then Volkonsky had got his massive arms around a great block of fractured rock and eased it upwards from the rubble which seemed to completely choke the stairwell. Suddenly it had come loose, at which Gulharov had added his own not inconsiderable muscle to the task. Together they'd heaved the block up and over the rim of the excavation—at which the debris at their feet had sighed and settled down a little, and a blast of foul air had rushed up into their faces!

They'd jumped back, startled, but still there had been no threat in it, no sense of impending danger. After a moment, taking Gulharov's arm to steady himself, the big Russian foreman had stepped down from the already uncovered stone steps onto the now dubious surface of the material blocking the descent. Still clinging to Gulharov he'd stamped first one foot, then the other—and at once gone down with a cry of alarm up to his waist in the stuff as it suddenly shifted and gave way under him!

Then the earth had seemed to rumble and shudder a little; Volkonsky had clung to Gulharov for dear life; Quint and Krakovitch had thrown themselves flat and reached down from above to grab hold of the ganger under his armpits. But he'd been quite safe, for already his feet had found purchase on unseen steps below.

And as they'd all four watched in astonishment, so the choking debris around Volkonsky's thighs had settled down, collapsing in upon itself, sinking like quicksand into the hollow depths of the stairwell. Hollow, yes! The stairs had not been completely choked but merely plugged, and now the plug had been removed.

"Now it's our turn," Quint had said when the dust had settled and they could breathe freely. "You and me, Felix. We can't let Mikhail go down there ahead of us, for he has no idea what he's up against. If there is still an element of danger attached to it, we should be the first ones down there."

They'd climbed down beside Volkonsky, paused and looked at each other. "We're unarmed," Krakovitch had pointed out.

Up above, Sergei Gulharov had produced an automatic pistol, passed it down to them. Volkonsky saw it, laughed. He spoke to Krakovitch who smiled.

Quint asked, "What did he say?"

"He said, why do we need a gun if we're seeking treasure?" Krakovitch answered.

"Tell him we're scared of spiders!" said Quint; and taking the gun, he had started down the littered steps. What good bullets would be if the vampires were still extant he couldn't have said, but at least the feel of the weapon in his hand was a comfort.

Blackened chunks of rock, large and small, cluttered the stairs so badly that Quint was often obliged to climb over them; but after turning through another full spiral, at last the steps were clear of all but small pieces of rubble, pebbles and sand sifted down from above. And at last he had been at the bottom, with Krakovitch and the others close on his heels. Light filtered down from above, but not much.

"It's no good," Quint had complained, shaking his head. "We can't go in there, not without proper light." His voice had echoed as in a tomb, which was what the place was. The place he spoke of was a room, a dungeon— *the* dungeon, for it could be no other place than Thibor's prison—beyond a low, arched stone doorway. Maybe Quint's reluctance had been his final attempt to back away from this thing, maybe not; whichever, the resourceful Gulharov had the answer. He'd produced a small, flat pocket torch, passed it to Quint who shone its beam ahead of him. There under the arch of the doorway, fossilized timber—ages-blackened fragments of oak—lying in a pile, with red splashes of rust marking the passing of defunct nails and bands of iron: all that remained of a once stout door. And beyond that, only darkness.

Then, stooping a little to avoid a keystone which had settled somewhat through the centuries, Quint had stepped warily under the archway, pausing just inside the dungeon. And there he'd aimed his torch in a slow circle to illumine each wall and corner of the place. The cell was quite large, larger than he'd expected; it had corners, niches, ledges and recesses where the beam of light couldn't follow, and it seemed cut from living rock.

Quint aimed the beam at the floor. Dust, the filtered dust of ages, lay uniformly thick everywhere. No footprint disturbed it. In roughly the centre of the floor, a humped formation of stone, possibly bedrock, strained grotesquely upwards. It seemed there was nothing here, and yet Quint's psychic intuition told him otherwise. His, and Krakovitch's too.

"We were right," Krakovitch's voice had echoed dolefully. He'd moved to come up alongside Quint. "They are finished. They were here and we sense them even now, but time has put paid to them.'' He'd moved forward, leaned his weight on the anomalous hump of rock—*which at once crumbled under his hand!*

In the next moment he'd jumped back with a cry of sheer horror, colliding with Quint, grabbing him and hugging him close. ''Oh God! Carl—*Carl!* It's not . . . not stone!''

Gulharov and Volkonsky, both of them suddenly electrified, had steadied Krakovitch while Quint shone his torch directly at the humped mass. Then, mouth gaping and heart fluttering, the Englishman had breathed, ''Did you sense . . . anything?''

The other shook his head, took a deep breath. ''No, no. My reaction, that was simply shock—not a warning. Thank God for that at least! My talent is working—*believe* me it is working—but it reveals nothing. I was shocked, just shocked . . .''

''But just *look* at this . . . this thing!'' Quint had been awed. He'd moved forward, carefully blow dust from the surface of the mass and used a handkerchief to dust it down. Parts of it, anyway. For even a perfunctory dusting had revealed—total horror!

The thing was slumped where in uncounted years past it had groped one last time upwards from the packed earth of the floor. It was one mass now—the mummified remains of one creature—but clearly it was *composed* of more than one person. Hunger and possibly madness had forced the issue: the hunger of the proto-flesh in the earth, the madness of Ehrig and the women. There had been no way out and, weak with hunger, the vampires had been unable to resist the advances of the mindless, subterranean ''creeper.'' It had probably taken them one by one, adding them to its bulk. And now that bulk lay here, fallen where it had finally, mercifully ''died.'' In the end, governed only by weak impulse and indeterminate instinct, perhaps it had attempted to reconstitute the others. Certainly there was evidence to that effect.

It had the breasts of women, and a half-formed male head, and many pseudohands. Eyes, bulging behind their closed lids, were everywhere. And mouths, some human and others inhuman. Yes, and there were other features much worse than these . . .

Emboldened, Gulharov and Volkonsky had come forward; the latter, before he could be cautioned, had reached out a hand and laid it upon a cold, shrivelled breast where it protruded alongside a flabby-lipped mouth. All was the colour of leather and looked solid enough, but no sooner had the big ganger touched the teat than it crumbled into dust. Volkonsky snatched back his hand with an oath, stepped back a pace. But Sergei Gulharov was much less timid. He knew something of these horrors, and the very thought of them infuriated him.

Cursing, he lashed out with his foot at the base of the thing where it sprouted from the floor, lashed out again and again. The others had made no attempt to stop him; it was his way of working it out of his system. He waded into the crumbling monstrosity, fists and feet pounding at it. And in a very little while nothing remained but billowing dust and a few fretted bones.

"Out!" Krakovitch had choked. "Let's get out of here before we suffocate. Carl." He'd clutched the other's arm. "Thank *God* it was dead!" And with their hands to their mouths, finally they'd climbed back up the stairwell into clean, healthy daylight.

"That . . . whatever it was, should be buried," Volkonsky had growled to Gulharov as they moved away from the ruins.

"Exactly!" Krakovitch had taken the opportunity to agree with him. "So as to be absolutely certain, it *has* to be buried. And that's where you come in . . ."

* * *

The four had been back to the ruins a second time since then, when Volkonsky had drilled holes, laid charges, unrolled a hundred yards of detonating cable and made electrical connections. And now they'd returned for the third and last time. And as before, Theo Dolgikh had followed them, which was why this would *be* the last time.

Now, from the cover of bushes back along the overgrown track near the cliff and its precarious ledge, the KGB man watched Volkonsky put down his firing box at the end of the prepared cable, watched as the party moved on towards the ruins, presumably for one last look.

This was Dolgikh's best chance, the moment the Russian agent had been waiting for. He checked his gun again, took off the safety and reholstered it, then quickly scrambled up the scree slope on his left and into a straggling stand of pines where the trees marched at the foot of the gaunt cliffs. If he used his cover to its best advantage, he could stay out of sight until the last minute. And so, moving with some agility beneath the trees, he quickly closed the distance between him and his intended victims as they approached the gutted ruins.

In order to maintain his cover in this way, Dolgikh occasionally had to lose sight of his quarry, but finally he reached the furthest extent of the cliff-hugging trees and was forced back down into the lesser undergrowth of the old track. From here the group of men at the ancient castle's walls were plainly visible, and if they should happen to look in Dolgikh's direction, they might also see him. But no, they stood silent one hundred yards away, lost in their own thoughts as they gazed upon that which they intended to destroy. All three of them were deep in thought.

Three? Dolgikh squinted, frowned, glanced quickly all about. He saw nothing out of the ordinary. Presumably the fourth man—that young fool, that traitor Gulharov—had entered through the broken exterior wall of the ruins and so passed out of sight. Whichever, Dolgikh knew that he now had all four men trapped. There was no way out at their end of the defile, and in any case they had to come back here to detonate the charges. Dolgikh's leering expression changed, turned into a grim smile. An especially sadistic thought had just occurred to him.

His original plan had been simple: surprise them, tell them he was investigating them for the KGB, have them tie each other up—finally hurl them one at a time from the castle's broken rim. It was a hell of a long way down. He'd make sure that part of the rotten wall went with them, to make it more convincing. Then, at a safe place, he'd climb down, make his way back to them and carefully remove their bindings. An "accident," as simple as that. There'd be no escape for them: the nylon cord in Dolgikh's pocket had a 200 lb. breaking strain! They probably wouldn't even be found for weeks, months, maybe never.

But Dolgikh was something of a vampire in his own right, except he fed on fear. Yes, and now he saw the opportunity to give his plan an elaborate twist. A little extra something for his own amusement.

He quickly kneeled, used his strong square teeth to strip the cable down to its copper cores, and connected up the firing box. Then, still on one knee, he called out loudly up the trail: "Gentlemen!"

The three turned, saw him. Quint and Krakovitch recognized him at once, looked stunned.

"Now what are we having here?" he laughed, holding up the box for them to see. "See? Someone is forgetting to make the connections—but I have done it for him!" He put down the box and drew up the plunger.

"For God's sake, be *careful* with that!" Carl Quint threw up his arms in warning, stumbled out of the ruins.

"Stay right where you are, Mr. Quint," Dolgikh shouted. And in Russian: "Krakovitch, you and that stupid ox of a foreman come to me. And no tricks, or I blow your English friend and Gulharov to bits!" He gave the T-shaped handle two savage right-hand twists. The box was now armed; only depress the plunger, and—

"Dolgikh, are you mad?" Krakovitch called back. "I'm here on official business. The Party Leader himself—"

"—Is a mumbling old fool!" Dolgikh finished for him. "As are you. And you'll be a dead fool if you don't do exactly as I say. Do it now, and bring that lumbering engineer with you. Quint, Mr. English mind-spy, you stay right there." He stood up, took out his gun and the nylon cord. Krakovitch and Volkonsky had put up their hands in the air, were slowly leaving the area of the ruins.

In the next split second Dolgikh sensed that something was wrong. He felt the tug of hot metal at his sleeve before he heard the *crack* of Sergei Gulharov's automatic. For when the others had gone forward to the ruins, Gulharov had stepped into a clump of bushes to answer a call of nature. He had seen and heard everything.

"Put up your gun!" he now yelled, coming at Dolgikh at a run. "The next shot goes in your belly!"

Gulharov had been trained, but not nearly as thoroughly as Theo Dolgikh, and he lacked the agent's killer instinct. Dolgikh fell to his knees again, straightened his gun arm toward Gulharov, aimed and squeezed the trigger of his weapon. Gulharov was nearly on him. He, too, had fired again. His shot went inches wide, but Dolgikh's was right on target. His snub-nosed bullet blew away half of Gulharov's head. Gulharov, dead on the instant, jerked to a halt, then took another stumbling step forward and crashed over like a felled tree—directly on to the firing box and its extended plunger!

Dolgikh hurled himself flat, felt a hot wind blow on him as hell opened up just one hundred yards away. Deafening sound blasted his ears, left them ringing with wild peals. He didn't see the actual explosion, or simultaneous series of explosions, but as the spray of soil and pebbles subsided and the earth stopped shaking he looked up—and then he did see the result. On the far side of the gorge the ruins of

Faethor's castle stood much as before, but on this side they had been reduced to so much rubble.

Craters smoked where the castle's roots were bedded in the mountain. A landslide of shale and fractured rock was still tumbling from the cliff onto the wide, pitted ledge, burying deep the last traces of whatever secrets had been there. And of Krakovitch. Quint and Volkonsky—

Nothing whatsoever. Flesh isn't nearly as strong as rock . . .

Dolgikh stood up, brushed himself down, heaved Gulharov's corpse off the detonating box. he grabbed Gulharov's legs and dragged his body to the smouldering ruins, then toppled him from the cliff. An "accident," a genuine accident.

On his way back down the track, the KGB man rolled up what was left of the cable; he also collected Gulharov's gun and the box. Half-way down the ledge where it hugged the cliff he threw all of these things into the dark gurgling ravine. It was finished now, all of it. Before he got back to Moscow he would have thought up an excuse, a reason why Gerenko's supposed "weapon," whatever it had been, no longer existed. That was a pity.

But on the other hand—Dolgikh congratulated himself that at least half of his mission had been accomplished successfully. And very satisfactorily . . .

8:00 P.M., at the Château Bronnitsy.

Ivan Gerenko lay in a shallow sleep on a cot in his inner office. Down below, in the sterility of the brain-washing laboratory, Alec Kyle also lay asleep. His body, anyway. But since there was no longer a mind in there, it was hardly Kyle any longer. Mentally, he had been drained to less than a husk. The information this had released to Zek Föener had been staggering. This Harry Keogh, if he had still lived, would have been an awesome enemy. But trapped in the brain of his own child, he was no longer a problem. Later, maybe, when (and if) the child had grown into a man . . .

As for INTESP: Föener was now privy to that entire organization's machinery. Nothing remained secret. Kyle had been the controller, and what he had known Zek Föener was heir to. Which was why, as the technicians dismantled their instruments and left Kyle's body naked and drained even of instinct, she hurried to report something of her findings—and one thing in particular—to Ivan Gerenko.

Zekintha Föener's father was East German. Her mother had been Greek, from Zakinthos in the Ionian Sea. When her mother died, Zek had gone to her father in Posen, to the university where he worked in parapsychology. Her psychic ability, which he had always suspected in her when she was a child, had become immediately apparent to him. He had reported the fact of her telepathic talent to the College of Parapsychological Studies on Brasov Prospekt in Moscow, and had been summoned to attend with Zek so that she could be tested. That was how she had come to E-Branch, where she had rapidly made herself invaluable.

Föener was five-nine, slim, blonde and blue-eyed. Her hair shone and bounced on her shoulders when she walked. Her Château uniform fitted her like a glove, accentuating the delicate curves of her figure. She climbed the stone stairs to Krakovitch's (no, she corrected herself, to Gerenko's) office, entered the anteroom and knocked firmly on the closed inner door.

Gerenko heard her knock, forced himself awake and struggled to sit up. In his shrivelled frame he tired easily, slept often but poorly. Sleep was one way of prolonging a life which doctors had told him would be short. It was the ultimate irony: men could not kill him, but his own frailty surely would. At only thirty-seven he already looked sixty, a shrunken monkey of a man. But still a man.

"Come in," he wheezed, as he sucked air into his fragile lungs.

Outside the door, while Gerenko had come more surely awake, Zek Föener had broken a trust. It was an unwritten rule at the Château that telepaths would not deliberately spy on the minds of their colleagues. That was all very well and only decent in normal conditions, normal circumstances. But on this occasion there were gross abnormalities, things which Föener must track down to her satisfaction.

For one, the way Gerenko had literally *taken over* Krakovitch's job. It wasn't as if he stood in for him at all, but had in fact replaced him—permanently! Föener had liked Krakovitch; from Kyle she had learned about Theo Dolgikh's surveillance activities in Genoa; Kyle and Krakovitch had been working together on—

"Come in!" Gerenko repeated, breaking her chain of thought, but not before everything had fallen together. Gerenko's ambition burned bright in her mind, bright and ugly. And his *intention,* to use those . . . those Things which Krakovitch was quite rightly bent on destroying . . .

She drew air deeply and entered the office, staring at Gerenko where he lay in the dark on his cot, propped up on one elbow.

He put on a bedside lamp and blinked as his weak eyes accustomed themselves. "Yes? What is it, Zek?"

"Where's Theo Dolgikh?" She waded straight in. No preliminaries, no formalities.

"What?" He blinked at her. "Is something wrong, Zek?"

"Many things, perhaps. I said—"

"I heard what you said," he snapped. "And what has it to do with you where Dolgikh is?"

"I saw him for the first time, with you, on the morning that Felix Krakovitch left for Italy—*after* he left," she answered. "Following which he was absent until he brought Alec Kyle back here. But Kyle wasn't working against us. He was working with Krakovitch. For the good of the world."

Gerenko swung his brittle legs carefully off the cot onto

the floor. "He should only have been working for the good of the USSR," he said.

"Like you?" she came back at once, her voice sharp as broken glass. "I know now what they were doing, Comrade. Something that had to be done, for safety and sanity. Not for themselves, but for mankind."

Gerenko eased himself to his feet. He wore child's pyjamas, looked frail as a twig as he made for his great desk. "Are you accusing me, Zek?"

"Yes!" She was relentless, furious. "Kyle was our opponent, but he personally had not declared war on us. We aren't *at* war, Comrade. And we've murdered him. No, *you* have murdered him—to foster your own ambitions!"

Gerenko climbed into his chair, put on a desk lamp and aimed its light at her. He steepled his hands in front of him, shook his head almost sadly. "You accuse me? And yet you were party to it. You drained his mind."

"I did not!" She came forward. Her face was working, full of anger. 'I merely read his thoughts as they flooded out of him. Your technicians drained him."

Unbelievably, Gerenko chuckled. "Mechanical necromancy, yes."

She slammed her hand flat down on the desk top. "But he wasn't dead!"

Gerenko's shrivelled lips curled into a sneer. "He is now, or as good as . . ."

"Krakovitch is loyal, and he's Russian." She wouldn't be stopped. "And yet you'll murder him too. And that really would be murder! You must be mad!" And in that she had hit upon the truth. For Gerenko's warps weren't only in his body.

"That—is—*enough!*" he snarled. "Now you listen to me, Comrade. You speak of my ambition. But if I grow strong, Russia herself grows that much stronger. Yes, for we are one and the same. You? You've not been Russian long enough to know that. This country's strength lies in its people! Krakovitch was weak, and— "

"Was?" Her arms trembled where she leaned forward, knuckles white on the edge of his desk.

He suddenly felt that she had grown very dangerous. He would make one last effort. "Listen, Zek. The Party Leader is a weak old man. He can't go on much longer. The *next* leader, however—"

"Andropov?" Her eyes went wide. "I can read it in your mind, Comrade. Is that how it will be? That KGB thug? *The man you already call your master!*"

Gerenko's faded eyes suddenly narrowed, their slits blazing with his own anger. "When Brezhnev is gone—"

"But he isn't, not yet!" She was shouting now. "And when he learns of this . . ."

That was an error, a bad one. Even Brezhnev couldn't harm Gerenko, not personally, not physically. But he could have it done for him—at a distance. He could have Gerenko's state flat in Moscow booby-trapped. Once a booby-trap is set, no man's hand is involved. From then on the thing is entirely automatic. Or Gerenko could wake up one morning and find himself behind bars— and then they could forget to feed him! His talent did have certain limitations.

He stood up In his child's hand was an automatic, taken from a drawer in the desk. His voice was a whisper. "Now you will listen to me," he said, "and I will tell you exactly how it is going to be. First, you won't speak of this matter or even mention it again, not to anyone. You've been sworn to secrecy here at the Château. Break your trust and I'll break you! Second: you say we are not at war. But you have a short memory. The British espers declared war against E-Branch nine months ago. And they came close to destroying the organization utterly! You were new here then; you were away somewhere, holidaying with your father. You saw nothing of it. But let me tell you that if this Harry Keogh of theirs were still alive . . ."

He paused for breath, and Föener bit her tongue to keep

from telling him the truth: that indeed Harry Keogh *was* still alive, however helpless.

"Third," he finally continued, "I could kill you now—on the spot, shoot you dead—and no one would even question me about it. If they did, I would say that I had had my suspicions about you for a long time. I would tell them that your work had driven you mad, and that you threatened me, threatened E-Branch. You are quite correct, Zek, the Party Leader puts a deal of faith in the branch. He is fond of it. Under old Gregor Borowitz it served him well. What, a woman, mad, running around loose here, threatening irreparable damage? Of course I should shoot her! And I will—if you don't mark each word I say most carefully. Do you think anyone would believe your accusation? Where's the proof? In your head? In your *addled* head! Oh, they just might believe, I'll grant you that—but what if they didn't? And would I sit still and simply let you have it all your own way? Would Theo Dolgikh sit still for that? You have an easy time here, Zek. Ah, but there are other jobs in other places for a strong young woman in the USSR. After your—rehabilitation?—doubtless they'd find you one . . ." Again he paused, put away the gun. He saw that he had made his point.

"Now get out of here, but don't leave the Château. I want a report on everything you learned from Kyle. Everything. The initial report may be brief, an outline. I'll have that by midday tomorrow. The final report will be detailed down to the last minutia. Do you understand?"

She stood looking at him, bit her lip.

"Well?"

Finally, she nodded blinked away tears of frustration, turned on her heel. On her way out, he softly said, "Zek," and she paused. But she didn't face him. "Zek, you have a great future. Remember that. And really, that's the only choice you have. A great future—or none at all."

Then she left and closed the door behind her.

She went to her own small suite of rooms, the austere

quarters she used when she was not on duty, and threw herself down on her bed. To hell with his report. She'd do it in her own time, if she did it at all. For what use would she be to Gerenko once he knew what she knew?

After a little while she managed to compose herself and tried to sleep. But though she was weary to death, she tried in vain . . .

Chapter Sixteen

WEDNESDAY, 11:45 P.M.—FIFTEEN MINUTES TO MIDNIGHT IN Hartlepool on England's north-east coast—and a thin drizzling rain turning the empty streets shiny black. The last bus for the colliery villages along the coast had left the town half an hour ago; the pubs and cinemas had all turned out; grey cats slinked in the alleys and a last handful of people headed for their homes on a night when it simply wasn't worth being out.

But in a certain house on the Blackhall Road there was a muted measure of activity. In the garret flat, Brenda Keogh had fed her baby son and put him down for the night and was now preparing herself for bed. In the hitherto empty first floor flat, Darcy Clarke and Guy Roberts sat in near-darkness, Roberts nodding off to sleep and Clarke listening with an anxious awareness to the timbers of the old house creaking as they settled for the night. Downstairs in the ground floor flat, its permanent "residents," two Special Branch men, were playing cards while a uniformed policeman made coffee and looked on. In the entrance hall a second uniformed officer kept his vigil just inside the door, smoking a slightly damp and ill-made cigarette while he sat in an uncomfortable wooden chair and wondered for the tenth time just what he was doing here.

To the Special Branch men it was old hat: they were here for the protection of the girl in the garret flat. She didn't know it, but they weren't just good neighbours, they were her minders. Hers and little Harry's. They'd looked after her for the better part of a year, and in all of that time no one had so much as blinked at her; theirs must be the cushiest, best paid number in the entire length and breadth of the security business! As for the two uniformed men: they were on overtime, kept over from the middle shift to do "special" duties. They should have gone off home at 10:00 P.M., but it appeared there was this bloody maniac on the loose, and the girl upstairs was thought to be one of his targets. That was all they'd been told. All very mysterious.

On the other hand, in the flat above, Clarke and Roberts knew exactly why they were here—and also what they were up against. Roberts uttered a quiet snort and his head lolled where he sat close to the curtained window in the living-room. He gave a grunt and straightened himself up a little, and in the next moment began to nod again. Clarke scowled at him without malice, turned up his collar and rubbed his hands for warmth. The room felt damp and cold.

Clarke would have liked to put on a light but didn't dare; this flat was supposed to be empty and that was the way it must appear. No fires, no lights, as little movement as possible. All they'd allowed themselves by way of comfort was an electric kettle and a jar of instant coffee. Well, a little more than that. Comforting too was the fact that earlier in the day a flame thrower had been delivered to Roberts, and both men had crossbows.

Clarke picked up his crossbow now and looked at it. It was loaded, with the safety on. How dearly he would love to sight it on Yulian Bodescu's black heart. He scowled again and put the weapon down, lit up and drew deeply on one of his rare cigarettes. He was feeling tired and miserable, and not a little nervous. That was probably to be expected, but he put it down to the fact that he'd been taking his coffee blacker and blacker, until he felt sure his blood must now be at least seventy-five per cent pure caffeine! He's been here since the early hours of the morning, and so far—nothing. At least he had that much to be thankful for . . .

Down in the entrance hall, Constable Dave Collins quietly opened the door of the flat, looked into the living-room. "Stand in for me, Joe," he said to his colleague. "Five minutes for a breath of fresh air. I'm going to stretch my legs down the road a bit."

The other glanced once more at the Special Branch men at their game, stood up and began buttoning his jacket. He picked up his helmet and followed his friend out into the hall, then unlocked the door and let him out into the street. "Fresh air?" he called after him. "You're joking. Looks like there's a fog coming up to me!"

Joe Baker watched his colleague stride off down the road, went back inside and closed the door. He should by rights lock it but was satisfied to throw home the single, small stainless steel bolt. He took his seat beside an occasional table bearing a heap of junk mail and some old newspapers—*and* a tin of cigarette tobacco and papers! Joe grinned, rolled himself a "free" one. He'd just smoked the cigarette down when he heard footsteps at the door and a single, quiet knock.

He got up, unbolted the door, opened it and looked out. His colleague stood with his back to the door, rubbing his hands and glancing up and down the road. A fine film of moisture gleamed black on his raincoat and helmet. Joe flipped the stub of his cigarette out into the night and said, "That was a long five—"

But that was *all* he said. For in the next moment the

figure on the threshold had turned and grabbed him in
hands huge and powerful as iron bands—and he'd taken
one look at the face under the helmet and knew that it
wasn't Dave Collins! It wasn't anybody human at all!

These were his last thoughts as Yulian Bodescu effortlessly bent Joe's head back and sank his incredible teeth
into his throat. They closed like a mantrap on his pounding
jugular and severed it. He was dead in a moment, throat
torn out and neck broken.

Yulian lowered him to the floor, turned and closed the
door to the street. He pushed home the light bolt; that
would suffice. It had been the work of mere seconds, a
most efficient murder. Blood stained Bodescu's mouth as
he snarled silently at the door of the ground floor flat. He
reached out his vampire senses and sent them beyond the
closed door. Two men in there, close together, busy with
whatever they were doing and totally unaware of their
danger. But not for long.

Yulian opened the door and without pause strode into
the room. He saw the Special Branch officers seated at
their card table. They looked up smiling, saw him, his
helmet and raincoat, and casually returned to their game—
then looked again! But too late. Yulian was in the room,
pacing forward, reaching a taloned hand to pick up a
service automatic with its silencer already screwed in position. He would have preferred to kill in his own way, but
he supposed that this was as good as any. The officers had
barely drawn breath, were scarcely risen to their feet, before
he'd fired at them point-blank, half-emptying the weapon's
magazine into their cringing, shuddering bodies . . .

Darcy Clarke had been on the point of falling asleep;
perhaps for a little while he had been asleep, but then
something had woken him up. He lifted his head, all of his
senses at once alert. Something downstairs in the hall? A
door closing? Furtive footsteps on the stairs? It could have

been any of these things. But how long ago—seconds or minutes?

The telephone rang and shocked him upright, rigid as a pillar in his chair. Heart pounding, he reached for the phone, but Guy Roberts's hand closed on it first. "I woke up a minute before you." Roberts whispered, his voice hoarse in the darkness. "Darcy, I think something's up!"

He put the handset to his ear, said: "Roberts?"

Clarke heard a tinny voice from the telephone, but couldn't make out what it said. But he saw Roberts give a massive start and heard his whooshing intake of breath.

"Jesus!" Roberts exploded into life. He slammed the phone down, came rearing unsteadily to his feet. "That was Layard," he panted. "He's found the bastard again—*and guess where he is!*"

Clarke didn't have to guess, for his talent had taken over. It was telling him to get the hell out of this house; it was even *propelling* him towards the door. But only for a moment, for his talent "knew" that there was danger out there on the landing, and now it was heading Darcy towards the window!

Clarke knew what was happening. He fought it, grabbed up his crossbow, forced himself to follow Robert's bulk to the door of the flat.

Out on the first floor landing, Yulian had already sensed the hated espers in the room. He knew who they were, and how dangerous they were. An old upright piano stood on broken castors with its back to the handrail at the top of the stairs. It must weigh almost a fifth of a ton, but that was hardly an obstacle to the vampire. He grasped it, gave a grunt, and dragged it bodily into place in front of the door. Its castors snapped off and went skittering, their broken housings ripping up the carpet as Yulian finally got the piano positioned to his satisfaction.

No sooner was he finished than Roberts was on the other side of the door, trying to push it open. "Shit!" Roberts snarled. "It can only be him, and he's trapped us in here! Darcy, the door opens outwards—give me a hand . . ."

They thrust their shoulders at the door together, and at last heard the piano's broken claws squealing on the scored floorboards. A gap appeared, and Roberts thrust out an arm into darkness, got a grip on the top of the piano and started to haul himself up and over it. He dragged his crossbow after him, with Clarke pushing from behind.

"Where the hell are those idiots from downstairs?" Roberts panted.

"Hurry, for Christ's sake!" Clarke urged him on. "He'll be up the stairs by now . . ." But he wasn't. The landing light came on.

Sprawled on top of the piano, Roberts's eyes stood out like shiny pebbles in his face as he gazed directly into the awful visage of Yulian Bodescu. The vampire wrenched Roberts's crossbow from fingers made immobile through shock. He turned the weapon and fired its bolt directly into the gap of the door behind the piano. Then he gurgled something from a throat clotted with blood, and began to methodically batter at Roberts's head. The wire string of the crossbow hummed with the speed and force of his blows.

Roberts had screamed once—one high, shrill scream—before he felt silent under Yulian's onslaught. Blow after blow the vampire rained on him, until his head was a raw red pulp that dripped brains onto the piano's keyboard. And only then did he stop.

Inside the room, Clarke had heard the *thrumm* of the bolt where it missed him by a hairsbreadth. And looking out through the gap in the door, half-blinded by the light, he had seen what this nightmare Thing had done to Roberts. Numb with horror, nevertheless he tried to line up his own weapon for a shot, but in the next moment Yulian had thrust Roberts's corpse back inside the room on top of Clarke, and rammed the piano back up against the door. And that was when Clarke broke: he couldn't fight that

Thing out there *and* his talent! The latter wouldn't let him. Instead he dropped the crossbow, stumbled back inside the flat and sought a window looking down on the street outside.

There was no longer any coherency left in him; all he wanted to do was get away. As far and as swiftly as possible . . .

In the garret flatlet, Brenda Keogh had been asleep for only twenty minutes. A scream—like the welling cry of a tortured animal—had snatched her awake, brought her tumbling out of bed. At first she thought it was Harry, but then she heard scuffling sounds from downstairs and a noise like the slamming of a door. What on earth was going on down there?

She went a little unsteadily to her door, opened it and leaned out to listen for any recurrence of the sounds. But all was silent now, and the tiny landing stood in darkness—a darkness which suddenly flowed forward to send her crashing back into the room! And now Yulian was within an ace of his revenge, and his coughing growl was full of triumph as he gazed with a wolf's eyes on the girl sprawled upon the floor.

Brenda saw him and knew she must be nightmaring. She *must* be, for nothing like this should live and breathe and move in any sane waking world!

The creature was or had been a man; certainly he stood upright, however forward-sloping. His arms were . . . long! And the hands at the ends of those arms were huge and clawlike, with projecting nails. The face was something unbelievable. It might have been the face of a wolf, but it was hairless and there were other anomalies which also suggested a bat. His ears grew flat to the sides of his head; they were long and projected higher than the rearward sloping, elongated skull. His nose—no, his *snout*—was wrinkled, convoluted, with black, gaping nostrils. The skin of the whole was scaly and his yellow eyes, scarletpupilled, were deep sunken in black sockets. And his *jaws!* . . . his *teeth!*

Yulian Bodescu *was* Wamphyri, and he made no effort to hide it. That essence of vampire in him had found the perfect receptacle, had worked on him like yeast in a potent brew. He was at the peak of his strength, his power, and he knew it. In everything he had done, no trace had been left which might definitely identify him as the author of the crime. INTESP would know it, of course, but no court could ever be convinced. And INTESP, as Yulian had discovered, was far from omnipotent. Indeed, it was impotent. Its members were merely human, and fearful; he would hunt them down one by one until he'd destroyed the entire organization. He would even set himself a target: say, one month, to be rid of all of them for good.

But first there was the child of this woman, that scrap of life which contained his one and only peer in powers—his helpless peer . . .

Yulian swept upon the girl where she cringed, locked his beast's fist in her hair and half dragged her to her feet. "Where?" his gurgling voice questioned. "The child—where?"

Brenda's mouth fell open. Harry? This monster wanted Harry? Her eyes widened, flashed involuntarily towards the baby's tiny room—and the vampire's eyes lit with knowledge as he followed her glance. "*No!*" she cried, and drew breath for a scream of sheer terror—which she never uttered.

Yulian threw her down and her head banged against the polished floorboards. She lost consciousness at once and he stepped over her, loped to the open door of the small room . . .

In the middle flat, struggling blindly with an old sash window which seemed jammed, Darcy Clarke suddenly felt his terror drain out of him; or if not his terror, certainly his urge to flee. His talent's demands were ebbing, which could only mean that the danger was receding. But how? Yulian Bodescu was still in the house, wasn't he? As sanity returned, Clarke stopped trembling, found a switch and put on the light. Adrenalin flooded into his system. Now he could focus his eyes again, could see the catches with which the window had been made secure. He released them and, unprotesting, the window slid upward along its grooves. Clarke sighed his relief; at least he now had an emergency exit. He glanced out of the window, down into the midnight road—and froze.

At first his eyes refused to accept what they were seeing. Then he gasped his horror and felt the flesh creep on his shoulders and back. The road outside the house was filling with people! Silent streams of them were converging, massing together. They were coming out of the cemetery gates, over its front wall; men, women and children. All silent, crossing the road to gather in front of the house. But worse than the sight of them was their silence. For they were quiet as the graves they had so recently vacated!

Their stench drifted up to Clarke on the damp night air, the overpowering, stomach-wrenching reek of moulder and advanced decay and rotting flesh. Eyes popping, he watched them. They were in their graveclothes, some of them recently dead, and others . . . others who had been dead for a long time. They flopped over the cemetery wall, squelched out of its gate, shuffled across the road. And now one of them was knocking on the house door, seeking entry.

Clarke might have thought he was mad, and indeed that thought occurred to him, but in the back of his mind he knew and remembered that Harry Keogh was a Necroscope. He knew Keogh's history: a man who could talk to the dead, whom the dead respected, even loved. What's more, Keogh could raise the dead up when he had need of them. And didn't he have need of them now? That was it! This was Harry's doing. It was the only possible answer.

The crowd at the door began to turn their grey, fretted

heads upward. They looked at Clarke, beckoned to him, pointed at the door. They wanted him to let them in—and Clarke knew why. *Perhaps I'm mad after all*, he thought, as he ran back through the flat to the door. *It's past midnight and there's a vampire on the loose, and I'm going downstairs to let a horde of dead men come inside!*

But the door of the flat was immobile as ever, with the piano still wedged against it on the landing outside. Clarke put his shoulder to it and shoved until he thought his heart would burst. The door was giving way, but only an inch at a time. He simply didn't have the bulk . . .

. . . But Guy Roberts did.

Clarke didn't know his dead friend had stood up until he saw him there at his side, helping to force the door open. Roberts—his head a crimson jelly where it flopped on his shoulders, with the broken skull showing through—inexorably thrusting forward, filled with a strength from beyond the grave!

And then Clarke simply fainted away . . .

The two Harrys had looked out through the infant's eyes into the face of terror itself, the face of Yulian Bodescu. Crouched over the baby's cot, the leering malignancy of his eyes spoke all too clearly of his intention.

Finished! Harry Keogh thought. *All done, and it ends like this.*

No, another voice, not his own, had spoken in his mind. *No it doesn't. Through you I've learned what I had to learn. I don't need you that way any more. But I do still need you as a father. So go, save yourself.*

It could only have been one person speaking to him, doing it now, for the first time, when there was no longer any time to question the hows and whys of it. For Harry had felt the child's restraints falling from him like broken chains, leaving him free again. Free to will his incorporeal mind into the safety of the Möbius continuum. He could have gone right there and then, leaving his baby son to face whatever was coming. He *could* have gone—but he couldn't!

Bodescu's jaws had yawned open like a pit, revealing a snake's tongue flickering behind the dagger teeth.

Go! little Harry had said again, with more urgency.

You're my son! Harry had cried. *Damn you, I can't go! I can't leave you to this!*

Leave me to this? It had been as if the infant couldn't follow his reasoning. But then he did, and said, *But did you think I was going to stay here?*

The beast's taloned hands were reaching for the child in his cot.

Yulian saw now that Harry Jr. was . . . was more than a child. Harry Keogh was in him, yes, but it was even more than that. The baby boy looked at him, stared at him with wide, moist, innocent eyes—and was totally unafraid. Or were those eyes innocent? And for the first time since Harkley House, Yulian knew something of fear. He drew back a fraction, then checked himself. This was what he was here for, wasn't it? Best to get it done with, and quickly. Again he reached for the baby.

Little Harry had turned his small round head this way and that, seeking a Möbius door. There was one beside him, floating up out of his pillows. It was easy, instinct, in his genes. It had been there all along. His control over his mind was awesome; over his body, much less certain. But he'd been able to manage this much. Bunching inexpert muscles, he'd curled himself up, rolled into and through the Möbius door. The vampire's hands and jaws had closed on thin air!

Yulian strained back and away from the cot as if it had suddenly burst into flames. He gaped—then pounced upon the cot's covers, tearing them to shreds. Nothing! The child had simply disappeared! One of Harry Keogh's tricks, the work of a Necroscope.

Not me, Yulian, said Harry softly from behind him. *Not*

this time. He did it all for himself. And that's not all he can do.

Yulian whirled, saw Harry's naked figure outlined in glowing blue neon mesh, advanced menacingly upon him. He passed *through* the manifestation, found himself tearing at nothing. "What?" he gurgled. "*What?*"

Harry was behind him again. *You're finished, Yulian,* he told him then, with a deal of satisfaction. *Whatever evil you've created, we can undo it. We can't give life back to those you've destroyed, but we can give some of them their revenge.*

"We?" The vampire spoke round the snake in his mouth, his words dripping like acid. "There's no 'we,' there's only you. And if it takes me forever, I'll—"

You don't have forever. Harry shook his head. *In fact, you've no time left at all!*

There was a soft but concerted shuffling of footsteps on the landing and up the stairs; something, no, a good many somethings, were coming into the flat. Yulian swept out of the tiny bedroom into the flat's main room and skidded to a halt. Brenda Keogh no longer lay where he had tossed her, but Yulian barely noticed that.

The Keogh manifestation, suspended in thin air, moved after the vampire to watch the confrontation.

A policeman, his throat torn out, was leading them. And with steps slow and staggering, but full of purpose, they came on. *You can kill the living, Yulian,* Harry told the mewling vampire, *but you can't kill the dead.*

"You . . ." Yulian turned to him again. "You called them up!"

No, Harry shook his head. *My son called them up. He must have been talking to them for quite some little time. And they've grown to care for him as much as they care for me.*

"*No!*" Bodescu rushed to the window, saw that it was old and no longer opened. One of the corpses, a thing that shed maggots with every step, lurched after him. In its bony hand it carried Darcy Clarke's crossbow. Others had long wooden staves, taken from cemetery fences. Animated corruption was now spewing into the room like pus from a ruptured boil.

It's all over, Yulian, said Harry.

Bodescu turned on them all, scowled his denial. No, it wasn't over yet. What were they anyway but a mirage and a mob of dead men? "Keogh, you bodiless bastard!" he snarled. "And did you think you were the only one with powers?"

He crouched down, spread his shoulders, laughed in their faces. His neck elongated, the flesh rippling with a life of its own. His terrible head was now like that of some primal pterodactyl. His body seemed to flutter, flattening in depth and increasing in width until his clothes, unable to contain it, tore into so many rags around him. He reached out his arms and lengthened them, forming a blasphemous cross, then grew a webbing of wing down each side of his body. With greater case, more fluency far than ever Faethor Ferenczy had possessed, he completely remoulded his vampire flesh. And where moments before a manlike being had stood, now a huge batlike creature confronted its hunters.

Then . . . the thing that was Yulian Bodescu turned and launched itself at the thin-latticed panes of the wide bay window.

Don't let him get away! Harry told them; but without need, for that wasn't their intention.

Yulian went out through the latticework, showering glass and fragments of painted woodwork down into the road. Now he formed an aerofoil, curving his monstrous body like a straining kite to catch a night wind blowing up from the west. But the avenger with the crossbow stood in the gap of the broken window and aimed his weapon. A corpse without eyes should not see, but in their weird pseudolife these pieces of crumbling flesh enjoyed all of the senses they'd known in life. And this one had been a marksman.

He fired, and the bolt took Yulian in his spine, halfway down his rubbery back. *The heart,* Harry admonished. *You should have gone for his heart.* But in the end, it was all to work out the same.

Yulian cried out, the raucous, ringing cry of a wounded beast. He bent his body in a contortion of agony, lost his control, sank like a crippled bird towards the graveyard. He tried to maintain his flight, but the bolt had severed his spine and that would take time to mend. There was no time left. Yulian fell into the cemetery, crashing into the damp shrubbery; and at once the crumbling dead turned in their tracks and began to file out of the garret flat, shuffling in pursuit.

Down the stairs they went, some with their flesh sloughing from their bones, and others who couldn't help but leave bits behind, which followed of their own accord. Harry went with them, with all of the dead he'd befriended, oh—how long ago?—when he'd lived here and new friends he hadn't even spoken to yet.

There were two young policemen among them, who'd never return home to their wives; and another two from Special Branch, with bullet holes like scarlet flowers blooming in their clothing; and there was a fat man called Guy Roberts, whose head wasn't much of anything any more but whose heart was in the right place. Roberts had come to Hartlepool with a job to do, which he expected to finish right now.

Down the stairs, out of the door and across the road they all went, and into the graveyard. There were plenty of stragglers there who hadn't made it over the road to the flat, who simply weren't in any condition to do so. But when Yulian had fallen they'd ringed him about, advancing on him with their staves and threatening in their mute, mouldering way.

Through the heart, Harry told them when he arrived.

Damn it, Harry, but he won't keep still! one of them protested. *His hide's like rubber, too, and these staves are blunt.*

Maybe this is the answer. Another corpse, recently dead came forward. This was Constable Dave Collins, who walked all aslant because Yulian had broken his back in an alley not a hundred yards down the road. In his hands he carried the cemetery caretaker's sickle, a little rusty from lying in the long grass under the graveyard wall.

That's the way, Harry agreed, ignoring Yulian's hoarse screaming. *The stake, the sword, and the fire.*

I've got the last. Someone whose head had collapsed utterly, Guy Roberts, stumbled forward dragging heavy tanks and a hose—an army flame-thrower! And if Yulian had screamed before, now he did so in earnest. The dead payed him no heed. They piled onto him and held him down, and in his extreme of terror—even Yulian Bodescu, terrified—he reshaped his vampire body to that of a man. It was a mistake, for now they could find his heart more easily. One of them brought a piece of a broken headstone for a hammer, and at last a stave was driven home. Pinned down like some ugly butterfly. Yulian writhed and shrieked, but it was nearly over now.

Dave Collins, looking on, sighed and said, *An hour ago I was a policeman, and now it seems I'm to be an executioner.*

It's a unanimous verdict, Dave, Harry reminded him.

And like the Grim Reaper himself, so Dave Collins advanced and took Yulian's head as cleanly as possible, even though he had to strike more than once or twice. After that it was Guy Roberts's turn; he worked on the now silent vampire with roaring, gouting, blistering, cleansing fire until there was really nothing much left of him at all. And he didn't stop until his tanks were empty. By then the dead were dispersing, back to their riven graves.

It was time for Harry to move on. The wind had blown Yulian's fog away, the stench of putrefaction, too, and

stars were shining in the night sky. Harry's work was
finished here, but elsewhere there was still a great deal to
be done.

He thanked the dead, one and all, and found a Möbius
door . . .

Harry was almost used to the Möbius continuum now, but
he suspected that most human minds would find it
unendurable. For it was always nowhere and nowhen on
the space-time Möbius strip; but a man with the right
equations, the right sort of mind, could use it to ride
anywhere and everywhen. Before that, of course, he would
need to conquer his fear of the dark.

For in the physical universe there are degrees of darkness, and Nature seems to abhor all of them much as she
abhors a vacuum. The metaphysical Möbius continuum,
however, is made of darkness. That is all it consists of.
Beyond the Möbius doors lies the very Primal Darkness
itself, which existed before the material universe began.

Harry might be at the core of a black hole, except a
black hole has enormous gravity and this place had none.
It had no gravity because it contained no mass; it was
immaterial as thought itself, yet like thought it was a
force. It had powers which reacted to Harry's presence and
worked to expel him, like a mote caught in its eye. He was
a foreign body, which the Möbius continuum must reject.

At least, that was how it had used to be. But this time
Harry sensed that things were different.

Previously there had always been this sensation of
matterless forces pushing at him, attempting to dislodge
him from the unreal back into the real. And he had never
dared to let that happen except where or when he desired it
to happen, else he might well emerge in a place or time
totally untenable. But now: now it seemed to him that
those same forces were bending a little, perhaps even
jostling each other to accommodate him. And in Harry's

unfettered, incorporeal mind, he believed he knew why. Intuition told him that this was his—yes, his metamorphosis!

From real to unreal, from a flesh and blood being to an immaterial awareness, from a living person to—a ghost? Harry had always refused to accept that premise, that he was in fact dead, but now he began to fear that it might indeed be so. And mightn't that explain why the dead loved him so? The fact that he was one of theirs?

He rejected the idea angrily. Angry with himself. No, for the dead had loved him before this, when he was still a man full-fleshed. And that was a thought which also angered him. *I still am a man!* he told himself, but with far less authority. For now that he'd conjured it, the idea of a subtle metamorphosis was growing in him.

Something less than a year ago he had argued with August Ferdinand Möbius about a possible relationship between the physical and metaphysical universes. Möbius, in his grave in a Leipzig cemetery, had insisted that the two were entirely separate, unable to impose themselves in any way one upon the other. They might occasionally rub up against each other, the action producing reaction on both sides—such as "ghosts" or "psychic experiences" on the physical plane—but they could never overlap and *never* run concurrent.

And as for jumping from one to the other and back again . . .

But Harry had been the anomaly, the fly in Möbius's ointment, the spanner in the works. Or perhaps the exception that proves the rule?

All of that, however, had been when he had form, when he was corporeal. And now? Perhaps now the rule was at last asserting itself, ironing out the discrepancy. Harry *belonged* here; he was no longer physical but metaphysical, and so should remain here. Here forever, riding the unimaginable and scientifically impossible flux of forces in the abstract Möbius continuum. Perhaps he was becoming one with the place.

Word association: force-flux—force fields—lines of force— lines of life. The bright blue lines of life extending forward beyond the doors to future time! And suddenly Harry remembered something and wondered how it could possibly have slipped so far to the back of his mind. The Möbius strip *couldn't* claim him, not yet anyway, because he had a future. Hadn't he seen it for himself?

He could even witness it again if he wished, by simply finding a future-time door. Or perhaps this time it wouldn't be so simple. What if the Möbius continuum should claim him while he traversed time? That was an unbearable thought: to hurtle into the future forever! But no need to take the risk, for Harry could remember it well enough:

The scarlet life-line drifting closer, angling in towards his own and Harry Junior's blue threads. Yulian Bodescu, surely?

And then the infant's life-thread abruptly veering away from his father's, racing off at a tangent. That must have been his escape from the vampire, the moment when he'd first used the Möbius continuum in his own right. After that—then there'd been that impossible collision:

That strange blue life-thread, dimming, crumbling, disintegrating, converging with Harry's own thread out of nowhere. The two had seemed to bend towards each other as by some mutual attraction, before slamming together in a neon blaze and speeding on as one thread. Briefly Harry had felt the presence—or the faint, fading echo—of another mind; but then it was gone, extinct, and his thread rushing on alone . . .

Yes, and he had recognized that dying echo of a mind!

Now he knew for sure where he must go, who he must seek out. And with something less than his usual dexterity, he found his way to INTESP HQ in London . . .

The top floor—self-contained suites of offices, labs, private quarters and a communal recreation room—which comprised INTESP HQ were in turmoil. Fifteen minutes ago something had occurred which, despite the nature of the HQ and the various talents of its personnel, was completely beyond all previous experience. There had been no warning; the thing had not telegraphed itself to INTESP's telepaths, precogs or other psychic sensitives; it had simply "happened," and left the espers running round in circles like ants in a disturbed nest.

"It" had been the arrival of Harry Keogh Jr. and his mother.

The first INTESP had known of it was when all the security alarms went off simultaneously. Indicators had shown that the intruder was in the top office, Alec Kyle's control room. No one but John Grieve had been in that room since Kyle flew to Italy, and the place was now secured. There couldn't possibly be anybody in there.

It could be a fault in the alarm system, of course, but . . . and *then* had come the first real intimations of what was happening. All of INTESP's espers had felt it at the same time: a powerful presence, a mental giant in their midst, here at HQ. Harry Keogh?

Finally they'd got the door to Kyle's office open—and found mother and child curled up together in the middle of the office carpet. Nothing physical had ever manifested itself in this way before; not here at INTESP, anyway. When Keogh himself had visited Kyle here, he had been incorporeal, without substance, a mere impression of the man Keogh had been. But these people were real, solid, alive and breathing. They had been teleported here.

The "why" of it was obvious: to escape Bodescu. As for the "how," that would have to wait. Mother and child—and therefore INTESP itself—were safe, and that was the main thing.

At first it had been thought that Brenda Keogh was simply asleep; but when Grieve carefully examined her he found the large soft lump at the back of her head and guessed she was concussed. As for the baby: he had looked around, alert and wide-eyed, appeared a little startled but not unduly afraid, lying in his mother's relaxed arms sucking his thumb! Not much wrong with him.

With the greatest care and attention to their task, the espers had then carried the pair to staff accommodation and put them to bed, and a doctor had been summoned. Then INTESP's buzzing members had concentrated themselves in the ops room to talk it over. Which was when Harry came on the scene.

While his coming was startling, if anything it was less of a shock and more of an anticlimax; the previous materialization had prepared them for it. It might even be said that he was expected. John Grieve had just taken the ops room podium and turned the lights down a little when Harry appeared. He came in the form all of the espers had heard about but which few of them, and none present, had ever seen: a faint mesh of luminous blue filaments—almost a hologram—in the image of a man. And again that psychic shock-wave went out, telling them all that they were in the presence of a metaphysical Power.

John Grieve felt it, too, but he was the last of them to actually see Harry, for he'd appeared on the podium's platform slightly to Grieve's rear. Then the permanent Duty Officer heard the concerted gasp that went up from his small audience where they'd taken their seats, and he turned his head.

"My God!" he said, staggering a little.

No, said Harry, *just Harry Keogh. Are you all right?*"

Grieve had almost fallen from the podium, only finding his balance at the last moment. He steadied himself, said, "Yes, I think so," then he held up his hand to quiet the buzz of excited, expectant conversation. "What's happening, Harry?" He got down off the podium and backed away.

Try not to be frightened, Harry told them all. This was a ritual he was getting used to. *I'm one of you, remember?*

"We're not frightened, Harry," Ken Layard found his voice. "Just . . . cautious."

I'm looking for Alec Kyle, said Harry. *Is he back yet?*

"No," Grieve shook his head, turned his face away a little. "And he probably won't be. But your wife and son got here OK."

The Keogh manifestation sighed, visibly relaxed. This told him the extent of the baby's delving into his mind. *Good!* he said,—*about Brenda and the baby, I mean. I knew they'd be somewhere safe, but this place has to be the safest . . .*

The handful of espers were now on their feet, had come forward to the base of the raised platform. "But didn't you, er, *send* them here?" Grieve was puzzled.

Harry shook his neon head. *That was the baby's doing. He brought them both here, through the Möbius continuum. You'd better look after that one, for he's going to be a hell of an asset! Listen, there are things that can't wait, so explanations will have to. Tell me about Alec.*

Grieve did, and Layard added, "I know he's there, at the Château, but I read him like . . . well, like he's dead."

That hit Harry hard. That strange blue life-thread, dimming, crumbling, disintegrating. Alec Kyle!

There are things you'll want to know, he told them, apparently in a hurry now. *Things you have every right to know. First, Yulian Bodescu is dead.*

Someone whistled his appreciation, and Layard cried, "Christ, that's wonderful!"

It was Harry's turn to avert his face. *Guy Roberts is dead, too,* he said.

For a moment there was silence, then someone asked, "Darcy Clarke?"

He's fine, Harry answered, *as far as I know. Listen, everything else will have to wait. I've got to go now. But I've a feeling I'll be seeing all of you again.*

He collapsed in upon himself to a single point of radiant blue light, and disappeared . . .

* * *

Harry knew the route to the Château Bronnitsy well enough, but the Möbius continuum fought him all the way. It fought to retain him, to keep him to itself. The longer he remained unbodied, the worse it would become, until finally he'd be trapped in the endless night of an alien dimension. But not yet.

Alec Kyle was not dead and Harry knew it; if he had been then Harry could simply reach out his mind and talk to him, as he talked to all the dead. But though he tried—however tentatively at first, cringingly—mercifully there was no contact. This made him bolder; he tried harder, putting every effort into contacting Kyle's mind, while yet hoping that he'd fail. But this time—

—Harry felt horror wash over him as indeed he picked up the faint, failing echo of the man he had known. An echo, yes: a despairing, fading cry tailing off into nothing. But it was all the beacon Harry needed, and he homed in on it in a moment.

Then . . . it was as if he were caught in a maelstrom! It was Harry Jr. all over again, but ten times worse, and this time there was no resisting it. Harry did not have to fight free of the Möbius continuum but was ripped out of it intact. Torn from it and inserted—

Elsewhere!

It hadn't been easy but Zek Föener had eventually fallen asleep, only to toss and turn for hours in the throes of sheerest nightmare. Finally she'd started awake in the small hours of the morning and looked all about in the darkness of her spartan room. For the first time since coming to the Château Bronnitsy the place seemed alien to her; her job here was empty now; it offered neither reward nor satisfaction. Indeed it was evil. It was evil because the people she worked for were evil. Under Felix Krakovitch things had been different, but under Ivan Gerenko . . . his very name had become a bad taste in Zek's mouth. Her life would be impossible if he took control here. And as for that squat, murderous toad Theo Dolgikh . . .

Zek had got up, splashed cold water in her face, made her way down to the cellars which housed the Château's various experimental laboratories. On her way, on the stairs and in a corridor, she'd passed a night-duty technician and an esper; both had nodded their respect but she'd hardly noticed, merely brushed by them and continued on her way. She had her own respects to pay, to a man as good as dead.

Letting herself into the mind-lab, she'd taken a steel chair and sat beside Alec Kyle, touched his pale flesh. His pulse was erratic, the rise and fall of his chest weak and abnormal. He was almost totally brain-dead, and less than twenty-four hours from now . . . The authorities in West Berlin wouldn't know who he was or what had killed him. Murder, pure and simple.

And she had been part of it. She had been duped, told that Kyle was a spy, an enemy whose secrets were of the utmost importance to the Soviet Union, while in reality they were only of the utmost importance to Ivan Gerenko. She had defended herself before that sick creature, made excuses when he said she'd been party to it—but there was no defence against her own conscience.

Oh, it was easy for Gerenko and the thousands like him, who only ever read reports. Zek read *minds*, and that was a different matter entirely. A mind is not a book; books only describe emotions, they rarely make you feel them. But to a telepath the emotion is real, raw and powerful as the story itself. She hadn't simply read Alec Kyle's stolen diary, she'd read his life. And in doing so she had helped to steal it.

An enemy, yes, she supposed he'd been that, in that he held allegiance to another country, a different code. But a threat? Oh, in higher echelons of his government there were doubtless personalities who would wish to see Russia devolve, become subservient. But Kyle wasn't a militarist,

he'd been no subversive strategist worrying at the foundations of Communist identity and society. No, he'd been
humanitarian, with an overwhelming belief that all men
were brothers—or should be. And his only desire had been
to maintain a balance. In his work for the British E-Branch
he'd been used, much as Zek herself was now being used,
when both of them could have been working towards
greater things.

And where was Alec Kyle now? Nowhere. His body
was here, but his mind—a very fine mind—was gone
forever.

Eyes filming, Zek looked up, looked scathingly at the
machinery backed up against the sterile walls. Vampires?
The world was full of them. What of these machines,
which had sucked out his knowledge and sluiced it all
away forever? But a machine can't feel guilt, which is an
entirely human emotion . . .

She came to a decision: if it were at all possible, she'd
find a way to break free of E-Branch. There had been
cases before where telepaths lost their talent, so why
shouldn't she? If she could fake it, convince Gerenko that
she was no longer of any use to this sinister organization,
then—

Zek's train of thought stopped right there. Under her
fingertips where they lay on Kyle's wrist, his pulse had
suddenly grown steady and strong; his chest was now
rising and falling rhythmically; his mind . . . *his* mind?

No, the mind of another! An astonishing wave of psychic power washed outwards from him. It wasn't telepathy—
wasn't anything Zek had felt before—but whatever it was,
it was strong! She snatched back her hand and sprang to
her feet, found her legs wobbly as jelly, and stood gulping, staring at the man lying on the operating table that
should have been his deathbed. His thoughts, at first jumbled, finally fell into a rhythm of their own.

It isn't my body, Harry told himself, without knowing
that someone else was listening, *but it's a good one and*

it's going free! There's nothing left of you, Alec, but there's still a chance for me—a good chance for Harry Keogh. God, Alec, wherever you are now, forgive me!

His identity was in Zek's mind and she knew she'd made no mistake. Her legs began to buckle under her. Then the figure—whoever, *how*ever it was—on the table opened its eyes and sat up, and that finished the job. For a moment she passed out, two or three ticks of the clock, but sufficient time in which to slump to the floor. Time enough, too, for him to swing his legs off the table and go down on one knee beside her. He rubbed her wrists briskly and she felt it, felt his warm hands on her suddenly cold flesh. His warm, alive, strong hands.

"I'm Harry Keogh," he said, as her eyes fluttered open.

Zek had learned a little English from British tourists on Zakinthos. "I . . . I know," she said. "And I . . . I'm crazy!"

He looked at her, at her grey Château uniform with its single diagonal yellow stripe across the heart, looked all around at the room and its instruments, finally looked—with a great deal of wonder—at his own naked self. Yes, at *his* self, now. And to her he said, accusingly, "Did you have something to do with this?"

Zek stood up, looked away from him. She was still shaky, not quite certain of her sanity. It was as if he read her mind but in fact he merely guessed. "No," he said, "you're not crazy. I am who you think I am. And I asked you a question: did you destroy Alec Kyle's mind?"

"I was part of it," she finally admitted. "But not with . . . that." Her blue eyes flickered towards the machinery, back to Harry. "I'm a telepath. I read his thoughts while they . . ."

"While they erased them?"

She hung her head, then lifted it and blinked away tears. "Why have you come here? They'll kill you, too!"

Harry looked down at himself. He was becoming aware

of his nakedness. At first it had been like wearing a new
suit of clothes, but now he saw it was only flesh. His
flesh. "You haven't sounded the alarm," he said.

"I haven't done anything—yet," she answered, shrugging helplessly. "Maybe you're wrong and I am crazy . . ."

"What's your name?"

She told him.

"Listen, Zek," he said. "I've been here before, did you
know that?"

She nodded. Oh, yes, she'd known about that. And
about the devastation he'd wrought.

"Well, I'm going now—but I'll be back. Probably soon.
Too soon for you to do anything about it. If you know
what happened last time I was here you'll heed my warning: don't stay here. Be anywhere else, but not here. Not
when I come back. Do you understand?"

"Going?" She began to feel hysterical, felt ungovern-
able laughter welling inside. "You think you're going
somewhere, Harry Keogh? Surely you know that you're in
the heart of Russia!" She half turned away, turned back
again. "You haven't a chance in—"

Or perhaps he did have a chance. For Harry was no
longer there . . .

Harry called out Carl Quint's name into the Möbius continuum, and was at once rewarded with an answer. *We're
here, Harry. We've been expecting you, sooner or later.*

We? Harry felt his heart sink.

*Myself, Felix Krakovitch, Sergei Gulharov and Mikhail
Volkonsky. Theo Dolgikh got all of us. You know Felix and
Sergei, of course, but you haven't met Mikhail yet. You'll
like him. He's a real character! Hey—what about Alec?
How did he make out?*

"No better than you," said Harry, homing in on them.

He emerged from the infinite Möbius strip into the
blasted ruins of Faethor Ferenczy's Carpathian castle. It
was just after 3:00 A.M. and clouds were fleeing under the

moon, turning the wide ledge over the gorge into a land of phantom shadows. The wind off the Ukrainian plain was cold on Harry's naked flesh.

So Alec copped it too, eh? Quint's dead voice had turned sour. But then he brightened. *Maybe we'll be able to look him up!*

"No," said Harry. "No, you won't. I don't think you'll ever find him. I don't think anybody will." And he explained his meaning.

You have to square things up, Harry, said Quint when he'd finished.

"It can't be put right," Harry told him. "But it can be avenged. Last time I warned them, this time I have to wipe them out. Total! That's why I came here, to see if I could motivate myself. Taking life isn't my scene. I've done it, but it's a mess. I'd prefer the dead to love me."

Most of us always will, Harry, Quint told him.

"After what I did to Bronnitsy last time," Harry continued, "I wasn't sure I could do it again. Now I know I can."

Felix Krakovitch had been silent until now. *I haven't the right to try and stop you, Harry,* he said, *but there are some good people there.*

"Like Zek Föener?"

She's one of them, yes.

"I've already told her to get out of it. I think she will."

Well (Harry could hear Krakovitch's sigh, and almost picture his nod). *I'm glad for that at least . . .*

"Now I suppose it's time I got mobile," said Harry. "Carl, maybe you can tell me: does E-Branch have access to compact high explosive?"

Why, Quint replied, *the branch can get hold of just about anything, given a little time!*

"Hmm," Harry mused. "I was hoping to do it a bit faster than that. Even tonight."

Now Mikhail Volkonsky spoke up: *Harry, does this mean you're going after that maniac who killed us? If so, maybe I can help you. I've done a lot of blasting in my time—mainly with gelignite, but I've also used the other stuff. In Kolomyya, there's a place where they keep it safe, Detonators, too, and I can explain how to use them.*

Harry nodded, seated himself on the stump of a crumbling wall at the edge of the gorge, allowed himself a grim, humourless smile. "Keep talking, Mikhail," he said. "I'm all ears . . ."

Something brought Ivan Gerenko awake. He couldn't have said what it was, just the feeling that something wasn't right. He dressed as quickly as possible, got the night Duty Officer on the intercom and asked if anything was wrong. Apparently nothing was. And Theo Dolgikh was due back any time now.

As Gerenko switched off the intercom, he glanced out of his great, curving, bulletproof window. And then he held his breath. Down there in the night, silvered by moonlight, a figure moved furtively away from the Château's main building. A female figure. She was wearing a coat over her uniform, but Gerenko knew who it was. Zek Föener.

She was using the narrow vehicular access road; she had to, for the fields all around were mined and set with trip-wires. She tried to walk light and easy, casual, but there was that in her movements which spoke of stealth. She must have booked out, presumably on the pretext of being unable to sleep. Or maybe she really couldn't sleep, was simply out for a walk and a little night air. Gerenko snorted. Oh, indeed? A long walk, presumably—probably right to Leonid Brezhnev himself, in Moscow!

He hurried down the winding stone stairs, took the key to his duty vehicle from the watchkeeper at the door, and set off in pursuit. Overhead, to the west, the lights of a helicopter signalled its approach: Theo Dolgikh, hopefully with a good excuse for the mess he'd earlier hinted at on the phone!

Two-thirds of the way to the massive perimeter wall that

surrounded the entire grounds, Gerenko caught up with the girl, pulled up alongside and slowed to a halt. She smiled, shielded her eyes from the dazzle of the headlights—then saw who was hunched behind the wheel. Her smile died on her face.

Gerenko slid open his window. "Going somewhere, Fräulein Föener, my dear?" he said . . .

Ten minutes earlier Harry had stepped out of the Möbius continuum into one of the Château's pillbox gun emplacements. He'd been there before and knew the exact locations of all six, and guessed that they'd only be manned in the event of an alert. Since that might well be the current state of readiness if Kyle's absence had been discovered, he carried a loaded automatic pistol in the pocket of an overcoat he'd stolen from a peg in the ordnance dump in Kolomyya.

Across his shoulders he bore the weight of a bulky sausage-shaped bag that weighed all of one hundred pounds. Putting it down, he unzipped it and took out the first of a dozen gauze-wrapped cheeses: that was how he thought of the stuff, like soft grey cheese, except it smelled a lot worse. He moulded the ultra-high-explosive plastic over a sealed ammunition box, stuck in a timer-detonator and set the explosion for ten minutes' time. This had taken him maybe thirty seconds; he couldn't be sure for he had no watch. Then he moved on to the next pillbox, where this time he set the detonation for nine minutes, and so on . . .

Less than five minutes later he began to repeat the process inside the Château itself. First he went to the mind-lab, where he materialized beside the operating table. It seemed strange that he (yes, *he*, now) had been lying on that table something less than three-quarters of an hour ago! Sweating, he stuffed UHEP into the gap between two of the filthy machines they'd used to drain Kyle's mind, set the detonator, picked up his much lighter bag and stepped through a Möbius door.

Emerging into a corridor in the accommodation area, he met face to face with a security guard doing his rounds! The man looked tired, shoulders drooping where he ambled down the corridor for the fifth time that night. Then he looked up and saw Harry, and his hand went straight for the gun at his hip.

Harry didn't know how his new body would react to physical violence; this was when he'd find out. He'd learned his stuff long ago from one of the first friends he'd ever made among the dead: "Sergeant" Graham Lane, an ex-Army PT instructor at his old school, who'd died in a climbing accident on the beach cliffs. "Sergeant" had taught him a lot and Harry hadn't forgotten it.

His hand shot out and trapped the guard's hand where it snatched at the pistol, jamming it back down into its holster. At the same time he drove his knee into the man's groin and butted him in the face. The guard made some noise but not much. And then he was out like a light.

Harry set another charge right there in the corridor; but now he noticed just how badly his hands were shaking, how profusely he was sweating. He wondered how much time he had left, considered the possibility of getting caught in his own fireworks.

He made one more jump—straight into the Château's central Duty Room—and in the instant of emerging caught the Duty Officer a blow that knocked him clean out of his swivel chair. The man hadn't even had time to look up. Moulding the rest of his UHEP onto the top of the desk between the radio and a switchboard, Harry fixed a final detonator and straightened up—and looked straight down the barrel of a Kalashnikov rifle!

On the other side of the raised counter, unnoticed, a young security guard had been dozing in a chair. This was obvious from his gaping mouth and dazed expression. The sound of the Duty Officer hitting the floor must have roused him. Harry didn't know how awake he was, how much he'd seen or understood, but he did know he was in big trouble. He'd only set one minute on the last detonator!

As the guard gabbled a startled question in gasping Russian, Harry shrugged and made a sour face, pointed at a spot just behind the other. It was an old ploy, he knew, but the old ones are often the best. And sure enough it worked. The guard jerked his head that way, turned the ugly snout of his weapon, too—

And when he turned back Harry was no longer there. Which was just as well, for his ten minutes were up . . .

The pillboxes went up like Chinese firecrackers, blowing their concrete lids off and bursting their walls. The first explosion—the intense flash if not the blast itself, which was minimal at this distance—caused Zek Föener to stagger and cower back where she was about to climb up into Gerenko's jeep. Then the *crack* and rumbling roar sounded, and the earth gave the first and least of many shudders. Anti-personnel land mines, fatally disturbed in the fields around, began to go off, spouting fountains of dirt and turf. It was like a bombing raid.

"What?" Gerenko turned in his seat and looked back, couldn't believe what he was seeing. "The pillboxes?" He shielded his eyes against the blaze of light.

"Harry Keogh!" Zek breathed, but to herself.

Then the main building went; its lower walls of massive stone seemed to inhale and go on inhaling. They bowed outwards, and finally blew apart in white light and golden fire! This time Zek *did* feel the blast: it tossed her down on the road and stung her hands where she held them up before her face.

The Château Bronnitsy was slowly settling down into itself. A sandcastle caught in the first wave of a swelling tide, it crumbled like so much chalk. Volcanic fires burned in its guts, and spewed out through its cratered walls; and as the upper storeys and towers fell inwards, so there came secondary blasts to throw them up again. Already the

Château was a total ruin, but then the big one In the Duty Room added its voice to the cacophony of destruction.

By this time Zek had managed to climb into the jeep beside Gerenko. They felt a huge fist batter at the rear of the vehicle, shove it forward; felt their ears savaged by the massive detonation, shuttered their eyes against a sudden incendiary glare. A brilliant fireball like the breath of hell turned everything to a negative photograph, blotted out the entire scene and made night into blinding day, then slowly faded and revealed the truth—that the Château Bronnitsy was no more. Bits of it, from pebbles to huge blocks of concrete, still rained to earth. Black smoke curled up across the moon; white and yellow fire seethed and roiled in the gutted ruins; a mere handful of figures stumbled about like crippled flies, trying to make their way outwards from the centre of the inferno.

Gerenko, stunned, had stalled the jeep and it wouldn't start again. Now he got out, ordered Zek out, too. The helicopter had veered sharply away as the first explosion occurred; it circled, came down and landed with a bump on the road near the perimeter wall. Theo Dolgikh spoke briefly to the pilot, climbed out and advanced at a run. Zek Föener and Gerenko made their way staggeringly towards him.

"For Alec," said Harry Keogh softly to himself.

He stood in the shadows at the foot of the perimeter wall and watched the three people moving towards the helicopter. He took note of the two men—one the mere husk of a man and the other a hulking brute—and the way they manhandled the girl into the chopper. Then the machine lifted off and Harry was alone with the night and his hideous handiwork. But like an after-image, a mental picture of those two men kept superimposing itself over the leaping flames. Harry didn't know who they were, but his intuition told him that these two above all others ought not to have escaped the holocaust.

He'd have to speak to Carl Quint and Felix Krakovitch about them . . .

Epilogue

THREE DAYS LATER IVAN GERENKO, THEO DOLGIKH AND ZEK Föener stood on the scarred rim of the gorge in the Carpathians and gazed gloomily on a great mound of scree and rubble, where only the stumps of the ancient castle's massive outer walls protruded. The scene was desolate as only these mountains can be, with jagged crests and peaks all around, an eerie wind moaning up off the plain, and birds of prey circling slowly in a sky ribboned with cloud. It was evening and the light was beginning to fade, but Gerenko had insisted upon seeing the site. There was nothing they could do tonight, but at least it would give him an idea of what must be done tomorrow.

Gerenko was here because Leonid Brezhnev had given him one week to come up with the answer—one all-inclusive answer—to the destruction of the Château Bronnitsy; Dolgikh because Yuri Andropov also required answers; Zek in order that Gerenko could keep an eye on her. She *said* she had lost her talent on the night of the as yet unexplained inferno—and worse, that all memory of

461

what she'd learned from Alec Kyle had also been burned
out of her—but Gerenko thought not. In which case he
couldn't be sure that if she were left on her own in
Moscow she'd keep her mouth shut.

But most importantly, and if she *were* lying, she was
here because she was the world's foremost close-range
telepath. If danger threatened from any source, Zek Föener
would probably know it first; and so her actions would be
Gerenko's indicator that all was well—or otherwise. After
what had happened at the Château one must look to one's
personal safety, and a mind such as Zek's could well be of
the utmost importance.

"Nothing," she said now, frowning at the grey ruins,
her forehead furrowed. "Nothing at all. But even if there
were something here I couldn't read it! Not now. I've told
you, Ivan, my talent has been destroyed. It burned up in
that great bonfire and now . . . I can't even remember
what it was like."

She told a part-truth: her talent was intact, all right—she
knew that from the seething cauldron of Gerenko's mind,
and the cesspool of Dolgikh's—but she really couldn't
detect anything else. Only a Necroscope may talk to the
dead or hear them talking to each other.

"Nothing!" Gerenko repeated her, his voice rasping.
He kicked at the dirt and sent pebbles flying. "Then it's a
black day for us."

"For you, Comrade, perhaps," said Dolgikh, turning
up the collar of his coat. "But you're up against the Party
Leader, who happens to have lost a lot. Andropov may not
have gained anything, but he certainly hasn't lost much.
Not that he'll notice, anyway. And there's no point in him
taking it out of my hide. As for E-Branch; he's waged war
with you espers for years, and now you're finished. No
skin off his nose. He won't agonize over it, take my
word."

Gerenko turned on him. "You fool! So you'll return to
simple thuggery, will you? And how far will that get you?

You could have gone up in the world, Theo, with me. Right to the top. But now?''

At the back of the ruins in the heaped shale and fallen scree, something stirred. The rubble formed a small mound, cracked open, and foul gases filtered up into the evening air. A bloodied hand, that of a corpse, scrabbled for a moment until it found purchase in the rocks. The two men and the girl heard nothing.

Dolgikh scowled at the smaller man. "Comrade, I'm not sure I want to go anywhere with you," he said. "I prefer the company of men—and sometimes women." He glanced at Zek Föener and licked his lips. "But I warn you, be careful who you're calling a fool. Head of E-Branch? You're head of nothing now. Just another citizen, and a poor specimen at that.''

"Idiot!" Gerenko muttered, turning away from Dolgikh. "Dolt! Why, if you'd been at the Château that night I'd suspect you of being involved in that mess, too! You're too bloody *good* at blowing things up, Theo!''

Dolgikh caught his slender arm, turned him about. Gerenko's talent was alerted . . . but so far the KGB man intended no real harm. "Listen, you spindly thing," Dolgikh spat the words out. "You think you're so high and mighty, but you forget that I've still got enough on you to put you away for the rest of your days!''

Back in the ruins, his movements covered by their arguing, Mikhail Volkonsky got to his knees and then dragged himself to his feet. He'd lost an arm and shoulder and most of his face, but the rest of him still worked. He shuffled awkwardly into the shadow of the cliff, drew closer to the three live ones.

"But it's mutual, Theo, it's mutual!" Gerenko mocked the KGB agent. "And it isn't only you I can damage but your boss, too. How would Andropov fare if I let it out that he'd been trying to interfere with branch work again? And how would *you* fare after that? Overseer in a salt mine, that's where you'd be, Theo!''

"Why you runt!" Dolgikh swelled up huge. He raised his fist . . . and a strange expectant *something* filled the air. However blunt his senses, Dolgikh felt it too. "Why, I could— "

Gerenko faced him squarely. "But that's just the point, Theo. You couldn't! Neither you nor any other man. Try it and see for yourself. It's *waiting* for you to try, Theo. Go on, strike me if you dare. You'll be lucky if you merely miss, fall over in the stones and break your arm. But if you're unlucky this wall could fall on you and crush you. Your superior physical strength? *Pah!* I . . ." He paused and the sneer fell from his face. "*What was that?*"

Dolgikh lowered his threatening hand, listened. There was only the keening of the wind. "I heard nothing," he said.

"I did," said Zek Föener, shivering. "Rocks falling into the gorge. Come on, let's get out of here. The shadows are lengthening, and that ledge back there was bad enough in full daylight. Why are you arguing, anyway? What's done is done."

"*Shh!*" said Dolgikh, his eyes going wide. He leaned forward, pointing. "Now I hear it—from over there. Sliding shale, maybe . . ."

At the rim of the gorge, back along the track and hidden by the undergrowth, blunt grey fingers came up from the depths. Sergei Gulharov's shattered head came up slowly and stiffly; then a shoulder, and an arm thrown far forward to take the strain and give him leverage. Silent as a shadow now, he drew himself up onto firm, flat ground.

"The temperature is falling fast," said Gerenko with a shudder, perhaps feeling the chill. "I've had enough for tonight. Tomorrow we'll take another look, and if it's quite hopeless we can decide what to do then." Wheezing with the effort and gritting his small teeth, he started back down the trail. "But this is all a great pity. I had hoped to salvage something, if only a little face . . ."

Dolgikh grinned after him, calling out: "We're pretty

close to the border, Comrade. Have you ever thought of defecting?'' When Gerenko failed to answer, he muttered, "Shrivelled little shit!" Then he put his hand on Zek's shoulder and she felt his fingers bite. "Well, Zek, shall we join him, or perhaps we'll hang back a little and do some stargazing, eh?"

She looked up at him first in astonishment, then outrage. "My *God!*" she said. "I'd prefer the company of pigs!"

Before he could reply she'd turned away. She started after Gerenko—then jerked to a halt, freezing in her tracks. Someone was coming up the trail towards them, closing on Gerenko. And even in the failing light it was obvious that the someone was a dead man. Lord God—he had only half a head!

Dolgikh saw him, too, and knew him. He recognized his fouled clothing, the damage a snub-nosed bullet had done to his head. "Mother!" he gulped. "Oh, mother!"

Zek screamed. Screamed again as a huge bloody hand passed over her shoulder, grabbed Theo Dolgikh by the collar and spun him round. Dolgikh's eyes stood out in his face. Behind the girl he saw a second corpse: Mikhail Volkonsky. And, God—Volkonsky had taken hold of him with his one remaining arm!

Like a startled cat, Zek bounded out from between them, fleeing after Gerenko. She didn't hear the mental voices of the dead, saying:

Oh, yes, these are the ones, Harry! But she did hear his answer:

Then I can't stop you taking your revenge. And she knew who was speaking, and guessed who he was speaking to.

"Harry Keogh!" she screamed, flinging herself breakneck down the track. "God, oh, God, you're worse than all of us together!"

Until a moment ago Harry had been beyond Zek's reach both mental and physical, hidden in the metaphysical Möbius

continuum. Now he stepped out of the shadows directly in
her path, so that she flew gasping into his arms. For a
moment she thought he was another dead man and pounded
at his chest; but then she felt his warmth, the beat of his
heart against her breast, and heard his voice. "Easy, Zek,
easy."

Wild-eyed, she pulled back from him. He held her
arms. "Easy, I said. If you go running like that you'll hurt
yourself."

"You . . . you're *commanding* them!" she accused.

He shook his head in denial. "No, I only called them
up. I'm not calling the shots. What they do is for
themselves."

"What they do?" Breathlessly she looked back towards
the ruined castle, where mad, frenzied shadows fought and
tore. She glanced down the track: Gerenko had somehow
avoided Gulharov's lunges (his talent, of course), but the
dead man was limping after him. Winds tugged at Gulharov,
threatening to blow him back into the gorge, and thorns
tore at his legs trying to trip him—but still he pursued.

"Nothing can hurt that one," Zek gasped. "Living or
dead, men are only men. They can't touch him."

"But he *can* be hurt," said Harry. "He can be frightened, too, made incautious. And it's growing dark; the
ledge back there is narrow and dangerous; there can easily
be an accident. That's what my friends are hoping, that
there'll be an accident."

"Your . . . friends!" Hysteria lifted her voice.

Gunshots sounded from the ruins, and Dolgikh's hoarse
screaming. He wasn't simply shouting but screaming, like
a terrified animal, for he'd just discovered that you can't
kill the dead. Harry covered Zek's ears, drew her head to
his shoulder, her face buried in his neck. He didn't want
her to see or hear. *He* didn't want to see or hear, and so
stared out over the gorge instead.

Weaker than he'd ever been before in his life, weak
with terror, Theo Dolgikh was being dragged towards the

rim of the almost sheer drop. Mikhail Volkonsky, on the other hand, was as strong as he'd ever been in life, and he no longer felt pain. With his one good arm round Dolgikh's neck, the huge ganger had him in a necklock which he wouldn't release until the man was dead. And now they were almost there, battling ferociously on the very edge of the gorge. Which was when Felix Krakovitch and Carl Quint showed up.

Blown to pieces, the two hadn't been able to do much until now; but finally Quint's arms—only his arms—had dragged themselves up from below, and Felix's upper torso, limbless, had wriggled its way out of the castle's debris. As the arms of Quint came up over the rim and grabbed Dolgikh, and as Felix's severed, sluglike cadaver wriggled into view and began to bite at him, so he gave up. He drew air for one last scream, filled his lungs to brimming—and the scream simply died on his lips, the merest gurgle of sound. Then he closed his eyes and sighed, and all of the air whooshed out of him.

But they made sure anyway, and with one last effort dragged him over the edge into space. His body pinwheeled down the face of the cliff, bounding from one projection to the next, all the way to the bottom.

Harry uncovered Zek's head, said, "He's finished—Dolgikh, I mean."

"I know," she answered with a half-sob. "I read it in your mind. And Harry, it's cold in there . . ."

He gave a grim nod.

Haarrry? A distant voice came to him as he released her—one that only he and the dead could hear—one he knew and had thought never to hear again. *Do you hear me, Haarrry?*

I hear you, Faethor of the Wamphyri, he answered. *What is it you want?*

Noooo—it's what you want, Haarrry. You want Ivan Gerenko dead. Well, now I give you his life.

Harry was puzzled. *I haven't asked any favours of you, not this time.*

But they did. Faethor's voice was a grim chuckle. *The dead!*

Now Felix Krakovitch spoke up from the bottom of the gorge: *I asked him to help, Harry. I knew you couldn't kill Gerenko, no more than we can. Not directly. But indirectly . . . ?*

I don't understand. Harry shook his head.

Then look up at the ridge there, over the ledge, said Faethor.

Harry looked. Silhouetted against the dying day, a straggling line of scarecrow figures stood silent on the high, precarious ridge. They were fretted, skeletal, crumbling— but they stood there and awaited the Old Ferengi's command. *My ever faithful, my Szgany!* said Faethor, that once-mightiest of all the Wamphyri. *They have been coming here for centuries—coming here, waiting for me, dying and being buried here—but I never returned. Over them, whose blood is my blood, my power is as great as yours is over the commoner dead, Harry Keogh. And so I have called them up.*

But why? Harry demanded. *You owe me nothing now, Faethor.*

I loved these lands, the vampire answered. *Perhaps you cannot understand that, but if I ever loved it was this land, this place. Thibor could tell you how much I loved it . . .*

Now Harry understood. *Gerenko . . . invaded your territory!*

The vampire's growl was deep and merciless. *He sent a man here who was responsible for reducing my house to dust! My last vestige on earth! And now there is nothing to show that I ever existed at all! How then shall I reward him? Ahhh! But how did I reward Thibor?*

Harry saw what was coming. *You buried Thibor,* he answered.

So be it! cried Faethor. And he gave the Szgany on the ridge his final command—that they throw themselves down!

Half-way along the ledge, Ivan Gerenko heard the clattering of ancient, leather-clad bones and fearfully looked up. Down from that high place they fell, breaking up as they came; skulls and scraps of bone and flaps of fretted flesh, a rain of dead things that might drown him in mummied remains.

"You can't hurt me!" Gerenko gibbered, covering his wrinkled head as the first ghastly fragments thudded down onto the ledge. "Not even dead men . . . can . . . hurt me?"

But it wasn't their intention to hurt him; they didn't even know he was there; they'd simply obeyed Faethor and hurled themselves down. And after that it was out of their hands, those of them who had hands. The clattering cascade continued, echoing loudly; and over and above the pelting of gristly bones, now there swelled a new sound: a terrible grumbling and groaning, but in no way the groaning of the dead. They were the groans of riven rock, of sliding shale and scree and accumulated debris. Avalanche!

And even as that fact dawned on Gerenko, so the face of the cliff fell on him and he was swept away . . .

Long after the dust had settled and the last rumbling echo faded away, Harry Keogh stood with Zek and watched the rim of the moon come up over the mountains. "It will light your way," he told her. "Take care, Zek."

She was still in his arms, had needed to be there else she might have fallen. Now she struggled free, wordlessly left him and headed for the scree-buried ledge. At first she stumbled, then straightened up and went with more certainty, more resolve. She would pick her way over the fallen cliff to the bottom of the gorge, then follow the stream down to the new road.

"Take care," Harry called after her again. "And Zek, don't ever come up against me or mine again."

She made no answer, looked straight ahead. But to herself: *Oh, no, I'll not do that. Not against you, Harry Keogh—Necroscope!*